# The Shanaandr

## Breaking Destiny

# T.R. Chowdhury &
# T.M. Crim

TR MOON ECLIPSE

Winter Wolf PUBLICATIONS

| Cincinnati, Ohio

Copyright © 2021, T.R. Chowdhury & T.M. Crim
First edition: 2012 Loconeal Publishing
First Winter Wolf edition: 2021
Cover Art © 2021, by Lindsay Archer
Interior Image Art © 2021, by Carol Phillips
Edited by Jennifer Midkiff
Interior Design by Tracy Ross

Published by TriMoon Eclipse,
An imprint of Winter Wolf Publications, LLC

ISBN: 978-1-945039-07-2 (paperback)

## Shadow Over Shandahar:

Dark Storm Rising
Echoes of Time
Whispers of Prophecy
Breaking Destiny
Embers at Dawn
Heroes' Fate

## Dark Mists of Ansalar:

Blood of Dragons
Shade of the Fallen
Forging the Bond

## The Troubadour's Inn:

*(Collections of short stories, poems, and artwork)*
Tales from the Hapless Cenloryan

## Other Work by T.R. Chowdhury
## (aka Tracy Renée Ross)

## Chronicles of Rithalion

Elvish Jewel
Dragon Vessel
Fire Heart

## Cat Tales:

The Dream Thief
The Time Swiper

# DEDICATION

This book is for the people who have stuck with us throughout the years, the fans of our world who have become more than just our readers, but our friends. Without your continued support, your patience, and your kindness, Ted and I wouldn't be where we are today. So thank you... thank you all for making our lives brighter and more fullfilled. And above all, thank for making us feel loved and appreciated.

~ Tracy

# TABLE OF CONTENTS

## PART I

## PART II

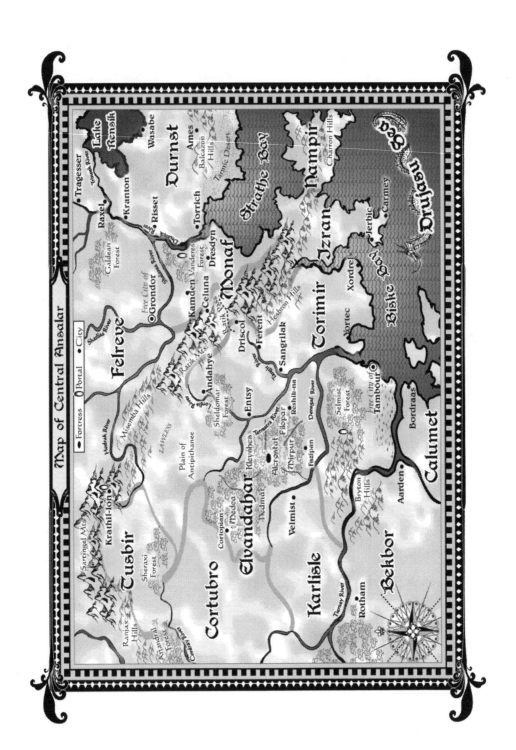

Map of Central Ansalar

● Fortress ◎ Portal ● City

*Child of light, child of dark...*
*Into a land covered with shadows*
*The Warrior of Destiny will come.*
*With a talisman of magnificent power*
*The undead Lord will once more know mortality,*
*He from whose loins she arose.*
*And from behind the aegis of the Protector*
*She will survive the temptation of power.*
*But the Master awaits, and with his magic*
*Bring forth his army of abominations.*
*And upon this battlefield of darkness*
*A war will be waged that will determine*
*The fate of the world forever...*

\* Excerpt from the Chardelis Prophecies

# PART ONE

## PROLOGUE

### 32 THALIREN CY543

Sydonnia moved through the wood, his labored breath misting into the chilly air. It had become strangely quiet, and he no longer had the auditory perception of the grisly conflict he'd left behind. A part of him was relieved to no longer hear the frightening howls that chilled him to the core of his being, and the terrified cries of men fighting a menace they had never encountered before. But the other part of him realized he'd wandered too far, and that he needed to get back to the comrades who relied on him to fight at their side. He slowed to a stop and turned in place, his eyes straining to see into the surrounding trees, trying to recall what had drawn him so far in the first place.

With the sleeve of his studded leather tunic, Sydonnia wiped at the sweat threatening to run into his eyes. The strong scent of blood filled his nostrils and he was suddenly reminded of the man to whom it belonged. Lanstar had died a terrible death, and the tortured screams of his fellow ranger would haunt Sydonnia as long as he lived. Even now Servial continued to hold his longsword defensively before him, a weapon uncharacteristic for one of his profession to carry. On several occasions, Servial had teased him mercilessly about it. Sydonnia couldn't help wondering why his brother cared so much.

Sydonnia shook his head and felt a surge of resentment. During their several days journey to the Terrestra, he had confronted Servial about ladies Lilandria and Keilah. He was aware of the relationship Servial had begun to entertain with the former prior to their business in Sangrilak, as well as the romantic inclination he had shown the latter once returning to Elvandahar. Again Sydonnia had been faced with another stellar example of his brother's philandering ways. But this time, it hit too close to home. In spite of the short time he'd known her, Keilah was his good friend. And Lilandria... well, Sydonnia was in love with Lilandria.

Servial had easily downplayed the allegations. In the ensuing argument, Servial had claimed that nothing had transpired between himself and Keilah. He then made Sydonnia out to be a fool, a lovesick pup who couldn't understand the depth of feeling that had arisen between himself and the Lady Lilandria. And then Servial had asked Sydonnia how he ever could imagine Lily, or anyone else, feeling anything but pity for a man who had delusions of reality.

After hearing what Servial had to say, Sydonnia struggled to keep from smashing his fist into his brother's face. The strength it took for him to simply turn and walk away was extraordinary. He knew for a fact that Servial harbored amorous intentions towards Keilah, and that the man had been more than willing to discard Lilandria in lieu of the mystery that characterized the beautiful stranger. From the moment the brothers had met her, the young woman was an enigma to them both. It was more than just Keilah's rather striking appearance, but the fact that she kept vital information about herself shrouded in secrecy. Servial had tried in vain to wrest the information from her, while Sydonnia simply accepted it for what it was.

By the gods, other than Lily, he had never befriended a woman like Keilah Laremion before. There was something about her, for she seemed to have the ability to look into a man's eyes and see his innermost soul. It was why she didn't fall into his brother's seductive snare, and why she so easily befriended Servial's corubis companion. She had obviously seen something special in Sydonnia, and it made him wonder about himself.

Two days before he and Servial were dispatched to the Terrestra River with the other rangers in their quadrant of Filopar, Keilah's brother had arrived. She had cried when they spoke their farewells, and Sydonnia remembered feeling his heart break. He would miss her friendship, for they had become close during the fortnight spent in one another's company. And at that moment, as Keilah was being led away from Merithyn Village, something deep inside had told Sydonnia that all the tears she shed were for *him*.

Sydonnia abruptly brought his focus back to the present, breathing another warm gust into the surrounding cold air. He felt a sense of foreboding, and once again he questioned why he had wandered so far away from comrades who needed his strength in their brutal battle. The enemy was something the rangers had never experienced before, monsters that stood between seven and eight feet tall, each bearing a strange resemblance to alothere, wemic, or kyrrean. Armed with tooth and claw, they were unnaturally strong and agile, and their ability to withstand ordinary weaponry was phenomenal. It was painfully obvious they had once been faelin. Now they were despicable beings harboring little or no regret upon murdering men and women who were once their brethren. Hells, Sydonnia hadn't meant to abandon his fellow rangers, but he'd felt oddly compelled to make his way deeper into the wood.

Strangely, in the fore of his mind was the anger he felt towards Servial.

Sydonnia suddenly heard a sinister voice emanating from the trees behind him. It was deep, and spoke in barely a whisper. *"I can feel your anger."*

Sydonnia swung around, blade brandished before him. He felt the breath catch in his throat, and his heart skipped a beat. From out of the shadowed forest stepped a figure cloaked entirely in the folds of a dark robe. Even the face was within a deep hood.

*"I can feel your hate."*

Sydonnia stepped back as the figure proceeded towards him. A chuckle emerged from inside the hood, and the voice spoke with a strange sibilant quality. "I chossse you, Sssydonnia Timberlyn. You are everything I want... everything I *need* to complete what I ssset out to accomplish."

Sydonnia shook his head. "Who the Hells are you? How do you know my name?"

The figure stopped. Sydonnia could somehow sense that the face hidden within the depths of the hood was smiling. "I am Gaknar, Mehta of the Daemundai. Already you have met sssome of my petsss. But *they* are nothing compared to what *you* will be."

Sydonnia swallowed past the lump that had formed in his throat. He shook his head, struggling to keep his apprehension under control. He spoke with false confidence, hoping it would be a deterrent. "I want nothing from you. Go find somebody else, someone who might actually give a damn."

Once again, Sydonnia heard a faint chuckle from within the folds of the dark hood. "I think not. I know you, Sssydonnia, whether you want it or not. I am your dessstiny."

Sydonnia nervously tightened his grip on the sword hilt. His hand was sweaty inside the leather glove he wore, and he was glad he had thought to don it that morning, for the weapon would surely have slipped from his palm by now. Once more, the figure slowly advanced. Sydonnia held his ground, keeping his sword between them. From within the voluminous folds of the cloak, hands with wickedly curved claws appeared. Sydonnia felt his eyes widen, but when he tried to retreat, he found himself held in place by some unseen force. He fought to control a surge of fear, knowing that if he allowed it to overwhelm him, the enemy would certainly persevere.

"Even now I can feel it," Gaknar hissed. "Your anger isss consssuming. Give in to your hate. It will show you a new path."

Sydonnia stoically watched the cloaked figure approach. A yellow-ish fluid dripped from the claws of one hand. Strangely, he felt the anger within him stirring. He wondered about it for a moment, for it should be the last thing on his mind in his present situation. But it seemed as though the cloaked man was bringing it out of him. And until now, Sydonnia had never realized there was a part of him that actually *hated* his brother.

Sydonnia shook his head free of the thought. *No!* He didn't truly hate Servial. He was simply angry with him. Anger and hate were two very different things. Sydonnia was better than that, better than to allow such a base emotion to cloud his mind when Servial was out there this very moment, fighting for his life.

Gaknar laughed, an eerie sound that sent prickles down Sydonnia's spine. "You cannot resssissst me. Sssuch futility will get you nowhere."

Suddenly the robed figure was standing before him. Sydonnia had no time to react as the dripping, clawed hand lunged forward more swiftly than any mortal. He caught a glimpse of the visage within the depths of the hood as the claws met his vulnerable throat. If he had the inclination, he would have recognized the hideousness of it. Instead Sydonnia was grasping at the deep wounds at his neck, struggling to keep his life's blood from soaking the front of his tunic. Sydonnia fell to his knees and the world around him began to shift and waver.

*So this is what it is like to die...*

Sydonnia slumped to the ground. The warm wetness flowed from between his fingers to dampen the leafy forest floor. He fought to breathe, felt himself drowning in his own blood. He then sensed something sweeping through him, something strangely invigorating.

And then the pain came.

# FIGHTING DAEMONS

**D**ramati at his side, Sirion was breathless as he staggered from the portal, moving aside to make room for those he hoped would come after him. Looking back at the hazy, shimmering blue wall, he could easily see that it was collapsing, and a slice of fear swept through him as he considered the fate of those who might have entered it too late. He didn't know what the consequences were, didn't want to know, and hoped he would never find out. The portal had been held together only by the will of the sorcerer Dinim, and not only looked, but had felt, unstable during his passage. It had been painful, not to the body as much as the soul. Sirion fought with intense vertigo for a moment, released a breath he didn't realize he'd been holding when the bladesinger, Armond, and the archer, Dartanyen, stumbled into view. Both men looked a bit worse for wear, but seemed unscathed.

With the aid of the light from the fading portal, Sirion's amber gaze swept the chamber for the rest of the Wildrunners, first settling onto Triath. The man appeared unaffected, perhaps due to the daemon locked in his soul behind the dark eyepatch he always wore. He was cradling his lover, Tianna, as she retched quietly, huddled on the floor. Sirion hoped she would recover quickly, for she was the only healer among them.

The others seemed to have fared better. Naemmious blinked his dark brown eyes quickly, muscles twitching under his bronze skin. His half-orocish ancestry may have given him a higher constitution, but passage through the unstable gate had winded something deeper inside. Sirion's sister, Anya, long-bow clutched in her hand, leaned against a stone wall. She breathed deeply, then choked on loose strands of her red hair and spat them out.

Sorn and Amethyst had been the ones to enter the portal before Sirion. Sorn, the half-Cimmerian faelin, had already found a shadowed nook and blended into the dark recess while his rogue apprentice, Amethyst, looked like the passage had not affected her at all. Her dark hair was dirty from the road, but her brown eyes were bright and concerned for Tianna though she kept her distance.

Sirion turned to the man beside him, his partner to walk through the portal, and let go of his arm. Sirion realized, too late, that he must have been holding Sabian up, for the spell caster collapsed and began retching next to Tianna, his dark complexion making his pale skin seem almost blue for a moment.

Then, from behind him, there was a sound that defied description.

Sirion turned to see Sheridana and Dinim finally emerging from the portal. Both hit the floor with a grunt as the last bits of glistening blue faded out, thrusting the chamber into darkness. With a hiss, a torch flared to life, and Armond's face was thrust into stark relief where he stood over their fallen comrades. Dinim was unconscious, his formidable arcane powers dulled behind half closed eyes, his black hair flipped over his pointed ears and across the lower half of his face like a veil. However, Sheridana blinked up at them from cerulean blue irises as Dartanyen moved to stand behind Armond. "Thank the gods you made it," the archer said.

Hearing movement from the passageway leading into the portal chamber, Sirion turned just as two men entered. He recognized them   as Brothers Verdec and Mattias, two of the highest ranked within the druid order, and ready for battle. Sirion rushed to greet them, the world spinning wildly as he raised his hands and made a wordless cry of peace. Both were very powerful druids and would be able to defend the apoptos against any unwanted interlopers that might arrive via the portal system. When the men saw that it was only Sirion and members of his group, they instantly relaxed. With a swift glance, they noted that not all was well with the party. Mattias moved to his side while Verdec went to aid Dinim.

Sirion stumbled and Brother Mattias steadied him, concern etched on his features deep within his hooded robes. "Timberlyn, what is it? No one has suffered this much with the hidden path to Krathil-lon since–"

Sirion shook his head and cut him off. "The Selmist Portal is gone. Destroyed. One of us had to open it alone, without aid of the brackets and mirror." Sirion turned back to look at Dinim and the other druid. Verdec gave a nod and Sirion breathed deeply. The sorcerer lived. Dinim had stretched himself to his limit to hold open the portal. He felt walls in his heart against catastophe lower, and relief at their survival come flooding in. With it came strength, and the feeling of unsteadiness ebbed.

Verdec rose and approached Sirion and Mattias. Sirion clasped arms with both men in formal greeting, then they dispensed with the formalities and shared an embrace. He noticed the questioning looks of the druids as they took in the state of he and his companions, but he waved off all inquiries. There was too much to tell: their grand battle against the dark queen, their loss of the one artifact that might help them in their battle against Aasarak, their capture by the orocs and subsequent imprisonment, their harrowing escapes from all of these, and their trek across open ground with few supplies and less equipment. All of that would have to wait. They looked like beggers, smelled like animals, and they had to see to Dinim and Tianna first after speaking to his old mentor.

"Please, I should see Dremathian..." Sirion trailed off, the brothers' expressions shifting to utmost solemnity.

Brother Verdec shook his head. "He is still in recovery. He becomes stronger every day, but we have been worried for him."

Sirion frowned. "What is he recovering from? What has happened?"

Brother Matthias shook his head. "Don't you know? We thought it was the reason why you are here."

Sirion's frown deepened. "I know nothing. Our reasons for being here are entirely our own. Pray, tell me what has happened."

"Perhaps Father should be the one to tell you. Come, we will take you to him," said Verdec.

Sirion nodded at the druids, then gestured for the rest of the group to fall in behind. Naemmious carried an unconscious Dinim in his arms as they made their way out of the bowels of the apoptos. The heavily forested glen of Krathil-lon was alive on every side. It was the bastion of the druids, and he breathed in lungfuls of the rich air swept clean by the mountains all around. The place always had an aura of peace that reached into the very soul, and he had not realized the constant strain of tension inside himself until now when it eased. Sirion had spent his entire life in the wooded places of the world, and this was where he felt most at home.

Once out in the open, the druids noticed that Naemmious' cargo had not made any sign of stirring even though the others had all but recovered.

"Your companion is more injured than he first appeared. Let us see to your accommodations and get him some of the healing he needs. Once you have had a chance to bathe, eat, and rest, we will take you to Father Dremathian," suggested Verdec.

Sirion shook his head. "No. I should see Dremathian right away, but my comrades will accept your offer." Sirion then turned to Dartanyen and Sheridana. "Rest up. I will return when I have seen my friend."

Dartanyen nodded and the rest of the Wildrunners followed Brother Matthias, while Sirion continued to follow Verdec. They walked through the apoptos to the center where most of the druids' ceremonies and rituals took place, then went beyond it to a series of humble quarters.

Verdec gestured for Sirion to precede him into one of the chambers. It was no different than any of the others, simply furnished with very little decor. Dremathian smiled when Sirion entered. "My good friend! It is so wonderful that you have come."

Dremathian sat up in his bed and gestured Sirion near with a bandaged hand. Sirion approached. In all of the years he had known Dremathian, he had never known him to be sick or injured. He couldn't help the dismay from reflecting in his eyes. Dremathian was quick to see it, and he patted the bed beside him, urging Sirion to seat himself there.

"Father, I had no idea that anything had happened. It is merely coincidence that I am here."

Dremathian frowned. "Sirion, haven't I taught you anything? Nothing is coincidence."

Sirion nodded contritely. "I'm sorry. I have a tendency to forget–"

Dremathian quickly laid a hand on Sirion's arm. "No, my friend. I am sorry. I forget that you do not exist here with us, and as such, have other things to occupy your mind. Of course, you wouldn't remember *everything*..."

Sirion grinned when he saw the twinkle in Dremathian's blue eyes and then nodded. "Please tell me what has befallen you. My mind wearies of not knowing."

Dremathian sighed deeply. "We went to battle… and lost."

Sirion frowned. "What battle? Why did I not hear of it?"

"News of tragedy flies fast, but not that fast. It happened only the day before yesterday," said Dremathian.

"Whom did you fight? I thought that druids were not inclined to do battle."

"All forces of life and light must rally to this cause." Dremathian's eyes widened and developed a faraway look. "The world quivers with the march of this army. The air reeks of death and decay, the stench overwhelming as the army passes. Rotting flesh hangs from their bones, and they moan as though in pain. They do not move as normal people would, but stagger along to the cadence of the one who controls them. There are hundreds and thousands of them, and where they walk, there is only death and destruction. Nothing can stop them but to tear them to pieces, but even then, the parts often have a life of their own."

Dremathian turned his haunted eyes to Sirion. "I called together all of the Orders on this continent. They met here in Krathil-lon, and shortly after, we went to meet the undead army. I used all of my strength in the fight, but it was to no avail. We were forced to retreat back to Krathil-lon. We lost many of our brothers to the fight, and many more lie here, needing healing assistance that we do not have the manpower to give."

Sirion put a hand on top of Dremathian's. "Don't worry. We will help in any way we can."

Dremathian nodded. "They keep me here in this bed despite my insistence to be out of it so I may aid those who truly need the help."

Sirion patted the hand beneath his. "Dremathian, you are important to your people. Let them take care of you as they see fit. When they feel that you are ready, you can help the others in need."

"By then, it may be too late."

"Then perhaps their passing was meant to be."

Dremathian shook his head and looked away from Sirion. "You sound too much like me. Perhaps I taught you too well."

Sirion forced a chuckle. "Perhaps. But I still have a lot to learn."

"You should have stayed here with us, like I asked you to," said Dremathian sulkily.

Sirion heard his own thoughts given voice and lurched a bit inside. "You know that I could not."

"Yes, I know. But let an old man have his say, why don't you?"

"Of course, Father," said Sirion in a submissive tone.

"Oh, stop that. I know that you are too wild to keep within the bonds the Order would place on you." Dremathian paused. "But please tell me that you brought your delightful companion with you, the gifted one, Adrianna."

Sirion felt his body tense. It was unexpected, this reaction he had had to hearing her name. "I'm sorry, but she isn't with us. She is in training with someone by the name of Tallachienan Chroalthone."

Dremathian nodded. "Ah, yes. Master Tallachienan. I shouldn't be surprised that he would have her. She is quite Talented, that one. Tallachienan would have been a fool not to take her. She will learn much from him."

"That is what we hope."

The druid closed his eyes and spoke wearily, suddenly very tired and very old. "Have no fear. When she returns from her training, she will have power that you can not imagine."

Sirion nodded mutely. For the first time in several days, he thought about Adrianna. Since his ordeal with the goddess, he had struck her from his mind. He had nearly betrayed her, and he couldn't easily forgive himself. He ached without her near, and he wondered if she fared well without him. He waited for the day that she would return to him, and he hoped that she wouldn't be quite as different as everyone seemed to think she would be.

The days passed into weeks. Adrianna delved back into her studies, her experiences with Servial and Sydonnia Timberlyn slowly becoming a distant memory. Unfortunately, there were some parts of the recent past that refused to recede. It was a constant battle to push them from her mind: Tallachienan's hands moving over her flesh, his lips at her throat, and the hard press of his body pushing her against the wall of the daladin in Elvandahar. It didn't help that she was in his presence more than ever as the intensity of her training went up another notch. No longer were there lecture classes dedicated to things like physics, mathematics, ancient languages, or mineral composition. She was expected to use all the knowledge she had accrued from those classes over the earlier years of her training to now aid her solely on making her more efficient, more skilled, and more adept with her spellcasting.

Adrianna's sessions with the Master came and went. He gave her no reprieve, pushing her hard during her first session since returning to the citadel, and then driving her relentlessly since then. Despite her efforts to ignore it, there was a tension that had developed between them, one that hadn't existed before her excursion home. She supposed it would be expected and natural. Two people didn't have an intimate encounter and then go back to normal, even if one of those people happened to be a god.

Adrianna focused extensively on her work. Once again, she felt that she had little time for her friends, and even less for eating and sleeping. In spite of her intentions to keep her friends closer upon her return from her rebellious Travel away from the citadel, she soon realized it was almost impossible to keep up the rigorous pace. The illness that plagued her prior to going home began to trouble her only a scant three weeks after her return. The chills she recognized as fever, and the fatigue was her body telling her it was desperate for sleep. Once the fever started, she lost her appetite and regular meals slowly began to make their way out of her agenda. After a while she noticed her pants would no longer stay elevated above her navel, and she wore her cloak almost continuously in the hopes of keeping the chill away.

However, there were other things Adrianna did to preserve her health. She read tomes that taught her how to make healing drinks that could take away her fever and restore her vitality. She made the draughts and drank them, hoping they would keep her illness at bay. She reached out to Xebrinarth more and more often. The link between them was weak, but it was there, and she could feel the sense of love that flowed through it. She could also sense his worry, for while she was in Elvandahar he'd been unable to access the link. She imagined what that must have felt like, and she was suffused with guilt. She wouldn't be able to explain it all until next she saw him, but she somehow knew he would understand. However, in the future, she would endeavor to not make her Bondmate worry like that ever again.

Meanwhile, the strange visions she had begun to experience prior to her leave-taking had returned. Her dreams had increased at least threefold and she began to think that someone, or something, was trying to show her something. The visions came so often, and the dreams were so real. The line between dreams and reality had begun to dissolve and she was changing, becoming someone more than just Adrianna Serine Darnesse.

Adrianna walked briskly down the hall, her fingertips lightly touching the walls as she passed. She had foregone the disk, as she was wont to do nowadays, choosing to walk instead. It gave her the opportunity to touch the walls of the citadel, which she loved to do, for they afforded her some warmth in the chilliness that pervaded.

Abruptly she stopped.

To her left there was a stairway. She frowned. *I've never seen this here before; I wonder where it goes?* She placed a foot on the top step, but hesitated. *I have to meet the Master for a spellcasting session. He hates it when I'm late. But I have a few moments to spare. It certainly won't take that long to indulge my curiosity.*

Adrianna continued down the stairs. In truth, the citadel had done this every once in a while, shown her passageways she'd never seen before. They usually led to some secret place the citadel felt comfortable revealing to her. Once it was a waterfall made of gold-veined marble, another time a shrine to gods and goddesses whose likeness she'd never seen before. The difference this time was that she had someplace else to be, and she was compelled to make her way downstairs to a place she had never been before in spite of the consequences.

Down, down into the depths of the citadel she went. Once she reached the lowest level, she moved through the corridor that stretched ahead of her. It was dark, and she cast a *Light* spell. She didn't have to create the light itself, but simply create a small portal and take it from one of the rooms above. The light circled her as she moved, easily showing her what lay in ahead.

*Hells, this place is creepy.*

Large, intricately woven spiderwebs stetched across the corridor. She marveled at the thing that would have made them, and within a few moments she decided to leave. For the life of her, she could neither understand why the citadel would have chosen to show her this place, nor could she recall why she'd been so terribly compelled to go down there in the first place. Not only that, she would probably be late for her spellcasting session and forced to endure the Master's ire. Muttering a string of epithets under her breath, she turned around to head back to the staircase.

*Click, click, click.*

Adrianna froze and stared into the darkness ahead, her senses screaming at her in warning of impending danger. She heard a scraping noise followed by a series of other unfamiliar sounds.

Then she heard it again. *Click click click.*

Her breath hitched in her throat when, from out of the shadows before her, emerged a terrible creature she thought would have existed only in her worst nightmares. The legs were spread all around the body, each one touching the walls of the surrounding corridor. The head was big, but not nearly as large as the abdomen, which seemed to take up the entire hallway.

*Oh gods...*

Adrianna forced herself to breathe, forced herself to rapidly assess the situation as her every instinct told her to run. At this vantage point, she could see no way she would be able to squeeze past the creature if she were to find the chance. Either she would have to run in the other direction, or immobilize the spider and climb over it in order to reach the staircase she knew lay beyond.

Giving into her impulses, Adrianna spun on her heel. She sprinted down the hallway and away from the staircase that had brought her there, careening around the first turn she came to. The sinister sounds the spider made as it moved through the corridor dogged her footsteps, making her move faster than she ever thought possible though a place so dark, her only light given by the circling orb that sped along with her. She knew it was very possible she would become lost, especially when the corridor branched off into three more, but it didn't trump her fear of the thing that followed.

Adrianna went down one side passage and then another. Before long, she had no idea how many turns she'd taken. Her thoughts were borne of desperation. *Why in the Nine Hells does Master Tallachienan have a monstrous spider in the corridors beneath his citadel, a series of passages that seem more and more like a dungeon maze? Why does he have a dungeon at all?*

Her strength flagging, Adrianna lost herself in a few more passageways before finally stopping. She couldn't run forever. Taking a few deep breaths, she turned back around to meet her fate.

Within moments, the spider was upon her. It stared at her from multiple eyes, eerily assessing her potential. She cast a *Cloaking* spell, taking the scene of the wall behind her and using it to obscure her location. As long as she didn't move much, the spider wouldn't be able to see her before she could do it some kind of damage.

Adrianna cast a *Flamesphere* spell, watching as it struck the spider's large abdomen. The monster emitted a shrill shriek before it turned towards her, immediately discovering her location. Adrianna managed to jump out of the way as it angled its abdomen towards her and shot out a stream of white material. She realized afterward that it was the same material it used for its web, the sticky white stuff clinging to the wall that had once been behind her.

Adrianna focused on another spell as the spider readied itself for its next attack. The electrical energy coursed from a storm atop a mountain in one of the Heavens and out of her fingertips, hitting it in the head. She heard the eyes sizzle, and once more the creature emitted a shriek. Then it was rushing her, its legs carrying it to her as quickly as the lightning she had just cast. The flexible front legs sought to capture her, and she could see the poison dripping from the fangs at its gaping maw. She was barely able to dodge the creature within the narrow confines of the corridor, succeeding only because it had been blinded by her spell. It scuttled past her, but more swiftly than she would have thought possible, it was turning around and rushing back.

But Adrianna was also fast, her blood singing through her veins with the rush of battle. She waited, and as one of the legs got close enough, she crouched low and found the courage to reach out...

The spell discharged, the monstrous limb shifting color as it solidified into ice. Adrianna scurried away and heard the *splat* of webbing material hitting the wall nearby, making her curse beneath her labored breaths. Then, in spite of the darkness, she spied something lying in the corridor in the near distance. Desperate for anything that might help, she lurched to her feet. She rushed over, and to her surprise, it was an old, dusty shortsword.

Without hesitation, she picked up the blade. Hearing the creature behind her, Adrianna spun around and aimed her blow at the leg she had frozen. The sword arced through the air and landed on the intended target. The limb shattered with the impact, pieces of it flying in all directions. The monster faltered and stumbled, screaming as it lunged for her. Once more, Adrianna was fortunate and managed to scramble away at the last moment. However, the spider found a way to angle its abdomen towards her, and again the white material issued forth.

This time Adrianna wasn't able to entirely escape the spray. She screamed as the sticky substance caught her free arm and pinned it to the nearest wall.

Her heart slammed against her ribcage as she struggled against the sticky web. The material was too strong for her to break, but it hadn't affected her sword arm. As the spider lunged, she swung the blade, masterfully stabbing the creature in one of its withered eyes. It screamed and lurched back, but it was only a moment later before it was lunging again. Adrianna swung the blade once more, this time stabbing it in another eye. Fluid poured from the wounds and the creature scuttled back.

It was at that moment the spider seemed indecisive. *Dear gods, please leave. Please leave...*

Suddenly it attacked yet again. It was a bit slower, but she barely had the strength to stab it again in one of its many eyes. Emitting one last shriek, the spider shrank away and made its way back down the corridor from whence it had come.

Breathing heavily, Adrianna leaned against the wall. Sweat ran down her temples, trickled between her breasts and down the furrow of her back. *I'll rest here for just a brief moment and then leave before the monster changes its mind and comes back to finish me off.* She looked down at the blade in her hand. *Dear gods, thank you so much for the gift. And the skill I used to wield it...*

She had never heard of unnamed gods bestowing skill upon someone, for only the most devout priests or priestesses deserved this honor, but it felt like a miracle and she wasn't about to complain. She had wielded the blade as though she had studied it for many years, wielded it the way her sister would have.

With no small amount of effort, she hauled herself off of the wall, and just as she was about to walk away, she felt a pull on her arm. Adrianna gave a silent scream and struggled, trying desperately to pull away from the web material that bound her to the stone. She cried for a few moments, tears as silent as her screams, not wanting to bring the creature back to her. She then remembered the sword.

*You can do it...*

Her sword arm ached and trembled with the effort, but she awkwardly held it over the sticky strands and began to cut. More sweat coursed down her back to soak her tunic, down her face to drip onto the stone floor. Her breath came in ragged gasps and her body shook with the chill.

Again, the blade saved her as she ultimately cut her way to freedom, and when finally it was done, Adrianna dropped the sword and allowed her body to sink to the floor beside it. The clang of metal on rock was jarring and not what she had intended. Her every instinct yelled at her to leave this place, but her legs refused to answer the command and she felt the cold as she lay there. Her teeth began to chatter, and as she curled within herself, she grabbed the sword lying nearby. She brought it close to her chest as she drew her knees up and put her head down.

*Just in case the spider comes back for me, just in case, just in case...*

Then, in spite of attempts to remain lucid, she slipped into darkness.

With confusion reigning in his mind, Tallachienan moved quickly through the dungeon corridor. He had left his laboratory and brought himself to Adrianna's rescue, knowing her continued presence down there spelled danger. He didn't recall seeing her make contact with any of the venom, so he didn't understand what her wound could possibly be.

Adrianna had fought against his spider. She hadn't vanquished it, but she had wounded it to the point that it had retreated. Within his Vision Orb, he'd seen the battle and watched her wield a blade as though artfully trained in its use. The last time he'd seen the girl use a blade like that was in the last Cycle, never in this one. He had expected to see her cut herself free from the web and then find a way out of the dungeons. Instead, he watched her slump to the floor. Within moments, she was as if lifeless.

Finally, Tallachienan was kneeling over the fallen young woman. She was curled around herself as an infant would be within its mother's womb. Her face was flushed, and her body trembled. He reached out, placing his hand over her brow. *Damnation! She is burning up!*

Swiftly, he picked her up from the chilly floor. She clutched the shortsword in a death-grip and he had to pry it from her fingers in order to slide it beneath his sash. Carrying her securely within his arms, he brought Adrianna up from the dungeons and took her to Master Warlin, the healer he was fortunate enough to have residing within the citadel. Within only a few moments, the man had assessed her. Adrianna was not ill as a result of spider venom. It was something else. With his prayers and magic, Warlin found no infection, cancer, or internal injury that would cause her to be sick. She just simply was, and there was precious little he could do for her.

With rising concern, Tallachienan watched as Master Warlin worked over his apprentice. He glanced down at the blade situated against his side, finding it vaguely familiar. For a moment he thought of where he could have seen it before, but soon discarded all thoughts of the sword, returning his attention to the young woman on the bed. She looked so small, so fragile lying there, that his heart went out to her. *What had happened to cause this? How long had she been sick before she finally collapsed... after his test of all things?*

Tallachienan sighed as he remembered what Trebexal had told him. Indeed, perhaps Adrianna had begun to wither away behind the cold stone walls of his citadel. Maybe she needed more than what he could provide, her Hinterlean heritage demanding fresh air and wide-open spaces. Guiltily, Tallachienan regarded the pale woman lying on the bed and knew that he had made a grievous mistake. He had ignored her needs, basic needs that any other man would have met. In the previous Cycles he had never been so harsh, even going so far as to provide beautiful gardens in which she could sit and study. There was one that had been her favorite. He had allowed it to perish with all the others when he lost her the last Cycle.

Behind him, Tallachienan heard the door open, and Pylar strode into the room. "Through our link I could feel that something had happened to Adrianna. Is she alright?"

Tallachienan noted the concern in his Bondmate's voice. The dragon cared deeply for Adrianna; the woman couldn't ask for a better champion.

"She will be," he replied somberly.

Pylar sighed with relief. "That is good news. I was worried."

Tallachienan nodded, almost as though to himself. "So was I."

Pylar placed himself on the other side of Adrianna's bed and took her hand. He leaned forward and whispered into her ear. Tallachienan had to strain to hear the softly spoken words; he wouldn't have heard them at all if he didn't try so hard. "I am here for you, my friend. Always I am here for you."

Tallachienan sensed the love emanating from the dragon, and with a sudden rush of understanding he realized that she held some kind of power over him, much as she did with her human and faelin friends. And thinking back on it now, there were other dragons which were also drawn to her somehow.

Tallachienan rose from his position beside Adrianna's bed. He knew her companions would be coming soon, they who had befriended her these several years of training. Then there was the citadel... he could feel the place reacting to her illness, responding to her as no other place could. As he began to turn away, he realized he didn't really want to leave, wished that he could stay by her side. The intense feelings he had for Adrianna surged through him, almost overpowering him with their magnitude.

Tallachienan quickly reined himself in, taking his emotions under control. He walked out of the infirmary and made his way towards his chambers. He wanted her, wanted her with an intensity he recalled from the last Cycle. He had fought these emotions for far too long, and was now willing to embrace them. His days of setting aside his own needs and desires were over. In spite of the man she had left behind in her normal time, Tallachienan would take Adrianna as his own. He would make certain she defeated Aasarak this time, and afterward he would keep her by his side as his consort.

And they would remain together for all eternity.

Sirion followed Dremathian into the room. The ranger was relieved his mentor was feeling better, but now there was another thing to worry about. Word had come that Tianna was sick, and the archdruid was quick to answer the call. She sat removed from the other people within the infirmary, her body slumped, her face pale. Sirion felt a stab of guilt. She had been there offering her abilities as a healer in order to help all of those who were injured in their fight against what they had come to realize was Aasarak's army. She had been uncharacteristically unwilling, but Sirion had peristed. Once they were at her side, they could see that she was, indeed, quite ill. Somehow, she had contracted something during her days at work and he had been the one to ask her there.

She wiped away the sweat that beaded her brow with a cloth and then glanced up at Dremathian when he pulled over a chair and seated himself beside her. His brow furrowed with concern. "How long did you say that you have been feeling this way?"

"Since yesterday," she replied. "It's much worse today. But to be honest, I've been feeling strangely for a few weeks now."

Dremathian frowned. "Strange, how?"

"Just not myself. I haven't been as alert as I used to be, and I feel... I don't know... slow."

Tianna looked up at Sirion standing there beside Dremathian. Her eyes seemed unusually bright, almost glassy like she'd been crying. Dremathian leaned in close to her, and when he asked her to breathe on him, she gave him an odd look. However, she obeyed his command, and when Dremathian returned to his former position, he had a look of alarm on his face.

"Sirion, this woman is under the effects of the shagendra root! She has been poisoned!"

Sirion's eyes widen with surprise, but his mind connected the pieces to a puzzle. This would be the reason for her recent strange behavior. Historically, she'd always been the first one to step forward when anyone might require her aid. But this time, Sirion had to approach her about it. Tianna had seemed almost reluctant to act as a healer for the druids who had been wounded in the battle against Aasarak's army, and had looked to Triath, and for some reason, Sabian, for guidance.

Sirion's mind ran with this newfound information. Triath had been acting strangely as well. Naturally, Sirion began to wonder if the same affliction had struck his friend. Sirion gripped Dremathian's shoulder and when he had the other man's attention, told him that they had to go see Triath immediately. They left Tianna in the capable hands of Brother Silas with assurances that he would give her something to help cleanse her body of the root. As they hurried away, she vomited into a bucket sitting next to the bench she was using, and Sirion felt torn. He wanted to stay with Tianna, but he knew that Triath may need him more.

Dremathian didn't argue and soon they were rushing down the hall in the direction of Triath's room. When they reached it, Sirion knocked loudly on the door. With a gruff command to enter, the men stepped inside. When they saw Triath lying there in his bed, it almost blew them away. The room smelled strongly of vomit, and when they approached, they could see that he was fevered. Just like Tianna, he was withdrawing from the addictive properties of the shagendra root.

Once standing beside Triath, Sirion felt Dremathian become tense. It was the first time the druid had met his good friend, and he knew that this wasn't the best of circumstances. Sirion turned to Dremathian, and when he saw the expression on the man's face, his blood turned cold. Dremathian's gray eyes were hard as steel. "Sirion, you know that this is a sacred place. How could you bring this man here?"

Sirion frowned. "Father, this man is one of my dearest friends. Why *wouldn't* I bring him here?"

Dremathian's expression turned incredulous. "Don't you know? This man is tainted!"

Suddenly Sirion knew what Dremathian was talking about. It was the daemon essence that resided within Triath, that thing that had made an eye reform in a socket where there should be none. Sirion then nodded. "Yes, you are right. I wasn't thinking. But Father, Triath is a good man. He can't help what has happened to him."

Dremathian inhaled deeply. He then turned back to the man lying on the bed, a man who watched them with a fevered gaze. It was then Sirion realized that there was more going on here than just Shagendra withdrawal. There was an aura about Triath, an evil that surrounded him. Sirion was no priest, but he knew that the daemon within Triath was gaining a foothold and would soon consume his friend forever. That is, if he lived long enough.

Dremathian cautiously moved to the other side of the bed. Triath followed him with his eye, but made no other movement. He breathed heavily and sweat matted the hair to his scalp. Suddenly, Triath sat up just enough to vomit over the side, then weakly returned to his former position. His complexion was pallid, and when he turned his eye to Sirion, he could see the helplessness reflected there.

Dremathian stood over the man lying on the bed. He could almost taste the bitter scent of the shagendra as it seeped from Triath's skin. However, this man wasn't just suffering from simple withdrawal. Dremathian placed a cool hand over Triath's forehead, felt the heat emanating from him. It abruptly became so clear...

Triath was in a battle for his life.

Somewhere, somehow, the daemon's essence had entered Triath's body. It fought to break free and gain ultimate possession. Triath was ill because the spirits within him were too disparate, constantly working against one another, disrupting the biology of the overall organism. *Triath was dying.*

Dremathian was suddenly swept away to another time. He remembered Sirion lying before him in the form of a large canine. Dremathian had done everything he could to help his friend, and it almost hadn't been enough. It was a situation similar to this one, where the body was wearing away because the spirits that inhabited it were unable to coexist. In Sirion's case, the man was supposed to have dominion over the beast. The animal had somehow taken over, and it had been slowly killing Sirion.

In Triath's case, no one side was 'supposed' to have dominion over the other. Once the essence of the daemon was inside of him, Triath had become something more than just a simple mortal man. But Triath wanted nothing of the daemon. He fought against it, and when the daemonic essence fought back, chaos ensued. Triath was losing his battle because he refused to accept the new being he had become, a being that was different than anything Dremathian had ever seen before, a being he had heard about only in rare texts and parchments he had encountered in his travels.

Dremathian leaned over the man on the bed. "Triath, I will try to help you, but you have to trust me."

Like a coiled snake, Triath's hand shot up from its place at his side and gripped Dremathian's wrist. "No one can help me now."

Dremathian slowly shook his head. "No, you are wrong. You can help yourself."

Triath's eye bore into his, searching him for any sign of doubt. Finding none, he released Dremathian and closed the eye. He seemed to be sleeping for a moment, but all of a sudden, his body began to convulse. Sirion rushed over and held Triath down on one side while Dremathian held him on the other. When the seizure finally passed, Dremathian looked at Sirion over the unconscious body between them.

"Let's get him to the meditation chamber," he said. "We can place a bed pallet there. I will help him all I can, but it is essentially up to Triath if he chooses to live or die."

Sirion nodded, saying nothing. He trusted that his friend would do all that he could for Triath. Between the two of them, they carried the limp body to the meditation chamber. On their way, they passed other druids whom Dremathian recruited to make a bed for Triath. By the time they got there, the bed had been prepared. Sirion and Dremathian laid him out on it, then Dremathian asked Sirion to leave.

For many hours Sirion wandered aimlessly through the apoptos. His mind ruminated over the past few weeks since the group had become reunited. Right away he had noticed that something was amiss with Triath. Other people had noticed it too, but said nothing. They feared that it might be the daemon within, slowly gaining a foothold. However, Sirion thought it was much more than that. There was foul play afoot, and he was determined to oust the instigator.

Sirion eventually found himself standing in front of the door to Sorn's room. He knocked, and upon hearing a welcome, he entered. The other man looked up from his activity, which seemed to be an inspection of his tools and equipment. Walking over, Sirion saw an assortment of lock picks, some strangely shaped keys, some bits of wire of varying widths, vials containing various powders and liquids, and some odd devices, the possible uses of which he couldn't discern.

Sorn moved his dark hair over one pointed ear and watched him through hard violet eyes before he gestured for Sirion to sit across from him and waited. When he was ready, Sirion spoke of what had recently taken place with Tianna and Triath. With avid interest, yet no emotional reaction, Sorn listened. When Sirion was finished, he came straight to the point. "You think there is a traitor in our midst and want me to find out who has been poisoning them."

Sirion nodded. "I hear you are the man for the job."

Sorn grinned lopsidedly and nodded. "Indeed, I am. I also have an apprentice. She is quite accomplished for her age and rank."

"I trust you, old friend. Amethyst is welcome to help you in any way she can."

Sorn's expression became somber. "I will let you know something within two days."

Sirion rose from the bed. He knew that he needn't tell Sorn to keep quiet about what he knew about Triath and Tianna. "I would see whoever has done this to Triath pay for what he has done."

Sorn quirked an eyebrow. "What if it isn't a man?"

Sirion felt his expression harden. "Treat her the same way as you would a man."

It wasn't long before Sirion was wandering the halls again, his thoughts with the friend that lay inside the meditation chamber. In the past they had their share of arguments, but always knew each would have the other's back in battle. Like he had told Dremathian, Triath was a good man who had been caught up in a very unfortunate circumstance.

In spite of their differences, Sirion could only hope that Triath would live.

*Triath slowly walked across a field of gray. It was springy beneath his feet, and perhaps if he were a child, he would have tried jumping up and down on it. In his mind, his thoughts tumbled about haphazardly. First they skimmed over his childhood and adolescence. Much of that period of his life was as nondescript as the gray he trod upon. However, he had to admit that there were defining moments that altered the course of his life. It was his decision to become a rogue mercenary when he met the rest of the* people that would come to be known as the Wildrunners. First, he had met Arn and Naemmious, a most unlikely pair if ever he met one. Next came Sorn, Laura, and then finally Anya. The six of them had many adventures, or misadventures, before Sirion joined them. Right away the ranger had been a thorn in Triath's side, another dominant male in his sphere of influence. It wasn't much longer before they came across the young Denedrian girl, Breesa, and then the Cimmerean mage, Dinim.

Several moon cycles later the group got into some trouble, and Triath found himself in a battle against something he had never encountered before. It was a daemon... not just any daemon, but a merzillith. The mind-flayer was strong, exceedingly so, but it was injured. Triath managed to deal it a fatal blow... and then it happened. Just as the daemon expired, it chanted the words of great power. Triath felt it immediately; the strands of the magic circled him, grabbed hold of him, and reached deep inside. It touched that beating part of him, the life force that ran through his body. He remembered stumbling away from the fallen daemon, the marks of their fight marring his flesh. Blood poured from the hole that had once been his eye, and deep scores ran above and below it. Yet, the other wounds ran deeper than that, the ones that could only be seen by his innermost mind. Something resided within him, dark and brooding.

And it waited.

Triath looked up from his memories. In the nondescript distance, he began to see something emerge. He loped across the gray expanse, not stopping, not tiring. Finally, he reached it and saw that it was a raised dais. In the middle of it lay a man. Stepping up to it, Triath could see that the man was himself.

Triath recoiled. He looked like he was dead, the flesh pale and the lips almost blue. Then he began to sense another presence there with him. Glancing around, he saw a creature he had hoped never to see again. It was the daemon he had met all of those long moon cycles ago. It was the mind-flayer.

The merzillith was man-sized and clothed within layers of hooded dark robes. The only thing visible was the face, the leathery dark flesh surrounding two red eyes. The nose was absent, but from beneath two slit nostrils emerged five thick tentacles that extended down its chest. They were the only things moving as the daemon stood there, watching him.

Triath froze. He took stock of himself: the tight leather pants he wore, the belt around his waist that carried his dagger and short sword, and the silk shirt and leather vest. He had another dagger in his right boot, easily accessible in a fight, and enchanted by Dinim. He had his psionic powers as well, but somehow, he thought that they would be no use against the creature from whom they came.

"What do you want?" Triath finally spoke. It was an attempt to quiet the voices in his mind just as much as it was to discover the intentions of the daemon.

The voice came to him in his mind, just as he remembered it from all of those moon cycles ago. It was slightly sibilant. "To finish what wasss ssstarted."

Triath shook his head. "That battle has long been over. I defeated you."

Triath felt the creature's amusement as it answered. "You call thisss defeat? I have been with you all of thisss time, a part of me carried with you. Now I will exssert the control that I ssso richly dessserve."

Triath felt his anger welling up. "What have you done to me?" he screamed. "I will kill you just as I did before." Without another thought, Triath lunged towards the merzillith, drawing his short sword from the scabbard at his side. The blade hissed as it was pulled free. Just as Triath was within range, the daemon pulled out his own weapon, wickedly curved, with forks of steel emerging from the main blade so as to open an opponent's bowel with one savage twist.

However, Triath's sword had been enchanted by Dinim. The blade began to hum as it flewed throught the air in his grasp, suffusing his limbs with the speed of lightning. Triath swung at his enemy and sliced into him before pulling back and away, all within one fluid strike. The merzillith was slower, but he had a strength about him that Triath knew all daemon-kind possessed. He bowed under the force of the blow the merzillith delivered, but then he stepped out of reach in order to execute another strike.

It was soon apparent to Triath that he had been correct when he assumed that he would be unable to use his psionic ability against the daemon. However, it also became clear that the merzillith could not use it either. Triath found himself galvanized by this discovery, and it urged him to greater heights as he dueled with his enemy. He blocked out the persistent voices in his mind, focusing on his battle.

Triath didn't know for how long he fought the merzillith. Hours passed, perhaps days. He felt himself becoming weaker, but felt the same from his opponent. He kept thinking that all he had to do was remain steadfast in his endeavor. He would eventually persevere over the daemon and then go back to the normal existence he had before the psionic power came to him, before the daemon eye grew in his head, and before the ill-fated battle took place. He would never be the handsome, debonair man he had been before, but at least he would be free of the daemon's taint.

More time went by. Triath became weak and his opponent equally so. They glared at one another across the small space between them. The gray

medium beneath their feet was smeared red and black with blood, testimony of the ferocity of their battle. Glancing around, he saw that they had worked their way close to the dais upon which his body lay. He noticed something strange about it, and when he focused on it, he saw that it appeared somehow faded.

Triath frowned and returned his attention to the merzillith. It just stood there, watching him. Keeping his eyes on the daemon, Triath stumbled and fell to his knees. The voices within his head suddenly came to the fore, soothing yet insistent. They were telling him something. Triath struggled to keep his eyes open, tried to focus upon the daemon. The merzillith had also fallen and was making no move to rise. Triath remembered to position his arm beneath his head as he fell the rest of the way onto the ground.

Triath, you must accept your fate. It is your destiny.

You must be strong. Embrace the being that you have become.

You must let go of what once was to make room for what will be.

Triath knew he was dying. That was why the body laying upon the dais was losing its substance. It would soon fade away into nothing, and he would no longer be a part of the mortal world. He heard the voices in his mind more clearly now, urging him onward, to overcome his resentment of the daemon essence within him, and to become one with it. They tempted him with memories of the mortal world: his friendships with his comrades, his love for Tianna, his desire to see an end to the shadows that threatened to overcome Shandahar. Triath thought that perhaps it wouldn't be so bad to live the rest of his life with the powers of the merzillith...

Triath opened his weary eyes. The daemon continued to lie on the ground a short distance away. With the rest of the energy left within him, Triath crawled across the space that separated them, and then reached out to touch the daemon.

Triath felt himself suddenly thrust into nameless space. He floated within the gray void, felt the evil surrounding him. He felt the presence of the daemon in his mind, pulling him towards the evil. At first Triath resisted, countering the pull of the daemon. He heard a sibilant chuckle and then the voice. "You fool. You fought me for ssso long that you have no ssstrength left to you."

Triath floundered, hearing the ring of truth in the daemon's words. He knew that he was weak. He felt powerless against the pull of evil and knew that it would just be easier to take the path of least resistance. But then he heard the voices within his mind once more showing him the right way. They encouraged him to continue to be strong and to fight for what he believed in.

Triath renewed his struggles. The daemon hissed in anger, promising to see the end of him. Yet, Triath fought on, pushing against the darkness that *had begun to permeate his soul since the daemonic essence entered him. He embraced the new being he had become, but rejected the alignment that sought to accompany it. Finding a well of strength that he never knew he had, Triath resisted the lure of darkness and corruption and pushed the remaining taint of evil from his soul.*

*Suddenly, there was silence. The daemon was gone, as were the voices in his mind. He finally relaxed his defenses, fatigue rushing up to envelop him. Now he could sleep, truly sleep for the first time in gods only knew how long.*

# A Meeting of Cycles

Adrianna slowly awoke. She opened her eyes to find she was laying in her own bed, the familiar pillows situated all around. She was alone, but knew she hadn't always been. If she really put her mind to it, she could recall the many visits from Pylar, Myan, Tridium, Yasmin, Dlamini, and even Coaxtl. Adrianna sat up, pulling away the blankets and furs. She inhaled deeply and noticed the air smelled fresh. She expected it would have been musty, with a hint of the illness she had endured. Instead, it was crisp and clean, as though the windows had been kept ajar. Moreover, when she looked over to such windows, she noticed that, indeed, the apertures were open, inviting the fresh air from the outside to permeate her chamber.

Smiling, Adrianna swung her legs over the side of the bed, placing her feet onto the cold floor. However, she didn't mind the chill as she stood and made her way over to the open windows. Once there she leaned upon the sill, allowing the mild afternoon breeze to ruffle her hair. By the gods, she actually felt well, not the sickly apparition she had recently become. Vaguely, she remembered a battle with a terrible monster, a huge spider that had pinned her to the wall with its sticky web. She remembered finding a sword...

Adrianna frowned in confusion. *That doesn't seem right. I have never been the best swordsman, even after my practices with Tridium.*

She turned when she heard the door open. Pylar entered and strode over to the window to join her there, putting his arms around her when he reached her side.

"It is good to see you up and about again, my friend."

Adrianna gripped his arm and shook her head. "Pylar, what was wrong with me?"

"No one knows, not even Master Warlin."

"Then who is to say that the illness won't return?" she asked with a frown.

Pylar's eyes clouded with concern. "No one. It is entirely possible that you could fall ill once more."

Adrianna looked away and back out the window at the barren landscape that stretched beyond. Slowly, she shook her head. "I haven't felt this well since I first came to study here."

Adrianna heard Pylar give a deep inhalation, felt a change in the aura surrounding him. He knew things that he would never tell her, things he had always known. The realization didn't come as a surprise to her, for above all else he was Master Tallachienan's Bondmate. Yet, even after her discovery of his true identity, Adrianna had always believed he was a true friend, and that Pylar would never knowingly sacrifice her well-being in order to keep his secrets.

Adrianna fought to keep herself in check. She looked down at the hands that gripped the window sill, noticed the long scar that marred the otherwise flawless flesh of her right forearm. It was an older scar, one she had noticed once before during another of her "visions", as she thought of them. Her head began to spin. She knew they weren't real, for they came and went as they pleased, yet there was the scar on her arm. Briefly she thought to ask Pylar if he saw the healed wound, but could not bear the look in his eyes if he saw nothing. And then there were the dreams that robbed her of rest. Perhaps her dreams had some connection to the visions, and maybe something was at play that was beyond her scope of understanding.

Regardless, standing there at the window, Adrianna knew something in her had changed. She was different somehow...

"I am famished." Adrianna made the announcement offhandedly, wanting Pylar to leave her to herself. She knew he would gladly obtain nourishment for her, and she needed a few moments alone to reflect. However, she was surprised to note that the statement wasn't entirely a fabrication. For the first time in a long time, she was indeed hungry.

Pylar smiled. "Let me go to the kitchens for you. I will bring a meal to your room."

Adrianna nodded with a small forced smile. "That would be lovely, thank you." She watched as he left her chamber, closing the door gently behind him. The knowledge that Pylar withheld information was disturbing, but Adrianna knew he cared about her, loved her even. His dedication to Tallachienan was worthy and she respected that.

Adrianna turned away from the window and made her way over to the looking glass. She stood before it, taking in the image staring back at her. Slowly, she began to remove her nightdress, unlacing the ribbon in the front and then slipping the garment over her head. When she finally stood naked before the glass, Adrianna took in her appearance. She saw her eyes widen, noticing that the scar between her breasts was no longer there. She stepped closer to the image in the glass, touching her fingertips to her chest where the mark was supposed to be. She felt no indication of the past injury, yet vividly remembered receiving it when she was raped on her journey to Andahye.

Adrianna looked away from her chest, noticing the scar on her forearm. The memory of this injury did not come so easily, but to her surprise, it was there in her mind, waiting to be tapped.

*Adrianna parried yet another blow from her opponent. She was beginning to tire, she could feel it as her reflexes slowed and her muscles burned with the effort it took to block the attacks. She no longer had the energy to take the offensive, but she hated to simply let her opponent win without more of a fight. He was an excellent swordsman, better than Dinim and just as good as the Master.*

*Her opponent swung his blade once more. Adrianna made the move to block it, but her arm was just too tired. Her wrist twisted involuntarily, and her arm fell into the swing of his sword. Despite his efforts to alter its trajectory, the blade cut into her arm, leaving a deep cut. Adrianna heard her own sword clatter to the floor as she gasped and put her other hand over the wound. She watched in fascination as the blood welled between her fingers and began to drip onto the pale stone underfoot...*

Adrianna shook her head, clearing it of the memory, a memory she didn't recall ever having before. She looked back into the glass, suddenly noticing other things that were different about her. It was the lines of her face, the set of her jaw, and the curve of her mouth. Shaking her head, she stepped away from the glass and made her way to the closet. She chose an intricately woven gown, one she had never worn before. She had always thought it too expensive for her tastes, but now imagined it might look nice on her.

Standing once again before the glass, Adrianna slipped the garment over her head. When she saw the image staring back at her, she noticed how well she filled out the gown. It was beautiful. The deep green fabric was the perfect color against her skin, and the weave was so soft, she could have spent the rest of the day simply rubbing it between her fingers. Yet, it was a loose weave, and Adrianna belatedly realized that she should perhaps wear a sleeveless under-tunic beneath the gown. Much of her flesh was visible, and although one couldn't pick out the details, it was enough to make her think twice about the decision to keep it on. Much to her surprise, there was a part of her that wanted to continue wearing the gown as it was, especially knowing that there was no harm in it since she had no plans to leave her chamber. She shook her head in response to her silliness, but before she could make her way back over to the closet, there was a knock on the door.

Tridium and Yasmin were walking into the room before she could issue a welcome to enter.

Gladly, Adrianna embraced her friends. They were happy to see her hale and whole after her long illness. After discovering that she had been only semi-conscious for over a fortnight, Adrianna began to realize the worry she must have caused. The women raved over the gown she wore, and despite the conservative part of her that warned against it, Adrianna decided to wear the gown without the under-tunic, not really wanting to take the time to find one. The women invited her to take the evening meal with them and she accepted, for she felt suffused with new energy by the presence of her friends and wished for more.

"But where is Myan?" she asked.

"He said that he would meet us in the dining hall," said Tridium.

Adrianna nodded, stepping up onto the floating disk Yasmin had called for them to take. As the disk carried them towards their destination, Adrianna looked about herself, feeling somehow much more comfortable with her surroundings than she ever had before. The citadel seemed much more familiar to her, and as they passed the side corridors, she knew where each one ended. There was a part of her that recognized she had been down those hallways before, but then there was another part of her that knew she had not.

Once they reached the dining hall, Myan was waiting at one of the tables. When he saw Adrianna, he smiled and rose from his seat. He stepped away from the table to join them as they made their way over, taking Adria's arm and helping her to seat herself. Meanwhile, she noticed his gaze roving over the gown she wore, and once again she wondered if she should have worn that under-tunic beneath it.

The companions shared the meal Alak brought out to them. The food was wonderful, the ptarmigan having been brushed with a delicate sauce, the roots tender, and the tubers mildly seasoned. Afterwards, the comrades partook of some wine and simply sat and enjoyed one another's company. After a while, Adrianna began to feel tired, and just as she was about to say something to her friends, she noticed Pylar standing near the entrance to the dining room.

Adrianna rose and excused herself, quickly making her way over to Pylar. When she approached, she suddenly remembered that he had gone to obtain some food for her and that he had probably returned to her chambers to find her gone. "Pylar, I am so sorry. Tridium and Yasmin came to see me. They invited me to dinner, and I am ashamed to say that I forgot about you." Adrianna stepped up to him, taking his hand in hers.

Pylar only shook his head and smiled. "My dear, don't fret about me so much. You have every right to enjoy some time with your friends. I came only to tell you that the Master wishes an audience with you."

Pylar pressed his lips into a thin line. It was bad timing... Tallachienan wanting to speak with Adrianna just when she was starting to relax with her comrades. But Pylar had agreed to hunt her down and bring her back to his chambers.

Adrianna nodded. "Allow me to let the others know, and I will be right back."

Pylar watched her as she went back to the table. Tridium, Myan, and Yasmin all stood and offered her an embrace before they all seated themselves again. Myan cast a dark scowl at Pylar as he led Adrianna from the dining hall. Pylar really couldn't blame the man for being irate. Hells, he felt something of the same protective anger for Adrianna, himself. Hailing a disk, Pylar and Adrianna rode towards Master Tallachienan's chambers. He had noticed the gown that she wore, and after a while, he realized it was reminiscent of something she would have worn in the last Cycle. It was most definitely the most elaborate attire he had seen on her, and he thought she looked rather enchanting. As they neared Tallachienan's chambers, Pylar was reminded of the confrontation to come. *Damnation.* He knew that Tallachienan was having a difficult time keeping himself from her, and Pylar had the distinct feeling that his Bondmate was letting down his guard. This heralded the emergence of a different relationship between them, although Adrianna had yet to find that out. Most likely, tonight would be that time. Pylar could only wait to see how everything would unfold.

Finally, the disk stopped before Master Tallachienan's personal chambers. If he recalled it properly, in all her years at the citadel during this Cycle, Adrianna had never been there before. She dismounted the disk and when Pylar didn't do the same, she turned towards him questioningly.

"Master Tallachienan wishes to speak with you privately. He will escort you back to your chambers when you have completed your discussion. I will see you tomorrow." Pylar tried to keep an encouraging expression on his face as he spoke, not wanting to give away any of his unease.

Adrianna nodded. "All right. I will see you tomorrow, then."

Pylar inclined his head before he sped away on the disk. She watched him as he left, a disquieting feeling stealing over her. She had been very sick for a long time, and she didn't know what to expect from this meeting. What the Hells was Master Tallachienan doing by calling her to his chambers when he had never bothered to do so before? She knew that there was this *thing* between them, yet here she was, standing outside the door to his suite, about to go in there... alone.

It seemed somewhat ominous.

*This is silly*, she chided herself. *What could possibly happen? Surely there have been other times we were alone together outside of our spellcasting sessions.* Adrianna wracked her mind for a moment, trying to remember. When she finally recalled a time or two, she very thoughtfully reminded herself that they hadn't been alone in his chambers.

Adrianna knocked gently on the door and a moment later, she heard Master Tallachienan's voice calling her to enter. She found him standing beside his desk, pouring two glasses of dark wine. As she stepped further into the room, he smiled and beckoned for her to sit on the large cushioned sofa to his right. Tallachienan brought the glasses over, holding both out so she could choose the one she wanted. He then sat down on the other side of the sofa and took a sip of the vintage. Adrianna did the same, and once she had a chance to experience the full flavor, she found it reminded her of the wine she and her companions had shared the evening of the ball. Great, just what she needed... remembrances of the night Master Tallachienan abandoned her out in the middle of the dance floor.

Adrianna slowly lowered the glass from her mouth, staring down at her hands. She began to feel self-conscious, her attention suddenly drawn to the gown she wore. *Damn*, she knew she should have put something underneath it. She wondered why he hadn't yet spoken, but she didn't want to look up for fear that he would somehow read her emotions. But even more, why was she there, and why he was serving her his finest wine?

"I am glad to see that you are doing well."

His voice startled her for a moment, but she was quick to recover.

"I think all I needed was a bit more sleep. I feel as good as new." Adrianna answered without looking up at him, rubbing the pad of her thumb against the rim of her glass. She wished that he would just get to the point of this meeting so she could rejoin her friends.

The room was silent for a moment. Then, "I think it was more than that, but I will settle for your explanation. It sounds better than the real one."

Adrianna became still, ceasing even the movement of her thumb and the breaths she took. Did she hear him right? Was Master Tallachienan admitting that perhaps he had a hand in the reason why she became so sick? Moreover, if he could be so forthright, then so could she. "Yes, and the real reason is so much more complicated than that."

Again, silence reigned. "I was worried about you."

This time Adrianna couldn't keep herself from looking up. She found her gaze locking onto his, and she saw the naked emotion simmering just below the surface. It reminded her of what she saw when she danced with him the night of the ball, something that lay... waiting. Once again, just as it had that night, it was almost like time slowed down. Her world collided with his, a mortal's existence entwining with that of a god.

And then, all of a sudden, it was coming back to her...

Memories of herself in this same place, but another time. She felt the love she and Tallachienan shared, the passion between them, and the deep commitment. She remembered training with him by day, and at night she came to this very room, beyond the curtained panel along the far wall, and into the bedchamber beyond. She remembered the feel of his lips on her mouth, on her neck, and then other places. She remembered his hands caressing her, the sensation of his body pressed against hers with nothing between them...

With no small effort, Adrianna dragged herself out of the memories. She rose from the sofa, her hand shaking as she held the wine glass.

"Adrianna, are you all right?" Tallachienan's voice rang with concern as he stood up beside her, putting one hand at her elbow while taking the wine with the other. This time, he behaved as a gentleman should, instead of forcing himself on her as he had while they were in Elvandahar. Yet, she had responded to him in spite of his aggressive actions. To this day, she still couldn't quite figure out what had happened between them and why.

Adrianna suddenly felt overwhelmed. *What is happening? My mind is filled with someone else's memories, a woman Tallachienan had loved, one who had loved him in return. Then there are the strange visions I have been experiencing, and dreams that are so vivid they could be real.*

He must have caught some of the expressions passing over her face because Tallachienan spoke again. "Adrianna, please tell me what is wrong."

Adrianna realized that he was standing before her and that he gripped both of her arms in his hands. She looked up at him again, unable to stop the tears. "Tallachienan, something is wrong with me. I..."

It took her a moment to realize what she had done. It was the same mistake she had made that night in Elvandahar before he started to ravish her. She had used his given name. She choked on her next words, saw the conflict in his eyes. He was genuinely worried about her, and she could see that he wanted to help. However, she could see something else there as well, something that he fought against... and lost.

Tallachienan's voice cracked as he made a reply. "Adrianna, there is nothing wrong with you."

Tallachienan whispered something in an unfamiliar tongue and then he was pressing his lips to hers, kissing her ardently. Adrianna's reaction was immediate, responding to him as she did in her newfound memories, giving in to the passion of the moment. He kissed her with none of the aggression she remembered from the last time. Yet, he claimed her mouth with his, taking all that she had to give, and much, much more. Tallachienan pulled her to him, ran his hands down her sides, then over her rounded bottom and up her back. As Adrianna felt her mind begin to

43

spiral away, she tangled her hands in his thick hair, loosening it from the thin strip of soft leather that bound it. He trailed kisses from her face down to her neck, and she felt her belly clench in anticipation.

"Gods, I was so worried about you after the test," Tallachienan breathed the words at the hollow of her neck, his voice husky and deep. He began to say something else, but the words were lost as he brought his mouth back to hers.

Sluggishly, Adrianna's mind mulled over his words. She ran her hands over his chest and then back up to his face, touching his lips where they embraced hers. *Test? What test?*

Suddenly, her mind found a moment of clarity, and she spoke the words aloud. "What test?"

Tallachienan continued to kiss her as he replied, "The test you completed before you passed out on my dungeon floor."

Adrianna felt herself become still. Tallachienan immediately noticed the change in her demeanor and stopped. Yet, he continued to hold her close, his warm breath moving a tendril of hair against her face. Then she made the connection. The spider. *The big ugly spider she had faced in the maze beneath the citadel had been a test.*

Adrianna pulled herself out of Tallachienan's embrace and turned away from him, putting a hand up to her mouth. Hellfire! She could have died, especially considering the condition she was in when she was forced to take his gods-forsaken test. She found her anger rising, as well as her disappointment. What was she thinking, kissing him like this? Alone in the middle of his study?

"I have to go..." Adrianna quickly walked across the room towards his door.

"Adrianna... stop."

Tallachienan's voice was gruff and authoritative. Adrianna just shook her head and imagined herself chuckling. He thought he would take control of the situation, somehow regain the authority he lost when he shattered the spell he had over her with a simple kiss. She had been wrong all of those moon cycles ago when she accused him of no longer being a man. She had seen another side of him. He was no longer the all-powerful Master. He had become mortal, and much of her awe had evaporated. He couldn't control her the way he had before. She forbade it.

Adrianna heard him curse as she rushed to the door. She opened it before Tallachienan could maneuver himself in her way, slipping out of his grasp as he attempted to grab her arm. She began to sprint down the hallway, tears clouding her vision. She knew that all of this was for nothing. With his power, he would easily catch her, and then... Adrianna struck the thoughts from her mind as ran as fast as her feet could carry her. When she saw him emerge from the hallway to her right, she slowed herself just enough to career down a corridor to her left.

Adrianna felt the sobs rising in her chest and then into her throat to close off her breath. *Why is this happening? What have I done in my life to deserve all of this? I had thought that being an apprentice to Master Tallachienan would be one of the best things that could have happened to me, and a great honor. But Tallachienan is going insane, and me with him. It has been one thing after another from the moment I entered this place.*

Adrianna turned down yet another hallway. At first, she thought that she would surely be lost, but then realized she wasn't. The corridor was familiar to her even though she knew it shouldn't be. She found herself looking for one door in particular, and when she found the one with the plant-like carvings, she opened it and stepped inside.

Just as she had that night so long ago, Adrianna found herself in what had once been a garden. She ran along the dark path, not stopping to look around. Finally, she stopped at a place that appeared as though it had once been a waterfall. She slumped down onto her knees and began to cry, her body shaking almost convulsively. She let the deluge overtake her for a while, and then attempted to take control of herself.

It wasn't until Adrianna recovered enough to form rational thoughts that she realized he was there. She'd known he would find her, but had still held onto the hope that he wouldn't. Tallachienan stepped off of the path and strode towards her imposingly, his every movement telling her that he was perturbed by her behavior. She steeled herself against him, telling herself that she would not allow him to bully her, much less seduce her again.

Adrianna sat up and regarded him as he stood over her. With all of the sympathy of a stone wall, Master Tallachienan looked down at her and shook his head. "I assume you are upset about the test I prepared for you to endure. You performed rather well, but I hadn't expected you to resort to a physical weapon in lieu of your magical training. I was slightly disappointed, but your performance was satisfactory enough."

Adrianna narrowed her eyes. Yes, the man that stood before her was her Master. However, she would no longer accept his absolute authority. The time for that was over. She had been witness to the loss of his control, a man who had preached the necessity of it to her day after day during their spellcasting sessions. Not only that, but she had become woefully aware of one of his weakness...herself.

Adrianna stood up and met his gaze defiantly. She then stepped up to Tallachienan, and before he could see what was coming, she slapped him across the face. "You bastard," she hissed.

Tallachienan's head turned from the impact, but almost immediately his cold gaze returned to her face. His hand snaked out and caught hold of her wrist. "You had best watch your footing on the ice you have chosen to walk across," he growled.

Adrianna jerked her arm free, only vaguely aware of the pain it caused. "No longer am I your pawn to simply be used and discarded. Since the day I arrived here, you have been a curse to me, and if I am to be banished as a result of my disrespect, then so be it."

Tallachienan's eyes narrowed. "Not even you could be so lucky. Yet, you have been the bane of my existence as well, and if I could, I would be rid of you. However, I have accepted my fate. Now you must accept yours."

Adrianna shook her head. "No. I choose my own fate."

Tallachienan laughed, the sound of it echoing harshly throughout the dead garden. "Like I said, you would never be so lucky." Once again, his hand quickly reached out to capture her wrist, holding it tight. He jerked her close and spoke to her in a low growl. "You are stuck with me, just as I am with you." Then he pushed her back, releasing her wrist as she stumbled backward onto the ground. A moment later, Tallachienan followed her down, his body lying over hers, one hand on either side of her head. "You are mine, always have been and always will be."

Adrianna put a hand on his chest, attempting to push him back. Once more he was the aggressor, attempting to claim what was not freely given. "No," she shouted. "Stay away from me. I will not succumb to you this time."

"I know you want to." Tallachienan's voice had changed. He sought to entice her to him, but she refused to oblige. "I can feel it every time I touch you." Tallachienan put his hand on her side near her breast, and even in the darkness, Adrianna could see that he had taken notice of the gown she wore.

Once again, Adrianna built up her resolve. For the second time, she felt her hand connect with his face. He was right; she *did* want him. She knew that much of it was because of his god-like power to *Charm*, his ability to seduce any mortal he wanted. However, it was also more than that; some aspect of her attraction was genuine. Right now, she hated that. Even more, she hated that he knew about it.

This time, Tallachienan's face didn't move, and his eyes bore into hers as he jerked her up from the ground. Savagely, she twisted away from him, her breaths beginning to come in ragged gasps. She could see that he was angry, but she could also see that he was experiencing other emotions as well. He was feeling a moment of indecision.

Between breaths, Adrianna finally found the words to speak again, her voice trembling. "I never want you to touch me again. I don't understand what you have done to me... don't want to understand. If your goal was to drive me crazy, you've succeeded. Now, just stay away from me. I want you to send me home as soon as you can arrange it."

Tallachienan just stood there as Adrianna rushed back along the path to the garden entrance. A part of him wanted to follow her, make her bend to his will. But the other part bid him stay. How she had been able to resist his *Charm* was confusing, and it had made him wonder if what he had been doing was the right thing.

Tallachienan slowly made his way back to his chamber. Once entering, the first thing he noticed were the two wine glasses sitting on the table in front of the sofa, both almost completely full. He sat down and picked one up, taking a long drink as he considered his situation. What was it about Adrianna that drew him so strongly? What was it that made her so special? It was more than just her graceful beauty, it was the person who resided within. Not for the first time he was tempted to contact Charlemagne, ask the god to view the events of Adrianna's life before he came for her. Tallachienan shook his head. It would take time to do that, possibly several days, not to mention the effort it would take from Charlemagne and the intense fatigue Tallachienan would suffer upon his return from the future.

Tallachienan drained the glass and picked up the other one. Once again he wondered how she was able to resist him. He had never noticed that ability in previous Cycles. Of course, he had never had to use his *Charm* so excessively in those Cycles, for she hadn't developed an aversion to him then as she did now. He sighed. Perhaps he deserved it, for he hadn't really been the epitome of kindness these past few years. And now she wanted him to send her home.

*Damn, she wasn't ready yet...*

The next time Adrianna awoke it was early in the afternoon. Sluggishly, she extracted herself from the blankets, wondering why she had slept so long. Certainly, she had been up half the night, and she was probably still recovering from her illness, but she had hoped her body would have at least *tried* to awaken at a normal time. She could only hope the sickness wouldn't revisit her, and the thought that it might sent her slumping back onto the bed. Memories of the previous night flashed through her mind: going to see Tallachienan in his personal chambers, experiencing the strange visions followed by his passionate kiss, learning about the test, her emotional flight to the garden, and their subsequent argument. She never did find out why he had called her to him in the first place.

Finally, Adrianna was up and she dressed in her customary long tunic and trousers. She noticed the scar still on her arm and wondered why it hadn't disappeared the way it always had before. She tried to think of what day it might be, and she belatedly realized she should have asked someone that question yesterday. Just as she was about to open the door to leave, someone knocked.

Adrianna admitted a solemn Pylar into her chambers. Neither spoke for a moment as Adrianna closed the door and turned to face him. He cleared his throat and finally brought his eyes to hers. "The Master wants me to tell you that he is prepared to take you back home later this evening. Currently he is making the preparations for the Travel."

Adrianna only nodded, regarding him intently. She knew that he was at least partially aware of what had happened the night before. She could see the sadness reflected in his golden gaze, as well as a mixture of other emotions she couldn't place.

Pylar stepped up to her, placing a hand on each of her shoulders. "I will miss you, my friend."

Adrianna nodded, casting her gaze to the floor. By the gods, he was actually going to let her go. But what about Xebrinarth? How would she be able to see him again? It was only because of Tallachienan's power that she had been able to meet him at all. Her heart cried out at the thought that she might never see her Bondmate again, and she found herself turning away from Pylar before he could see her tears.

Pylar turned her back around to face him, putting his arms around her as she began to cry. He held her that way for a while, and when her tears subsided, he gently wiped them from her face with the palm of his hand.

"Pylar, I'm so afraid."

Pylar nodded. "I know. But I want you to know that I will try to help you through this."

Adrianna shook her head. "No, it's not just what had happened between the Master and I. It is Xebrinarth."

Pylar let out an explosive breath, suddenly understanding. The connection between Bondmates was strong. Without one another, the Bonded pair would suffer greatly. Within his lifetime, Pylar had seen a few dragons perish without their Bondmates. Then there were others who withstood an abruption of the soul and were never the same again. Right now, living as they did, Adrianna and Xebrinarth placed great strain on themselves. The Bond was not meant for pairs who lived apart, especially worlds apart. Pylar felt they endured their separation rather well. From personal experience, he knew they were only able to share a weak link through which only the strongest emotions could be transmitted.

However, a Bonded pair could not live like that indefinitely. Currently, the only means they had to see one another was through the portals that Master Tallachienan could provide with his power. There was the rift, but its location wasn't common knowledge. Pylar didn't know what kind of effect it would have on Adrianna, but he guessed that Xebrinarth would probably die without her. He didn't want to see that happen.

"Adrianna, come with me."

He led her out of the chamber suite and called a disk. In silence, they rode it to his own chambers. Once there, Pylar opened the top drawer of his desk, knowing exactly where he had placed the device. It had been centuries since he used it last, but he remembered as if it was yesterday. Pylar handed the rune-inscribed metal band over to Adrianna, watched the expressions pass over her face before she finally asked.

"What is it?"

"It is a communication enhancement device. It will allow you to speak more with Xebrinarth, make it so you can feel your link more strongly. It will make it easier for the two of you to live apart, allow you to share your lives more fully. I know it isn't the final answer to your dilemma, but at least it is something."

Adrianna's eyes were wide with incredulity. "How did you come to have such a device?"

"Tallachienan created it when he was much younger, just beginning to approach the apex of his power. We were forced to live apart for a time, much like you and Xebrinarth. He was a genius, even then, and he produced it for me and gave it to me to wear."

Adrianna turned the metal over in her hands, scrutinizing it. Pylar used to wear it on the middle talon of his left claw. He watched as Adrianna placed the band over her left forearm and then closed it. The metal seared shut, molding itself to the shape of her arm. The runes glowed briefly and then returned to their natural state. They created an elaborate design on the band, making it appear to be a simple piece of decoration that looked very much like a band that Tallachienan wore on his own arm. The Master obviously no longer had need for it unless he was busy instructing his apprentices off-world. Yet he wore it almost every day, mayhap out of respect for the Bond he shared with Pylar.

"Pylar, are you sure you want to give this up?"

"For you, yes. I no longer need it, and I want for you to be as happy as possible."

Adrianna stepped close to him, wrapping her arms around his neck. "I love you so much, Pylar. You have no idea what this means to me."

Pylar rather thought he did, but he said nothing, merely stood within her embrace. She brushed her lips across his before stepping back and giving him a grin. "I am going to go give it a try."

Pylar nodded and then watched as she left his chamber. He suddenly felt bereft, and he wondered what would happen now. Tallachienan was going to lose her again. She wasn't ready for the fight ahead of her, and she would most likely be defeated. The world would be thrust into chaos and then would reset itself to be repeated all over again. Pylar felt his chest begin to ache, felt his throat begin to close over the lump forming there.

Once again, he would lose one of the best friends he had ever had.

Adrianna rode the disk back towards her chambers. She brushed her fingers over the smooth metal band on her arm, wondering if it would really work for her. She stopped the disk in the middle of the corridor, and then began to concentrate on her link with Xebrinarth. Suddenly, there was a blossom of sensation in her mind and a rapid influx of emotions. She felt the newfound strength of their link, felt her Bondmate's surprise and astonishment. When his words came tumbling into her mind, Adrianna couldn't help the joy from suffusing her, rushing through the link to Xebrinarth.

<Zahara... where are you? Let me come to you so I can fly you to my lair!> With the strengthening of their link, Xebrinarth had assumed she must be on Haldorr. She could sense his happiness, his intense desire to see her. She hated to let him down, but he would be almost as happy to discover that they would be able to communicate like this despite the worlds that separated them.

<Xebrin, I am not on Haldorr. I am still on Shandahar.>

Immediately she could sense his confusion, the thoughts tumbling around in his mind. <How is this possible? I am speaking to you as though you were here.>

<It is a gift given to us by Pylar. It is an artifact that enhances our ability to communicate.>

Xebrinarth was quiet for a moment before he responded. <Do you know what this means for us?>

Adrianna smiled to herself. <Indeed, I do. I can speak to you anytime I want, and you can do the same. It won't replace us not being able to see one another, but it is better than nothing.>

Once again Xebrinarth was quiet before he spoke again. <Zahara, we will no longer be able to see one another?>

Hearing the tone of his mind-voice, Adrianna felt her heart ache. Feelings of desolation and hopelessness filtered to her through the link, and once again she realized how much harder their separation was for her

Bondmate. Fear coursed through her, the reality of his situation finally becoming so much clearer. *Xebrinarth would die without her.*

<I don't know.> Adrianna didn't have the heart to tell him nay. <I will soon be leaving Master Tallachienan's citadel to return to my comrades.>

<Why don't you come here to be with me?> The tone of his voice was plaintive. Once again, she felt her heart ache.

<I can't... not yet. I have a duty, and I can't just abandon them. However, when my time with them is through, I will try to find a way to come to you.>

Adrianna sensed his reluctant acceptance. <There is more to this than you are telling me. I can sense it in your mind. But I will accept it for now. I love you, Zahara. Strive to keep yourself safe, for my life is in your hands.>

<I know, my friend. I am sorry that this has been so hard for you. If I could, I would make it otherwise.>

<No!> His voice rang stridently in her mind. <Never say that you would change anything about us. You are everything to me, and I could never regret what we have together.>

Adrianna nodded, a tear escaping her eye. She sent him a surge of love through their link, and then refocused on the disk, bidding it return to her chambers. As the disk carried her, she contemplated her situation. She would be returning to her companions before completing her training. She hoped that the training she had would be sufficient. It would have to be... she no longer had a choice.

After a while the disk stopped, and Adrianna looked around in surprise. The corridor was not immediately known to her, but after taking a look around, she got a vague sense of familiarity about the place. It was definitely not the location of her chamber, but there was a door before her. What she really wanted to do was tell the disk to return her to her chamber, but a part of her felt compelled to go through the door, curiosity having gotten the best of her.

Slowly Adrianna dismounted the disk. She half expected it to be locked, but when she turned the knob, the door easily opened to admit her. Adrianna walked into the dim chamber and looked around. It was much like her own, one that an apprentice would use. However, it was obvious that this particular chamber hadn't been used in a very long time. A layer of dust covered every surface, and the air tasted stale. Adrianna walked further into the room, the familiarity she sensed about the place getting stronger. Yes, this chamber was a component within her new memories. She walked towards the bookshelf, saw texts that were similar to the ones she currently used. She passed the canopied bed, allowing her fingertips to skim over the sheer fabric that formed a shroud around it.

She then made her way over to the desk, and once she reached it, pulled out the chair and seated herself there.

For a moment she just sat, the memories pooling in her mind. They told her this had once been her chamber, and that Dinim's quarters had been just down the hall. Adrianna shook her head. That couldn't be. She knew that Dinim was with the rest of the Wildrunners. Everything had become so confusing now, and she was finding it more and more difficult to separate her real memories from these others.

Adrianna's eyes skimmed over the desk. Along the back, there was a part that could be used to store stylus, ink, parchment, and any books that were currently being used in study. As her gaze roamed over the area, they came to rest on a small volume nestled in one of the compartments. Her interest piqued, she took it down and examined the cover. There was nothing adorning it, not even a title to indicate what might lie within.

Adrianna opened the book and began to riffle through the pages. Immediately, she realized it was a journal. Many of the pages were headed by a date and then followed by a series of entries that, as Adrianna could read, described the subject's experiences there at the citadel. Interestingly, she noticed that the dates were recent, and didn't correspond with the state of the chamber, nor the book itself, which appeared to be rather old. Adrianna frowned as she continued to flip through the pages: 20 Zredoren CY594, 9 Macaren CY594, 32 Macaren CY594... That was only a couple weeks ago! Her confusion deepened, another piece to a puzzle that had yet to be revealed. She thumbed to the back of the book, and one of the entries caught her attention.

*7 Tiseren CY594*

*I have finally figured it out. I'm in love Tallachienan. With every beat of my heart, I love him. I don't quite know how it came to be this way. I don't want to deny it, and wouldn't even if I had half the chance. When he touches me, the passion burns so deep that it threatens to consume me. By the look in his eyes, I feel that it is the same for him too. When we are together, there is no place in the world that I would rather be. When my duty is complete, and all is said and done, I want to return to the citadel...*

Adrianna looked up from the book, her mind going over what she just read. Whose journal was this anyway? Suddenly, the name of the woman who had loved Master Tallachienan so much was of paramount importance. She flipped to the front of the book, turned the first page and then the second. The name written there was familiar...

Adrianna Serine Darnesse.

She became still, felt the very air around her pause. It couldn't be... yet there it was, written in a style similar to her own. By the gods, what was happening?

Adrianna finally let out the breath she'd been holding and jumped up from the chair, almost knocking it to the floor. She felt a sudden compression in the air and then a tense expectancy, like something was about to happen. She felt her heart rate increase, turned in place, and suddenly saw the room as it must have once been. The canopy over the bed was a light green, and it billowed from the breeze that came in through the open window. The room was devoid of dust, and the place was bright with the small fires that gleamed from the wall sconces. Adrianna took in a ragged breath, felt the power that began to surround her.

She stumbled towards the door, catching herself against the nearest wall. The stone was warm, much as she had experienced it before, and a soothing sensation was transmitted to her. Something was happening here, something big. But somehow, she wasn't afraid, for the citadel told her that she needn't be.

All of a sudden, there was a shaft of light. From above it flowed down to Adrianna, and she lifted her face to its warmth. Her mind roiled with the confusion of the past years, and she wanted... no, *needed* to know what was happening, what message it was that she needed to receive. She lifted her arms into the air, her palms open in supplication. She would accept whatever it was that would happen. It seemed nothing short of crazy, but she knew she surely would be if she didn't discover the secret of Tallachienan's citadel.

The light enveloped her, enhanced the memories of which she had, heretofore, only experienced glimpses. She saw herself in what she now understood was sometime in the past. She had been there before, in the citadel, and had studied under Master Tallachienan. Dinim had been there as well. The memories coalesced, forming distinct time lines within her mind. From these memories, she gleaned a basic understanding of the Cycling of the world, and what it had come to mean for the inhabitants of Shandahar. The information was more than a shock to her, it was a revelation... the missing piece to the puzzle. All of the other pieces suddenly fit together, and understanding bloomed within her.

Suddenly, there was a wrenching sensation. She felt the light intensify, then the energy surrounding her began to pour into her body. She felt her mouth open and would have screamed, but she could emit no sound. She felt herself changing, altering to accommodate the spiritual essence that filtered into her. For a moment, time seemed to have no meaning, and she just hung in the air, weightless.

Then it was over. The light began to fade, and the room dimmed. Adrianna crumpled to the floor, unable to hold herself upright anymore. She just lay there, the chamber suddenly quiet. She heard the sound of her breaths as they moved in and out of her chest, felt the press of the cool stone floor against her palms.

She had been enlightened... the citadel had given her that. She wasn't just herself anymore. She was more than just the weak creature who had walked through the double doors of Tallachienan's citadel that day so long ago. She had been empowered. The citadel had given her that as well. The essences of her past selves now resided within her, giving her their strengths, their skills, *and their emotions.*

Adrianna slowly picked herself up from the floor. Looking out the window she could see that dusk was gathering. Soon, the Master would be sending her back into her own time so she could rejoin her comrades. It was difficult to remember why he was doing that, somehow knowing that her training wasn't yet complete. Thinking about it now, she suddenly realized it was no longer her desire. *What she desired was Tallachienan.*

Adrianna quickly left the chamber, hopping onto the disk that awaited. She sped through the corridors of the citadel, every one of them well-known to her. Her heart pounded in her chest, every fiber of her being humming in anticipation. She knew exactly where the Master's laboratory was located, and when she reached the doors, she jumped off of the disk before it could stop. Without bothering to announce herself, Adrianna swept into the room, her gaze immediately searching out Tallachienan. When her eyes finally came to rest on him at the far end of the laboratory, she stopped.

Tallachienan looked up from his spellbook. He had spent the main portion of his day preparing to send Adrianna back into her time. He had called upon Charlemagne, and the god was ready to come when the preparations were complete. Tallachienan had just sent Pylar to bring Adrianna to the laboratory. Either more time had passed than he realized, or Pylar was really, really fast.

Now, as Tallachienan looked at the disheveled countenance of the woman standing across the chamber, he felt a stirring of emotion. *Damnation*, he couldn't believe he was actually going to send her home. But she had requested it. He knew that, once again, he had treated her badly. At least in this he could honor her wishes. Yet, Tallachienan couldn't help feeling he was making a mistake. Her training was not yet complete, for he hadn't the opportunity to teach her some very important incantations. Unfortunately, time was no longer on his side, and Adrianna's tenure with him had come to an inauspicious close.

Tallachienan furrowed his brows thoughtfully and regarded her more closely. He noticed the rapid rise and fall of her chest, the dilation of her pupils, the naked emotion on her face. By the gods, what had happened to her? Tallachienan rose slowly from his desk, his eyes fastened to her face. There was something about the way she stood there, *as though she awaited something*.

It was then Tallachienan realized that Adrianna hadn't seen Pylar. The dragon would have entered alongside if he had been the one to bring her. Moreover, she would have brought some of her personal effects, knowing that she wouldn't be returning to the citadel. Tallachienan felt himself swallow, his throat having gone dry. There was something different about the Adrianna that stood across the room from him, a *knowingness* in her dark eyes that shook him to the core of his being.

And with it was unadulterated, naked desire.

Tallachienan stepped from behind the desk, his eyes still fastened onto hers. He felt a surge of his own desire, and with a sense of determination he swiftly walked towards her. It seemed to be what she was waiting for. Adrianna moved forward and joined him halfway across the room. When their bodies met, they wrapped one another in a powerful embrace.

Adrianna felt Tallachienan's arms come around her, and she reveled in the familiarity. He pulled her close and lifted her feet from the floor, turning in place for a moment before setting her back down. When he brought his lips to hers she welcomed the kiss, deepened it by threading her fingers into the hair near his neck and pulling him closer. Overcome by the power of her emotions, she pressed her body firmly into his. She felt his hands splay across her backside and her mind roiled with a passion that replaced all rational thought.

Everything else was forgotten. At that moment, all she knew was that she wanted Tallachienan Chroalthone... *and he wanted her.*

Adrianna rolled over in the bed, brought a pillow close, and inhaled at the beginning of a yawn. Midway through she stopped, recognizing the scent as not being her own. Adrianna's eyes snapped open, and she found herself in a chamber that wasn't hers. Bits and pieces from the evening before tumbled into her mind: her discovery of the musty chamber suite, the truths the citadel revealed to her, and the passionate night she shared with Tallachienan.

Adrianna frowned. Besides herself, the pillows, and the blankets, the bed was empty. Checking her internal clock, she realized that it was about midday, and she put her hands to her face. Damn, Tallachienan was probably in seminar with his Echelon 2 students. Obviously, she wasn't there. Realizing the irony of the situation, a burble of laughter rose in her throat and she shook her head.

It wasn't long before the amusement receded. Last night she had been out of control, caught up in the vortex of memories and emotions heralded by the merger of her past lives. Sitting there in the middle of the bed, Adrianna could sense the change in herself and she was scared. What would this mean for her? She felt her life spinning out of her hands, found herself a simple pawn in a game bigger than anything she could ever have comprehended on her own. This was more than just Tallachienan... more than just the Wildrunners. This was the history of the world, and she was caught up in events beyond all of the petty encumbrances she had known before.

Adrianna scooted to the edge of the bed and swung her legs over the side. As she moved, she caught sight of the band that enveloped her left forearm. Tallachienan must have noticed it, but said nothing. Of course, they had been so caught up... Even now, she could sense Xebrinarth through their link. He was a constant presence in her mind, and she knew that he must be aware of what occurred between her and the Master last night. The emotions had been too strong for him not to know. Thinking upon it now, she realized he could have easily interfered. Yet, he hadn't done so, signifying his respect for her and her right to privacy.

<Xebrinarth?> Adrianna gently probed the mind that touched hers.

<Zahara... it is so good to speak with you. I was wondering about you... knew that something was happening but not knowing how I should react. So, I stayed quiet.>

Adrianna smiled. <Thank you, my friend. I had enough to think about without having to explain everything to you as well. Actually, I don't think I would have been able.>

Xebrinarth paused for a moment. <There are many things I was able to perceive. That is the way it is with Bondmates. I hope you do not mind.>

<No, I don't mind, Xebrin. I am certain it is much the same for the Master and Pylar.>

She suddenly sensed unease through the link. <Zahara, please be careful. Something has been set in motion now, but I don't know exactly what. However, I *do* know that the path you have embarked upon is a dangerous one. You are no longer just his apprentice. You have become his Mistress, just as you were in the last Cycle.>

<What do you know of the Cycles?> she asked.

<Only what you do. The strength of your revelation was so powerful, I

received it as though I had been there myself.>

Adrianna nodded. She knew that Xebrinarth had cause to be worried about her, but she didn't want for him to fret unnecessarily. <I will be fine. Master Tallachienan can be a rational man. I am sure that we can work through this.>

Adrianna sensed the uncertainty in Xebrin's mind, but he said nothing. He sent his love through the link and then his mind was pulling away, focusing on something that required his attention. Adrianna got out of bed and pulled on the tunic and trousers she had worn the day before. She then took a disk back to her chambers. Once there, she bathed and donned a fresh set of clothes. She sat down in front of her desk and immediately her gaze focused on a book with the faded red binding, *Cycles of Prophecy*.

Adrianna pulled the volume out of the compartment and skimmed through the pages. This time, she read the text with new eyes, suddenly knowing to what the sages referred when they mentioned the Cycling of the world. As she read, she began to understand that the world had been through four such Cycles already, and was currently in its fifth Cycle. This information tied strongly with what had recently been revealed to her. She knew that she had been in Tallachienan's citadel during the fourth Cycle and thought that she might have been there in the third as well. She had no memories of the first and second Cycles and assumed she hadn't known Master Tallachienan in those, much less been in his citadel. Continuing to read, she found that only those of great power could withstand the changing of a Cycle. Adrianna realized that Tallachienan was most likely one of those people. Moreover, if Tallachienan could withstand the Cycling, then possibly so could Pylar. That would have to mean that both of them had known the Adrianna from the third and fourth Cycles.

Adrianna felt her hands shaking as she turned through a few more pages. It was scary to know that one of her best friends had known her before, many centuries ago. She wondered what it must have been like for Pylar, seeing her again after so long when she first entered the citadel at Tallachienan's side. It was only then that Adrianna wondered what had happened to her in the last Cycle.

A sense of foreboding swept over her. She dug back through her memories, trying to discover what the future held for her. However, all she could remember was up to the last day she spent in the citadel. After that, she remembered nothing. She realized that this made sense, for it was the citadel who bestowed the memories upon her, and how would it know what happened to her if she was no longer there?

Adrianna glanced back down at the book lying before her. It was turned to a new page, one she hadn't read before. She realized it was another of Johannan Chardelis' prophecies.

> *Child of light, child of dark...*
> *Into a land covered with shadows*
> *The Warrior of Destiny will come.*
> *With a talisman of magnificent power*
> *The undead Lord will once again know mortality,*
> *He from whose loins she arose.*
> *And from behind the aegis of the Protector*
> *She will survive the temptation of power.*
> *But the Master awaits, and with his magic*
> *Bring forth his army of abominations.*
> *And upon this battlefield of darkness*
> *A war will be waged that will determine*
> *The fate of the world forever...*

Adrianna stared at the words, reading them over again. She felt the shaking begin anew, felt her heart beat faster in her chest. No, this couldn't be. But there it was, the words plain as day before her. *With a talisman of magnificent power, the undead Lord will once more know mortality...* Without a shadow of a doubt Adrianna knew who that undead Lord was.

It was her father, Thane Darnesse.

*...from behind the aegis of the Protector she will survive the temptation of power...* Adrianna swallowed convulsively. Without Sirion there acting as her anchor, she would never have been able to resist the lure of the Ring of Aboleth. He had protected her as no one else could...

Adrianna shook her head. This prophecy sounded like it was about *her.* But it couldn't be... could it? Adrianna breathed deeply. Didn't that mean that the other ones could be about her as well?

Adrianna quickly shut the book, trapping the prophecy once more between the pages. By the gods, what did all of this mean? So many of her questions had been answered, and things suddenly seemed to fit together like the scenes in a story. She swept a hand over her forehead, and it came away damp with sweat. She had read the dates in the book, knew that it was always around the same year that the Cycles changed. The year was very familiar, for it was the one she had left behind when the Master took her back into time to study Dimensionalism. The world was due for the coming of another Cycle, doomed to repeat itself for a sixth time.

That is, unless someone were to try and stop it.

# THE DEPRAVITY OF POWER

Deep within the bowels of the cavern, Tholana licked her wounds behind the walls of the sanctuary of her dark fortress. Vile thoughts flitted through her mind, thoughts that focused on the atrocities she wished to visit upon Adrianna Darnesse. The resulting pain would make the girl scream, and Tholana so much wanted to hear that sound again. She had heard it once before, a time many years ago as the girl made her way to Andahaye.

Tholana smiled to herself. It had been a plan made impromptu, one made up of the simplest resources available and the ripe conditions under which she could use them. Those resources were the dirty mercenary human men she came across in the Sheldomar Forest, men who had seen many days without a woman, and many more days spent without the means to buy the favor of one even if they came across one willing to provide. They were a somewhat desperate lot, and didn't really have much respect for those of the female persuasion. Under ordinary circumstances, the dark queen would have dealt them a slow and agonizing death. But this time... this time she just whispered to them the location of a pretty young girl traveling in the darkest part of the forest in the paltry company of an old man who could use only the most basic of magicks.

It was the first Cycle she had wanted to make such a move against Adrianna Darnesse, for it was only in the previous Cycle the woman had become Tallachienan's mistress, a place that rightfully belonged to Tholana. Long ago, Tallachienan had broken a pledge he had made when he refused to accept Tholana as his consort after she held true to her own promise to heal his mortally ill sister. Lady Briyana Chrolathone went on to live many more years at Tallachienan's side, while Tholana was left to pick up the shattered pieces of her prideful heart.

Hidden within some nearby brush, Tholana had gleefully watched the terrible ambush play out. Much to his credit, the old man had helped in any way he could, but was easily dispatched. One of the men knocked Adrianna unconscious and they took her back to their encampment. Once there, she was tossed to the side until she awakened. They could have easily had their way with her while she slept, but it seemed they felt the pleasure would be so much more enjoyable if she was awake to offer resistance. Of course Tholana couldn't blame them, for she felt much the same way.

Tholana had watched the men take their turns with Adrianna, the girl's screams making her loins tighten spasmodically. Tallachienan had been a fool to keep the girl outside the shadow of his protection this *cycle*, especially when she and Adrianna had fought so brutally in the bailey of his citadel in the *fourth*. A normal man would have recounted that event and taken precautions. But Tallachienan was no normal man. When he ultimately lost Adrianna in her battle against Aasarak, he had broken down.

Of course, Tallachienan's idiocy had been a benefit to Tholana. If the man had been on guard, Tholana would never have experienced the pleasure of hearing the exquisite agony of Adrianna's tortured cries. And when the mercenaries left her broken body to die in the forest, Tholana thought it was the end of the young woman who would warm Tallachienan's bedfurs.

Imagine her surprise when Tholana discovered otherwise many years later when one of her priestesses brought to her attention the presence of a girl with the same name traveling with a group of people connected with the Wildrunners. She had subsequently sent out a company of her priests to attack the group, some of the best ones she had at her disposal. Only two of them returned to her, one of them her most Talented illusionist. By the story he told, he had scared the girl witless... digging into the depths of her mind to find her deepest fear and then use it against her during the battle. He had conjured the likeness of the leader of the band of mercenaries that had attacked her as a young girl, had even replicated the man's voice and had him speak to her. When the illusory mercenary touched Adrianna, she had felt it as if it was real.

The knowledge that Adrianna had been seriously affected by her experience as a younger girl in the Sheldomar Forest gratified Tholana. However, it wouldn't bring back the priests she had lost to the group of young comrades who stood by Adrianna's side. Only one of them had fallen, the halfen they called Bussimot, while over two-thirds of hers had met a similar demise.

Tholana rose from the cushioned sofa upon which she had been seated. She untied the laces of her robe and allowed the garment to fall as she continued walking towards the heated pool that lay in the chamber beyond this one. Once there, she stepped into the warm bubbly waters, making her way ever deeper until everything beneath her eyes was submerged. Her thoughts shifted away from Adrianna and to the man whom she had recently attempted to seduce, a man who had somehow resisted the power of her *Charm* in spite of his ordinary status. No one had ever been able to do that before, even with a bloodline that touted the presence of an ancestor begotten by one of the gods.

Sirion Timberlyn had proven to be something special, and Tholana had every intention of discovering why that was.

When Tholana first learned of the relationship between Adrianna and the Hinterlean ranger, she had been very pleased. Tallachienan would be sorely put out when he realized his young apprentice had been a willing visitor in the bed of another man. Meanwhile, Tholana decided she would find the man and take him for herself. When she discovered the infidelity of her betrothed, Adrianna would be heartbroken, much as Tholana was when she learned Tallachienan had taken her to his bed the last Cycle.

But Sirion had resisted her. It made him so much more appealing, not to mention, he was the most handsome Hinterlean she had ever come across. The ranger became an instant enigma to her, and made her want him all the more. But the small group with whom Sirion traveled, rejoined their comrades.

The newcomers had suspected something about Tholana and those who bore an allegiance to her. However, it wasn't they who ultimately ousted her; in spite of her *Persuasion*, it was Sirion. Then, in the battle that ensued, Sirion and his comrades managed to defeat Tholana and her priests and priestesses.

Enraged, the dark queen had been forced to leave the scene.

And now here she was, thinking about what she should do next. Sirion had escaped her, but not without first bending to her will. If she could somehow show Adrianna the image of her and Sirion together, and then find the means of elaborating on it a bit, it just might prove to do enough harm to make Tholana happy. Of course, that pleasure would be very transient. Adrianna was merely one of the many ornaments that decorated Shandahar to be reborn with every Cycling of the world. Just like in the fourth cycle, Adrianna would leave her master. She would go to face Lord Aasarak again and lose just as she had the Cycles before. The world would repeat itself, and the sixth Cycle would begin.

And Tholana liked it because she became so much more powerful with each Cycle...

Knowing Tallachienan, he just might prove to be just as much a fool in the next Cycle as was in this one. Meanwhile, Tholana was always one to learn from her mistakes. *In the sixth, she would be certain Adrianna was dead before leaving her behind.*

Adrianna cursed eloquently in Hinterlic and then shook her head as though to clear it. She was distracted, even more so than she had been during the last several days. Despite the precipitous changes that influenced her life, she still sought to maintain her studies and focus on her training. As she learned to deal with the new aspects of herself, the initial shock was beginning to wear off and the emotions of her past selves weren't quite so intense. Either that, or she was learning to deal with them better. As her mind slowly became unveiled, she began to lose focus, thoughts of her situation infiltrating her awareness. With that, she started questioning herself.

Since her first night with Tallachienan, many things had changed. Yet, she was quick to discover that other things had not. It was the consistency of some of these things that kept her from going insane. Her friends knew there was something going on with her, and they had noticed a change in Master Tallachienan as well. They didn't know what had happened, but sensed there was a connection between the two that wasn't there before. Yet, they were still Adrianna's friends, and she knew that she could rely on them. For almost six years now they had lived together in the citadel, and they had become close. She was glad to know that some things would never change.

Adrianna still attended seminars and had her spellcasting sessions with the Master. After that first night, two days had passed before she had a session with Tallachienan. Within that time, she didn't see him, and when she took the disk to the practice chamber, her belly was tied in knots. The moment she stepped into that room, she could feel the change in the man who stood in the center of it. As they got to work, a tension had begun to build between them, distracting them from the session. It ended with nothing pertaining to magic getting accomplished.

Despite their union earlier in the day, Tallachienan had come to her that night and almost every night thereafter. After the first two or three times, she had found herself staring into the darkness of her bedchamber, waiting for him to come. When he was there, she reveled in his touch and the pleasure he inspired. It seemed that he couldn't keep himself from her, much the same way she didn't want him to. Inasmuch, the nightly trysts kept the sexual tension at a minimum during spellcasting sessions, giving them the chance to proceed with her training.

However, it wasn't long before things began to change again. Adrianna knew that she loved Tallachienan, there was never a question of that. However, since her emotions began to recede, and rationality returned, Adrianna began to remember other aspects of her life. It wasn't that she had forgotten them, merely that they had been set aside for a while. Her newfound understanding of the Cycling of the world had never been far from her mind, and her thoughts revisited the fact that she didn't have a lot of time. Sure, she was in the past, and that had helped her to obtain the training that she needed. Yet, she still knew that she needed to get back to the Wildrunners, and in particular, Sirion.

Adrianna closed the text she was trying to read. She sighed and leaned back on the pillow behind her. What in the Hells was she doing? What did she think was going to happen? Tallachienan was a god, and she a mortal. She had her entire natural life before her. With his power, she was certain Tallachienan could do things to extend it. However, she knew this wasn't what she really wanted, much as she knew that it wasn't Tallachienan with whom she wished to spend the rest of her life. That man resided in another time, and despite the passion Tallachienan had invoked within her, it was to her memories of Sirion she clung. Her love for the ranger had not abated, and now that the overwhelming emotions from her past selves were falling away, she was beginning to feel that familiar ache to be with him once more.

When the essences of herself from the third and fourth Cycles became infused within her, Adrianna had been overpowered by them. Memories of Tallachienan from the fourth Cycle dominated, and when she went to him that night, he had accepted her with wholehearted abandon. But now she remembered her love and dedication to Sirion, a man who was Promised to be her husband. Memories of the fourth Cycle no longer overwhelmed her, and she could think more clearly. Tallachienan had never asked about her change of heart that day, why she decided to stay at the citadel after their fight even when he was all too ready to send her home. Now, any thoughts of guilt associated with her union with him while betrothed to Sirion were swamped by her wondering how she would tell Tallachienan that their current arrangement was no longer feasible. How would she tell a man who loved her so deeply that she desired another?

There was a knock on the door, and when she called out, Pylar entered. She sat up in the bed as he walked over. Adrianna saw precious little of him as of late, and she hadn't seen Myan, Tridium, or Yasmin except in seminar. His expression was hooded as he settled himself on the edge of the bed, and they regarded one another mutely for a few moments.

Pylar looked at his friend. She wasn't the same person she was before... something had happened to change her, and he knew it was something entirely separate from the Master. Her shift in behavior was noteworthy, for she had been more than ready to leave the citadel that night after she fought with Tallachienan. The Master had even prepared a portal to send her home.

Pylar knew what she had become. As Tallachienan's Bondmate, he would never have been able to miss it. Adrianna was the consort of a god, much like she had become in the previous cycle. But in the fourth it had been vastly different. Tallachienan had kept things in perspective, knew that she would be facing her destiny. Pylar sensed that he wasn't entirely in control of himself this time. Yes, Tallachienan knew that Adrianna had to meet her destiny in this Cycle as well, but there was a complexity this Cycle that hadn't been there in the last.

*Sirion Timberlyn.*

"I am worried about you, Adrianna."

She nodded. "Things have become so much clearer to me today."

"Why today? And why did things change for you so quickly? You had to know that Tallachienan wanted you, would take you with the smallest provocation."

Adrianna shook her head. "You might think me crazy, but the citadel... it did something to me. It made me remember the previous Cycles. I know that, in my time, the end of this Cycle is coming."

Pylar's gaze sharpened on her. He had always known there was something about this place, something extraordinary. Yet, he never imagined it would have the ability to do something like this.

Adrianna continued. "I found out about the Cycling because the citadel gave me the memories of myself in the other two Cycles I was here. They overwhelmed me, and I became caught up in them. I wasn't myself, and I didn't care to step softly around the Master." Adrianna lowered her eyes, almost as though in shame. "I wanted him to take me," she whispered.

Pylar swallowed heavily and shook his head.

"Now that the initial fervor has died away, I can think for myself again. I don't want to sit here and say that I made a mistake, but in part, it is the truth. Tallachienan knows nothing of my reasons for coming to him that night, and if I had been in my right mind, I would never have done it. I am afraid he won't want to accept it when I tell him that I should leave the citadel."

Pylar nodded. He shared her fear. Tallachienan wouldn't want her to leave, more for personal reasons than those related to destiny. He knew that Tallachienan wasn't always the most rational of men, especially when it came to Adrianna. But Pylar would stand by her the best that he could. He wouldn't be the one to tell her that it might be a battle with Tallachienan to let her to go, fearing that to do so would serve only to defeat her instead of strengthening her resolve.

Adrianna rose from the bed. "I need to get ready. Please tell Tallachienan that I need to speak with him. I will meet him in his personal chambers in an hour."

Pylar nodded and left. It was strange to hear Adrianna speak with such conviction in her voice, with so much confidence. She had given Pylar a command without realizing it, and she expected Tallachienan to do as she asked of him. Indeed, Adrianna would have made a fine Mistress for the Master. But it just wasn't written in her destiny.

Sirion knelt on the floor of the meditation chamber. It was empty save for him, for they had taken Triath away the day before. Dremathian said he would recover; Triath had succeeded in overcoming the evil tendencies of the daemon essence by accepting the new being he had become. Only the psionic abilities Triath had begun to harness were left behind, as well as a few other abilities that would only make themselves known with the passage of time.

Sensing Sorn's presence, Sirion rose and turned. Walking across the chamber, Sirion grabbed his clothing from the table he passed. He slipped the tunic over his head and then pulled on the vest. Sorn waited patiently for him to complete this activity, and when he had Sirion's complete attention, he spoke.

"We found something."

Sirion blinked and his gaze sharpened onto his friend, expressing that he wanted Sorn to continue.

"We checked everyone, including Anya and Naemmious. Only Sabian was found to be of any interest to us." Sorn pulled a pouch out from within the folds of his cloak. "We found this in his travel pack, as well as some other questionable items."

Sirion opened the pouch and removed the smaller bags contained within. He opened each of them and inhaled. He knew when he came to the right one. It was the powdered shagendra root that Sabian had been using against Triath and Tianna. Sirion closed the bags and then placed them back into the pouch. He handed it back to Sorn, who then offered him a rolled piece of parchment. Sirion took it, and when he saw the image drawn upon it, he felt his breath catch in his throat. The symbol belonged to the Daemundai, an ancient cult of daemon worshippers with which he was unfortunately familiar.

With the sect's failure to bring Tharizdune into Shandahar, and the subsequent death of the cult leader, Gaknar, the order must have been thrown into a state of internal chaos. Someone had obviously stepped up to take Gaknar's place. That person was allied with a mage, one Sabian Makonnen, and had obtained his allegiance. Adrianna and her comrades had caught the order's attention, most likely courtesy of Sirion and the original Wildrunners before the battle with Tharizdune and Gaknar. Sabian had been sent as a spy, and in the process, he uncovered the truth about Triath. With such a unique prize, Sabian would be venerated for bringing Triath into the fold. It was almost unheard of for a human to acquire the essence of a daemon and live to tell the tale.

So, Sabian had poisoned Triath, and since Tianna had become close to the other man, Sabian had chosen to poison her as well. Sirion remembered Sabian's suggestion that they travel to Krathil-lon on foot as opposed to taking the portal. Most likely, the sorcerer had contacted his brethren and hoped that he would meet up with them. Perhaps the root would have put Triath under Sabian's sway enough that he would have been able to urge Triath into the fold without a fight.

A saudden realization came to Sirion's mind and his jaws tensed. The destroyed portal brackets. Sabian had probably been behind that as well, hoping to force the group to travel to Krathil-lon on foot as he initially insisted.

Sirion drew his lips into a thin line. It was Sabian who had been manipulating Triath. Under Sabian's guidance, the daemon had begun to control the man, warping his perceptions, and changing him into someone other than the person Sirion remembered. Sabian would have succeeded long ago if it had not been for the stalwart bulwark of Traith's will. However, all of that was now over, and Triath was alive. But Sirion didn't know if he thought Sabian should be.

"We need to show this to Dremathian," said Sirion.

Sorn nodded. "The rest of the group deserves to know what has been going on. They don't even know how close Triath came to death."

Sirion shook his head pensively. "No. They can't know until Sabian has been detained. I don't want him to get scared and try to leave."

Sorn shrugged. "We would just catch him and bring him back."

Sirion glared at him from under lowered brows. "You mean that Anya and I would track him, then capture him and bring him back."

Sorn grinned. "Yeah, I suppose."

Sirion shook his head. "No, thank you. We will take him here, after Dremathian has seen what we have to show him. Then we will let the druids decide what to do with him."

Sorn frowned. "What do you mean? He is Daemundai, and a traitor. He *should* die."

Sirion sighed. He wanted the same thing, but he knew the druids wouldn't see it that way. Despite Sabian's alignment and transgressions against the group, they would not put him to death. It just wasn't their way. Druids always chose the path of life, unless something extraordinary dictated against it. And right now, they were in Krathil-lon, a druidic stronghold. They would not want the taint of murder to permeate the sanctity of this place. Sirion could understand their wishes because he had learned their ways as a younger man.

The rest of the Wildrunners wouldn't be quite so sympathetic.

The days blurred into one another, and her world became dark. She had become a shadow of herself, a specter that walked the halls of the citadel. She went through the motions, an attempt at some normalcy in a life that had become anything but. She kept to herself, spending her days closed away in the libraries or in her chambers. These were the only choices she had left to her, for the Master had stripped most of the others away.

Well over a fortnight ago, Adrianna had met Tallachienan in his chambers. She started from the beginning, telling him about the nature of the citadel... how it seemed to communicate with her sometimes through the dreams and visions she'd experienced. Then she told him about the other Cycles, how the citadel had stored the memories, or the 'essence', of herself from those Cycles and channeled it into her present being. She explained her heightened emotional state, and that she remembered what had happened between them in the fourth Cycle...

*Tallachienan regarded her silently from dark lavender eyes, his thumb and forefinger rubbing over his chin. "Why didn't you tell me about this before?" he said solemnly.*

*She shook her head. "I didn't know how to explain it, and at the time, it really didn't seem to matter. I was so overcome with emotion, all I could think about was my desire to be with you."*

*Tallachienan's gaze softened. He stepped up to Adrianna and pulled her into his arms. Then he kissed her softly, seductively. She couldn't help giving in to the passion he invoked, reveling in the feel of his hands on her body and his lips over hers. However, when he began to steer them into his bedchamber, Adrianna stopped him. She pulled away and took a deep breath, knowing she needed to tell him the rest. "Since that first night, I've come to realize something." She hesitated before continuing. "This isn't what I want. Before coming here, my life had already begun taking me in another direction, down a path vastly different than the one you are offering me."*

*Tallachienan frowned. "What are you talking about?" he asked in a low voice.*

*"I'm Promised to someone already, a man I love very much."*

*Tallachienan nodded. "Ah, yes. The ranger Sirion Timberlyn. Dinim told me a little about him during our correspondence before I took you as my apprentice."*

*She heard the slightly condescending tone to his voice and the sudden chill in his demeanor only verified what she already knew. He was angry.*

*Adrianna took a deep breath. "It is my wish that we put an end to the liaison we have begun to share."*

*Tallachienan turned away to walk to a small table atop of which sat a small cask of wine. "You think it will be easy, then."*

*It was more a statement than a question, but Adrianna made a reply anyway. "No, I don't think it will be easy. I understand if you want to terminate my training and send me home."*

*Tallachienan turned back to face her, his eyes glittering dangerously. She felt a prickling sensation on her scalp, a warning she often experienced when danger was near. He shook his head and gave a low chuckle. "No, you needn't do that. We will continue your training, and when the time comes, you will face Aasarak with your comrades. After, I will come for you, and you will never leave me again."*

*Adrianna felt her breath catch in her throat. The expression on his face was frightening, one borne of obsession. Oh gods, this can't be. She shook her head in denial. "N... no. I want to stay with Sirion. He loves me and..."*

*Tallachienan's face was full of rage as he swept his arm across the table, forcefully sending the cask and glasses to the floor. The cask burst upon impact, the contents splattering in every direction, and the glasses shattered into thousands of tiny shards that became submerged in the spreading dark red pool on the floor. "I love you!" he shouted in a strident voice. "And I won't let you go, especially not into the arms of a simple mortal! How you could possibly favor him above me is confounding!"*

*Adrianna's heart pounded against her ribcage as he approached her. Before she could even think about moving out of his way, Tallachienan had his arms around her in a vice-like grip, and his lips covered hers...*

After that, she remembered very little. She recalled that she offered some resistance, but there was very little contest. Tallachienan was a powerful man, accustomed to getting what he wanted. He used his powers of *Persuasion*, and her will was stripped away. She found herself wanting to stay with him in the citadel, never wanting to leave his side, and she felt a hunger deep within, a burning for him that was quenched only by their physical union.

However, as the days passed, Adrianna somehow managed to defy him. Every day she fought against the bonds of his *Persuasion*, pushing at him, making him use his power against her time and time again. Deep within her mind, she continued to hear Xebrinarth. He was her rock; that place in her mind that offered stability and hope. The Master's power made it hard for her to speak to him fully, but at least his thoughts filtered through to her, as well as his love and his will to see her through.

Sometimes, Pylar would come to her. He would make her eat when she otherwise would not. She knew that her friends were worried about her and that they had gone to Pylar. They hoped that he would be able to tell them what was happening to her, give them an explanation for her withdrawal. Yet, he could tell them nothing. At some point, Adrianna discovered that Tridium had even gone to the Master. Tallachienan had only brushed her off, telling her that there was nothing wrong with Adrianna, and that she should tend to her studies.

More time passed. She didn't know how much, only that it did. Every night, Adrianna went to the Master. Tallachienan brought her to her knees with the pleasure of his lovemaking, strengthening her desire for him through the *Persuasion*. At first, she had been able to resist him with all of her strength, but finally, she just didn't have any left. It didn't take him long to overcome her completely... only a few days. Whittled down to nothing, Adrianna simply gave in to the Master's power.

The days came and went. Each day merged into the next. She no longer saw to her studies, and her training was placed on hiatus. The Master waited for her to break completely. She would accept her fate, and then he would lift the *Persuasion*. He would continue her training, send her off to fight Aasarak, and then bring her back to the citadel afterwards. For Adrianna, there were no choices left in life to make. She lived only for the battle that she would fight with her companions. She would strive to do her part to help them defeat Aasarak and give the world a chance for a future.

She could only hope she would also have a future when all was said and finished.

Sirion contemplated the game board. There were a number of moves that he could make, but he was having a difficult time deciding which one. The rest of the game pivoted on this decision and he didn't want to be too hasty. His sister sat across from him, also watching the board. Anyanka was a shrewd competitor, and she would be swift to take advantage of any move he executed.

Sirion and Sorn had taken their information about Sabian to Dremathian. The druid had wasted no time in gathering some of his higher-ranking Brothers and then accompanying them to Sabian's room. They took the mage by surprise, and he hadn't the chance to cast any spells before they had him bound and gagged. They kept him in confinement until the rest of the Wildrunners could be gathered, and when everyone was together, Sabian had been brought before them.

Sabian had known it would be futile to deny his guilt. When the druids went through his packs, they had found his talisman and the orb he used to commune with his Daemundai brethren. Once he was questioned, Sabian had told them much of what Sirion had already suspected. Glancing over at Dinim, Sirion had seen the disgust written there, along with the anger of betrayal. It was Dinim who had brought Sabian into the group, and he likely felt responsible for what had happened. However, his anger outweighed the guilt, and knowing the things that Sabian had done in order to accomplish his goals, Sirion knew that Dinim would sooner see the end of Sabian Makonnen.

Yet, death was not to be Sabian's destiny at this point in time. Just as Sirion had thought, the druids wouldn't allow him to be executed within the silver glen of Krathil-lon. Naemmious, Sorn, and Armond were the biggest advocates for his death, but only gave brief grumbles of discontent beneath their breath. It was decided that the talisman would be destroyed, along with the communion orb. Sabian would be exiled from Krathil-lon, sent far away from his brethren. It would take him many moon cycles to return to them, maybe even a year. Sirion hated to see him set free, but he knew that he couldn't argue. They were within the jurisdiction of Father Dremathian, and as such, forced to honor his decrees.

Everyone had followed the procession as Sabian was taken to the portal room beneath the apoptos. Dremathian flipped through the pages of the tome before he found the one he wanted. It was a place that Sirion had never seen, much less heard of, some place on the eastern continent. As Dremathian began to speak the words on the page, Tianna had stepped up to Sabian and slapped him across the face. Sirion knew it was for Triath, for the man hadn't recovered enough to be there with them. Brothers Silas and Verdec had then dragged Sabian up to the portal that was forming. When it was complete, they had thrust him, still bound, into the swirling wall of color.

Sirion saw his move. He shook of thoughts of Sabian and then made it before he looked up to see Anya frown. Sirion grinned to himself. Triath was recovering well from his ordeal. He had even returned to being the same obstinate man that Sirion met when he first joined up with the original Wildrunners. Tianna continued to help out as she could with the druids who had been injured in the fight against Aasarak's army. However, most of her work was near completion. Now all they could do was wait. Without Adrianna, the group was not complete.

Anya made her move. Having predicted it, Sirion was fast to move another of his pieces. Anya's frown deepened. She hated to be predictable.

Sirion felt a surge of affection for his sister. As children, they had been nearly inseparable, but when their father began to train Sirion to be a ranger, all of that had changed. Now, they had only a hint of that old camaraderie. They weren't so close anymore, but a bond remained between them. Sirion thought it would be nice to rebuild what they had once shared when they had a chance to go home and live some semblance of a normal life.

Sirion knew they were running out of time. Aasarak's army was marching, unchecked across the land. Every day people were dying, and no one was there to stop it. Sirion and Dartanyen had decided to give Triath another three or four days to recuperate, but then they would leave. Dremathian knew where Aasarak had made his lair; the druid could feel the world crying out from that place. Even the rock and the soil agonized, and the life had left that place long ago. Sirion hoped Adrianna would be rejoining them soon because they needed the skills that she would bring to the fight...

...and because he missed her.

Tallachienan flinched inwardly when Pylar slammed the door closed behind him. The dragon was angry; he could sense the strong emotion thrumming through their link. He was through merely protesting on Adrianna's behalf, and today Pylar had contested Tallachienan's sanity. Pylar was in a position to see the situation from every perspective, and Tallachienan could sense his Bondmate's fear. Adrianna had given up fighting him, but Pylar believed it was more than that. She was giving up on life.

Tallachienan never imagined things would turn out this way. When Adrianna came to him that night about three weeks ago, he thought he had her. He never stopped to wonder why she came to him after being so angry the night before. He didn't care, just as long as she was in his arms. But now he realized that he should have questioned it. Now that he looked back on it, her behavior had indeed been inconsistent. However, he had been so consumed by his own emotions, he wasn't thinking clearly. Later, when she confided what had happed to her; that the citadel had somehow altered her state of being, he'd reacted irrationally. When she then expressed a need to leave the citadel, he responded with the first thing that came to his mind... his power.

Tallachienan had been using his powers of *Persuasion* to make her want to stay with him at the citadel, and now he was beginning to wonder about the integrity of that action.

Tallachienan walked across the chamber and seated himself in his favorite chair. Somehow, she had resisted him. Tallachienan found himself in awe of her ability to do that. She shouldn't have been able to do so; any normal mortal would simply have succumbed to him. With all of the will left to her, Adrianna fought him, forcing him to exert more and more of his influence over her. Truth be told, the energy it cost drained him, and he found himself sleeping a bit longer at the end of every day. Hells, how did she do it? This question led Tallachienan to do the research he should have done decades ago. He went to his personal library and took the genealogies down from the shelf. He added to them every so often, but it had been quite a while since he bothered to touch them.

Tallachienan looked back into Adrianna's family history. He skimmed over her father's birth-line, but finding nothing of interest there, he went to the mother's side. It was there he found himself the most intrigued. The Lady Gemma Farwyn had a sister, a younger one by the name of Sharra. They were the daughters of a very influential Savanlean family. A woman by the name of Salirya Songwoven was their mother. Tallachienan drew his brows together in contemplation. That name was vaguely familiar to him, but the genealogy became broken, and he wasn't able to accurately follow Salirya's maternal birth-line.

He rummaged around through the histories and lineages, eventually coming to a place where it referred to another book. Tallachienan went to his shelf and pulled down another genealogy, a much older one, and opened it to the appropriate pages. After reading for a while, he found another chart, one that was incomplete after the turn of the second common century. There was reference of the birth of a female child born in the same common year as Salirya, to a woman by the name of Arkevna. Upon further investigation, he believed that child to be Salirya.

Deep in thought, Tallachienan looked up from the book. If Salirya was indeed the daughter of Arkevna, then that explained Adrianna's ability to withstand his god-given powers. It would mean that she was a descendant of the gods as well, and privy to certain immunities. It would give her certain inherent abilities that were dependent upon the god from whom she shared her descent. Arkevna was the daughter of Odion and Ilistia, two of the Ancients. Odion himself was Tallachienan's own sire, and as such, had bequeathed a great amount of potential to his son. As the daughter of two ancients, Arkevna had her own share of power. Most likely, she went by another name as a goddess and Tallachienan was curious as to who that would be. Regardless, she had passed her power down to her daughter, Salirya. Then, Salirya had passed it to Gemma, who in turn passed it to *her* daughter.

Throughout the centuries, the ancient blood would have been diluted, but not so much that Adrianna wouldn't have her own share of power. Tallachienan shook his head. Adrianna had no idea what she was, the potential that lay untapped within her. He rubbed his hands over his face.

Here he was, forcing his will on her. She had finally stopped fighting him, and now he could only hope that she would be able to recover from their battle.

Tallachienan stood up from the table, closed the genealogies, and returned them to the shelf. He knew what he needed to do. He would release her from the prison of his *Persuasion* and hope that he hadn't damaged her. If she had been a simple mortal, it wouldn't have been an issue. However, for a god to influence another so strongly could be detrimental, especially for one like Adrianna who was untrained in her abilities.

Tallachienan donned the cloak that hung near the door and then took himself to Adrianna's chambers. Outside her door he hesitated, making certain he composed himself before entering. He felt his loss keenly, for he knew he had lost any chance he would ever have of her coming back to him. He had made a grave blunder when he used his power to influence her, and in truth, she might never forgive him. His thoughts shifted to her battle with Aasarak. In a few moon cycles it might not matter.

Tallachienan swallowed past the ache in his throat as he knocked on the door. He didn't hear a response and knocked again. When he still received no response, he entered the chamber. The small shaft of light that entered through the closed curtains over the window only dimly lit the room. Tallachienan would never have noticed her lying on the bed if he hadn't seen a slight shift of the linens as Adrianna moved. The air in the room smelled stagnant, and he could feel the despair all around him. He suddenly realized what he had wrought, and Tallachienan found it no small wonder that Pylar was so angry.

Tallachienan walked over to the bed and then gingerly sat on the edge. He didn't have to touch Adrianna for her to know that it was he who graced her with his presence. He heard the increase in her respiration, and when she awakened, he watched as she shrank away from him. Tallachienan felt his heart almost stop in his chest. *What have I done?* He had brought this woman, whom he claimed to love, down to nothing. She wasn't even a husk of what she was before their battle of wills.

"Adrianna, I release you from my spell. You are free," he whispered. Tallachienan didn't need to concentrate upon the *Persuasion* to lift it. With those words said, it was simply gone, the strands of the invisible bonds floating away from her. However, Adrianna did nothing. She merely lay there on the bed as far away from him as she could get without falling off.

Tallachienan watched her for a moment and then reached out to her. He touched the top of her hand, caressing it softly with his fingertip. "I am sorry for what I have done. I want you to know that I did it because I love you so much. I hope that one day you will understand and forgive me."

At first Adrianna said nothing. She just lay there, unresponsive. Several moments passed before she moved her eyes to look at him. Awareness had returned to them, and they regarded him coldly. Then she spoke in a thin voice equally as chill. "I want you to get out. Stay away from me Tallachienan."

With a heavy heart, Tallachienan merely nodded and rose from the bed. He looked down at her for a moment before moving towards the door. Once reaching it, he turned back. His voice almost broke. "I will send Pylar to you." Then he turned and left.

# Training for the End

S he sat in front of the window, looking out over the boring gray landscape. For the moment it was all Adrianna cared to do. Even freed from the prison of Tallachienan's *Persuasion*, she didn't feel quite right. Her mental sharpness was gone, and her awareness dulled. Once more in control of her own emotions, she didn't know what to feel. Lackluster was the most appropriate term for her state of being, so much that she couldn't even motivate herself enough to leave the damned suite.

Adrianna narrowed her eyes when she sensed Tallachienan's presence in the chamber. Despite her command that he leave her alone, he had come to see her the past three days, usually in the company of Pylar. She had never acknowledged him, merely pretended he wasn't there. He would lean against the farthest wall for a while and watch her, almost as though he was assessing her for something. She recognized his efforts to keep his distance, and she might have appreciated the gesture if he hadn't betrayed her in such a brutal way.

This time he came alone. She felt a jangling of her nerves, her mind anxiously responding to a perceived danger. She couldn't help fearing that he would take her again, that she would succumb to him just as she always had before. She looked over her shoulder and saw Tallachienan leaning there against the wall nearest the entry, his arms crossed at his chest. He watched her quietly from lavender eyes, perhaps waiting for her to finally say something.

"What do you want?" She asked the question even though she really didn't care about an answer.

Tallachienan fluidly extricated himself from the wall and approached her. She struggled to remain as she was, having at least enough wits about her to feel that she didn't want to show him exactly how much he affected her. But he must have seen something reflected in her eyes, for he stopped half way across the room.

"Adrianna, I know you wish to make preparations to return home, but I urge you to consider staying here until your training is complete."

Adrianna narrowed her eyes into slits. "Why in the Hells would I consider doing that?" she asked icily in a low voice.

"The things that I have to teach you... they could be of great help to you in your upcoming battle with Aasarak."

Adrianna turned away from him. "I think I have *learned* enough from you Tallachienan."

Tallachienan pressed his lips into a thin line. "You are right to be angry with me, and even more so to question my motives. But your life, and the lives of your companions, are now at stake," he replied coldly. "What if something I have yet to teach you could save them? What if it means the difference between success and defeat in the end? Don't you care about that anymore?"

Adrianna kept her back turned to him for a few moments after he spoke, contemplating his words. Of course, he was right; her training was incomplete. These last things he could teach her... if they might influence the turn of the battle, then she should stay. But she so much didn't want to.

Adrianna slowly turned back around to face him. The lines of strain were deep on Tallachienan's face and she suddenly realized that he suffered for what he had done. The hollows beneath his eyes spoke volumes, and his expression was haunted. He regretted what had happened, and all Adrianna had to do was find it in her heart to forgive him.

Tallachienan kept his silence as she regarded him. She kept her face expressionless, not wanting to give him an inkling of what she was thinking. However, he seemed to know it when she made the decision to stay, perhaps from the curling of her fingers into a fist. She could see it in the relieved stance he took, the slow exhalation of breath.

"We must have an agreement," she said. "You will meet me on my terms." Tallachienan gave a stoic nod. "State such terms, then."

"I will be the one to decide when our sessions are to begin and end. I keep my own pace, and I don't need you or anyone else trying to change that for me. I have decided that classes and seminars are over. I have neither the time nor the inclination for them. The remainder of this training is to be done as quickly as possible. I have spent long enough away from my comrades and the man who is Promised to be my husband. I know that time hasn't passed for them the way it has with me, but it is for my benefit that I return to my own time as soon as possible."

Tallachienan seemed to contemplate her words for a moment. He had probably thought she would insist on him keeping his distance from her. Yet, she was essentially telling him to spend most of his waking moments with her in order to hasten what remained of her training. Somewhere deep inside, she must have realized he would no longer bring her harm. Despite what he had done, she had forgiven him, and despite his arrogance and power, she knew that a good man lay within the broken pieces of the person she had come to know. She somehow recognized that fact even though he had never proven it to her with his actions towards her. Perhaps it was the dream she had of him so long ago, the one where he promised to live the rest of his life with a woman he didn't love, all because he wanted his sister to become well again.

"Fine," said Tallachienan. "When do you wish to meet?"

"I will see you early tomorrow morning in the Practice Chamber," she replied.

Tallachienan silently nodded before turning on his heel. Adrianna watched him leave and then made her way over to the bed. Truthfully, she hated sleeping on it now because it brought back so many unwanted memories. Unfortunately, it was either that, the chair, or the floor. One night it had been a pile of blankets and pillows. Pylar had offered her one of the innumerable rooms in the citadel, but she had stubornly refused. It felt like giving ground to her master; another way she could be owned by him was giving up her space.

She shook her head and stepped up to the bed. It was when she began pulling the pillows towards her that her toes made contact with something underneath it. She furrowed her brows and knelt beside the bed, thrusting her hand into the space beneath. She gasped the object and pulled it out, instantly recognizing it as the sword she wielded against the spider during Tallachienan's test. The weapon was sheathed within a simple scabbard that had been constructed impromptu. She wondered who had ordered it made, and thought it must have been Pylar. Adrianna drew the sword from the sheath and saw that it had been cleaned and polished. The blade glinted at her from beneath the light streaming through the open window, and she noticed the intricate decorative engraving on the hilt. It was such a beautiful weapon, and a shame it had been misplaced in the dreary dungeon filled with spiderwebs. But now it was hers, and she would keep it with her when she returned to the Wildrunners. She would have a belt made so that she could carry it at her hip. She didn't think it would be a burden, for it felt so light in her hand.

Adrianna laid the sword on the desk and decided to climb into the bed after all. Besides, she needed to be as comfortable as possible in her sleep because on the 'morrow, her training would begin anew. At her insistence,

Tallachienan would convene on her timetable. She would spend most of her day in his company, and then return to her chambers to study and practice what she learned. Her determination was solid. She would complete her training and return to her comrades as soon as possible. And she would have Sirion by her side once more.

Tholana manipulated the strands of her *Dreamthread*, weaving the words of power into each one. Ezkebrion stood nearby, deep in concentration. The young god had agreed to help her, but only because he lusted after the potential chaos that could ensue as a result of their actions... that, and the promise of the pleasure of her body for the next seven days. She provided him with such opulent luxury for he had been the one to discover Adrianna's location when Tholana herself had been unable. Certainly, the girl resided within Tallachienan's citadel, *only it was many years in the past.*

Tholana chuckled malevolently. Charlemagne wasn't the only one with the ability to manipulate time. Tholana knew that Ezkebrion hadn't near the power of the older god, but it was enough. Tholana would send the images she had stored in the *thread* to Adrianna, and they would seem so real, the young woman would perceive them as the truth. Everything in the scene was accurate with the exception of one detail, the detail that would shatter her hopes about Sirion Timberlyn into a thousand pieces.

"The hole is ready my lady. Let us make haste," said Ezkebrion.

Tholana stepped closer to her companion, continuing the words to her spell. She recognized the strength it had taken for Ezkebrion to create the aperture by the haggard look on his face. She began to concentrate on the next phase of her endeavor, completing the *Dreamthread* and casting it through the small, black wyrm-hole. With her mind, Tholana carefully guided it through the years until it finally reached its intended recipient...

*Adrianna took in the trees all around her. The air was cool as she walked slowly among them. She heard the whisper of the winds through the leaves, and smelled the scent of the campfires behind her. As she walked deeper into the wood, she began to hear something different: heavy breathing and low moaning sounds. Only a moment later, she was taking in the scene of a man and a woman in the throes of passion. The woman was the epitome of beauty, and somehow familiar to her. The same applied to the man. His hair was colored a deep red, and his skin tone was a golden bronze.*

*Adrianna stood helplessly by as Sirion kissed the woman, his hands seeking access to her body through the layers of their clothing. The woman trailed her hands over his back down to his hips, then brought them to the front of his trousers. Adrianna felt the breath catch in her throat, followed by the warm wetness of her tears as they fell down her face.*

*The moaning intensified, and moments later the couple began to strain against one another. Not much was visible to her past cloaks and other clothing items, but it was blatantly obvious what they were doing. Adrianna felt her heart break into hundreds of tiny shards. She knew that she should just turn away, but she couldn't, her body refusing to obey her commands. The woman slowly turned her head and looked over to Adrianna standing there among the trees. With a wicked gleam in her eyes, she curved her full lips up into a smile of triumph...*

Adrianna jerked awake, her heart beating fast in her chest. Her mind reeled with what she had seen, and the pain of the lump in her throat intensified. She put trembling hands over her eyes, drew her knees up to her chest, and began to cry.

The dream was so vivid, she knew it had to be real. It wasn't just a construct of her mind, but her strange gift for *Seeing* things showing her what would come to pass. In her Time, it seemed that Sirion had moved on without her. She supposed she really couldn't blame him. Hells, she hadn't even stayed to give him a farewell when Tallachienan came to take her for her training. Yet, her heart ached with what she had seen, for she had hoped Sirion would remain steadfast and unwavering in his love for her.

Even though she had not.

Adrianna sat up in the bed, then put her hands to her head and groaned. The pain pounded at her temples, spreading across her forehead and behind her eyes. With this type of pain, she didn't see how she would be able to train with Tallachienan that day. Checking her internal clock, she knew it to be in the very early hours of the morning. Well, at least she had some time left to rest before she had to meet him.

Adrianna lay back down and pulled the blankets up, over, and around her. She tried to sleep, but her thoughts kept returning to Sirion. Residual tears crawled down her cheeks and onto the linens. Her body trembled with emotion, her loss sweeping over her like a wave. With Sirion, she had felt a completion she had never known before. To have that suddenly stripped away made her feel empty inside.

Adrianna's mind rolled over the course of their short relationship. It had a rather tumultuous beginning, with an almost nonexistent middle. And the end, well, that still had yet to be determined. She remembered the warmth of him next to her in the night, the way his hand would always come to rest on her belly, and the feel of his breath at the curve of her neck. She liked his protective nature and the way she always felt safe when he was near. She missed the scent of him, slightly musky with a spicy overtone. Not the least, she loved the way he made her feel... as an equal, his partner in life.

Even with the passage of over six years, she still felt the same way about him. However, it was obviously not the same for Sirion. She found it difficult to believe, especially in light of things he had told her about his past. In her early days, before she left Sangrilak to study in Andahye, he remembered seeing her about the city and had always wished he knew her. Then, during all of those years she was in Andahye, Sirion had wondered about her. When she finally returned home, the woman she had become blew him away.

Yet, all of that seemed to be over now. Adrianna curled herself deep within the blankets and furs. Her head pounded ferociously and she closed her eyes to the pain. She focused on regulating her breathing and then relaxing her muscles. The next thing she knew, Pylar was there beside her, gently shaking her shoulder, telling her that she was late for her session with the Master.

Adrianna leaped out of bed. The headache was still there, lurking just below the surface. As she quickly dressed herself in fresh clothing, she asked Pylar to get her some rathis tea. She hoped that it would help quiet the pain and it from becoming worse as she practiced. She knew that Tallachienan was most likely upset by her tardiness, but she waited for Pylar to bring her the tea. She didn't want to have to cut the session short because of a stupid headache.

When Adrianna finally arrived, Tallachienan was indeed irate. However, he said nothing as they got to work. The first day passed, and then the next, and the next. Since making their arrangement, Tallachienan no longer harassed Adrianna about her efforts, most likely figuring that it was up to her how much she chose to push herself. No longer was he merely her instructor, telling her what to do and how to do it. He was a mentor and a guide, showing her how things were done and then leaving her to figure out the complexities. He was a tool, the key to unlocking the potential she carried deep inside. Tallachienan had finally become the master she always hoped he would be.

For several more weeks, Tallachienan imparted to her the knowledge of the Dimensionalist, slowly concluding everything he had been teaching her for the past several years. He showed her the intricacies of opening portals, how to use certain objects to concentrate her power, and how to use others to channel that power. He taught her the arcane language to use as she chanted her spells and the different ways in which she could harness her magic. He taught her the various media she could use to aid in her spellcasting, the basics of how to enchant a weapon, and more. Adrianna pushed herself to maximum capacity, much harder than Tallachienan ever had before.

And she became stronger.

Adrianna's sessions took up the entirety of her days, and even into the nights. She rarely saw her friends anymore, but spoke to Xebrinarth before she crawled into bed every night. He was aware of what had transpired between herself and Master Tallachienan, and also knew she sought to complete her training so she could return to her companions. There was something that Adrianna had come to realize, a hardship that Xebrinarth would need to endure. When she went forward into the future to rejoin the Wildrunners, Xebrinarth would be forced to remain in *this* time. Decades would pass, and they would have no contact with one another. He would be forced to live without her until Adrianna was thrust back into her own time.

If she calculated correctly, it meant that over one hundred years would pass on Haldorr.

This realization made Adrianna worry for her Bondmate. She already knew how difficult it was for him to live without her near. She thought about asking Tallachienan to ask Trebexal if Xebrin could come to the citadel and then send him with her into her own time. But somehow, she knew what the answer would be. Their Bonding was barely tolerated by the dragon Elders, and she should expect no favors from them, Trebexal, or Tallachienan. Many would say that Xebrinarth settled his fate when he made the mistake of choosing her as his Bondmate. However, it was too late for recriminations now. Adrianna rather hoped that the Elders would look past it and simply reach out to a dragon in need. Adrianna wouldn't hold her breath, and she knew that Xebrin wouldn't either. She knew she had to tell him what would happen when she left, and it was just a matter of when...

Adrianna knew when her training was coming to a close. It must have been something in Tallachienan's demeanor that translated itself to her. Or perhaps, it was simply her subconscious telling her that, for now, she had learned almost all she could from him. She was happy that it was near completion and that she would soon be returning home, but there was a part of her that was saddened as well.

And then one day it hit her... a realization that struck her to her core. She had wondered about her ability to forgive Tallachienan so readily, had wondered why she thought he could possibly have goodness within him. She remembered the surge of feelings that had drowned her senses when she was enlightened by the citadel. The other Adriannas' lives were from other Cycles, not truly hers. Standing there, at that moment, she realized this Tallachienan was not a Cycled verion of himself. He was *the same man*. This was a man who had loved versions of her over and over. His memories were his own, and loss of her in each Cycle had brought him to the brink of madness. His love for her had done that. Loss of her had done that. He had done evil, but now he recognized it, saw it, and knew it inside of himself. It had almost destroyed her, but they were not wounds caused by anger, but a lonliness she could never fully understand. With that understanding, something had changed between herself and the Master, and she was suddenly loath to give it away.

It was friendship.

After the terribleness that lay between them, it came softly on feathered feet. When the realization washed over them, they were left feeling refreshed, like they had walked beneath a cleansing waterfall. After all of these years, the Master had let his guard down, allowing his true colors to shine through the dense shell that had become his exterior during the centuries that separated this Cycle from the last.

Inasmuch, Adrianna and Tallachienan spent her last days at the citadel in relative contentment. There were many times when they took their meals together, and even conversed about things other than the arcane. Somehow, he had endeared himself to her, and she began to feel that, if she chose, she might find happiness there in Tallachienan's citadel after all... after the battle with Aasarak was through. She knew that her relationship with Sirion was probably over, but she couldn't make such a decision while she continued to grieve over his loss. Moreover, there was something that continued to tell her that, although she seemed to have found her niche at the citadel, it was not her destiny to stay. So she made her preparations to leave, never to return to its Master as his consort.

Then one night she dreamed. Just like the last, it was one of those dreams that was so vivid, she knew it had to be real. It was her gift of *Sight* once more showing her what would come. Somehow, Adrianna knew that she saw the future, for it could be nothing but.

*Adrianna sat across from him at the table. A short stack of books rested to her right while a similar stack lay at Tallachienan's left. She was tired of reading these old musty tomes and she needed something, anything, to break the monotony. She looked up at her companion, took in the expression of concentration that furrowed his dark brows. Hells, he looked so serious sitting there...*

*She glanced down at the stylus held between her fingers, smiled to herself, and tapped the blunt end of it atop the table.*

*Nothing happened. Tallachienan didn't bother looking up from the yellowed pages of the huge book open before him. Damnation, the thing was almost as big as a small child.*

*Adrianna tapped the end of the stylus down on the table a second time. When she got no response, she did it again. Finally, she was faced with the desired result. Tallachienan looked up at her from dark lavender eyes. "Is something wrong?"*

*Adrianna shook her head and gave him an impish smile.*

*With a sigh he returned his attention to the book. She frowned. She had expected much more of a response. She didn't quite know what the response should be, only that it be much more interesting.*

*She tapped the end of the stylus once more on the table.*

*Tallachienan instantly brought his gaze up to meet hers. She could feel instant ire emanating from him and again she smiled to herself. He raised an eyebrow as he regarded her and his lips pulled into a thin line. "You know, we can stop anytime. It's not my problem we are seeking an answer for."*

*Adrianna arched her own brow. "But it could be," she said. "We have yet to determine how the rest of the system might now be involved."*

*Tallachienan crossed his arms at his chest and leaned back in his chair. She could only imagine what he was thinking. After a moment he narrowed his eyes. "I think you want this to be my problem."*

*Adrianna grinned. "Now why would I want such a thing? Wouldn't that make our circumstances so much more ominous?"*

*It was at that moment Dinim entered the library. He shook his head when he saw Tallachienan's expression. "You two arguing again? What's it about his time?" He put the scrolls he carried onto the table and folded his arms across his chest.*

*Tallachienan waved a hand in Adrianna's direction. "It's her. She takes nothing in earnest anymore. And she wants to blame me for all her problems."*

*Adrianna tossed the stylus onto the table. "No, Dinim, it's him. How he can sit there for so long and say absolutely nothing is so beyond me!" She then gave a disdainful sniff. "And he is the cause of my problems... not all of them, but many."*

*Dinim only rolled his eyes. "Are you people serious?"*

*Adrianna gave a deep sigh and rose from her place at the table. She maneuvered herself from the tight spot and stepped up to her friend. She placed a hand on his chest. "I am serious, but only because..." She paused, knowing what she wanted to say but wondering if she should. It was then she felt a movement from inside of her, and she glanced down at her slightly distended abdomen...*

Adrianna blinked herself awake, placing a hand at her belly. It was flat, just as it should be. She wondered about the dream. It wasn't a memory from the third or fourth Cycles, for it had a different quality about it. She had felt the camaraderie with Tallachienan in spite of their difference in opinion. She wondered about the pregnancy...

Dispelling the remnants, Adrianna shook her head free of the dream and rose from the bed. This was one of the last days she would spend in the citadel. Tallachienan was already working on the portal that would send her back to her own time. She would spend a portion of the day with her friends and with Pylar. Then she would tell Xebrinarth all she needed to say about the reality of her return home.

It didn't take her long to prepare her travel pack, and after a while Pylar came to help her finish. She could sense he was sad to see her leave, but he was also happy. She could tell he was pleased with the way things had worked out between the Master and herself, and she perceived the pride he felt burning all around him. Yet, there was another emotion she sensed as well, one he fought to hide. *It was fear.*

The emotion dampened some of Pylar's happiness at seeing her leave the citadel as one of Tallachienan's finest journeymen, and it nibbled at the edges of her nerves. However, she didn't ask the dragon about it. She didn't want to ruin their last hours together bickering about emotions he tried so hard to keep from her. When the time came for her to meet with Myan, Tridium, and Yasmin, she invited Pylar to join them. He was more than happy to oblige.

The friends spent the remainder of the day and into the evening in one another's company. All knew it could very well be the last time they saw one another for a long time. They still didn't know what had happened between herself and the Master. Adrianna didn't see why they should. Knowledge of that sort was unnecessary, and would only make it difficult for them to pursue their own studies. One day, she hoped they would come and find her when they completed their work at the citadel.

Finally, the friends bid one another farewell. Once back in her chambers, Adrianna prepared herself for bed. When she went to move her travel pack, she saw that her newly acquired sword lay next to it. The plain scabbard was gone, replaced by one that had been designed specifically for the blade. It was beautifully decorated, strict attention paid to the finer details. She wondered who had thought to have it made, but then realized she was being silly. Of course, Tallachienan had done it. With tears in her eyes, she smoothed her fingertips over the artistry before setting it aside. She climbed into the bed and hoped that sleep would come swiftly and uninterrupted.

The next morning, Adrianna stepped into the laboratory. Her travel pack was slung over one shoulder, and the sword belted at her hip. Tallachienan stood before a portal bracket, one that she had never seen used before. She had only seen him cast his portals out of thin air, without the use of any concentrators. But she knew that this time was different. There was another element to this portal that was absent in all of the others she had seen him cast. *This one would be taking her through time.*

Earlier that morning, Adrianna had spoken at length to Xebrinarth. In silence, he had listened as she told him she was from a time in the future, and that Tallachienan had taken her from it when he began her training. She told him that Tallachienan would soon be sending her back to her own time, and that Xebrinarth would be forced to live many long years without her.

It had been difficult for Adrianna to experience the emotions that bombarded her. Desolation and loneliness were paramount. Xebrin wondered how he would live so long without feeling her in his mind. Adrianna had told him to wait for her, to simply hold on until the day she could speak with him once more. She had begged him not to leave her, for if he were to die, then she would have the rest of her life to live without him.

Only after Xebrinarth had made his promise to her did Adrianna finally begin to think about her leave-taking. She had packed away her belongings the day before, so she spent the rest of her time wandering the halls of the citadel. Before long, Pylar had come for her. She gathered her travel pack and other accessories before riding a disk with him to Tallachienan's laboratory. Once there, Adrianna had fiercely embraced him. It was Pylar she would miss the most. He knew everything about her, and besides the Master, still considered her his dearest friend.

Tallachienan turned when Adrianna walked across the room towards him. As she neared, she could tell he was very tired. His gaze was conflicted as he moved away from the portal bracket to meet her. He was silent for a few moments before he spoke, his eyes roving over her face as though he was burning it into his memory.

"There are just a few things I need to say about the journey you are about to take."

Tallachienan watched Adrianna nod her head. His heart ached with the pain of her leaving. Even though he knew she wasn't his to keep and that she loved another, he desperately wanted to see her live through her fight with Aasarak. Tallachienan glanced down at the sword at her hip. He had taken it just last evening while Adrianna enjoyed some time with her friends. He'd given it a proper scabbard, a gift he had made specially for her...

...but not before *Enchanting* the blade.

Tallachienan knew the Chardelis Prophecies. He had read other prophecies as well, but the ones from Johannan Chardelis had a ring of truth to them he had found in few others. They foretold of one who would be the Sworn Protector to the Warrior of Destiny. Tallachienan imagined that perhaps this Protector loved the Warrior, and maybe he shared a certain closeness with her. Tallachienan had taken the sword and cast a spell on it, one of his own devising. He put all of his care into the intricacies of the spell, weaved it into the elemental substance of the weapon. When he was finished, Tallachienan sheathed the blade in its new scabbard and placed it on the bed next to her travel pack so there would be no chance its wielder would leave it behind.

"Lord Charlemagne has taken a look into time and chosen the best place for you to rejoin your comrades. It will be the druid stronghold of Krathil-lon. For them, only six moon cycles have passed since I first took you for your training. I am not entirely certain why he chose not to return you to them at an earlier date, but I am not one to repudiate Charlemagne. In all matters of time, he is the Master."

Adrianna nodded again.

"The Travel itself will be different than it was when I brought you here. Traveling backward in time is relatively easy compared to Traveling forward. As you make your way through the portal, you will feel a painful wrenching sensation. Then, once you have been deposited, you will have only a short amount of time to search for your comrades before the convulsions begin. They will start out weak. At their fullest strength, you will feel like you are going to die. However, you will live through the pain. It is merely your body adjusting to Traveling forward through the fabric of time."

Tallachienan looked deep into Adrianna's eyes as he emphasized his words. He saw hers widen as she began to comprehend what he was telling her. "Won't the portal take me to the location of the Wildrunners?"

Tallachienan nodded. "Yes, but we can only be so precise. Lord Charlemagne did the best he could with your exact placement. The power it takes in order to execute an endeavor such as this one is overwhelming."

In light of what she would be forced to endure, Adrianna was especially pleased with the location. She loved the silverwood glen, and the druids who lived there would certainly discover her presence quickly. It was good that the Wildrunners had made their way to Father Dremathian's domain. She could think of no better place to rest before their confrontation with Aasarak.

Tallachienan gestured towards her arm, the one that wore the serpentine talisman. Adrianna lifted her sleeve, and when the serpent was exposed, Tallachienan placed his hands over it, much as he did the day he rendered it powerless within the confines of the citadel. Now he was releasing that *Suppression* spell. The place beneath his palms glowed briefly. Adrianna immediately noticed a difference in the object, felt a warmth suffuse the golden coils. The serpent's ruby eyes glittered at her before she covered it with the sleeve of her tunic.

Adrianna looked up to see Tallachienan watching her intently. "Come, let me begin the incantation to open the portal. Charlemagne's spell has already been cast into the brackets, making it possible for me to complete your *Timewalk* without his physical presence."

Tallachienan made to move towards the portal bracket, but Adrianna's hand on his arm stopped him. Tallachienan turned around to face her. "Tallachienan, I have a question to ask you." She used his given name, for they were now friends, and status had ceased to mean anything between them.

Tallachienan closed his eyes and then nodded. "If it is within my ability to do so, I will give you an answer." He then looked at her again, his eyes intent upon her face.

Adrianna gave a heavy swallow, wondering if she really wanted to know the answer. "What happened in the other Cycles? How did the battles with Aasarak end?"

Tallachienan didn't want to answer her. He should have known she would ask him this question. He could have formulated an answer to it beforehand, so that he wouldn't feel as sick as he did now. Yet, he knew that he needed to tell her the truth. She deserved that much.

Tallachienan fought to remain expressionless and monotone as he answered her. "You died. Aasarak destroyed you, and his empire slowly grew and eventually took over the whole of Ansalar. At the end of every Cycle, he has reigned supreme over this land."

Adrianna stared mutely at him for a moment before nodding her head. "That is why Pylar looks at me the way he does, and why you..." She stopped, unable to complete what she had to say.

Tallachienan closed the space between them and grasped her arms. "But I still have hope." His voice was gruff as he replied. Tallachienan fought the ache in his throat as he continued. "I know that I haven't been the best master for you, but the things that I taught you are valuable. You learned them well... very well. I have faith in you, Adrianna."

Adrianna looked up at him with eyes that shimmered with unshed tears. Countless expressions passed over her face in that moment, and he could see a glimmer of regret in her eyes. "I will always remember what you have done for me. I wish that I had..."

Tallachienan put a forefinger over her lips and shook his head. "Shhhh. All of that is history. Now all we have before us is the future. Let us concentrate on that for awhile. If you ever have need of me... ever... I will always be here." Tallachienan gave a small smile.

Adrianna drew a shaky breath and stepped towards him. Tallachienan wrapped her in his embrace, and for several moments they stood there, each taking strength from the other. Just like the Cycle before, Tallachienan felt his heart breaking into a thousand pieces. Yet, he spoke nothing of it to the woman in his arms. Just as he had said, he wouldn't think of the past. For once he would look ahead, and hope for the future that could be.

Finally, they stepped apart. Tallachienan gripped each of her shoulders in his hands. "Come, my dear friend. It is time for you to go home."

Xebrinarth sat alone deep inside the mountain. It was his prison, a maze of vast labyrinths that had become his home. The place was one of rare beauty, a gem-laden cavern meant for a king. Water flowed from the surface and made a river from which he drank, and his supply of meat was endless, the animals coming often to the cavern beneath his mountain. The air somehow remained fresh, mayhap from some hidden vents he never had the luck to find.

However, the mountain was isolated, warded, and shielded. His thoughts could reach no dragon, and neither could theirs reach him. In every way he was alone, and had been thusly for many years. Adrianna had been gone for almost twenty when they came to take him. The Elders told Xebrin that he could not be trusted, and that they could not take the chance he would go to her when Adrianna finally contacted him again. They knew things that he did not. That bothered him. Yet, they were certain that Adrianna would return to him. That made him happy.

So, Xebrinarth continued to wait. He did not lie down and die, as he had wanted to do so many times those first couple of decades. The Elders had given him the hope he needed to live. He knew that Adrianna would return to him one day. He knew it because the Elders feared it so much that they locked him into the prison of this mountain. Perhaps they hoped that he would wither away and die of natural causes. Then his blood would not be on their consciences...

Regardless, his dearest hope was that the voice of his beloved Bond-mate would be able to reach him in spite of the shields. Then he would at least have that to last him the remaining centuries of his life.

Xebrinarth sat. For many years he continued to exist in isolation beneath his mountain. But this day someone came. She passed like silk through the wards, effortlessly spoke to him with her mind despite the shields. Her hide was the color of darkest black, and her eyes molten silver. He thought that she must be Degethozak, but she was much larger than any he had ever seen before.

"I have come to set you free." Her voice was melodic in quality, almost mesmerizing. He felt he could become lost in it if she spoke for too long.

"Who are you? Where did you come from? How did you get inside my mountain, and why do you wish to free me?" Xebrinarth asked the questions despite the compulsion to simply follow her out of the mountain.

The black dragon smiled. "Only one question I will answer, young one. I wish to free you because it is simply my desire to do so. The rest you do not need to know. Accept this gift I have given you. Go and hide yourself until your Bondmate calls for you. Then go to her, wherever she may be..."

# Bᴀᴄᴋ ɪɴ Tɪᴍᴇ

**A**drianna slowly regained consciousness. She felt grass beneath her palms, smelled the freshness of the air, and heard the sounds of a surrounding forest. She opened her eyes and an image of large tree trunks swam into focus. She levered herself up from the ground, felt her consciousness waver for a moment, and then turned to vomit in the grass. The nausea was anticipated, for she remembered Tallachienan's words of caution before she stepped into the portal. She also remembered she only had a limited amount of time to find her companions before she succumbed to the Travel Sickness. However, her first thought was for Xebrinarth, who had lived over a century without her.

Adrianna anxiously concentrated on her link with Xebrinarth, hoping that he still lived. She had asked him to wait for her, but she knew that it might have been too much for him. When she felt the link still there, even after so long, her heart was joyous. <Xebrinarth, my friend. Are you there?>

Suddenly she sensed him in her mind, felt the intensity of his emotion. His elation swept through her like a river, and she heard the thoughts that accompanied it. All of his suffering hadn't been in vain! He had placed all his faith in her and now she was there in his mind after so very long! She slumped back down on the grass and cried, the years of his agony washing over her. Adrianna felt her heart break a hundred times, the pain being so much more even than what she experienced when she dreamed of Sirion's betrayal.

<Zahara, is it really you? After all of this time, have you finally returned to me?>

Adrianna choked on another sob. <Xebrin, I told you that I would return. I asked you to believe in me.>

<But I did believe in you... I did! Look, I have survived these one hundred and four years without you, waiting for you to speak to me yet again. And now, here you are. What a happy day this is for me!>

Adrianna nodded, even though she knew he could not see her. She felt a strange cramping in her belly, knew that her time was running out before the sickness overcame her.

<Xebrinarth, I wish that I could continue to speak with you. I know that you need me, but I don't have much time. I must find my companions

before this illness overcomes me. You will sense the sickness as it consumes me, but please don't worry. The Master assured me it would pass, and that I will live through the pain.>

Xebrinarth nodded. <I remember. Go to your healer. Perhaps she can help ease some of the pain.>

Adrianna nodded. <Yes, that is a good idea. Maybe Tianna can help me.>

<Go... find your companions and contact me again when you can.>

Adrianna sensed the strength that it took for him to say those words. His love surged to her through the link and then his mind receded from hers. Throughout much of her life, she had always considered herself the unlucky one. But when she found Xebrinarth, that had all changed. Now, she knew she was one of the luckiest people on Shandahar.

Adrianna rose from the ground, putting a hand on her forehead in an attempt to quell the slight sense of vertigo that overcame her. Then she stumbled forward, her pack slung over her shoulder and her sword thumping against her thigh as she moved through the silver wood of Krathil-lon. She hoped to find someone soon or she would be suffering through the illness alone.

Adrianna suddenly felt another cramp ripple through her belly, the pain radiating up her torso and down to her pelvis, and her head began to ache. Damnation... this was all happening too fast! She felt the tears, wet and hot, begin to stream down her face. She didn't want to suffer through this alone. Tallachienan's words echoed through her mind... *"The intensity of the pain will steal your breath away and you will feel like you are dying."*

"Hello? Is anyone out here? Please, I need help." Adrianna spoke the words as loud as she could as she increased her walk into a slow jog. She kept the pace for only a few minutes before the cramping returned, this time more intensely. The pain rippled all the way to her chest and it was hard to breathe. She had to stop for a moment with her hand against the trunk of a nearby tree until the sensation subsided. Then she was moving again, hopefully in the direction of the apoptos.

Several more moments passed. She looked around, hoping to see a familiar landmark, but all the trees looked the same. "Sirion? Dartanyen? Armond? Is anyone out here? Please..." Adrianna felt her voice crack as the next wave hit her. She hissed between her teeth, the pain now radiating from her abdomen and chest down her arms and legs. She fell onto the ground, cowered there for a few moments before rising. The pain in her head had intensified, and her vision was blurred at the periphery.

"Hello? Please, I'm sick. I need help." Adrianna jogged onward for a short while longer, barely managing to dodge the trees as she swept by. She no longer used her strength to speak, saving it to withstand the next wave. More swiftly than she imagined it would, the pain struck her again. The intensity of it rushed over her like a torrent, and this time she screamed before falling to her knees. She accepted the unfortunate reality that she would be forced to endure the sickness alone. Tallachienan had told her that she would survive. She would cling to that hope. She felt the reassuring presence of her Bondmate, a soothing beacon in her mind. Yes, for him she would endure, for he had been through so much more in the past decades.

Adrianna slipped down into the grass. Above her, the silver trees swayed with the wind. Vaguely she thought she heard a shout, and then the sound of footfalls coming closer. She felt someone kneeling beside her, picking her shoulders and head up off the ground. The face of a man swam within her line of vision, and it took Adrianna a moment to realize it was Sirion. *By the gods, he is just as handsome as he was the day I left him. It hurts to know he has found another, but I am so happy to see him. He will take care of me, make sure I make it somewhere safe.*

She heard Sirion shout for Dramati as he put his other arm beneath her legs. Adrianna reached out a hand, grasping the front of his tunic in her fist. She felt the next wave of pain begin to crest over her as she focused on his fear filled gaze.

"Take me to Tianna. Please, take me to Tianna." She barely got the words out before she screamed once more, the agony forcing it from her throat. Sirion picked her up and began to run, carrying her out of the forest. Adrianna wrapped her arms around his neck, feeling safe, truly safe, for the first time in so many years.

It was peacefully quiet. A cool breeze passed through, carrying the scent of nearby lirylacs. Adrianna awoke to find herself lying in a bed. She looked around, seeing that she was in a small room. She continued to lie there for quite some time, simply taking in the ambiance of the place. She knew that she was in Krathil-lon, somewhere in the apoptos. She vaguely remembered the pain of the sickness she had endured, the intensity of it making her cry like an infant, breaking her down to the point that she actually wanted her life to end. But then Tianna had been there, Father Dremathian, and Xebrinarth. She found the strength to rise above the agony, and then fell into a trance-like sleep.

Adrianna slowly sat up in the bed. None of the pain accosted her, and she realized it was finally passed. She had thought that it would never end, but here she was with nothing left of it but a fading memory. She suddenly sensed movement just outside the door to the room. It opened to admit Tianna, who carried an armful of fresh linens. At first, the other woman was unaware of Adrianna's wakefulness as she bustled quietly around the room. However, it didn't take long for her to realize that someone watched. Tianna looked towards the bed, and when she saw Adrianna's eyes on her, Tianna's mouth turned up into a smile. She rushed over to the bed, sat on the edge, and took Adrianna's hand. "By the gods, we were so worried about you. I'm glad I was able to help, if even it was just a little."

Adrianna felt her breath catch in her throat. It had been so long since she had seen Tianna last, and having her there now tugged at Adrianna's heart. She remembered the good times they had shared before their mutual love for Sirion came between them. Tianna had still been so despondent when last they had shared company, and now her friend looked down at her from tear-filled eyes that reflected nothing but happiness.

"You... helped me?" Adrianna's words were broken and thick.

Tianna nodded. "Father Dremathian and I sent you to sleep so the pain wouldn't consume you so much. It seemed to help a little, for your mind wasn't quite so aware." Tianna's eyebrows then drew together into a frown. "What caused such pain, Adrianna? What happened to you?"

Adrianna felt her own brows pull together. It would take a lot to explain everything to her friend, and she didn't know if she had the energy to do it. "I will have to tell you some time." Her tongue still felt thick, even though the words were no longer broken.

Tianna nodded. "You must still be tired. You have been asleep for a few days now. The pain seems to have abated, and has been gone for at least a day or two. Just rest. I will let the others know that you have awakened."

"Could you get me some water?" Adrianna hoped that it would help the strange sensation in her mouth.

Tianna reached beside her and took a mug from the small table situated there. "I actually have a restorative draught for you to take." She smiled. "Don't worry, it's not that bad; I tasted it myself." Tianna placed it to Adrianna's mouth, holding it while she drank. When she was finished, Tianna took another moment to smooth the furs comfortably around her.

"It is good to see you, Tianna. It's been so long."

Tianna smiled and shook her head. "Not too terribly long; only a few moon cycles. But it does seem like longer, does it not?"

Adrianna only nodded, scooting back down in the bed and pulling the covers up to her chin. If only Tianna knew how long she had been away, how many years she had been without the Wildrunners. She felt her eyelids begin to drift shut against her will, and when next she awakened, Tianna was no longer there. Adrianna sat up, feeling stronger than the last time she was awake. She wondered how much time had passed since then.

Adrianna swung her legs over the side of the bed, and when she stood up, she found herself falling. She clutched the bedpost, willing her legs to straighten and stop shaking from the effort it took for them to hold her up. She wondered what was wrong with her, and then came to the realization that it must have something to do with the *Travel Sickness*. She heard a knock on the door, but before she could say anything, Sheridana was entering the room. Her eyes lit up when she saw Adrianna standing near the bed and rushed over. Sheridana wrapped her arms around Adrianna in a gentle embrace and then helped her to sit back down.

"Adria, I've missed you so much! We were all so worried when Sirion brought you back here."

Adrianna nodded, her throat unexpectedly closing up. *Sirion. Where is he?* She knew he had moved on without her and found another with whom he could share his affection, but did he care so little for her that he couldn't even come to see her?

Sheridana took Adrianna's hands and then regarded her intently. Adrianna became slightly tense under the scrutiny, and then finally said, "Sheri, I missed you too, but you're looking at me like you haven't seen me in years." Once again Adrianna noticed the thickness of her tongue, and when she gestured to the mug on the bedstand, Sheridana appropriated it and handed it to her. This time it was filled with water. As she drank, Sheridana continued to stare.

When Adrianna finally lowered the mug, Sheridana reached out a hand and brushed some errant strands of hair away from Adrianna's face. "It seems like it's been years," whispered Sheridana. "And you have changed... aged somehow. I can see these lines on your face that were never there before. And you are thin... thinner than I have ever seen you." Sheridana traced around the corners of Adrianna's mouth and alongside her eyes.

Adrianna stared at her sister. *Can it be that, somewhere deep inside, my twin knows how long I have been gone? Is the connection between us that strong?*

"And there is a change in the aura that surrounds you. Even though we haven't spoken about your time away, I know you're not the same person you were when we parted ways six moon cycles ago."

Adrianna took Sheri's hand into her lap, enveloping it with both of hers. "You are right. I've been gone a long time."

Sheridana's eyes stopped their perusal and flew to meet Adrianna's gaze. "How long?"

"Almost seven years."

Sheridana was silent for a moment. "I knew it." She lowered her eyes from Adrianna's and was quiet again for a while before she continued. "It must have been difficult." She then looked back up at her. "He must have been very hard on you."

Adrianna pulled her brows into a frown. "Who?"

"Your Master. I expected you to tell me that you have been away much longer than that, for you appear to have aged at least a decade."

Adrianna nodded. "Yes, he was a difficult Master." This time it was she who broke the eye contact. She didn't want her sister to see the shadows in her eyes, the hardship she had endured in Tallachienan's citadel.

Then she remembered. Adrianna pointed to the pack that rested on the chair near the window. "Sheridana, I have something to show you. Could you bring my pack?"

Sheridana brought the pack and Adrianna opened it to remove the book she had heisted from the citadel, *Cycles of Prophecy*. She opened the volume to the appropriate page and then laid it in her sister's lap. Sheri stared at it for a moment before looking up at her sister. "Adria, I can't read this."

Adrianna looked from her sister to the book and then remembered that Sheridana could only read in Common. This book was written in Savanlean, one of the faelin languages she had learned as an apprentice under Master Tallek. She tended to forget that many people could only read in their native tongue, or knew not how to read at all.

Adrianna cleared her throat. "It is a prophecy, written by a Savanlean scholar over three hundred years ago." She read the prophecy to her sister, the one she had read the day after the citadel gave her its revelation. When she was finished, she gave Sheri some time to digest the words, watching her sister's face for any clues to her thoughts.

Finally, Sheri looked up into Adrianna's eyes. Her expression was solemn and her expression haunted. "I think that you should show this to Dinim."

Adrianna was taken aback. She had read the text to Sheridana so that her sister could offer her thoughts on the prophecy. Instead, she told Adrianna to show the prophecy to Dinim. Six moon cycles ago, Sheri would never have made that suggestion. It showed Adrianna that she wasn't the only one who had changed during the time they were apart.

Adrianna nodded. "I will, but I want to know what you think about it first."

Sheri shook her head. "I don't know what to think. You came back to us in the throes of great pain, told me that you have been gone for over six years instead of six moon cycles, and then show me this... this strange mixture of words that sounds like..."

Sheri went silent.

"Sounds like what?" Adrianna pressed.

Sheridana frowned. "It sounds like a description of you when you wielded the Ring of Aboleth against our father."

Adrianna nodded. "I know. I just wanted to get someone else's opinion. I thought maybe I was going crazy..."

Sheri interrupted her. "Adrianna, I'm scared. What's happening here? What have you brought back with you from that place where you were?" Sheridana's voice was accusing.

Adrianna frowned. "What do you mean? You think that I've brought a curse back with me? That's ridiculous!"

Sheridana shook her head and sighed. "Yes, you're right. Our bad fortune started quite a while ago as we made our way back from the temple."

Adrianna's eyes brightened. "The rod was in a temple? Ooooh! How did that go? Has Dinim figured out how to use it?"

Sheri stared at Adrianna from desolate eyes. "No. The rod was destroyed when we went into the temple to get it."

Adrianna did a quick intake of breath, and then slowly let it out. Damn. She wasn't expecting this news. She had rather hoped that they would have something of arcane value to use when they met Aasarak. Suddenly feeling tired, she lay back on the bed and stared up at the ceiling.

Sheri lay next to her for a few moments. Neither one of them spoke in the pervading silence. Finally, Sheridana touched her shoulder with a gentle hand. "I'm going to let you get some rest. I'll come back in a couple of hours and bring you something to eat."

Adrianna nodded and then gestured around herself. "Could you help me?"

Sheri nodded and helped Adrianna into a more comfortable position. She then smoothed the furs over her the way Tianna had when last she was awake. Adrianna closed her eyes and heard the door softly close as Sheri left the room. Despite her fatigue, it took her a while to fall asleep. Her mind was restless with the knowledge that they were in big trouble. Without the rod, they had no real weapon against the Deathmaster. All they had were the skills and Talents of the members of the group.

Every Cycle before, it hadn't been enough...

Adrianna walked slowly down the corridor. She was lucky, for the room Dinim had acquired for his use during the Wildrunners' stay in Krathillon was close to her own. The only reason she knew was because Tianna had happened to mention it during her next visit. Dremathian had been in accompaniment, making certain she was resting comfortably and eating heartily. Dartanyen and Armond had then come to see her, their crazy antics making her smile. In her own time, even Amethyst had come, creeping in without Adrianna hearing a single sound until the girl stood beside her bed.

"Adrianna, it's so good to see you with us again," she spoke so low it was almost a whisper.

Adrianna couldn't help smiling with the sincerity she heard in the girl's voice. Amethyst gently sat beside her on the bed, tentatively reaching out to touch a curl of her hair where it lay in a pale mess all around her shoulders. "It was hard when you left."

She regarded Amethyst intently, sensing the solemnity pervading the air around them. "I know, and I'm really sorry..."

Amethyst quickly shook her head and interrupted. "No. You have no reason to apologize because it wasn't your fault. You had to go."

Adrianna continued to look at Amethyst, knowing there was something more she needed to say. "I know it isn't my business, but..." she paused for a moment before continuing, "...Sirion needs you."

Adrianna nodded, immediately feeling a sense of loss sweep over her. He still hadn't come to see her. Then, in a show of affection she had never experienced with Amethyst before, the girl leaned over to give her a brief kiss on the forehead. "I missed you, Adria." More swiftly than she would have imagined, the girl had risen from her place on the bed, moved across the room, and slipped out the door.

Now, as Adrianna struggled to reach her destination, she knew she never would have made it if it were any further. Her legs shook as she moved, straining with the effort it took them just to keep her upright. Tianna had told her the convulsions she endured for so long had weakened them, but then swiftly assured her that their strength would return in time. Adrianna was very much looking forward to it.

She finally stopped before the door belonging to Dinim's chamber and knocked. His familiar voice bid her enter, and she swallowed nervously before pushing it open. Adrianna walked into a room very similar to her own, and once glancing around, she saw Dinim sitting at the small desk across from the bed. His eyes widened with surprise when he saw her, and he quickly rose and crossed the room to take her arm, leading her to the bed and sitting her down on it. She couldn't contain her sigh of relief when she felt her muscles finally relax from the strain of keeping her upright.

Dinim looked down at her with a worried frown. "Adrianna, I didn't expect to see you about so soon. You suffered so much on your return to us. I thought you would be still abed."

She nodded. "I should be, but I needed to come see you." Adrianna regarded him intently as she spoke. She was surprised to see how haggard he looked. He was paler than she remembered, and the dark circles under his eyes more pronounced. He was thin, she could tell despite the billowing tunic and trousers he wore. In part, she knew his decline was because of her. She had noticed it before the group split ways, before she went to study with Master Tallachienan.

Back then, the pain of his betrayal had been too fresh, but now almost seven years had gone by. Not only was she able to forgive Dinim for what he had done, she had nearly forgotten it. For so long she had heard praises sung about the young Dinim Coabra from all the masters in the citadel, and she knew him to be a commendable man. Adrianna also carried memories of him from the third and fourth Cycles. They had shared an intimate relationship in the third, and even though they didn't share anything like that in this Cycle, she found that she didn't want to just discard all she knew he was and what he could have been. She cared a great deal for Dinim, and she wanted to try to bridge the rift that had come between them.

Dinim took the chair on which he had been sitting when she entered the room and pulled it closer to the bed. He turned it around and seated himself on it, resting his forearms on the back. He then gave her a small smile. "What has happened that requires you to come in search of me?"

His gaze locked onto hers, a resigned expression on his face. Adrianna could feel the sadness emanating from him, and she knew he thought she visited only to discuss business. Seeing him now, after so long, the memories welled up inside of her. It was the curve of his expressive mouth, how he regarded her from dashing lavender eyes, and the way he cocked his head slightly to the right. She remembered laughing with him in the back of one of the wagons of a gypsy caravan, and the funny way he had made amends with her after his foolish introduction to her sister.

Adrianna breathed deeply, her thoughts having stolen away her ability to form coherent speech. She then lowered her eyes, unconsciously placing a hand on top of the book she brought. Her primary reason for seeing him was the prophecy, but there were so many things she wanted to say. "I heard about the Rod of Atlenbos. It meant so much to us. How did it happen?"

Dinim gave a heavy sigh. "It was trapped, and when the group stepped over the magical seal on the temple floor, a mechanism was activated."

Adrianna shook her head. "Couldn't you warn them?"

Dinim also shook his head. "There was a spell in effect that took hold of me before I could enter the chamber. I was asleep before I hit the floor."

Adrianna nodded and then was quiet for a moment as she collected her thoughts. It was important that she tell Dinim everything she knew. It was possible that he knew some of it already, but simply kept it to himself. "Do you know what a Cycle is?"

Once more Adrianna watched him intently for any change in his expression. He suddenly became more alert, and his eyes seemed to brighten. "Perhaps. What do you know of the subject?"

Adrianna felt her eyes narrow slightly. She wondered what he knew and if he had any intention of treating her as his equal. She suddenly recalled how their fighting had started; he hadn't respected her opinions, and felt her an unworthy equal in battle. She decided to give him the benefit of the doubt, just this time.

Adrianna held up the book. "I know a lot about the Cycling of Shandahar."

Dinim's eyes widened. He reached out a tentative hand and then took the book from her. He caressed the faded binding, and then put the book to his nose, breathing deeply.

"We are currently in the fifth Cycle," she said.

Dinim nodded. "I thought as much. I have read texts that have only alluded to the Cycling of the world, and unable to find one that describes it in detail. I know only bits and pieces, and some of that may not even be fact."

"Not all of what I know is described in the book."

Dinim regarded her intently. "Then how do you know the rest?"

Adrianna hesitated. She didn't know how to tell him that the citadel had provided her with the information, not knowing what he knew of the place. Tallachienan had conceded that there was something extra-ordinary about the citadel, but he hadn't elaborated.

"It is something I discovered while I studied with the Master."

Dinim smiled. "It's interesting to hear you refer to Tallachienan as your Master. I knew you before he did, told him about you. He took my advice when I told him that you would be a good apprentice."

"You told him that?"

"Of course. You have great Talent. I would say that you are a Prime."

"What is a Prime?" she asked.

"Someone whose Talent excels above that of most others."

"Are you a Prime?"

Dinim nodded. "Yes."

Adrianna was silent, taking in his words. Dinim thought that he had known her before the Master. He knew very little about the Cycles. Either that, or he hadn't thought much about how it worked. She would have to educate him.

"Like I said, we are in the fifth Cycle. Many of the events that have taken place this Cycle have taken place already in previous Cycles."

Dinim was quiet for a few moments before speaking again. "But not everything."

"No. There are some small changes between the Cycles, most likely as a result of immortal intervention." Adrianna paused before she continued. "There are some people who are capable of withstanding the turn of a Cycle. Master Tallachienan is one of those people."

Dinim nodded. "So, he knew you in previous Cycles... knew *me* in previous Cycles."

Adrianna nodded.

Dinim looked past her as he continued to ponder her words. She could see him piecing together some of the pieces of the puzzle, saw it in the expressions that flitted across his face. "Most likely, we knew one another in previous Cycles as well."

Adrianna nodded again. Something must have passed over her face because he stopped to look at her.

"What is it? Tell me what you know."

Adrianna knew that she had to tell him, knew that it was one of the reasons why she had sought him out. She needed to do more than offer him her forgiveness. She needed to let him know that they had once shared something between them and that she carried those memories with her. She didn't know exactly how much she could tell him, but she needed to at least try. "Something happened to me within Tallachienan's citadel."

Dinim stared at her for a moment. "What was it?"

"Somehow, I was able to obtain my memories from previous Cycles." Adrianna kept it at that, not willing to give him the details of her revelation. Perhaps later, when their time wasn't so pressing.

Once again, Dinim was silent. She also remained quiet, letting Dinim think through what she had just told him. Several moments passed before he replied. "So, you have memories of yourself in the fourth Cycle?"

Adrianna nodded. "And the third Cycle."

"So, what happened at the end of those two Cycles?"

"I don't know. I only remember the time I spent in the citadel."

Dinim nodded pensively. "So, each Cycle is slightly different, eh? The gods have been playing a role with each subsequent Cycle, and now here we are the fifth time around. Does anyone know why this started happening in the first place?"

Adrianna shook her head. That was one question for which she had never been able to find the answer. However, her attention was focused upon another issue, one that Dinim had not yet addressed. If she had memories of the previous two Cycles, did she have memories of him as well?

Yet, Dinim was quick to make the connection. "So, do you happen to remember me in the third and fourth Cycles?"

Even though she had prepared herself for the question, expected it even, she found herself floundering for the right words. "Yes. We studied together at the citadel."

Dinim grinned. "I bet we had some good times."

Adrianna smiled in return. "Indeed, we did. I only wish that you could remember it as I do." Adrianna stopped, feeling a slight wrenching in her chest. Dinim would never have the memories she had. She was the only one who would ever remember what had been between them. To him, it had never happened, or it had happened to an entirely different man. Only she would think of that man as Dinim despite the fact that he was dead and gone for several centuries.

Adrianna refocused her gaze onto Dinim's face, only to find him regarding her intently. He knew that she was keeping some things from him, but he didn't pursue it. Instead, he turned back to the book in his hands and opened it.

"There is more to that book than just some information about the Cycles." she said.

Dinim glanced up at her. "Perhaps some prophecies?" He grinned slightly as he pointed out the word to her on the binding.

Adrianna grinned in response. Of course, he would have figured that the book contained prophecy. She felt herself starting to relax a little, beginning to experience a little bit of the camaraderie they had once shared before their fighting had started.

"The ones mentioned in this book were given by a man with the name of Johannan Chardelis."

"Oh yes. I have heard of him," said Dinim. "He was a prophet of some renown who lived near the turn of the second century."

Adrianna gestured to the book. "I read some of his prophecies. I was hoping that you could read them as well, and then tell me what you think."

He nodded. "All right. Show me where they are."

Adrianna showed Dinim the appropriate pages. She leaned back on the bed as she waited for him to read the text. After a few moments, she began to watch his face, wanting to see what type of reaction he would have. She saw his eyes widen and then he began to flip back and forth between the pages containing the three prophecies. By the expression on his face, she knew that if his complexion could have become even paler, it would have.

Finally, he looked up at her, his eyes haunted. "Adrianna, you know that these prophecies are about us... about *you*..."

Her tone was grim. "Actually, I was hoping that you would tell me that they weren't."

Dinim swallowed convulsively and turned to one of the prophecies. He rose from his chair and then seated himself next to her on the bed. Adrianna attempted to straighten herself, but Dinim only shook his head, situated his arm and shoulder behind her back, and pulled her against him.

Dinim thrust the book before her and began to read. "*The world will Cycle and the fifth will come...* Chardelis is referring to this Cycle." Dinim paused and then continued. "*Fourteen they will be, a number of strength...* remember, we used to be fourteen, before Zorg died. In the next verse that is mentioned... *One will be taken away in death...*"

Adrianna nodded. She felt her own eyes begin to widen, realization finally setting in.

Dinim went on to another verse. "*The third carries a daemon deep inside...* Adrianna, Chardelis is referring to Triath. In his earlier days with the Wildrunners, he battled a daemon. To this day, he carries the essence of the daemon within him and even has some of the powers that type of daemon possesses. And look down here." Dinim pointed to yet another verse. "*Clerics will fight alongside assassins... And faelin, human, and oroc...* Tianna is a cleric, Sorn is an assassin, and Naemmious is of orocish descent."

Silence reigned for a moment as Adrianna collected her thoughts. But once again, Dinim spoke. "Adrianna, there is no doubt to whom this prophecy is referring."

Adrianna frowned. "But who is the Dreamer?"

Dinim stared at her for a moment, his expression telling her he wondered if she was truly serious. "It's the same person as the Warrior spoken about in the other prophecies." Dinim then turned to one of them. "*The Warrior of Destiny will come... With a talisman of magnificent power...*"

Adrianna pulled her lips into her mouth, an attempt to keep her emotions at bay. Denial was futile. She would accept her fate, but she didn't have to like it. Despite her attempts, the tears fell down her face. Then she shook her head. "I am no warrior. I'm not strong enough to be what this prophecy says I should be."

Adrianna heard the bitterness in her voice, knowing her words to be the truth. She felt Dinim's hand at her jaw and then he was moving her to face him. She stared into eyes full of sadness and regret. Dinim shook his head. "You are wrong. You are everything that prophecy says you are. You are the Child, the Warrior, and the Dreamer. Without even really knowing why, we have rallied to you, and here we are, preparing ourselves to fight the Deathmaster. You are strong, have proven it time and time again, despite the odds against you. You will lead us into this fight, and with your magic, we will defeat Aasarak."

Adrianna shook her head yet again. "What have I done that has changed your opinion of me so much?"

Dinim rubbed his thumb across her cheek, wiping away the wetness there. "I was a fool. I let my emotions control me, allowed them to dictate my thoughts and actions. I could have killed you, and I have known regret every day of my life since then. I have lived without your friendship for only a few moon cycles now, but it seems like many years have gone by. What I am trying to say is that my opinion of you never changed. I never had a poor opinion of you to begin with. Only then, I had no way to tell you how I truly felt. But now, with everything that has happened, and in light of what I have learned, I know that I need to tell you these things."

"Dinim, you must know I have already forgiven you." Adrianna reached up to cup the hand at her jaw.

Dinim shook his head. "But I can't forgive myself."

Adrianna frowned. "But you must. I need you to be strong."

"I know. But I just don't know if I have the strength left in me anymore."

Adrianna deepened her frown. "I have endured so much so we can win this fight. Am I really hearing you say that you are giving up? For over six years I have studied under Master Tallachienan. Mercilessly, he taught me everything he could before I left his citadel. I come back home to discover that the rod has been lost, and our most powerful sorcerer may be almost useless?"

"What do you mean, six years have passed?" Dinim interjected.

Adrianna gave a heavy sigh. "The Master knew our time here in the present was limited. He took me back into the past so that I would have the time necessary to learn all he had to teach me before our battle. For me, over six years have gone by, while for you it's been only a few moon cycles. That's why I suffered so much on my return from his citadel. My body was reacting to being thrust forward in time by almost fifty-two years."

"Xebrinarth said he waited one hundred and four years."

She nodded. "Remember, time passes differently in the Heavens than it does here."

Dinim nodded, then stared at her for a moment. Tallachienan was more powerful than he thought; either that, or he had great connections. Tallachienan obviously knew that Adrianna's role in the upcoming battle with Aasarak was of paramount importance. Otherwise, he wouldn't have bothered to go through the effort to take her back in time. He glanced back down at the book in his hands, knowing they still didn't have all the facts. However, he had a feeling that the book contained much of the information they needed to know.

Dinim rose from his position on the bed. "How much of this have you read?"

"Not enough. I've only had the chance to read a few of the chapters; some of them I skimmed through, and a couple I haven't been able to look at yet."

"Let me borrow this for the evening. Get some rest tonight and I will come to you tomorrow. By then I can tell you all I have gleaned from this book."

Adrianna nodded. "I guess you can tell I'm pretty tired."

Dinim grinned. "It's all right. Based on what you described to me, I'm surprised you've been able to make it this long without falling asleep already."

Adrianna stood up from the bed, Dinim holding onto her supportively. Once realizing her legs couldn't sustain her weight, he lifted her in his arms and carried her back to her own room. He gently deposited her on the bed, and noticing a plate of food on the desk, brought it over. He watched as Adrianna took a chunk of bread and then drank the water that sat on the nightstand. After making sure she was comfortable, Dinim then bade her a good rest. Adrianna was closing her eyes before he managed to leave the room.

# Destiny of the Fourteen

Adrianna slowly walked the periphery outside the apoptos. It was early morning and the first rays of dawn had begun to crest over the horizon. The cold wind blew through her hair, attempting to burrow into her cloak. The season would be changing soon, the icy grip of winter slowly loosening its hold. But until then, the night and early morning hours would still be cold. Adrianna wrapped the fur lined cloak more tightly around her to shut it out.

After Dinim carried her back to her room, she had slept for the rest of the day and into the night. She had awoken sometime in the wee hours, hunger driving her out of bed to seek the plate of food she remembered sitting on the desk. Ravenously, she ate what remained of the bread, cheese, and papas fruit. She tried to settle back down for the remainder of the night, only to find herself unable to sleep. She felt her strength returning and her legs had not shaken so much when she got up to get the food. After a while, she decided that despite the darkness she would go for a walk. She needed the physical stimulation, and perhaps it would tire her enough that she would be able to sleep again. She wistfully thought about dancing. Aside from the times she had danced in the gypsy encampment and at the ball at Tallachienan's citadel, she had not danced in years.

Adrianna had found her clothes resting inside the chest at the foot of the bed, as well as her pack, belt pouches, and sword. She donned the tunic and trousers, momentarily considering the belt with her pouches and sword. She quickly discarded that idea. Heavens, she was only going for a walk... what did she need with spell components and a blade here within the sanctified confines of Krathil-lon?

Adrianna chuckled to herself as she walked. Yes, indeed. What would she do with those things? Krathil-lon was highly fortified. There wasn't much that would have a chance to get a foothold. The power of the druids that resided here was too strong. And there was another reason why she felt so protected. It was the presence of Sirion.

Adrianna felt the familiar ache in her chest. She had tried to leave most of her pain behind in Tallachienan's citadel, but obviously she wasn't very successful. With him so near, Adrianna couldn't help feeling this way. She didn't understand why he wouldn't come to see her, especially since he had been the one to find her and bring her safely back to the apoptos. Even if he no longer had romantic inclinations towards her, didn't he at least respect the friendship that could still exist between them?

Suddenly Adrianna felt a stirring in her mind. It was Xebrinarth, responding to the strong emotion he felt through their link. He knew the cause of her distress, for they had spoken for quite some time before she went to see Dinim the day before. He sent her soothing thoughts, hoping to dispel some of the sadness she felt. He was sorry about Sirion, knew how much the man meant to her. He had once called Sirion her life mate, the person who would one day sire her children. Yet, that dream had become a distant memory, just like so many of the other dreams that had come before it.

Adrianna shuffled her feet, wondering how much longer it would take for her to continue the circuit around the apoptos. Hells, she was a fool to think she would be able to walk around the entire structure without even knowing how large it was. It was obviously too far, and she was beginning to get tired. She was so deep in her thoughts that she didn't realize someone was near, and when she finally perceived that she wasn't alone, the man was standing close enough to harm her if he chose.

Adrianna jerked her head up, her heart suddenly racing in her chest. By the gods, he had frightened her, coming out of the darkness that way. When she saw that the man who stood before her was Sirion, her heart did a curious flip. She put a hand to her chest and exhaled an exclamation.

"Sirion... you startled me."

Despite his pounding heart and his heightened sense of awareness, Sirion attempted to keep his face expressionless. Finally, she was awake and standing before him for the first time in far too long. He hadn't meant to frighten her, so sure that she would notice him as he approached her from out of the forest. But her faelin senses hadn't notified her of his presence, and he had forgotten that her senses may not be as they should be since she was still recovering from her illness.

Sirion had been shocked to find her alone in the woods when she returned, and even more to discover that she was in such agony. After calling for Dramati, the corubis had swiftly carried them to the apoptos. By that time, fear had overtaken Sirion. Something was seriously wrong with Adrianna. He yelled for someone to find Tianna and bring her to him. One of the nearby tyros rushed off, and when he returned, Father Dremathian and the rest of the Wildrunners were following closely behind. After examining her and praying to her goddess, Tianna could find nothing physically wrong with Adrianna. The malady that afflicted her was unnatural, beyond what Tianna could understand. Father Dremathian said the same. However, the two of them together decided that they could put Adrianna into a slumber, make it so that she didn't feel her pain so acutely.

Even in her deep sleep, Adrianna continued to convulse with pain. It took two days for it to pass, and after that she slept for another two days. Tianna came to him when Adrianna awoke for the first time, but by the time he made it to her room, Adrianna was sleeping again. He sat with her for a few hours, hoping that she would awaken again. When she didn't, he whispered in her ear that he would return the next day.

But that hadn't happened. Or it did, but every time he came, she was either not in her quarters or sleeping. He neither had the heart to wake her from her healing rest, nor the inclination to hunt her down. So now here he was, standing before Adrianna with a vague sense of disquiet. Just by looking into her eyes he could sense the change in her, a change he had been warned about by many of his comrades. Regarding him out of those dark eyes, she seemed so much older now, wiser. There was a solemnity that was never there before, and a reservedness. He didn't know how to respond to those things, or to ask questions he feared the answers to, so he said the first mundane thing to enter his mind.

Sirion shook his head. "I'm sorry. I didn't intend to alarm you."

Adrianna nodded. For a moment they just stood there, silently regarding one another. Under normal circumstances, she would have smiled a greeting, perhaps rushed to embrace him. However, this situation was anything but ordinary. She was no longer the same person that she was when she left, Sirion had moved on without her, and she had made her own mistakes to nullify their betrothal. No matter how much she tried to remind herself that she was under the influence of stronger forces when she made the decision to sleep with Tallachienan, she still couldn't eradicate all wrongdoing within herself. Even if Sirion himself had not chosen to take another to his bed, he had every right to break their betrothal based on her confessions alone.

Adrianna took a deep breath. "It's been a long time."

Again, more silence. Adrianna broke eye contact, spoke the words even though he might not feel the same, "I missed you."

The air itself seemed to become still for a moment. Adrianna's heart stuttered in her chest when he was suddenly reaching out to her, bridging the space between them. Sirion pulled her close and breathed into her hair. "Gods, Adria. I've been wanting to see you since yesterday morning."

She sighed deeply, settling herself into his side. She inhaled the familiar scent of him, never wanting it far from her again. "Then why didn't you come?"

"I *did* come, but you were either sleeping or not in your room."

Adrianna pulled away and looked into his face. "Why didn't you just wake me up?"

Sirion shook his head. "You were sleeping a healing sleep. In my right mind, I could never do that."

She almost whispered the words, her voice taking on a sad tone. "But I've been waiting for you."

Sirion pulled her close again and just held her there for a while, reveling in her presence. The cool winds swept against them and he tightened his embrace. A part of him had stagnated with her gone, had been only half the man he knew he could be. He would never let her go again, never.

"I am so glad that you found me in the forest," she said. "I was afraid no one would hear me."

"Why did your Master send you back like that? Why were you in so much pain?" Sirion asked, unable to keep the gruff tone from his voice.

Adrianna shook her head where it rested against his chest. "It wasn't his fault." Then she pulled away, looking into his eyes. "I have so many things I want to tell you."

Sirion noticed the tumult in her eyes and the minute trembling in her body before she turned away. He just stood there for a moment, a feeling of unease sweeping over him. He could sense the disturbance all around her, and he didn't know what to do. She was upset, that much was obvious. And when he noticed a tear falling down her face, he pulled her back around to look at him.

"*Shendori*, please tell me what's going on."

Adrianna pulled out of his embrace, refusing to be comforted. She shook her head, several more tears following the first one. "I can't. So many things have happened, and I can't think of what needs to be said first."

"That's all right," he said. "We can work through it all together."

Once more Adrianna shook her head. "No, not now... not yet." She sniffed and then wiped away the tears on her face. "Please, I am so terribly tired, Sirion. Can you help me back to my room?"

Mutely, Sirion nodded. Slowly he approached her, took her in his arms, and then lifted her up. Adrianna wrapped her arms around his neck as he carried her back into the apoptos. He felt the gentle shuddering of her body as her sobs began anew. His heart ached with the knowledge that she felt she couldn't confide in him, and once more he rued the day he'd let her go.

Once they reached her small chamber, he opened the door and carried her to the bed. When he lay her there, he stood over her for a moment, taking in the beauty of her face, the golden halo of her hair splayed all around, and the darkness of her tear-dampened eyes. He lowered his lips to hers and brushed them softly in a loving caress. He wanted more, but instead of pressing her, he slowly straightened and then walked out of the room, closing the door behind him.

Adrianna stared up at the ceiling. Her heart ached with the depth of her melancholy. What was Sirion doing, holding her and talking to her like that when he had moved on to another lover? But also, what was *she* doing? Certainly, she wanted to tell Sirion everything about the years she spent in the citadel, but she knew that she would also have to tell him about what happened between herself and the Master. That wasn't a story she was ready to tell him yet. She would gather her thoughts, and then talk to him another day.

Some day after she told the Wildrunners about the prophecies she had discovered...

Then she and Sirion could address the state of their relationship... if they even had one anymore.

The knock sounded for the second time, finally bringing her from troubled thoughts about Sirion, the prophecies, and anything else to do with the future. Then she heard Dinim's voice, "Adrianna, can I come in? It's important."

She approached the door and opened it just wide enough for Dinim to enter before closing it behind him. It was just before midday, and she'd been starting to wonder when he would come. Dinim swiftly moved to the bed and she followed. Adrianna then seated herself beside him. Dinim turned towards her, and by the intensity of his stare knew that he had nothing good to tell her.

"Adrianna, I have read the text in its entirety. Some things that I am about to say you will already know. The others you will not."

Adrianna gave a brusque nod. She was ready.

"The turning of this Cycle is near. With my knowledge of history, and by looking at the timeline of events leading up to the turns in the other four Cycles, it appears to coincide with what has been happening *now* in this Cycle. At first, the events leading up to the turning of a Cycle were unclear to me, but as I continued to study the text, it all began to fit together."

Adrianna nodded. This was the part she knew she didn't want to hear, but knew she must. This was where Dinim was going to tell her about her destiny.

"I still don't know how the Cycling started, but supposedly there is a way to end it. Many say that it has to do with the Balance, which must be tipped back towards equality. Others say it hasn't much to do with the Balance at all, but simply a series of events that must take place in order for the curse to be broken. "In every Cycle preceding this one, there has always been a small cohort of individuals that have gone against the Deathmaster. It has always been comprised by a young woman, whom they call the Dreamer, and her comrades. Sometimes she is also called the Warrior, and in one instance, the Child. But all the names refer to the same girl. In every Cycle thus far, she and her companions have failed. The reign of Aasarak then went unchecked, the world eventually plummeted into chaos and, after a while, the Cycle turned anew."

For a moment, Adrianna just sat there. "The Dreamer and her companions died in their battle." She made it a statement, for she already knew how the story ended. She had asked Tallachienan as much before she left his citadel. She watched as Dinim hesitated. Mayhap she knew more than he thought she would.

"Yes, but this Cycle, Johannan Chardelis prophesied about the Dreamer and her battle against Aasarak. It could mean that, this time, we actually have a chance."

Adrianna swallowed despite the lump lodged painfully in her throat. She wasn't heartened by Dinim's statement and had just realized she would be the one to tell her friends they would probably die in their fight against Aasarak. Some of them, she was sure, had already faced that reality. Regardless, she still had to tell them what she and Dinim already knew... they had always failed before. The one thing that may have helped them, the Rod of Atlenbos, was gone, and their chances of success were desolate.

Adrianna cocked her head to the side. "It's good to know that you have suddenly become an optimist."

Dinim shook his head. "No. Not just optimism. *Hope.* Without hope, what would we strive to live for?"

Adrianna sighed and then nodded. "I'm just afraid of letting everyone down. These prophesies build me up... Dinim, no matter what you say, I just don't think of myself this way."

Dinim put a hand on her shoulder. "That is what makes you so genuine. Believe me, there is no one better suited for a prophecy such as this one, than you."

Adrianna placed her hand on top of the one on her shoulder, grinning tremulously. "Well, at least I have one staunch supporter."

Dinim shook his head. "When all is said and done, I'll almost guarantee you have twelve."

Adrianna rose from the bed. "Well, we had best tell the others as soon as we can. The longer we stay here, the closer that Aasarak will be to completing his army."

Adrianna barely noticed Dinim's silence as she prepared to leave the chamber. She stepped into her boots and then placed a sash around her waist, sliding the loop of the scabbard through before she tied it. She completed the rest of her preparations before she picked up her sword and slid it into the sheath.

Dinim's questioning voice broke the silence. "Adria, where did you get that blade?"

She turned to face Dinim, saw the look of incredulity on his face. "I found it in the dungeons of Tallachienan's citadel. The Master prepared a test for me and lured me down there. I found myself up against a monstrous spider. I defeated it with an *Ice* spell and this sword I found lying on the floor. I've kept it ever since."

Dinim grinned widely. "It seems that you have become a warrior in more ways than one."

Adrianna drew her brows together for a moment, suddenly viewing herself the way Dinim did. Yes, she imagined he might see her that way. She carried a sword, had the skills of an amateur warrior. "Yes, well, I am not very good."

"You were good enough to wield it against your enemy and defeat it."

"I suppose," she acceded.

Dinim raised his hands from his sides. "That is the definition of a warrior— someone who wields a weapon of war and uses it effectively against the enemy." He then gestured towards the sword. "That blade once belonged to me."

Adrianna's eyes widened. "How did it ever find its way to the dungeons?"

"As I recall, that is where I lost it. I had my own test down there once."

Adrianna fingered the hilt. That was something, finding the sword that had been left there by Dinim, just to have it save her from the monster that was her test. She truly believed that, for she had been too weak from her sickness to summon her magic. The sword had definitely saved her life. Without it, she wouldn't have found something strong enough to shatter the spider's leg.

Without being told, Adrianna untied the sash. She removed the sheathed sword and held it out towards Dinim, offering the blade to its rightful owner. He said nothing for a moment before laying his hands over hers. He then slowly curved her fingers around the weapon.

"No. It is yours now. Besides, I have another." Dinim indicated the short sword at his hip.

Adrianna nodded mutely as she retied the sash around her waist. She then stepped closer to him and wrapped her arms around his neck. "Thank you, Dinim. The sword means so much to me. I'm so glad to have you as my friend again."

Dinim returned the embrace, holding her tightly in his arms. He breathed deeply, happy that they had finally come to terms with what happened before their battle with Thane. Finally, Adrianna released him and stepped away. She took her cloak from the nearby chair and proceeded to fasten it onto the reinforced shoulders of her tunic. He watched her for a moment, knowing that he needed to tell her something before they left to meet with the rest of the group.

*Adrianna didn't know that Aasarak had already completed his army...*

"Before we go, there are some things I think you need to know."

Adrianna looked up at him, taking in his solemn countenance. "What are they?"

Dinim solemnly stepped up to her and took the fasteners from her fingers. "Events in this Cycle have taken place much more swiftly than the ones before."

He paused for a moment before continuing. "Aasarak has already completed his army. As we speak, it is marching through the Kingdom of Cortubro, laying waste to whatever stands in its way."

Adrianna blinked and her dark eyes widened. Dinim watched the horror wash over her face as she shook her head. "No, this can't be happening already. How do you know? Have you seen it? Perhaps it isn't what you think. Maybe..."

Dinim sighed heavily. "Adrianna, there is no doubt as to the origins of this army."

"Then it is... they are..."

Dinim nodded. "They are abominations... dead, but not dead. They are the poor souls that Aasarak has brought out of the grave. Many of them are nothing but skeletons, while others are endowed with swaths of rotting flesh. They are human, faelin, halfen, and oroc. There are even some animals... thritean, kyrrean, bruin, corubis, and wemic."

"We need to stop them," Adrianna whispered the words from a dry throat. Dinim shook his head. "They can't be stopped. Even with an arm severed, a leg removed, a sword through the middle... they keep coming. Only when they lie in pieces on the ground will they lose their animation."

Adrianna suddenly turned away from him. She put a hand to her forehead as the gravity of the situation slammed into her. Meanwhile, Dinim kept his calm as he continued with what he had to say. "The druids knew when the army began its movement. The world seemed to shudder as it marched. All life sought to escape it. Only the birds were able to fly fast enough to come and tell the tale. The plants and animals in the path of the army withered and died, and when it encountered villages and towns, those were quick to succumb as well.

"Krathil-lon sent out a summons, and druids from around the continent rallied. This place was swarming with druids from Reshik-na, Halith-shin, and Dregil-zan. They went out to meet Aasarak's army." Once again Dinim paused for a moment. "The army was so vast... there were so many of the undead that the druids didn't have a chance. More than half of them fell before they retreated and returned home."

The room was suddenly quiet for a moment before she spoke. "How many druids are left?"

"Only a couple thousand," he replied.

"And the army. How big is it?"

"Dremathian says it was over twenty thousand strong when they met it. It is probably larger now."

She regarded him dejectedly. "Then we are too late."

Dinim shook his head. "No! It is never too late. But I just wanted you to know that Aasarak's army has already begun to march. I didn't want you to be shocked when you heard it from the others today when we go to meet them."

Adrianna gave a heavy sigh. "How is it not too late? If we even destroy Aasarak, will it stop the army?"

"No, I don't think so. But with Aasarak gone, at least the dead will no longer rise."

"How is he doing this? How has Aasarak been able to animate so many of the dead? How can he go to every individual to make the incantation that will bid it rise?" she asked.

"While I studied under Tallachienan, there was a time I was fascinated with necromancy. It was then that I learned about the Ring of Aboleth, as well as an artifact known as the Azmathion. The powers of this artifact are very difficult to harness, and one of those powers is very similar to that of the Ring of Aboleth. I am certain Aasarak has possession of the Azmathion and that he has learned to use many of its powers. One of those was the creation of the Azmathous, which we saw in the twisted guise of your father. Another is the power to raise the dead. By now he doesn't have to seek out each individual. He has the strength to focus the power of the Azmathion onto an *entire group* of individuals and make them rise to do his bidding." Dinim shook his head. "Heavens forbid he has mastered the ability to do it from afar."

Adrianna bowed her head with the weight of this newfound knowledge. What they were up against was far greater than just a master sorcerer deep within his lair. Even if they somehow defeated Aasarak, which was far unlikely, they would still have to find some way to incapacitate his undead legions. Hellfire, this was something that was going to take more than just her and the rest of the Wildrunners.

They needed their own army.

The Wildrunners gathered in the tsumee, one of the small ritual chambers slightly removed from the apoptos. Four stonework walls surrounded them, but no roof existed overhead, allowing the light of the first moon, Steralion, to shine down from the darkening sky. The air was warmer than it had been as of late, a herald to the coming of a new season. However, a fire had still been built, and the flames cast eerie shadows on the crudely built walls.

The group waited expectantly. Strewn somewhat haphazardly around the place were large flat rocks of varying shapes and sizes. They had situated themselves on these surfaces, not knowing what their intended use was for, but needing a place to sit. No one knew who had called them together, only that Dinim had come to each of them and asked them to come to this place at the appointed hour. Perhaps they thought it was Father Dremathian. The old druid sat farthest away from the fire, almost hidden in the shadows at the far side of the tsumee. Dramati sat next to him, contentedly enjoying the caress of the older man's fingers working their way into the thick fur at his neck.

Everyone's attention swung to Adrianna as she rose from her place. She spent a moment to take in the scene, wanting it to remain in her mind in the days ahead. It felt like a part of forever had passed since she had last seen them all together. Beside her was Sheridana, her long dark hair worn in its customary plait down her back. Her pale eyes reflected the weight that had settled over her since Adrianna revealed the prophecy. Tianna and Triath sat together on a rock against the nearest wall. She had heard that Triath was recently very ill, and close to death. She was glad to see him hale and whole. His arm was around Tianna's shoulders, and her head lay contentedly against his chest. Sorn and Anya sat next to one another on a stone outcropping, and Naemmious' large form leaned nearby. Adrianna had never been very familiar with him before, so now, coming back to the group after so long, his size seemed a bit imposing. Sirion leaned against an adjacent wall, bare arms crossed at his chest, amber eyes regarding her intently. The light of the fire cast into his coppery hair made it appear as flame. As always, her heart did a little lurch in her chest when she saw him. Armond leaned against the same wall, his gaze speculative. There was Amethyst, who stayed in the shadows outside the light cast by the fire, Dartanyen, and finally Dinim, who was the only one who had any idea of what she was about to say.

Once upon a time, Adrianna would have felt intimidated to address a group of people like this. She had allowed so many things to hold her back, especially fear. But over the years she had grown, leaped so many hurdles, and overcome so many more obstacles. As such, simple speeches had ceased to daunt her, even if they were of the negative quality. Her voice was crisp and clear as she spoke.

"Many moon cycles ago, I followed some of you into an underground temple. Since then, my life has been anything but my own. My father was hunting me, and in spite of the danger, you all followed me down that dark path. Back then, I only marginally understood the choice you made. Despite your contact with me, you still could have escaped the shadowed gaze of Lord Thane and gone your own way."

Adrianna paused for a brief moment and then continued. "But you didn't leave. And now, here we are, faced with an even larger threat. For the past six and a half years I have been studying with Master Tallachienan in his citadel." Adrianna paused again when everyone glanced at one another in confusion, continuing when no one said anything. "During that time, I have learned much about myself and the destiny that has been ordained for me. I understand so much more now than I did when we first met, and that leads me into what I need to tell you.

"Just as I have discovered the truth of my fate, so have I discovered yours. Our fates are entwined, each one of us dependent on the other. It wasn't just circumstance that brought us together that day so long ago in Sangrilak. It was destiny." Adrianna paused again for a moment. She glanced at Dinim, saw him nod his head for her to continue. She then looked at her sister and noticed that Sheri's eyes glimmered with something that Adrianna had never seen there before. It looked like respect, and perhaps some degree of admiration. She couldn't help feeling lifted, as though maybe she *could* rise to be what the prophecies made of her.

Adrianna heard her tone become more solemn. "I have discovered that this is not the first time we have gone to meet Aasarak. For centuries we have fought against him, more than you can imagine. Shandahar has been going through what many scholars have begun to refer to as 'Cycling'. The world has been repeating itself approximately every six hundred years, and so far, Shandahar has endured four such Cycles. We happen to now be in the fifth one.

"In every Cycle that has come before, we, as a group, have fought against Aasarak. As each of the Cycles has been slightly different, it is possible that not all of us were present during all of the battles. However, a core of us has always been there, and that core has always included me. For some reason, something or someone *somewhere* in the world has chosen me to be a pivotal member in the fight against Aasarak."

Adrianna stopped speaking when she heard Dinim's voice fill the chamber. He spoke the words of the prophecies, telling all three to their comrades. In silence, the Wildrunners heard what was spoken. Some of her companions remained stoic, showing no expression. Others whispered among themselves, the implications revealed by the prophesies leaving a disturbing aftertaste.

Adrianna picked up where Dinim left off. "I don't claim to know everything about what those prophesies say, but I am not fool enough to not realize they are speaking about me and most of you. In every other Cycle, we have failed in our fight against the Deathmaster. The same thing could happen this Cycle as well. Just like that fateful day in Sangrilak when you chose to follow me into an uncertain future, everyone now has a decision to make. I can't imagine anyone thinking less of a fellow comrade if they feel unable to stay in the company. However, it is my responsibility to battle Aasarak, and I will leave Krathil-lon at the break of dawn two mornings from tonight.

"There is much that we stand to lose in this fight, most notably our lives. But think of all that we stand to gain if we can defeat Aasarak. The Cycle won't change, and Shandahar will enter an era that it has never experienced before. The world will have a future. Our children and our children's children will live on to tell the tale of the battle we hope to win.

"Dinim says that I am the Child, the Warrior, and the Dreamer spoken about in the prophecies. I know in my heart that he is right. I am young, only having seen twenty and nine years in my life. In many ways, I am still a child. I will fight for a worthy cause; use the Talent and skills I have developed through the years to aid me. In this way, I have finally become a warrior. My dreams are powerful. They tell me things, show me things that have passed or have yet to pass. In this way, I am the Dreamer who has come to lead us into a fight not only for our lives, but for all of the lives around Shandahar."

Adrianna stopped speaking, a reality suddenly enveloping her. She was speaking to these people as though she was their leader. Her voice had been strident and clear, reaching out to everyone in the tsumee. She saw everyone staring at her now, their eyes bright in the firelight. She saw Dartanyen and Triath nodding their heads in silent acceptance and noticed the small grin pulling at the corners of Dinim's mouth. She inhaled deeply and then slowly let the air out. She was about to turn and leave when she noticed Tianna rise from her place beside Triath. Adrianna waited as Tianna approached. When she felt her friend's arms circle her in an embrace, she felt no small amount of surprise. "I am here to stand by you Adrianna."

Strong emotion suddenly swept through her, threatening to take her breath away. Adrianna held her friend close, so happy to have her there. But then she felt someone else standing beside her. It was Sheri, saying that she loved her. Tianna stepped aside and Dartanyen was there, clasping her shoulder and offering her his services, just as he did that day in Volstagg's inn so long ago.

Suddenly she realized the whole group was surrounding her. Each person reached out to touch her arm, pat her back, hold her hand, or offer an embrace. Adrianna felt her heart fill with the strength only the best of friends could give. Once again they were willing to follow her into the darkness, stand by her side wherever she led. Adrianna sensed Xebrinarth in her mind, felt the power of his emotion through their link. With a smile of happiness, Adrianna looked over her comrades, reveling in their camaraderie. Her eyes met Dinim's and he nodded, a knowing expression reflecting in their lavender depths. Somehow, he had known. He had foreseen how this night would play out.

It was then Adrianna sensed someone watching her. She turned and saw Sirion still leaning against the wall. His gaze caught hers and held. Just like always, she felt a wave of security sweep over her. He said nothing, just simply stood there, watching over her. Adrianna felt a feather-light brush against her soul, something she had experienced once before while in the city of Entsy, when she and Sirion finally came together for the first time.

It was the touch of destiny, telling her this was meant to be.

# FLIGHT INTO THE MOUNTAINS

## 10 TISEREN CY594

I t was just before daybreak when the Wildrunners walked out of the apoptos. Scattered about the meadow, their breaths pluming in the chilly air, were eight griffons, Dremathian's contribution towards a speedy journey to the northernmost arch of the Sartingel Mountains. The creatures crouched low in the tall grass, only the crown of feathers on their heads visible in the pre-dawn darkness. Adrianna smiled when she saw them, taking in their majestic beauty. She was heartened by their friendly presence, and grateful for their willingness to help.

From behind, Adrianna sensed someone's approach. She turned to see Father Dremathian and one of his brothers walking towards them. He inclined his head to the group, clasping Sirion's shoulder in a gesture of greeting. Dremathian's countenance was somber as he regarded them, and Adrianna recalled what had happened to many of the druids he called his brothers and sisters, the pain he must feel with their loss.

"Good morn to you all. Your sojourn here has been a pleasure and I feel sadness to see you go." Dremathian cleared his throat and then gestured to the man at his side. "This is Markon. He will lead you to Lord Aasarak's lair." Then he gestured towards the crouching griffons. "By air, it shouldn't take you too long to get there, maybe three or four days."

Sirion nodded and reached out a hand towards his friend. The two men clasped one another's arms. "Thank you for the help. It will save us at least two to three weeks of travel time."

Dremathian nodded. "I only wish that I could help more."

Adrianna stepped up to the men. "No Father, you have helped enough. Your aid has been invaluable, and I can't begin to express my gratitude."

Dremathian took her hand within his. "It's the least I can do, my dear. These griffons will keep you well for as long as you have need of them. Godspeed to you."

Dremathian embraced her briefly before she turned to rejoin the group. Adrianna felt a weight settle over her as everyone slowly approached the meadow. This was it, the day she had been preparing for. All of her comrades walked around her, no one having chosen the easy path during the past day spent in preparation. The griffons stood from their places in the grass, their golden fur shimmering in the rays of the newly rising sun. She stepped up to the nearest animal, stroking the soft fur on his face. The griffon pushed his large head against her hand, hoping to maximize the caress.

The rest of the group walked among the beasts, situating their lightly loaded packs onto the harnesses across each animal's withers. Adrianna knew the faelin would be riding two abreast and turned to call for Sheridana. Just then, Sirion stepped up next to her and took her arm.

"I will ride with you."

Startled, Adrianna looked at him, took in the solemn determination on his face. Then she looked down at the arm Sirion held tightly in his grip. Noticing her gaze, he released her and then busied himself with his packs.

Adrianna said nothing. The past two nights had been woefully uncomfortable. Hells, she had spent the last several years wishing she could be near him again, and now here she was hoping to get away from him. The irony of that was astounding.

*Adrianna walked through the apoptos back to her room. It was dark, the only light from the cloud covered moons and whatever remaining torches were lit along the passageway. It had been an eventful evening and she was tired. She needed to be well rested for the day after tomorrow. She and the rest of the Wildrunners would be leaving Krathil-lon on their journey to Aasarak's lair.*

*Adrianna suddenly heard movement in the corridor before her and she slowed her pace. When Sirion stepped out of the shadows she immediately relaxed. He approached and reached out to take her arm.*

*"Adrianna, your words were quite enlightening tonight." His voice was low as he drew her close.*

*She shook her head and gave a light chuckle. "I didn't even know what I would say until I was saying it."*

*"You have changed during the time you were gone... more than six years you said."*

*Adrianna nodded. "Yes, Master Tallachienan knew he didn't have enough time to teach me all the things he needed, so he took me back into the past. When he finally returned me to this time, I began to suffer from Travel Sickness, and it was then you found me."*

*He pulled her even closer, his eyes roving over her for a moment before returning to her face. "And you couldn't tell me this last night?"*

*Adrianna was quiet for a moment before she answered "I have many things to tell you, Sirion. I just don't know where to start yet."*

*Sirion only nodded. He gently ran his hand up and down her arm,* caressing her through the long sleeve of her tunic. She suddenly felt uncomfortable, not prepared to experience the emotions she would feel if she remained in his company.

"Sirion, I should go. I'm really tired, and we have a long day ahead tomorrow." Adrianna made to pull away, but Sirion tightened his grip.

"I think we should stay together. I will come with you to your room if you don't want to come to mine."

Adrianna felt her eyes widen. "What?"

Sirion nodded. "We will stay in your room then."

Adrianna was taken aback. By the gods, what was he thinking? She shook her head. "Wh... no. I don't need you to stay with me!" she said incredulously.

Sirion pulled his lips into a thin line, and his eyes darkened with emotion. "Perhaps I know more about your prophecy than you do."

Adrianna frowned. "What are you talking about?" In that moment, she thought he was going crazy and that something had pushed him over the edge. His grip on her arm had become tight, and it hurt.

"Adrianna, I am the Protector that is mentioned in your prophecies. It is my destiny, and my duty, to stand by you at all times."

Adrianna just stared at him for a moment, the words of the prophecy going through her mind. And from behind the aegis of the Protector she will survive the temptation of power... she will wield great power that can be harnessed only by the one man who has sworn his soul to her...

Adrianna swallowed heavily. By the gods, he was right. Why hadn't she realized it before? Yet, did it mean he needed to be a constant shadow every moment of every day and night? If so, how would she possibly escape these feelings she felt for him? How would she exist with him so near yet be unable to...

Adrianna shook her head. "Even if you are the Protector, you don't need to constantly be in my company," she said indignantly. "I am a big girl now. I think that I can sleep by myself."

Sirion also shook his head. "Not right now. There are things out there that would like to see your death, and I will not have your blood on my hands."

"But we are in Krathil-lon! What could possibly happen to me here?" she said with an exasperated tone.

"This is not open for discussion! I am staying with you tonight, whether you like it or not," he growled.

Adrianna stared at him, took in the determined edge to his jaw and the intensity of his gaze. He would give no quarter, and much too tired to argue, she merely turned and continued down the corridor to her room. She opened the door and stepped inside, Sirion following closely behind.

*For the remainder of the night, he stayed there. Once in bed, she slept under the covers and he on top. Sirion made no move to touch her. In turn, Adrianna made no effort to bridge the yawning distance that seemed to separate them more than ever before.*

With a slump to her shoulders, Adrianna watched the handsome ranger affix his packs to the griffon she had chosen to ride. She would suffer through his presence all day, force herself to remain aloof even though she really wanted throw herself into his arms, tell him how much she loved him, and have him take her to his bed. However, she couldn't do that. Her pride dictated that she not give in to her base emotions. Sirion had taken another lover, and she had slept with her master. So what if Sirion was the Protector mentioned in the prophecies? That didn't mean they were destined to marry and have children together.

But that wouldn't stop her from wishing that it did.

When everyone was ready, the Wildrunners mounted their feathery steeds. The griffons shrieked into the dawn, raising their voices to the opening of a new day. Dramati barked from his place beside Dremathian. He would be staying behind, for it would be difficult to travel with the corubis by air. It was obvious the animal didn't like the situation, but there was little choice.

Adrianna sat astride and patted the griffon's furry shoulder. When Sirion mounted behind her, she stiffened her body, unwilling to let herself lean into the warmth she knew he could offer. She sensed his momentary hesitation, but then the griffon was moving, bounding swiftly through the tall grasses. Before she realized it, the hindquarters were bunching for the leap. She felt the compression, felt Sirion press close and wrap a protective arm around her waist. Then they were airborne, mighty wings unfurling to beat at the air currents. She felt a warmth settle into her lower belly despite her adjustment to the ascent, evidence of her body's reaction to Sirion's nearness.

Once they were in the air and stabilized, Adrianna looked down from her perch. The apoptos and surrounding silver forest was spread below them. Rapidly they left its vicinity, flying north into the large mountain range. It was cold, and she wrapped her winter cloak tightly around her. She enjoyed the ride from the back of the griffon, but she missed Xebrinarth abominably. She reached out to him, hoping he wasn't upset that she flew on the back of another. She felt him chuckle through their link. He told her that she was a silly creature, but that this was one of the reasons why he loved her so much. He asked her where she was going, for she had quickly begun to learn to close her mind to him. She knew that Xebrinarth could easily breach the weak barriers that she had been able to erect, but he chose not to do so, instead allowing her the choice to share things with him in her own time. He didn't wish to press her, knowing that their relationship was built on mutual respect.

At first, Adrianna didn't know what to tell Xebrinarth. He knew that she had a duty to perform, but not the exact nature of that duty. He knew that it required all of her energy and attention, but not that it placed her life in jeopardy. She knew that she needed to tell him about it soon, be entirely honest with him. Tonight, she would do just that, but for now, she would allow herself to enjoy the view.

For most of the morning they flew. At midday they stopped to eat and to give the griffons a rest from their long flight. The air had become more chill, testament to their northerly route. Around them the mountains rose all around, their steep rocky cliffs reminding her of another mountain range much farther to the south and another battle they had fought together.

Early that evening, from her place on a nice flat rock, Adrianna watched her companions in silence. In countless ways, everyone was the same, but in so many more they had changed. Amethyst and Sorn displayed a healthy mentor and apprentice relationship. It seemed to be doing the girl much good, for she appeared to be more relaxed and even enjoyed some banter with other members of the group. Adrianna remembered the withdrawn person that she used to be, and was glad that Amethyst had found her niche.

Then there were Tianna and Triath. The two seemed to have found the perfect match in one another, and it was obvious to everyone that they were in love. Adrianna was glad that her friend had found what she was looking for, even if that person happened to *not* be Sirion Timberlyn. Tianna was once more the carefree person she had first met, and Adrianna was pleased to see her so happy.

Finally, there was Sheridana. It was apparent that she and Dartanyen had taken a dual leadership role. This was not surprising, since Adrianna had always seen the leader in Sheri before. Yet, there was something different about her sister, a melancholy that surrounded her, as well as a slight sense of anxiety. All too often, Adrianna noticed the hooded glances that Sheridana shared with Armond, and she realized a change in him as well. There was an attraction between them; that much Adrianna understood. However, they were not public about it, and many times didn't even seem to like one another because they argued so much.

Adrianna pulled away from her musings as Sheridana approached and sat beside her. Sheri's warm side was welcome, and Adrianna found herself nestling into it. Sheridana chuckled for a moment but then became somber. "Adria, what's going on between you and Sirion? I know it's been a long time for you, but I thought...?"

Adrianna looked up into her sister's face. Sheri's eyes were serious as they regarded her, and Adrianna wondered if her sister could possibly be unaware of Sirion's recent liaison. For just a moment, she considered not saying anything to Sheri about it, but then realized that she had to address the issue eventually. "Sheri, I know that Sirion has taken another woman to his bed."

Sheridana's eyes widened incredulously and she shook her head. "Who told you that?"

Adrianna shrugged. "No one. Last night I told you that I sometimes have dreams, visions that reveal things that have happened in the past or things that have yet to happen in the future. Well, while I was in my master's citadel, I had a dream that Sirion had taken another to his bed. She was very beautiful, with long black hair. Don't tell me that you haven't seen her."

Sheridana's expression was one of astonishment as she shook her head. "Adria, that wasn't just any woman, and Sirion did not go willingly to her. It wasn't until, it was too late that we realized her true identity. She was the goddess Tholana, using her powers of *Persuasion* to get Sirion to do her bidding. Even now we don't know why she chose him." Sheri became speculative for a moment and then continued. "Maybe she hoped to interfere with the prophecy, thinking that perhaps it might not come about with Sirion gone."

Adrianna stared, dumbstruck, at her sister. By the gods, now she knew why the woman had seemed so familiar to her. She was the same one from her dream of Tallachienan and his sister, the one whom he had promised to marry in return for healing Briyana. It was obvious Tallachienan hadn't held up his end of the bargain. If he had, Adrianna would surely have known it and at least seen Tholana's presence within his citadel a few times.

Adrianna was now overcome with guilt, and it had nothing to do with Master Tallachienan. She had erroneously assumed Sirion took another lover. She'd been stupid to not ask him about it, keeping her distance from him all this time when, in truth, he'd endured the same *Persuasive* power she had. The guilt was swiftly replaced with relief. He hadn't forsaken her after all, and mayhap still loved her the way she loved him. Adrianna shook her head. "Maybe I should have a talk with Sirion about it."

"I should say so," responded Sheridana.

Adrianna looked back up at her sister, her eyes narrowing at the mild rebuke she heard in Sheridana's tone. "Well, what about you and Armond?"

Adrianna caught the surprise reflected in Sheri's eyes before the other woman turned away. "I don't know what you mean."

Adrianna pushed at Sheri's side with her cloaked elbow. "Don't be coy with me. I can see that there is something there between the two of you."

Sheridana was silent for several moments before she turned back to Adrianna. "Oh, Adria. With Armond it has become so complicated..."

"Do you love him?"

Sheri shook her head. "I don't know. I'm so confused right now, and we fight all the time. It's a wonder that we can even get close enough to..."

With that, Sheridana turned away again and was silent. However, Adrianna was quick to understand to what Sheridana was alluding. She hissed under her breath and poked at Sheri's side again. "You've *shared his bed?*"

Sheri's voice was broken. "Adrianna, neither of us intended for it to happen, but it did. Now we seek one another out in the night, and when it's done, we go back to our separate sleeping places. We are terrible to one another during the day. Yet, in the night, under the cover of the darkness, he makes me feel so good, and I feel wanted... needed again."

Adrianna sighed heavily. She had to put herself in her sister's place, try to understand what it was like for Sheridana... to be the mother of a child whose father was dead and gone. Just like any other woman, Sheri needed to feel wanted and accepted, and if that person happened to be the one man who drove her to the edge of reason, then so be it.

Sheri continued. "And there is something else, something that I've been denying for the past fortnight. I don't know what to do, what to think..."

Adrianna put her arm around Sheri's shoulders, hearing a note of fear in her sister's voice. "What is it? What's wrong?"

Sheridana turned back to Adrianna, tears forming at the corners of her eyes. "I'm pregnant."

Adrianna suddenly felt like a warhammer was slamming into her chest. It took her a moment to remember to breathe, and then she let the air out in a big gush. All she could do was stare at Sheri from wide eyes, now understanding the fearful look on her sister's face.

After a few moments, both sisters looked away from one another, each of them not knowing what to say. They just huddled there for a while, and when the rest of the group prepared to continue their journey, Adrianna and Sheri rose from their spot, clasped one another's hands for a moment, and then went to their respective mounts.

Adrianna noticed Sirion watching her as she climbed into the saddle of their griffon, but she said nothing to him. Her thoughts tumbled haphazardly around in her mind, the ones concerning him having become lost among all the others. What she really needed was a good sleep, but she knew that she wouldn't be getting that anytime in the near future.

They were two days out of Krathil-lon. The group had stopped for the night, taken the evening meal, and were preparing themselves for sleep. Sheridana huddled beneath her furs near the fire. It was her night to take the first watch, but she was so tired, all she wanted to do was curl up beneath her furs and go to sleep. She knew it was because of the pregnancy, knew also that her condition was beginning to give her sickness over which she had no control. It reminded her of another time, another pregnancy when she hadn't realized what was happening, only knowing that something strange was going on inside her body.

Sheridana pressed a palm against her flat belly. She was in good physical fitness, and she wouldn't begin to show her condition for quite some time. She had been almost four months pregnant with Fitanni before she stopped denying the fact that she was with child. And she didn't begin to grow out of her trousers for another two moon cycles after that. This time, she knew right away that she was expecting, so in tune with her body and the sensations felt during pregnancy. Yet, her certainty was scary, for this wasn't a good time for this to happen. *The group needed her in their upcoming encounter, but if she went with them to meet the enemy, she knew that she placed the child at grave risk.*

Sheridana suddenly felt herself being watched. She looked away from the fire to see Armond staring at her from his bedroll across the flames. She knew he had noticed a change in her, and he even asked her about it. Yet, she would tell him nothing. She didn't want to complicate matters with him any more than what they were already. However, she would continue to go to him. Armond had become an addiction she couldn't resist. The same seemed to hold true for him as well. No wonder she'd become pregnant; she had been with him almost every other night since that first time. It often took faelin women a bit longer to conceive a child, but Sheri wasn't entirely faelin... there was a part of her that was also human. Sheri looked away from Armond as Dartanyen approached. His gaze reflected concern as he knelt down beside her. "I will take your shift again tonight. You look like you need the sleep."

Sheridana felt the protest forming in her mouth, and Dartanyen must have seen it as well, for he held up his hand. "No, I will hear no objections. Besides, I know you would do me the same courtesy."

Sheri only nodded then, saying nothing. *Damn.* When had Dartanyen become such a good friend? Without him, she would have had to take the last three nights worth of watches. He seemed to know that she couldn't handle the strain they would cause, and the group needed someone hale enough to remain alert throughout the shift. She was nothing less than grateful.

Dartanyen stood and walked to the other side of the fire, whereupon he started to talk to Armond. Sheri glanced around the encampment, noticing Adrianna sitting on her own bedroll. She seemed to be deep in thought, for her eyes had that faraway look. Sheri pursed her lips and shook her head in silence. She could tell that Adrianna still hadn't spoken with Sirion. The two had become so distant, and Sheri wondered if that was part of the reason why Adrianna felt she couldn't talk to him. But as an outsider looking in, Sheri could see the pained expression that passed over Sirion's face whenever he looked at Adrianna. She knew that her sister felt the same way, but Adrianna was somehow able to keep it in check.

All of a sudden, Adrianna was jumping up from her bedroll and rushing over to Dinim, who was busy reading one of his weird texts. Sheri frowned. She was glad that the two had come to terms with the past, but it definitely didn't help Adrianna's floundering relationship with Sirion. Sheri glanced quickly in the other man's direction and saw that, he too, had noticed Adrianna's activity. Even from this distance, Sheri could see the tightening of his jaw. Sirion still loved her sister, that much was for certain. But Sheri knew that Adrianna needed to talk with Sirion soon, or all could become lost between them.

Adrianna rushed over to Dinim's bedroll, excitement and hope foremost in her mind. If they could pull this off, they just might have a chance against Aasarak's army. For the past two days she had been thinking about it... how they would be able to find a way to stop the bloodshed that had already begun.

Last evening, she had contacted Xebrinarth. She told him the truth about herself, how she and the rest of the Wildrunners went to face a man who had control over the undead. She told him that she may not return from her battle, and that she was sorry that she had not told him before.

Xebrinarth had been beside himself. He wanted to come to her immediately, and when he realized that he could not, he roared in anger and defiance. Through their link, she tried to calm him, to make her Bondmate see reason. But he would have none of that. She felt the power of his emotion, the destruction that was in his mind. Adrianna could only sit by while Xebrinarth went on the hunt, destroying all within his path. She feared for him but knew that she could do nothing. Her Bondmate had to work through this himself.

All the next day, Adrianna had thought about Xebrinarth. She tried to contact him, but the dragon shut her out, not allowing her access to his mind. A terrible loneliness engulfed her, and it was made worse by the fact that she had yet to speak with Sirion. But she couldn't think about that now. She had to keep trying to get Xebrinarth to let her in. And then there was the battle that lay before her, and the army that marched, unchecked throughout the western kingdoms.

However, tonight she had a revelation. The last thing that Tallachienan taught her before she left his citadel was the fundamentals of how to open an access portal to another world. It would allow more than simple elements to pass through. It would be a difficult endeavor, one that she would never be able to accomplish on her own. However, as Dinim had once told her... she was a Prime, and he was a Prime. Maybe, between the two of them, they would have just enough power.

"Dinim... Dinim, I have to ask you something."

Dinim looked up from the book he was reading. "What is it?"

Adrianna knelt beside him on the bedroll. She quickly realized that she would have to start from the beginning so that he would better understand what she had to say. "You visited Haldorr during one of your Travels with the Master, did you not?"

Dinim gave her his undivided attention. "Yes. It was a wonderful place." Adrianna nodded. "The inhabitants are equally as wonderful."

Dinim also nodded, obviously wondering where she was going with this. "I agree."

Adrianna decided that she would just have out with it. "I took a Bondmate while I was there." She touched the band on her forearm. "Such is the reason for my wearing this band. It aids in my communication with him."

Dinim dropped the book and stared at her with wide eyes. "You mean to say that a drake chose you as his Bondmate?"

Adrianna nodded. "Yes. We went through the ceremony and everything."

"And Master Tallachienan allowed this?"

She frowned. "I don't see how he had any choice."

"By the gods, Adria. What were you thinking?"

Adrianna shook her head, dismissing Dinim's question. "Listen, I have an idea. How do you think Aasarak's army would respond to fire?"

Dinim shrugged. "I don't know. Perhaps it could have an impact."

Adrianna cleared her throat, ready to tell him about her solution to their problem. "I want to open a portal to Haldorr, bring the dragons through, and set them against the army."

Dinim only stared at her.

"I can't do it by myself, but maybe the two of us will just be able to pull it off."

Dinim continued to stare.

"I know that it would take most, if not all, of our power, but perhaps it will be worth it."

"It will *definitely* take all of our power, and I hope that you are thinking about doing this *after* our fight with Aasarak," he said with a scowl.

Adrianna shook her head. "No. I want to do it as soon as possible. The longer we wait, the more people are going to die. And maybe it will even offer a distraction to Aasarak, perhaps give him something more to think about than his battle with us."

"So, you will contact your Bondmate, tell him to prepare a force that will come through our portal?"

Adrianna nodded. "Then you think we can do it?"

"I don't know. Maybe."

"That other Dimensionalist did it, the one who opened the portals to allow Tharizdune to enter Shandahar. Remember, you told me all about it?"

"Yes, but he had five prisms to help concentrate his power. They hung from each of the brackets that had been built to encircle the portals that would form. We don't have that."

"But we have each other. It isn't just going to be one of us opening this portal."

"Let me think about it. I will let you know what I think tomorrow morning."

"If you think it can be done, will you do it?"

Dinim began to grin. She knew how he would respond, but it seemed that she needed to hear him say it anyway. "Only for you."

Adrianna smiled back, and then threw her arms around his neck. "Thank you, Dinim. I knew I could count on you." She then turned and made her way back to her own bedroll. Now, all she had to do was get Xebrinarth to talk to her again...

The next morning dawned crisp and cool. As the rest of the group prepared for the day, Dinim came to join Adrianna near the fire. "I think that we may be able to do it. Contact your dragon friend. We will need to give him time to rally our allies."

Adrianna's heart lurched in her chest. This was what she was hoping for. She smiled widely at Dinim, took his face in her hands, and kissed him heartily on the mouth. "Thank you. Whatever you need me to do to prepare to open the portal, I am at your disposal."

Dinim nodded. "It will indeed take some time. We will have to tell the group about our plan."

Adrianna nodded. "I will do it right after I speak with Xebrinarth."

Dinim nodded and then moved away from her back to his bedroll. She focused on the band around her arm, hoping that her Bondmate would answer her this time. His anger had cooled somewhat, but she could still feel his discontent.

<Xebrinarth, please hear me. It is important. I must speak with you.> Silence rang through the link she shared with the dragon.

Once again, Adrianna felt the feelings of loneliness that had become familiar to her the last couple of days. Adrianna felt herself choking up. Perhaps her Bondmate would never speak to her again. Maybe Xebrin wanted nothing more to do with her and she wore this band for nothing.

Adrianna placed her hand above the golden band, focusing her energy into its removal. Suddenly, a voice was in her mind, filling the void that had begun to creep through her soul. <Zahara, no!>

Adrianna removed her hand from the band, focusing instead on the voice of her Bondmate. She said nothing for a moment, simply basking in the presence that now filled her mind. Xebrinarth had returned to her.

<I never truly left you.> His voice was matter-of-fact.

<It felt like it.>

<I am sorry. I was angry and disappointed that you had not told me about your destiny earlier.>

<I know. I, too, am sorry. I intended no disrespect, nor to undermine our Bond.>

<I know that. I should never have treated you so unfairly after you told me about yourself. It might make you feel that you cannot tell me things in the future. I hope this is not the case.>

<I have nothing more to hide.>

Adrianna heard the sound of his contented sigh. But it was tinged with a note of grief. She knew that it had much to do with her, and she hoped that her news would help. <Xebrin, the reason why I needed you to speak with me was because I have something to tell you. I have a friend here, another Dimensionalist. The two of us are hoping to open a portal to Haldorr.>

<Zahara, that is wonderful!> Adrianna could feel his joy through their link.

<Yes, but it is for a reason even greater than that of simply bringing us together.> Adrianna opened her mind to her Bondmate, inviting him in. She didn't need to say anything, he would be able to see what her plan intended.

Xebrin was silent for a moment after he had seen what was in her mind.

Then, <I will rally the dragons as soon as possible.>

<You have two days. In the meantime, Dinim and I will prepare to open the portal.>

Adrianna felt the mental nod. Then Xebrinarth was gone, sending her his love before refocusing his attention elsewhere. She did the same, her eyes once more seeing what lay before them. She found herself staring at the band on her arm, and she reached out her hand to caress the warm metal.

"Where have you been?"

Adrianna jerked, startled to hear the voice so close. She turned her head to find Sirion sitting next to her, his gaze intense.

Adrianna only stared at him for a moment. He asked her where she had been. Obviously, she was sitting on her bedroll, but Sirion was not stupid. Her mind had been elsewhere.

"We need to stay here for the next two days." Adrianna watched Sirion's expression register surprise.

"I thought that it was our intention to reach Aasarak as soon as possible."

"But our reinforcements won't reach us for another two days."

Sirion regarded her speculatively. Adrianna could see him briefly contemplate the fact that she might be a few stones short of a Spinot game. "What reinforcements?"

Adrianna took in a deep breath. It had been easy for Dinim to accept that she had a dragon Bondmate. He knew of the existence of dragons because he had mentored under Tallachienan. However, Sirion had not. To him, dragons were merely creatures of legend. "During my training with Master Tallachienan, I made some powerful friends. Dinim and I plan to open a portal to bring them here. They will go to meet Aasarak's army while we go to fight the undead master himself. We hope that they will offer a distraction."

Sirion was quiet for a moment before he responded. "I think that is an excellent idea. We should tell the others."

Adrianna nodded.

"But that doesn't tell me where you were."

Adrianna caressed the band on her arm. "This artifact allows me to communicate with my comrades. I was speaking to them when you approached me." The half-lie came easily to Adrianna's lips. She didn't really know why she did it, except for the fact that she didn't feel like telling Sirion about her Bondmate until the dragon actually flew through her portal.

Sirion sat and watched as Adrianna went to tell the others of the new plan. More than ever, he felt the yawning rift between them. He so much wanted to reestablish what had once been there, and sometimes he imagined that she did too. But other times, like now, he felt that all she wanted was to keep him away. Adrianna had changed so much, he didn't even know if he knew her anymore. He couldn't really blame her. Six years had passed while she studied with Tallachienan. Sirion could only imagine himself in her position. He could easily say he would have retained his love for her in spite of time's passing, but realistically, he knew he wouldn't know what he would have done unless thrust in the same situation.

For quite some time Sirion looked on as Adrianna interacted with the rest of the group. It was so easy to see that Dartanyen, Armond, Tianna, Dinim, and Amethyst loved her. He could tell that Sorn felt much the same since he'd shared her company during their journey to Andahye. Triath, Naemmious and Anya would follow suit if given the chance. Adrianna was so charismatic, and that quality had grown during her time spent away. People were drawn to her like moths to a flame, and Sirion wasn't fool enough not to realize he was one of those moths too. He shook his head. He hadn't spent enough time with her before she left for training. Their relationship had been too young, and they didn't have enough time to really get to know one another. Now he was paying the price. In spite of the power he imagined lay at her behest, Sirion regretted the day he'd agreed to let her go.

# RALLY OF DRAGONS

Armond looked up from his swords just in time to see Sheridana bending over some nearby bushes. She retched several times, and after a few moments, finally straightened. His brows creased in concern. He had noticed a change in her as of late, saw that her complexion was unusually pale and the lines around her mouth pinched. She had been more withdrawn as well, a big difference from the ordinarily brassy woman he had come to know. Armond had asked her about it, but she responded rather elusively, telling him that she just wasn't feeling well and that she was sure she would be better in a few days. He knew that she was keeping something from him, but he just didn't know how to get her to tell him about it.

That morning, Adrianna had announced to the group that they would be staying in this location for the next two days. She told them that she had arranged for reinforcements that would go to meet Aasarak's army to the south while they continued north to the sorcerer's lair. They hoped that the attack on the army would cause Aasarak's attention to be diverted and that he wouldn't be as focused on his fight with the Wildrunners. Additionally, any power he might expend replenishing his forces could not be brought to bear on them.

Armond was less than optimistic about the plan. Adrianna's reinforcements would have to be quite extraordinary to fight an army of that magnitude. For most of the day, she spent her time with Dinim, the two mages enlisting the help of some of the others to help make a clearing. Afterwards, they sat with their books, and Armond imagined they studied the incantations that would perform the magic they desired.

While the spellcasters studied, the rest of the group sparred in mock battles, two against two and sometimes three against three. Armond thought the exercises were good practice, and he had joined in them for a while. He'd prepared himself for the challenge he imagined Sheri would force upon him, for she surely remembered that he owed her a rematch for the spar he'd forfeited several weeks ago before their capture by the orocs. However, as the afternoon came to a close and evening approached, he realized Sheri had no intention of joining in the sparring matches. Tianna and Triath left to prepare the evening meal, and Adrianna and Dinim were finally taking a break, settling themselves at the periphery of the arena. A wan Sheridana seated herself at Adrianna's other side, seeking a rest after having spent only a fraction the day at any type of practice, followed by the upheaval he'd just witnessed. It was so different from the energetic woman whom he'd taken to his bed almost every night since the first.

Armond frowned. Thinking about it now, he realized another disparity. Sheri had kept herself away from him the past few days.

He shook his head and shifted his attention to the arena. Sorn and Dartanyen were just finishing a match, and he heard Dinim entreating Adrianna to a spar. Armond immediately felt his interest piqued. He had never seen the two of them matched before, and the shortsword Adrianna now carried at her hip hadn't gone unnoticed.

Shaking her head, Adrianna finally acquiesced. The pair removed their cloaks and stepped into the arena. Once at combat readiness, they drew their blades, hailed one another, and then began the match. Armond couldn't help being impressed by what he saw. Adrianna was definitely no expert, but she wielded the weapon with grace and ease, as though she'd been doing it for many years. Armond knew that she had spent six years apart from them, but even then, with the skill she possessed, she would have had to practice at least every other day.

Armond glanced around at the rest of the group. They seemed to be just as surprised about Adrianna's skill. Not the least was Sirion. He watched the spar with avid interest, hardly taking his eyes off of Adrianna. Armond felt his heart go out to the man, knew his relationship with Adrianna wasn't what it was before they parted ways all those moon cycles ago. Adrianna had changed, and Armond knew that it was more than just weapon proficiency. It was her entire demeanor. Her self-confidence had grown, and with that, she took up the yoke of her responsibility with poise and style.

Armond watched as Dinim pressed into his opponent, offsetting her balance. Adrianna fell back, and Dinim stood over her with his sword at her throat. From her position on the ground, Adrianna grinned sheepishly up at him. Dinim extended his hand and hoisted her up. Adrianna sheathed her sword and then wiped the dust from her trousers.

Adrianna was taken a bit aback when everyone applauded and bid her a job well done, but then she remembered she hadn't possessed such skill with the sword before leaving them. With a flourish she bowed and she heard chuckles all around before the group began to disperse. She had been reluctant to face Dinim across the circle, her memories of the third Cycle having suddenly coming to the fore of her mind. But when he was so adamant, she couldn't refuse. Her fears had been unfounded, for the spar had been nothing like she remembered from the past. The relief made her take a deep breath and it was then her gaze caught Sirion watching her.

As always, her heart increased its tempo and her belly spasmed. He was so handsome standing there, in spite of his brooding countenance. His amber eyes were so pale they were mesmerizing. With no small amount of effort, Adrianna tore her eyes away from Sirion and made her way back to her books. Her heart felt that familiar ache, but she thrust it aside. She and Dinim had to get the incantations just right, and they had only the minimal materials required to open a portal such as this one. Not only that, but it had finally become apparent to them that they would only be able to open a man-sized portal; to open one large enough to fit a dragon would be impossible for them at their strength and skill level.

Well into the night, the mages practiced the incantations they would use to open their portal. When Adrianna finally settled down to sleep, she had only a few hours' rest before she needed to rise again for the next day. In the morning, she contacted Xebrinarth and told him that he and his allies would need to be in faelin form when they walked into the portal. She told him the exact time the portal would open, and where. She needed a place that she remembered from Haldorr, and that place happened to be Xebrin's lair. She could sense his fatigue, and she was sure he could feel the same from her. They didn't speak for long, merely assured themselves that the other was well enough, and then returned to their business.

All that day, Dinim and Adrianna continued to prepare to the exclusion of all else. The rest of the group left the mages to their own devices, and Tianna was kind enough to bring them their meals when it became apparent they wouldn't come to get the food themselves. Only when the sun finally sank below the horizon did they go to their bedrolls. They needed as much sleep as they could get before the morrow... gather as much strength as possible. Adrianna knew they would be severely weakened after the ordeal. They would need to rest after the portal had been closed, and she had explained all of that to Tianna and Sheridana earlier in the day.

Adrianna awoke early the next morning after a fitful sleep. She went to the banked fire to get a mug of tea from Tianna and waited for Dinim to join her. Only a few moments later, he was sitting beside her, sipping from his own mug. In the pre-dawn darkness, they sat there in companionable silence, finished the tea, and then went to the clearing that had been prepared. Dinim turned to her. "Adrianna, I've been thinking. This portal is going to cost the both of us a great deal of energy."

Adrianna shook her head. "I thought we agreed that it would be worth it."

"I know. But I'm thinking it would be best if most of the energy contribution came from me."

Adrianna was quick to protest. "No. It will be too dangerous. We agreed that this would be an equal venture."

"But that isn't truly feasible, now is it Adria? You must have enough energy for the fight against Aasarak. We are only about two days' ride to his lair."

"Maybe we can wait another couple of days so that we can..." He shook his head. "No, we have waited long enough."

"Then maybe I should make the greater energy contribution. You are more seasoned, have seen more battles than I."

"No." Dinim's voice was uncompromising. Adrianna frowned. "Why not?"

Dinim sighed heavily. "Because the prophecy says that it is only by the magic of the Warrior and the sworn Protector that Aasarak can be stopped."

"As I remember it, the prophecy says that it is the *army* that will be stopped by the magic of the Warrior and the sworn Protector," Adrianna responded grimly.

Dinim contemplated it for a moment. "Perhaps, but I still can't take the risk."

Adrianna sighed. She understood Dinim's reasoning. They could ill afford to make any mistakes. Too many lives were at stake. Then she nodded. "Fine, but we will be hard pressed without you in our ranks."

"I know. But we decided that this was worth it."

Adrianna gave him a small smile. "Yes, we did, didn't we?"

"I will keep the portal open for as long as I can, but once my strength runs out, promise me that you will not use your own energy to keep it open."

Adrianna nodded in affirmative.

"Most likely, I will fall unconscious after it is done. It has happened to many mages before me. Don't be too worried. I will recover."

She regarded him grimly. "Some never recover."

Dinim inclined his head. "But that is rare."

She pursed her lips. "Not rare for an endeavor such as this one."

"You aren't thinking about changing your mind, are you?" Dinim asked with a grin.

Adrianna shook her head solemnly, refusing to be drawn into his light banter. "No. But it doesn't mean I haven't thought about the fact I could lose you."

Dinim wiped the grin off of his face and then slowly closed the short distance between them. He put a hand on one shoulder while he brushed his fingertips across her opposite cheek. He gently took the errant strand of hair that fell there and pushed it away from her face. "You will never lose me." Then he lowered his head until his lips pressed to hers.

Dinim deepened the kiss only momentarily before releasing her. They stood there for a moment, looking into one another's eyes. The spell was dangerous because they were young, and their skill had yet to reach the appropriate level for spells such as this one to be attempted. Just as Dinim had placed his life at risk when he reopened the portals to return Tharizdune back to the Hells, the same applied here. Only this time, the risk would be greater because they had very few spell enhancement materials at their disposal.

Finally, they stepped apart. Dinim gave her a small smile. "We must begin now if we are to open the portal at the time you told your Bondmate to be ready."

Adrianna nodded. It was then she noticed that the rest of the group was standing at the periphery of the clearing. They looked tired and bedraggled, but they had come to see the arrival of their reinforcements. Adrianna knew what they expected, but there was no way she could tell them the truth of what would emerge from this portal.

Adrianna took her place on the other side of the clearing while Dinim remained on his side. They knelt, looked at one another for a moment, inhaled in synchrony, and then began the words to their incantation. Each one put a hand into a bag at their hip and drew forth a handful of crystal sand. Slowly they poured it onto the ground before them. Immediately the sand took on a greenish glow and the grains began to melt together into a liquid flowing mass. Each of them held their fore and middle fingers into their respective pools of molten crystal and began to draw the runes into the air before them.

Adrianna and Dinim lifted their voices. At first there was a small breeze, but it quickly became a wind that whipped at their hair and clothing. The completed runes circled them, glowing radiantly golden in the semi-darkness. The mages looked up into the sky and then raised their arms above them. A wail began to accompany the gale that swept around them, and the first incantation blended into the next one. The golden runes began to glow crimson, dancing in the winds of the maelstrom. Then, in the center of the clearing, a shimmering form began to take shape.

Sirion stared, wide eyed, at the scene before him. It reminded him of another time and another battle, one from which three of his comrades had never returned. He couldn't believe the power he felt concentrating there, and he realized exactly what Adrianna had learned while she was away from him. She had become a powerful sorceress in her own right, someone to be reckoned with. For this endeavor, she had sought the help of a fellow spellcaster, but Sirion had the distinct feeling that if the need arose, she would be able to cast spells that could kill a man with just the flick of a wrist. The timid girl he had once known had fallen away somewhere.

Sirion had awakened just before the rest of the group, with the exception of Dinim and Adrianna. He saw them walking over to the clearing and knew that they would soon be opening the portal. He and the rest of the Wildrunners quickly got themselves together and then began to gather at the periphery. Sirion had approached the scene just in time to catch the last of the exchange between Adrianna and Dinim. He watched as Dinim kissed her, and Sirion felt his heart sink, knowing that his fears had been real and that he had seen the last days of his relationship with her, the promises they had made to one another having died a crib death. However, another concern soon became foremost in his mind. He had heard Adrianna tell Dinim her fear that he would be lost, and Sirion had rather hoped that no one would be taken in this battle against Aasarak. He knew that it was a silly and unrealistic expectation, but it was his goal nevertheless.

Sirion swallowed his tears and his hurt, pushing past them to focus on this battle ahead. As the portal began to shimmer into existence, he felt awe. Within his own profession, he was known as a paragon, one of the best. Now he saw that Adrianna was the same within her own. She was still so young, and yet, she was able to rally the most powerful of magic to do her bidding. He didn't understand the logistics of what she did, but he knew that it took all of her skills and abilities to do it.

The shimmering glow of the portal became brighter. Adrianna began to feel the energy it took from her, sensed Dinim struggling to take on the brunt of that burden. With her training, she was now so much more attuned to other spellcasters, and she was astounded by the power Dinim had at his behest. They completed the incantation, and when they refocused their eyes onto the clearing, a fully formed opalescent portal stood between them. The blue, green, and lavender colors swirled about within; almost mesmerizing in quality. Yet, it wasn't long before the swirling pattern was broken as the first of Adrianna's reinforcements stepped through. A steady stream of naked men and women walked through the portal. They were led by Xebrinarth and came in twos and threes. Xebrinarth was aware of the energy it took for his Bondmate to keep the portal open, so he urged the others to make haste, telling them that the portal was near to closing.

And he was right. Dinim had reached the end of his endurance. Adrianna knew when he was unconscious without having to look at him. The full burden of keeping the portal open was suddenly thrust upon her.

140

She remembered the promise she had made, but thought again about it. She felt that she could hold the portal open for a few moments longer, but she dared not. Dinim had made a sacrifice, and she didn't want that to be in vain. Adrianna disengaged herself from the portal, and the opening immediately began to fade out. The last of the dragons were able to rush through, followed by Mordrex, as the portal closed.

Then there was silence. Only a shimmering remnant remained where once a portal had stood. Adrianna wavered on her feet and then felt someone catching her and laying her gently on the ground. She opened her eyes to see Sirion leaning over her. Behind him was Xebrin. "Dinim... how is he?"

"He lives, but he is unconscious," said Sirion. "Tianna is seeing to him."

"He warned me about that." Adrianna struggled to sit upright. Sirion helped her with an arm at her back. She then viewed the group that stood before her. They numbered about forty strong, a sufficient number she hoped would make a dent in Aasarak's army. She reached out a hand to her Bondmate and Xebrin came and knelt beside her. "I have missed you, Xebrin."

"And I have missed you as well, Zahara." Xebrin glanced at the dragons he had brought through the portal. They watched Adrianna intently, she being the one who had made the summons. In her name he had rallied them, opening his mind to all he encountered so that they could see what his Bondmate faced. All of them were young, many just out of adolescence. The older dragons, despite the temptation to join them, had stayed behind on Haldorr.

Adrianna smiled wanly. All Sirion could do was frown. She could imagine what he was thinking: *Who in the Hells are these people and where are their clothes? It isn't every day a man sees forty people walk through a magical portal with no clothes on. Perhaps the portal didn't allow them the luxury of keeping their clothes with them? And what about their weapons? How would they fight without weapons? The Wildrunners haven't the capacity to equip forty men and women.*

Xebrinarth turned back to Adrianna. <They are anxious to return to their natural forms. I must tell you that not all of them are of Helzethryn and Rezwithrys descent. There are some that are Degethozak. I assumed that, in this case, alignment was not an issue, just as long as we fought for the same cause.>

Adrianna gave him a mental nod. <You are right, Xebrinarth. Alignment is not an issue here. However, I can only hope that the Degethozak will not turn against us when the mission is completed.>

<I can make you no promises, but I don't think that it will be a

problem. They will go their own way after the battle is through, just as many of the Helzethryn and Rezwithrys,> said Xebrin.

<Ask them to wait for a few moments before resuming their natural forms. My comrades don't expect it, and might be alarmed by what they see. But the Wildrunners will understand when they see you for the first time, and will come to know that the others are dragons as well.>

Xebrin nodded. <It is good to see you, Zahara. I cannot wait to have you on my back again.>

<I have your harness in my travel pack.> Adrianna smiled and reached out to caress his face. A moment later he was stepping away from her. There was a blurring around his form and then it grew in size, lengthening and widening. It wasn't much longer before the golden form of her Bondmate stood before her. She heard Sirion's quick intake of breath, felt his body become still behind her.

Adrianna immediately noticed that Xebrinarth was different. He was a bit larger, and his color was a paler gold than she remembered. He caught Adrianna's thoughts and answered her unasked questions. <Remember, I have lived over a century without you. I am destined to age. A dragon's color lightens as he becomes older, and he becomes larger.>

Adrianna nodded and felt the familiar sadness that haunted her since returning to her own time. Xebrinarth had endured so much without her, and she wondered how she would ever be able to make that up to him. She then turned towards the Wildrunners. They stared at Xebrinarth from wide eyes, and it appeared that Naemmious had fainted. She suddenly remembered the first time she had seen Xebrinarth and understood the awe that her friends must be feeling. He was huge, at least four lloryk long. His talons were thick, and wickedly sharp, and the ridges that protruded from his head gave him a fierce countenance.

Adrianna felt her fatigue beating at her in waves, resisted the pull of temptation to go to her bedroll and sleep. It was important that she speak to her companions about what she had done, and then explain to them why she didn't tell them about the dragons before. She put her feet beneath her and slowly stood. Sirion steadied her with a firm hand at her back and waist. She could feel the tension emanating from him and could only imagine what he must be feeling. There once was a time she felt that she could tell him anything. But now they were so distant, and she had so many things she wanted to tell him that she didn't know where to start first.

Breaking away from Sirion, Adrianna walked over to Xebrinarth. He lowered his head to her. She stroked his forehead and then turned towards her comrades. "This is Xebrinarth. He is a friend that I met while studying with my master. We have a Bond that allows us to communicate telepathically. When I told him about our upcoming fight, he told me that he wished to aid us. That is when I got the idea to have a force go against Aasarak's army.

"Forty dragons have come through the portal. Currently, they are in their faelin forms. They will transform back into their natural forms when I give the signal. I want to give you a chance to become adjusted to the idea of being surrounded by forty dragons before they make the change."

Adrianna glanced at the griffons. The druid that Dremathian had sent to lead them to Aasarak stood with them. "The griffons may choose not to stay with us. Naturally, they will be afraid of the dragons once they have us surrounded." Adrianna then looked back towards her friends. All of them bore varying degrees of concern and alarm on their faces. "I know that I should have told you about the dragons before, but I knew that you would never believe me. Until I met one myself, I thought them only to be the stuff of myth and legend."

Adrianna stopped and regarded her comrades. They stood there in silence, glancing at one another and then back at Adrianna and the huge beast at her side. Finally, someone spoke. "By the gods, Adria. How much more do you have to say that will astound and amaze us?" said Dartanyen.

"Damnation, Naemmious fell like a stone," said Sorn, considering the uncontious half-oroc.

Armond bowed at the waist. "It is a pleasure to meet you, Xebrinarth."

Adrianna felt a trill of pleasure flit through her mind. <Tell him that the pleasure is all mine.>

Adrianna smiled at Armond and told him Xebrinarth's response. Dartanyen nodded. "Yes, Adrianna. You must introduce your friend to us more appropriately," he chastised roguishly.

Slowly, the group walked towards Adrianna and Xebrinarth. Naemmious, who was still on the ground, did not come. Neither did Amethyst, so overcome with fear and awe that she couldn't move from her place beside him. As the Wildrunners greeted her Bondmate, Adrianna felt a brief moment of contentment. Yes, this was how it should be, all of those she cared about the most standing right here beside her. She only wished that it were under better circumstances. Yet, she was pleased that the Wildrunners had accepted Xebrinarth so readily, and she knew then that it would be all right for the other dragons to begin their transformations.

It wasn't long before the area was littered with forty dragons. Their multi-hued hides shimmered splendidly in the rays of the newly risen sun. The colors ranged from bronze, gold and copper, to silver, blue, violet, green and black. The griffons vacated the area, just as Adrianna thought they would. However, she knew that Xebrinarth, Mordrexith, and

Saranath would have no problem flying them the rest of the way to Aasarak's lair.

It wasn't for quite some time that the excitement died down. Adrianna left Xebrinarth to deal with the conflict that was sure to arise between dragon races bearing contrasting alignments. Meanwhile, the Wildrunners began to prepare for the last day of their journey to Aasarak's lair. She stopped at Dinim's bedroll to see how he was doing. He seemed to be sleeping soundly, but Adrianna noticed the dark smudges beneath his eyes and the lines around his mouth. Even in sleep, he seemed to be feeling the strain of his energy depletion. After a while, she rose from his side and left him, intending to go to her own bedroll and rest.

Once reaching it, she found Sirion there waiting for her. He had his hands on his hips. By his stance and the expression in his eyes, she knew that avoidance was futile. However, she found she no longer wanted to evade him. More than anything, she wanted Sirion by her side again. She had grown weary of the distance between them, and she ached to have his arms around her.

Unfortunately, Sirion was no mind reader. He stepped towards her as she approached and took her arm firmly within his grasp. "We need to talk." His voice was laced with steel, and his eyes dared her to defy him. She had never seen Sirion so incensed with her before, and she felt a rush sweep through her.

Sirion pulled Adrianna away from the encampment, nodding gravely at Sorn as they passed. They walked between the large boulders and the scrubby trees that grew in between them, and when they were far enough away from the rest of the group, Sirion swung her around to face him and then released her arm. "Why didn't you tell me about the dragons? And don't give me the excuse you gave to the others. You *know* that I would have believed you."

Adrianna looked into Sirion's eyes. He was hurt and angry. It was understandable. "I didn't feel that I had the time to tell you. It would have opened up a much bigger conversation that I didn't have the inclination to share with you at the time."

Adrianna watched as Sirion wrestled with her explanation. His nostrils flared as he breathed and his mouth was drawn into a thin line. "It seems that you don't have a problem taking the time to explain things to Dinim."

Adrianna shook her head. "With Dinim it is different..."

Sirion emitted a low growl from deep within his throat as he grabbed her arm again. "Why have you never told me what lies between the two of you?"

Adrianna frowned. *What is he talking about? Perhaps he is referring to why I had spoken to Dinim about the prophecy before anyone else.*

"Dinim is a fellow mage. I thought that he would have knowledge..."

Sirion shook his head. "It wouldn't have taken you very long to explain things to me. And despite what once existed between us, you have kept me from you." Sirion paused as he attempted to collect himself. She had never seen him like this before, and she felt herself beginning to shake. She knew he wouldn't hurt her, but all of his pent-up energy was affecting her. "However, you have brought Dinim closer to you... chose to confide in him when you could have done so with me."

Adrianna pulled at the arm encased within his grip in reaction to the emotion she felt emanating from Sirion. She knew that she had to at least try to explain things to him. "With Dinim it isn't so complicated–"

"And why not?" Sirion interrupted with a raised voice. "I suppose it is with me?"

Adrianna felt her chest constrict with emotion, felt her lower lip tremble. "Yes. With Dinim it isn't so complicated..." Adrianna paused for emphasis, almost daring Sirion to interrupt her again. "... because I am not in love with him."

Silence reigned between them, thick and heavy in the air. Adrianna bit at her lower lip to keep it from giving her away. She didn't want to show Sirion how much he had shaken her. He released his grip on her arm, letting it drop back to her side. There was only momentary indecision on his face before he gently took her within his embrace and held her close. Adrianna dropped her guard, melting into his warmth. She tried to relax, but her stomach was curling into knots. For so long she had awaited him, and now that the time was come, she found that she was afraid.

Sirion ran his hands over her back, then up her sides and into her hair. He pulled her head back and she faced him. She saw the tumult in his eyes and the thinly veiled desire. Then his lips were descending to hers, claiming them in a gentle caress. Her body's response was immediate, and she felt her trembling increase as her own emotion began to take over. She had missed him so much, and her passion for him had remained undiminished. She had submitted herself to a god, slept in his bed and accepted him into her body. Yet, her passion for Tallachienan was never a fraction of what it was for Sirion, despite the *Persuasion* he had used on her and the spirits of the past that had influenced her. She loved Sirion with every fiber of her being, and nothing could take that away from her... except for Sirion himself.

Adrianna felt the tears gathering in her eyes, felt them begin to flow down her cheeks. Sirion simply kissed them away for her, gathered her close, and then laid her gently down on the only thatch of grass that existed around them. Adrianna reveled in his touch, the caress of his hands sweeping across her flesh as he unlaced her tunic and pulled it away. She took in the scent of his hair as it fell over his shoulder to caress her neck, felt the muscular contours of his chest and shoulders beneath her fingertips.

Sirion's lips paused at her ear. "I love you."

Adrianna felt the sincerity of those words. For so long she had waited for this moment, the time when they could finally be together again. She gave herself to him, and when they were finally spent, they just lay there in one another's arms. It was the only place Adrianna wanted to be.

The dragons arrayed themselves within the mountain reaches. They tended to keep proximity with those of their own race: the bronze, gold, and copper Helzethryn, the blue, purple, and silver Rezwithrys, and the dark green and black Degethozak. They looked to Xebrinarth for leadership, he being the one who brought them there. The differing alignment of the Degethozak caused trouble. The former two races tended towards neutrality and goodness while the latter had a propensity for chaos and evil. Xebrinarth diffused the bickering as much as he could, but it was bound to happen that a fight here and there would break out.

For the remainder of that day, Adrianna rested. Sirion eventually carried her back to the encampment, situating her within his bed furs. The dragon Xebrinarth stayed the closest to the encampment, watching over as though to protect it. In particular, he watched Adrianna as she slept. He would often go see to the other dragons that surrounded them, but he would always return to watch over his friend. Sirion wondered exactly what their relationship was, but knew that it was a question he might not find the answer for until after their ordeal with Aasarak. Dinim remained within his magic-induced coma, and appeared to have no plans of coming out of it. Adrianna slept the deep sleep of one who had overtaxed herself.

Late in the afternoon, Adrianna awoke. She was hungry, and when she found that Tianna had set something aside for her from the midday meal, Adrianna sent her friend a smile of gratitude. Glancing around camp, she saw that everyone was either resting or tending to their weapons and armor. In the close distance she could hear the sounds of the dragons. She saw the druid, Markon, tending to the one griffon that had chosen to stay, despite their presence. And in her mind, she felt Xebrinarth. When she was finished eating, he came to her. His large form filled the encampment, but he was careful not to disrupt anyone. He settled himself next to her and when she moved closer so that she could lean against his smooth side, he thrummed deep in his throat with pleasure.

For several moments they sat there, simply enjoying one another's company. Words couldn't express how pleased she felt that they were together. She couldn't help thinking it was meant to be; even though they'd been worlds apart, they found a way to be together. On the other side of the encampment, Adrianna watched her sister. Sheridana looked a trifle pale, and she wondered how much of that was a result of her condition. The situation bothered Adrianna, and she didn't quite know how to approach it. Before she could begin to ponder it, Xebrin was in her mind.

<That woman is with child,> he stated simply. Adrianna looked up at Xebrinarth and saw his golden gaze was on her sister.

Adrianna only nodded the affirmative, but Xebrin felt her response in his mind.

<You told me that you are to enter into battle. This woman, she is a part of your group?>

<Yes. She and Armond are our most accomplished swordsmen.>

Xebrin frowned. <This is dangerous. You told me so yourself.>

Adrianna nodded. <Yes.>

<But she is with child. She would risk her baby so as to fight this battle?>

Adrianna could sense the deep confusion within her Bondmate. Through their link, she could feel the reverence that he held for the unborn child that resided within Sheridana. He felt protective of that helpless little being, much as he would if it were his own egg or hatchling. She wondered if all dragons felt this way.

<Not so much the Degethozak.> Xebrin had divined her thoughts. <They have many more offspring than we do, and as such, tend not to treasure them as much. But to the Rezwithrys and the Helzethryn, children are a gift from the gods, and very precious. We take care so as not to risk them needlessly.>

Adrianna answered his question. <She sees no alternative but to fight with us. She knows how much we need her and what she could do for the battle.>

<But you do not feel the same.>

Adrianna was surprised. He could see many of her thoughts before she even knew them herself. <No. I do not feel that Sheri should fight with us. The child is of my flesh and blood. I would grieve if something were to happen to it. And I know that Sheri would never forgive herself.>

<Then tell her not to fight.>

Adrianna sighed. <I wish it were that easy.> Adrianna knew her sister. Sheridana would not leave them to fight without her. She would never forgive herself if they died in the battle and she wasn't there with them. With Sheri, it was a no-win situation.

Xebrinarth could hear her thoughts, she making no effort to shield them from him. However, he said nothing more. He curved his neck around, brought his head up next to his body and closed his eyes. While Xebrin rested, Adrianna sought out Sirion. She saw him sitting with Anya on the other side of the freshly made fire and began to make her way over to him. Anya smiled as she approached, but then excused herself. She and Dartanyen were going to try to hunt something down for dinner. Adrianna took the spot that the other woman vacated next to Sirion, sitting the opposite way on the fallen tree. He put his arm around her, pulling her in close to him for a moment. She formed the thoughts in her mind but then simply blurted them out.

"Sirion, Sheridana is pregnant and I don't know what to do about it."

Sirion regarded her from wide amber eyes. Then he shook his head. "How can that be? Are you sure?"

Adrianna smiled at his question and the expression on his face. He appeared genuinely confused. "Sirion, I think that you know how conception occurs. And yes, I am quite sure."

Sirion frowned and pulled his lips into a thin line. "You know what I meant," he chided gently.

Adrianna lost her smile. "Yes, I know."

"When did it happen? Does she know who the father is?"

Adrianna nodded. Sirion waited for her to elaborate, but she found herself loath to do so. She felt somehow guilty for telling someone else what Sheri had told her in confidence, even if it was just Sirion.

She pulled closer as though to embrace him, but when her lips came close to his ear, she told him the secret. Sirion slowly pulled back from her, his eyes clouded with concern. "He doesn't know?"

Adrianna shook her head.

Sirion was quiet for a while before he spoke again. "I don't think this would come as the best of news to him right now."

"I know. That is why Sheri doesn't want to tell him." Adrianna paused. "I agree with her. It could take his mind off of the fight and cause him to lose focus."

Sirion nodded. "What is she going to do?"

"That's just it. I think that she is still planning to fight with us, but I am not sure that I want her to do that."

"But how would you stop her?"

Adrianna frowned. "I don't know. That is why I came to you."

Sirion was silent for several long moments. "You will have to confront her, tell her that she shouldn't fight."

Adrianna shook her head. "You don't know my sister. She won't want to leave us. She knows how much she is needed in this fight."

"You must convince her."

"I don't think I can," Adrianna replied.

Once again Sirion was quiet. He watched Triath as he walked towards Tianna. She was sitting next to the fire, brewing a new batch of tea. Then he turned back to Adrianna. "Perhaps Triath will need to convince her."

Adrianna raised an eyebrow, regarding him skeptically.

"Triath has certain powers that give him the ability to affect the minds of others. He can 'push' her or *Suggest* to her that she should not fight with us. If that doesn't work, he can knock her unconscious with the power of his mind.

"Are you certain that it will work?"

"The *Suggestion* thing, no. But the knocking unconscious thing, yes," said Sirion.

"But Tianna will try to revive her."

Sirion shrugged. "Then we will simply have to let her in on the secret as well."

Adrianna inhaled deeply. She knew that what she was about to do would most likely cost her Sheridana's trust for the rest of their lives. She, Sirion, Triath, and Tianna would be taking away Sheri's free will. It bothered Adrianna greatly, but she hoped that, with time, Sheri would see reason, and would understand why she had to do it.

Adrianna nodded. "All right. Let's go ask Triath if he will do it, and Tianna if she will follow through with her part."

Triath and Tianna were surprised when Adrianna and Sirion called them away from the main encampment, and even more so when they discovered the reason. As Sirion told Triath his plan, he realized that this was the first time he had actively sought out Triath's help with anything. Even in their earlier days with the original Wildrunners, they had never been close, simply respecting one another from afar. Sirion always knew that he could count on Triath in battle, but always kept his distance, never willing to bridge that gap. Until now. Adrianna had brought that out in him, and he knew that it was good.

Sirion could see Triath making the same realization. However, the other man said nothing. He merely thought over Sirion's words for a few moments and then turned to Adrianna. "You know what you are asking me to do?"

Adrianna nodded. "I am asking you to use your power against another member of your company. It is a breach of protocol and greatly frowned upon. But I fear for my sister's life and the life of the child she carries."

Triath nodded. "It is commendable. This thing you ask of me, I would do it for nothing less. This is one of the only reasons that I can think of that would make me use my power against a comrade."

Adrianna stared up at the man before her and into his eyes, one of which was vastly different than when she had left for her training. Instead of a black orb, there now rested a beautifully iridescent silver eye. He claimed that it viewed the world much the same as the original, only with a few changes that were nothing like it had been when he struggled with the daemon. "I realize you don't know me, but you know my sister. For her you will do it?"

Triath nodded and placed his hand, palm up, in front of him. "For my friend, Sheridana, I will break protocol."

Adrianna placed her hand within his. "I thank you."

Triath curved his hand around Adrianna's, Sirion put his hand over theirs, and then Tianna's on top. "We are together then?" asked Sirion.

The foursome murmured their assent and then discussed their strategy. Sirion knew the rest of the group would not be pleased about the turn of events, but he saw no other choice. Sheridana would only be a liability in battle, especially to herself and to Armond if he were to discover her condition. Sirion could only hope that Sheri would find it in her heart to forgive them one day.

"You actually think I would even consider leaving you to fight this battle without me? Are you crazy?"

Adrianna looked at her sister, her heart sinking. It was turning out to be just as she imagined it would be, maybe evn a bit worse, as Sheridana continued her high-pitched diatribe. Sheridana's eyes were wide, bright with suppressed anger. Her face was flushed and her breathing was fast like she had run for several zacrol without rest.

"Do you have any idea what I've gone through to be here? What we have all been through? If you did, you'd not be sitting here telling me I shouldn't fight. I am one of your two best swordsmen. Dinim is already out of the fight. You can ill afford to spare anyone else!"

"Sheri, please, listen to reason. You are–"

"I know exactly what I am!" she spat. "And I can't believe you, of all people, are condemning me for it!" Sheridana put her face alongside Adrianna's, her voice just above a whisper. "Don't sit there and tell me you haven't shared Sirion's bedfurs! You are at just as much risk!"

Adrianna cast a quick covert glance around the wooded area. She had taken Sheri far enough from the encampment so as not to be overheard, but the possibility that they had been followed was always there. That is, followed by anyone other than Triath. He was lurking somewhere in the trees, waiting…waiting for things to get so out of control that he knew there was no bringing Sheridana back.

Adrianna nodded, conceding to Sheridana's point. "You are right. I don't have the herbs that would keep a pregnancy at bay at hand," she said in a low voice. "Indeed, I have placed myself at risk. However, my flux has been regular, and I had it just last week. It is unlikely I am with child. Unlike you."

Sheridana pulled back, her eyes glittering. "I will not abandon the group because of a mistake I made. I am one of the Fourteen. You need me, and I will be there."

"And what of Armond? What if he finds out? Don't you think that would affect him?"

Sheridana shook her head. "I...I don't know. But he won't find out."

"Even if he doesn't find out now, he will later, after the battle. You don't think he will piece it all together and realize that you kept this from him and put the child at risk? Even more, what if you are wounded and lose the child? What then?"

Sheri narrowed her eyes. "What? You don't think I've considered all this? Well, rest assured that I have, and understand that my conviction holds. My wish is to stand at your side until the end. For truthfully, if we don't stop Aasarak, there will be no future anyways, for any of us."

Adrianna had to grant that her sister had a good point. If they didn't defeat the Deathmaster the world would Cycle again. And what would happen in the sixth Cycle? Perhaps Aasarak would find a way to kill her in her childhood, or perhaps Thane, or even Tholana.

But what if they could do this without Sheridana having to imperil herself and the life of the child within her?

Adrianna wracked her mind. *Why am I so intent about saving this one child, when there are so many more at risk if we don't destroy Aasarak?* The fact that the child was a part of her family certainly played its part, but was that the whole of it? As Adrianna thought deeper, she knew that she was compelled to save the child regardless. It could be Tianna's child, Amethyst's, or one of the druid women of Krathil-lon. It went beyond kinship bonds, or even those of friendship. It was something more. She didn't know what it was, and she didn't have the time to dig deep enough to figure it out. But she had to accept it, and keep Sheridana as far from the fray as possible.

Adrianna's voice was imploring. "Sheri, I understand what you are saying. But the life you carry is important, not just for you, me, and Armond, but..."

"No! Sheridana's strident voice rang out. "This is my choice! It is my weight to bear, and I will do it with all my willpower and all my strength." Sheridana rose from her place beside Adrianna. "Now, I have some preparations to make. I'll see you back at the encampment."

"What's going on here? I heard shouting."

Adrianna let out a sigh of relief as Triath sauntered into view. He walked with calm assurance, hair tied neatly back from his shoulders, shirt fitting just right over his lean, muscular chest.

"It's nothing," mumbled Sheridana.

"It didn't sound like nothing. You seemed angry."

Sheri shook her head. "Don't worry about it. It's fine." She made to brush past Triath, but he stepped to the side to block her path.

"You seemed angry about something important."

Sheridana stopped and looked up at Triath. "What did you hear?"

His gaze was piercing as his eyes bore into Sheridana. "Enough." His expression told her that he knew about the pregnancy and Sheridana stiffened her spine and glared at him defiantly. Triath continued to regard her intently from blue eyes, his stance relaxed and assured. His gaze intensified as he continued. "The child you carry should not be subject to unnessary risk. It is best that you stay away from the fighting, return to Krathil-lon with Markon and Dinim."

Sheridana shook her head as though trying to shy away from a fly. She took a step back from Triath, and then another, shaking her head a second time. Adrianna watched as Sheridana resisted Triath's *Suggestion*, the strain causing her brows to furrow and her hands to clench into fists at her sides. Triath pressed harder, his body now a rigid line of tension.

Determination won out. Sheridana's shout rang through the air and Adriannna only hoped it didn't reach the encampment. "No! I will fight!"

A look of resignation passed over Triath's face for the briefest moment before Sheridana crumpled. He was there to catch her before she could fall, and he swung her up in his arms as Adrianna rushed to his side. Sheri hung limp in his grasp, her complexion pale. Trendils of dark hair that had escaped their plait stuck to the sides of her face and the back of her neck.

Adrianna looked up at Triath. "Will she be alright?"

He nodded. "I used a *Mindlash*. It has knocked her unconscious for now, but she could awaken at any time. We need ro make haste to Tianna so that she can put her to sleep."

With purposeful strides Triath carried Sheridana back to the camp, and with a heavy heart, Adrianna kept up at his side. On the lookout for their return, Tianna was the first to notice them. "By the gods! What happened?" she asked in an alarmed tone.

Adrianna shook her head, tears gathering in her eyes. "I don't know! We were just talking. All of a sudden, she said she didn't feel very well. She put a hand to her head, and a moment later she was falling over."

"Quickly Triath! Put her here."

Tianna unfurled the bedroll near her feet. Triath lay her down and Adrianna sank to the ground at her sister's side. She wiped the tears at her eyes, realizing they were not the false ones she thought she'd have to make herself shed. They were real, the knowledge of what she had done making her heart break. She watched as Tianna worked, heard her speak the words that would make Sheridana sleep, her voice so low it was a whisper.

It was several moments before Tianna was finished giving Sheridana a thorough look over. At the end, she shook her head, an expression of surprised confusion on her face. "I don't understand it. I can sense nothing amiss with her."

"You sense nothing? Nothing at all?" Adrianna looked up to see Armond standing beside her. His brow was creased with concern and his eyes reflected even more. The naked emotion written there took her aback, and it was then she realzed the man was in love with the woman lying between she and Tianna, very much so.

Tianna shook her head again. "All I know is that she is in a deep sleep and unlikely to come out of it soon."

Armond's response was strained. "A coma?"

"I don't know. But it is obvious she can not fight with us. We need to send her back to Krathil-lon with Dinim."

A hush fell over the area, everyone taking in the harshness of their new reality. Not only were they down their most experienced spellcaster, but a warrior as well. The oppressiveness descended upon Adrianna like a thick net, ensnaring her as easily as the spider webbing in Tallachienan's dungeon.

Atop Xebrinarth, Adrianna saw the large hole in the cliff face. It was just where Markon said it would be. Xebrinarth flew closer to the cavern to give his riders a better look. Just as it looked like he might fly right into the mountain, Xebrin banked to the right, the other four dragons following suit, and then flew around to the other side of it. He stayed low, and when he found a good place, he landed. It was bumpy, and Adrianna felt Sirion grip her more tightly around the waist. She grinned to herself, remembering the fearful exhilaration of her first ride on Xebrinarth. The dragon's laughter rumbled in her mind and she knew that he remembered as well.

That morning, after realizing that Sheridana would no longer be in their ranks, it had been difficult to get the rest of the group to rally. They bickered back and forth about whether or not they should wait and see if Sheridana would awaken, and the talk even went so far as to include waiting for Dinim to regain consciousness as well. Sirion had been the one to finally put an end to it all, reminding them that, even if both awakened from their slumber that day, that it might take several more before they were hale enough to participate in a battle such as this one. They didn't have the luxury of another week of waiting. Aasarak's army was continuing its march, becoming stronger and stronger, while they dithered around in irrational argument.

Adrianna shed more tears while the rest of the group looked at Sirion in shock and dismay. They then finished their preparations to take the rest of their journey to Aasarak's lair. The plan was for five of the dragons to take them there. Using his telepathic ability, Xebrinarth was able to pluck the basic location of the lair from Markon's mind. The druid then set to his task of finding a way to get himself and two unconscious people back to his home.

Calling a hawk to him, Markon wrote a message, affixed it to the bird's leg, and bade it go to Krathil-lon. The hawk would make it there in good time, and reinforcements would be sent to help him to get back home. It would be difficult for the griffon to carry the three of them, if not impossible, and they would have to let the animal rest often. Alone in the mountains, the dangers to them were great, and he knew that help was needed.

The group was loath to leave them, but they had no more time to spare. While Xebrinarth instructed the other thirty-five dragons on where they were to go in order to meet the undead army, Mordrexith, Saranath, Nordrahl and Fazarandrehl were loaded with their packs. These dragons would make a detour and take the Wildrunners the rest of the way to Aasarak's lair. Adrianna explained to everyone where they should sit, and how to hold on to the dragon whilst in flight. Finally, they were prepared.

All of the dragons wanted to see Adrianna before they flew to meet the army. Astride Xebrinarth, she met all of them. Each one greeted her as she approached, and when they brought their heads close, she touched each one on the muzzle. Even the Degethozak were humble. It was for her that they had Traveled between worlds, and for her that they would fight against this army of abominations. They were all followers of Adrianna and her cause. They would fight the good fight, and then go to live the remainder of their lives upon Shandahar.

Then everyone was ready and the dragon force took to the air. After them rose the five that carried the Wildrunners. With a heavy heart, Adrianna watched as the forms of Markon and the griffon faded away into the distance that began to separate them. Sirion sat behind her on Xebrinarth, Triath and Tianna rode Mordrexith, and Dartanyen and Armond sat astride Saranath. Upon the two Rezwithrys dragons that chose to accompany them, Sorn and Amethyst rode one, while Naemmious and Anya sat the other. It only took them the rest of the day to make it to the entrance to the lair, rather than the two days they had originally thought. Now, as they landed in a vicinity close by, the reality of their situation began to weigh heavily on Adrianna.

Xebrinarth offered her his leg as Adrianna began to slide off of his back. She felt a darkness descend upon her, and she was forced to lean against her Bondmate for support. This was her destiny. Finally, she had come to meet it, just as she had in all of the other Cycles before. However, Dinim was not there, and neither was Sheridana. Their strength in the upcoming battle was greatly needed. Dinim had already made his contribution to that fight by helping her to open the portal for the dragons. His part in the fight was done. For Sheridana, it just wasn't meant to be. Adrianna had made certain it would be that way.

<Zahara, let me take you away from this place. We can leave it and never look back.>

Adrianna turned towards Xebrinarth. He lowered his head so that he looked into her eyes. She put her hand on his jaw and stroked him there for a moment. Then she shook her head. <You know that I cannot. It is foretold in prophecy that I should be here, just as I have been in all of the Cycles before this one.>

<I can feel the evil of this place weighing on you. I wish to take it from you, to ease your burden.>

<But you have. Just by being here, you have made my destiny complete. Even though you will be many zacrol away, you will be fighting by my side.>

Xebrinarth lifted his head. <It is my greatest desire to see you again, Zahara.>

Adrianna felt a tear roll down her cheek. <It is my hope that you will hear my voice in your mind when our fight with Aasarak is finished.>

<We will come back for you and take you home. Then we will be together again, and no one will keep us apart.>

<Yes, we will always be together, you and I.>

Adrianna felt his rumble through their link, felt the undying love he had for her as he crouched low and then vaulted himself into the air. The other dragons followed. With a terrible lump in her throat, Adrianna watched them until they were but mere specks in the sky. She felt a hand on her shoulder and then turned to find herself within Sirion's embrace. He held her there for a moment while she collected herself. She was glad that he was there to offer his protection, support, and guidance. She knew that she would need it in the hours to come.

# Advent of a New Era

The Wildrunners found a suitable campsite father up the mountain. Sirion had scounted ahead while the others began to set up camp and was pleased to note that it probably wouln't take them long to reach their destination in the morning. After taking their evening meal, the group sat around the central fire. Silence reigned for a while, but it wasn't long before they were discussing the enemy.

"We would be fools to think that Aasarak is alone up here," said Triath.

Sirion nodded in agreement. "It's a good bet that he has some of his Azmathous at his disposal, and maybe even some of the poor souls whom he brought back to life so as to fill the ranks of his army."

"Father Dremathian referred to them as wraiths," said Tianna, her voice almost a whisper.

"Whatever they are, we have to be ready for them," Sirion replied.

"Anya and I still have many of the arrows that Dinim enchanted for us in our fight with Lord Thane. Dinim gave them the ability to drain the energy from those whom they struck. They seemed to work well against the Azmathous," said Dartanyen.

"It must have been experimental. Dinim wouldn't have known how the enchantment would affect the Azmathous," answered Adrianna.

Dartanyen shrugged and offered a grin. "Well, it worked. After a few hits, I could see the effect the arrows were having on our enemies."

Adrianna returned the smile and nodded. "That's good, another valuable weapon we can use against them."

Sorn narrowed his eyes. "No wonder I was able to defeat that death-rogue."

"As I recall, the monster had felt the wrath of two or three of our arrows before you encountered it," said Dartanyen, widening his smile.

"We need to remember that we don't have Destroyer with us this time," Naemmious reminded them glumly.

Dartanyen nodded, his expression turning solemn. "Yes, it was Sheri who delivered the final blow to Thane."

Adrianna felt her heart lurch into her throat. It was still hard for her to believe that Sheridana wasn't there. For the past six years she had always imagined her sister would be standing beside her in this battle. She could only hope that she had made the right choice by sending Sheri away. Adrianna caught Triath's gaze as he stared at her from across the fire. She knew that he was thinking the same thing.

Seated beside Sorn, Amethyst restlessly flipped her dagger into the air, catching it by the point with her fingertips when it fell. She remembered the battle with the Azmathous like it was yesterday. She had almost died in that fight, but back then she had been nothing. Now she was an accomplished rogue, armed with the many skills Sorn had imparted to her.

Amethyst had been through so much since she had first met up with the group all of those moon cycles ago. She felt at ease with these people, knew that they had accepted her a long while back. They didn't care where she came from, only where she was going. With them, she had found something that she had been looking for all of her life, something she had never really found with the Thieves Guild in Sangrilak. Family. And it was with her family she would be entering a battle in which she was needed.

And then there was Sorn. In the beginning, he had treated her as nothing more than a sewer rat that he needed to train for battle. It wasn't until she had begun to put all of her strength into the training that he started to display some, albeit reluctant, respect for her. His attitude towards her slowly changed, and somewhere along the way, he had come to be more to her than just a teacher and a mentor. He was the brother, uncle, or father she had never known.

Amethyst felt that she finally meant something to someone, and that in this endeavor, she had never been so needed in her entire life.

Amethyst reared forward into alertness as a swift chill swept through the encampment. All conversation ceased, and everyone was suddenly on edge. The air had a strange feeling to it, one that she couldn't really describe. However, it was quite familiar, and when she began to hear the keening wail being carried to them in the wind, she knew what it was.

Everyone jumped up from their positions around the fire. They rushed to their travel packs and quickly donned the accoutrements of their respective professions. The wail became louder, chilling them to the bone, causing an unnatural fear to suffuse them. The Azmathous were coming, the undead having somehow divined their location. Certainly, Aasarak had sent them, hoping to weaken them before their meeting on the morrow. As the terrible sound of the death wail reached its apex, the Wildrunners knew their time had run out. Just as Armond finished buckling his breastplate into place, the Azmathous were surrounding them.

They were just as Adrianna remembered. The only difference was that her father wasn't with them this time. He was dead and gone many moon cycles ago, his remains burned after the battle. They rode no shadow lloryk, surrounding them instead on foot. Somehow, they didn't seem as impressive as Thane and his group had been. But mayhap 'twas because that battle, at least for her, had been fought approximately seven years ago.

Adrianna had become so much bigger since then.

They were all warriors, each of them wearing black plate mail. Most of them wore helmets that covered the head and most of the face. Two of them did not. Looking at them, Adrianna could see that one of them had once been a woman. Her features were twisted by evil, and death had done the rest. Despite what she had become, Adrianna could still see the last vestiges of her beauty. All of them had their weapons drawn, and for a moment, they seemed to wait for some unseen signal.

As the lengthening shadows merged with the encroaching darkness, the Azmathous rushed the group. Adrianna was quick to cast her first spell, easily calling upon the *Lightning* she had learned how to harness at the beginning of her training with Master Tallachienan, correcting for this time and place. She directed it towards one of the death-knights and watched as it scorched him, blackening his armor and making any exposed flesh fall from the bones. Much to her horror and fascination, the knight continued to come towards the group with his cohorts... and the battle was joined.

Adrianna stepped back and watched as Sirion gripped his weapon at the center with both hands. Within moments, the quarterstaff had become two separate blades. Moving past her, the ranger swung at the charred death-knight. The enemy deflected the blow with his blackened longsword and made an attack of his own. Adrianna quickly stepped away from the struggle and began to chant the words to her next spell. She knew that she should cast something for her personal protection, and if she could, she would cast a protective spell over everyone in the group. She knew that it was unrealistic, but it didn't stop her from considering it.

Meanwhile, the lure of the *Flamesphere* was insurmountable.

Naemmious dodged the arrows that Dartanyen and Anya fired as he rushed his opponent, the big one with the massive battleaxe. Naemmious swung his mace as they got closer, and when his weapon struck the black chestplate, sparks flew off the enchanted metal. However, the mace was similarly enchanted, courtesy of a crazy old mage he and the original Wildrunners had met during one of their missions together. It left a huge dent in the chestplate of his opponent, resulting in the hideous scream that Naemmious remembered from their first fight with the Azmathous. He cringed inside, the keening making him want to cower on the ground at the monster's feet. Yet, Naemmious resisted the impulse, instead finding the strength to block the blow from his opponent's battleaxe. He stumbled beneath the might of the blow, but was quick to recover.

He renewed his attack, striking the knight on the shoulder as the enemy made an attempt to deflect it. Naemmious caught himself before he teetered off balance, and was in the perfect position to parry his opponent's next attack.

In the meantime, Naemmious caught Sorn and Amethyst out of the corner of his eye. Sorn swung his flail at an enemy riddled with arrows, only to watch the weapon glance off the protective armor. Sorn cursed, but then grinned when he saw Amethyst jump onto their opponent's back, plunging her dagger deep into the back of the neck. The wail was excruciating, and once again Naemmious could hardly keep himself from slamming his hands up over his ears.

The enemy gave a half-hearted swing at Sorn, but then began clawing at Amethyst with the intention of removing her from his back. Sorn found the distraction to be his best opportunity, and he swung the flail again. The barbs hooked themselves into the enemy's head-gear, and when Sorn pulled the weapon back, the helm came with it.

In dismay, Naemmious saw the helmet fly through the air towards him. It struck his upper arm just as he parried a blow from his own opponent. Naemmious followed up with an upward swing, managing to smash his mace into the head of his adversary. The knight went to its knees and then became dust just before it fell at Naemmious' feet. Meanwhile, Amethyst was thrown from her opponent's back only to collide into Sorn. Both went sprawling into a heap on the ground, where moments later, the offending knight was standing over them...

Naemmious watched a sphere of fire race towards the knight standing over Sorn and Amethyst. It could have originated from no one but Adrianna. While the enemy was consumed within the resulting conflagration, Sorn quickly unsheathed the shortsword at Amethyst's hip, lurched upwards, and sliced it across the knight's neck. The fiery head rolled off of the shoulders, and before the body hit the ground, it had become a smattering of dust.

With quick efficiency, Sirion had dispatched the dark knight that Adrianna had struck with her magical lightning. Then he turned and took stock of the situation. Dartanyen had discarded his bow in lieu of his shortsword, while Anya continued to selectively shoot hers when a good opening became available. With deadly accuracy, Sirion saw her arrows become embedded into another of the death-knights, one wielding a battleaxe. Sirion began to advance towards it when a large body slammed into him from the side.

With a *whoosh*, Sirion felt the breath leave his body. He fell onto the ground, the death-knight lying on top of him. The stench of rotting flesh clogged his nostrils and he felt his stomach roil. *Damn, not now!* He refused to be sick in the middle of a battle. Sirion struggled with the weight on top of him, and thankfully, the knight was equally as determined. Within moments, they rose from the ground and were circling one another menacingly.

However, the knight had forgotten his earlier opponent. Triath used the power of his *Psionic Force* again, and the knight found itself being thrown back another farlo. Triath nodded solemnly at Sirion as he passed, following the trajectory the enemy's body used as it flew through the air. The knight seemed confused, and it was obvious Triath was pleased. This would be to his advantage when he used his sword against it.

Nearby, Armond dodged another blow by his opponent. This one was good, very good. He seemed to have an aura of power about him that was absent from the other knights. Sirion thought that he just might be the leader, much like Thane was the leader of the last group of Azmathous they had encountered. Armond swung one blade, quickly followed by the other. It just so happened that his opposition was a master with two blades as well, and they moved around one another in a deadly dance. Armond sang to his blades, and even from a distance, Sirion felt the flow of magical energy towards the weapons. The swords began to move faster, Armond's arms following suit. It seemed the magic knew every move before the man could consciously think it.

But then something happened. There was a disturbance behind him, and Armond faltered. The man stumbled backwards into another death-knight, and the enemy's blade caressed his side. Armond grunted and lurched around to swing at this new foe. It was the lady knight Sirion had noticed at the beginning of the fight. Armond pressed into her, and then disengaged, swinging back around to engage the leader. Much to Armond's surprise, his adversary was gone. Armond quickly repositioned himself to deflect a blow from his female opponent...

Dartanyen knew that he was no match for the death-knight despite the two arrows that protruded from between the plates of its armor. Once more it swung its bronze-plated battleaxe, and Dartanyen was just quick enough to dodge the blow. He swung his shortsword, and when it raked across the knight's chestplate, he grimaced through clenched teeth. Then the axe was swinging towards him again. He knew that there was no chance he would be able to get out of the way in time as he raised his sword in an effort to block the axe.

Dartanyen buckled beneath the power behind the attack. The axe scraped against his blade and then continued to slice downwards and into his leg. He screamed in agony, the searing pain shooting up the leg and into his groin. Dartanyen lay on the ground, watched the knight as it loomed over him. Time seemed to slow down for a moment... the moment he realized that he was going to die. But just as the knight was getting ready to execute his final swing, Naemmious was there.

The big man slammed his mace into the knight's head. The metal helm crunched beneath the blow and the knight rocked to the side. Dartanyen struggled to sit upright despite the pain in his leg, but his vision kept clouding. He put his hand over the wound... felt the parted meat and the bone beneath. He resisted the urge to vomit as he pulled the muscle together, soon realizing the futility of his action as his hands quickly became too blood-slicked to hold the flesh together properly. He shuddered when he felt a hand on his shoulder, but was relieved when Tianna was kneeling beside him. With a hand to his chest, she bade him lie back on the ground. Dartanyen slumped backward and blacked out.

Tianna knelt over her comrade, a frown of worry creasing her brow. Dartanyen had lost a lot of blood before she could reach him, and the wound was a bad one. However, she had faith in her abilities and in her goddess. She prayed fervently over the faelin man before her, placing one hand over the parted flesh on his upper thigh and the other around the talisman at her neck. The familiar wave of power surged through her. Beneath her palm, Tianna could feel the blood cease to flow. She then took a strip of cloth and bound the wound. She would clean it and then heal it further after the battle.

Tianna looked up at Dartanyen's face, noting the paleness of his complexion. Yet, she wasn't so worried anymore. With the blood flow stopped, he would live to see their next battle. She glanced around the field and saw that the fight was over. Adrianna had created an orb of light for them to see by. The Wildrunners were scattered haphazardly over the encampment, their enemies nothing but piles of dark dust beginning to blow away in the wind.

Triath strode quickly over to her and then knelt with her beside Dartanyen. "Naemmious has a few cuts, as does Sirion. Other than that, everyone is fine," he said.

Tianna nodded. "Let's rebuild the fire and get the men over to it. Then I can work on everyone together."

Triath nodded to Armond and the other man came over. The two men picked Dartanyen up and carefully carried him to where their old fire had been disturbed by the melee. Only a few glowing embers remained of it. Anya busied herself with the task of rebuilding the fire, and it was only a short while later that the flames were lively again. Sorn scoured the area for the enchanted arrows that Anya and Dartanyen had used against the Azmathous as everyone began to finally settle down after the battle. After a short while, he came back and gave the arrows to Anya. He looked around the fire and then said, "Where is Amethyst?"

Everyone looked around the group sitting at the fire. Tianna frowned, not recalling having seen her since the beginning of the skirmish. Armond echoed her thoughts. "I haven't seen her since the beginning of the fight."

Sorn shook his head and strode away from the fire. Triath, Sirion, and Naemmious rose to join him. With a hand to his side, Armond also rose from his place. Tianna noticed and quickly made her way over to him. Once there she pulled his hand away. Blood had soaked through his tunic to form a large circle. "What in the Hells is this? Why didn't you tell me you needed healing?"

Armond pulled away from her. "I wanted to wait until you were done with the others. It's nothing."

Tianna hissed through her teeth. "Sit down. I will see to it now. A wound made by the undead is never 'nothing'."

As Armond silently obeyed, Triath and Sirion brought some torches and lit them at the fire before leaving to investigate the outskirts of the encampment and surrounding area. Anya and Adrianna were swift to join in the search while Tianna began to boil some water for a restorative tea.

Quite a while later, everyone met back at the fire, each of them taking a mug of her steaming brew before sitting down. All were silent until Sorn spoke with a tone of finality. "She has been taken."

Adrianna shook her head. "All of the Azmathous were destroyed. Who could have possibly taken her?"

"Did anyone see the knight that was wielding two longswords?" asked Armond. "His helm was unlike the others, covering only his head and leaving his face exposed."

The rest of the group shook their heads. "I saw him at the beginning of the melee, but I thought that you had him, Armond," said Naemmious.

"I did, but sometime during the fight he disappeared. I just assumed he'd been assaulted by one of Adrianna's spells, or that he had been crushed by you, Naemmious," replied Armond. "I think he was the leader."

"I don't recall this particular knight. This means it is very possible that he took Amethyst," said Adrianna.

Sorn clenched his hands into fists. "We need to go after her."

Sirion shook his head. "Sorn, are you crazy? We can't go after her right now. Most likely, the knight took her to Aasarak. We aren't prepared to fight him at this moment."

Sorn affixed him with a steely gaze, "But we can't just leave her."

"I agree. But we need to rest and allow Tianna to continue her healing of us," replied Sirion. "In the morning we will go to Aasarak's lair, but for now let's decide how we will fight the man when we meet him."

From where Tianna sat beside Dartanyen, she watched as Sorn reluctantly sat down at the fire. The urge to find his apprentice reflected strongly in his eyes, but he also realized the wisdom of Sirion's words. If they went after Amethyst now and met Aasarak, they would be defeated for certain. All he could do was wait until the morning. Meanwhile, she would continue her work with Dartanyen. He wouldn't be at his best, but definitely healed enough to participate in the fight.

Adrianna stared into the fire. She concentrated on the flames, willing them to give her the answers she needed. The group wasn't ready to meet Aasarak, and with the demoralizing capture of Amethyst, she feared for their lives. Unfortunately, the fire would give her no visions, and her mind was absent of divinations of the future. She mentally cursed her so-called gift in Hinterlic and then began to think of other, more mundane things she could do to try to give them an edge in their upcoming battle against Aasarak.

If, indeed, the Azmathous leader had taken Amethyst to the Deathmaster, then the knight would most likely be there when they met Aasarak. One member of the group would have to be the one to fight him, keep him away from the rest of the group while they concentrated on Aasarak. Adrianna looked over at Armond, watched him grimace when Tianna applied her salve to his side. Yes, Armond should be the one. She was sure that Sirion could have kept the knight occupied as well, but knowing him, she knew that he would want to be as close to her as possible during the fight.

Adrianna nestled into Sirion's warmth, and he put an arm around her shoulders to pull her closer. With Armond out of the picture, they would have less offensive to use against Aasarak. It would be only herself, Triath, Sirion, Naemmious, Anya, and Dartanyen. Tianna would remain in the defensive, and Sorn as well. Most likely, Amethyst would be incapacitated, and Adrianna could only hope that the girl was still alive.

Adrianna wracked her brain, and when the idea finally came to her, she almost discarded it. There was a spell that she had learned during her last days with Tallachienan. It wasn't anything special, it being a spell that any mage of her skill level could cast. Tallachienan had taught his apprentices many such spells, reminding them that it was a fool who learned only one discipline to the exclusion of all others. However, because Dimensionalist magic worked very differently from 'ordinary' spellcasting, it would take a lot of effort for her to cast the spell.

Adrianna glanced down beside her at the hip that Sirion pressed against hers. One of the blades that constituted the weapon he called Stalker was sheathed there. If she could enchant Stalker with the power of the spell, then Sirion could use his blades as a virtual shield. When Aasarak cast a spell at Sirion, the *Deflect Magic* spell that she would use upon Stalker would empower the blades when he held them before him. The spell would then retrace itself back to its caster. She knew that it wasn't much, but at least it was something. Maybe Aasarak would cast a spell that would be his own undoing.

Adrianna turned to him. "Sirion, give me your blades."

Sirion looked at her in surprise. "Why?"

"I want to cast an enchantment on Stalker before we meet Aasarak tomorrow."

Sirion pulled the swords free from the sheaths at his hips. "What kind of enchantment?"

"It will allow the weapon to deflect magic. At my skill level, I should be able to cast the spell strong enough to deflect magic even from a sorcerer as powerful as Aasarak."

Sirion frowned. "But won't that drain you of your strength?"

Adrianna smiled wanly. Sirion was learning things about her profession. Right now, she wished that he had not. "Yes, but I think that it could be a great benefit in our battle."

Sirion shook his head. "I don't know, Adria."

She pressed her lips into a thin line. Glancing around, she saw that the rest of the group was listening to their conversation. She thought about getting upset about the intrusion, but then remembered they had a stake in this too. It was everyone's lives that were on the line.

"Sirion, this will be one of my contributions to our fight. This is my profession, what I was trained to do. Please let me do my job." Adrianna looked him in the eyes as she spoke, emphasizing her determination. It was several moments before Sirion spoke again.

"You are right." Sirion paused and then give her a mirthless smile. "I tend to forget that your profession is so different from mine. I am sorry." Sirion placed the hilts of the shortswords together, end on end. Within moments, the weapon had transformed into a quarterstaff. He then kneeled and offered the weapon to her, bowing his head over it. "I am honored that you have chosen me to bear the burden of your enchantment."

Adrianna chuckled nervously. "What do you mean... burden?"

Sirion's eyes were intense as they regarded her. "It is the perfect enchantment for my weapon to have. As your sworn protector, it is I who will be the front line of defense."

Adrianna nodded and swallowed heavily. Sirion was right. She had inadvertently chosen him to be the recipient of her spell out of all of their comrades. It was her subconscious making her decisions now, following what had been foretold in prophecy.

Adrianna accepted the quarterstaff and began to make preparations for the enchantment. Sirion watched her for a moment as she riffled through her travel packs for the components that she would need, and his gaze fell on her sword. He had been meaning to have a look at it, but the time simply hadn't presented itself. Sirion took the sheathed weapon, noting the decorative hilt and scabbard. He then drew the blade, the hiss of the weapon leaving its sheath softly filling the abrupt silence that pervaded the encampment.

Sirion held the blade before him. The weapon glowed softly lavender in the night. It was beautiful, intricate runic designs making their way from the hilt down to the tip. All of a sudden, he felt a wrenching in his gut. It was painful for only a moment before a warmth surged through him. Sirion glanced from the sword to Adrianna, took in the beauty of her face, the gentle cant of her dark eyes, the fullness of her lips. Her pale, moon-lit hair glistened around her shoulders, the curls tumbling down her back. Her small body was slender and curved in all the right places. She was his soulmate.

Sirion felt his love for her flow forth. He returned his gaze to the sword, saw that it had begun to glow a bright purple. The intensity of his love surged through him and into the waiting blade. A low moan escaped his lips as he reveled in the joy he felt over having found her at last, the better half to his whole.

All of a sudden, he could hear the sounds from the encampment again, and Adrianna was leaning towards him, her expression one of concern. His muscles relaxed and he dropped the blade, the glow rapidly fading away. He brought his hands before his face, remembering the light that suffused them as power radiated into the blade. Now the weapon lay on the ground before him. Looking at it now, one would never guess that just a moment before it glowed with power.

But somehow, Sirion knew what had happened. Without words, the weapon had told him its intentions as it worked magic over his body. The sword had taken the power of his emotion, the love he had for Adrianna, and locked it within itself. When next Adrianna used the sword, his love would be there to protect her. Sirion reached out and took Adrianna's face within his hands. He kissed her tenderly, and once more felt a surge of love course through him.

"Sirion, what happened?" Adrianna broke the kiss and breathlessly pulled away.

Sirion shook his head. "It was your sword. I think it has been ensorcelled." Sirion told the lie easily. He didn't just *think* it was enchanted... he *knew* it was. He just didn't want to alarm her...

Adrianna shook her head as well. "It can't be. I used it while I was apprenticed at the citadel. It never showed an inkling of enchantment before."

Sirion shrugged nonchalantly, now fully recovered from his brush with sorcery at its greatest. "Then I don't know what happened."

Hesitantly, Adrianna returned to her business. Tianna had finished her ministrations, and the group was settling down for the night. She considered all she would need, meanwhile pushing away the feather-light sensation of uncertainty. She didn't know precisely how much of her strength it would take to cast the spell, for she had practiced it only once at the citadel before moving on to other things. She placed Sirion's quarterstaff across her lap and had already opened her spellbook to the appropriate page when she felt the presence of someone standing over her. Adrianna looked up into the somewhat monstrous visage of Naemmious.

The big warrior cleared his voice before he spoke. "Lady, I couldn't help but overhear your conversation with Sirion... that you need to use a lot of your strength to enchant his weapon."

Adrianna only nodded.

"Well, I am hoping I can be of help. As you can see, I am a big man with a lot of strength to spare. I want to give some of it to you so that you can enchant Sirion's weapon and still be able to fight with us tomorrow."

Adrianna felt her eyes widen with incredulity. She never imagined he would offer himself in such a way. She had heard of it done before, recorded in a book she'd read whilst in the library one day at Tallachienan's citadel. The text spoke of a man who gave some of his life-force so that his sorcerer companion could cast a difficult spell. A priest had been there, acting as a conduit between the two so that the exchange could be completed.

Adrianna regarded Naemmious for a few moments. Sirion glanced up from his activity and regarded them both. "I... are you sure that you want to do that?" she asked.

"Absolutely certain, milady," responded Naemmious.

Adrianna nodded. "I have heard of such a thing being done before, but I've never done it myself. We will need to ask Tianna for help."

Sirion silently rose to get Tianna while Adrianna shuffled around in her travel pack to withdraw a few more items she would need.

Naemmious' sacrifice would enable her to cast the enchantment on Stalker and then have the capacity to fight on the morrow with very little rest. It was a grand gesture, one that many would never have the intellect to consider. It seemed that Naemmious was cleverer than anyone probably thought.

A short while later, the trio removed themselves from the rest of the group, hoping to minimize any possible sleep interference they might cause. Tianna sat between Adrianna and Naemmious, placing a hand upon each of them the way Adrianna instructed. Adrianna was surprised that she recalled the precise words of the spell she needed to cast, looking it up briefly in her spellbook before beginning the incantation. Tianna began a prayer to her goddess. Adrianna drew some runes into the air...

Naemmious just sat there and waited.

Amethyst awoke to find herself in a strange place. Feeling cool stone beneath her, she sat up, looked around, and realized that she was in a cage. There was nothing inside except for her, and the bars gleamed eerily yellow in the darkness. She crawled over and hesitantly touched one with a fingertip. Nothing happened. She breathed a sigh of relief. At least the bars would not harm her if she happened to touch them.

Amethyst focused on the environment outside the cage. She didn't remember how she got there, or even where 'there' was. All she knew was that she had been grabbed from behind during the battle with the Azmathous, and when she began to struggle, she was knocked unconscious. Now she had a headache, a dull pain that she felt she could tolerate. She saw that she was in a huge cavern. Large spires rose from the floor and descended from the ceiling like teeth in the mouth of a gargantuan carnivore. In the stillness that pervaded, she could hear the sound of dripping water.

Appearing to be made of the surrounding darkness, a man stepped out of the shadows. He was about the size of a Hinterlean faelin, clothed entirely in black robes. A hood was pulled up over his head that was so deep, the face within couldn't be seen. In his hand he held a strangely shaped object. She felt her eyes widen when she recognized it for what it was. It was a puzzle artifact, an extremely elaborate and beautiful one! Amethyst stared at the eight-sided object from within her prison. Even from childhood, she remembered being very adept at discovering the secrets kept by all manner of puzzles, one of them being in the form ofone such as this. It was a skill, the thieves told her, a *gift* bestowed upon her by the gods in order to serve a greater purpose one day. Amethyst had scoffed at them then, but now, seeing a puzzle artifact like this, and knowing that this man was Lord Aasarak, Amethyst wondered at the wisdom of their words.

"Ah, so you have awakened, small one."

Amethyst's eyes darted from the artifact to the man who held it. His voice was deep and rich, and it almost seemed to echo around the cavern.

"I could feel that you and your companions were close, and I sent my Azmathous to weaken your group. Hodorin brought you to me, a surprise to say the least. He could have killed you, but I find that I am more pleased to see you behind the bars of my cage."

Amethyst held her tongue. It was something she had learned to do while she apprenticed under Sorn. Her heart hammered in her chest, and she realized that she was afraid. Aasarak approached the cage and she couldn't help but glance at the puzzle. It was elegant, and obviously made by a master in his craft. Amethyst's fingers itched to hold it, but as Aasarak made his way ever closer, she found herself moving away from the bars. She'd caught a glimpse of the armor he wore beneath his robes, armor made of bones. They didn't all appear to be human and faelin, but from animals as well. It was creepy to say the least, and she wanted as much distance between herself and this man as possible, artifact or no.

Amethyst watched Aasarak as he placed the puzzle artifact within the folds of his robes, making sure to see how far back he placed his hand, and at what height. If she were to somehow get free of the cage, she would lift the object from the mage and divine its secrets for herself in spite of the scary armor. She would wait for the Wildrunners to come for her, and once they were there, they would surely set her free. Then the artifact would be hers for the taking.

"Somehow you don't seem to be as despondent as I thought you might be," said Aasarak. "I suppose you think that your friends will come for you. They may come, but they will not live long." Aasarak chuckled. "Then you will have no one. I will watch you wither away behind these bars."

Once again, Amethyst held her tongue. She knew that her companions would come, and she knew that Sorn would get her out of this cage... even if it was the last thing he ever did.

The Wildrunners set their travel packs at the entrance to the cavern. The fetid air coming from within made many of them put their hands over their noses and mouths. Dartanyen lit some torches and handed one to Sirion, Naemmious, Tianna, and Triath. Sirion was the first to step inside, followed by Adrianna. Aside from having their weapons sheathed, everyone was alert and battle-ready. Everything they would need for the fight was either buckled around their hips or across their backs.

The group had walked but a farlo into the cavern when Adrianna felt the presence of Xebrinarth in her mind. Since leaving the Wildrunners at the lair, the five dragons had flown hard and fast to catch up with those who had gone before. Finally they were approaching the army. Xebrinarth fully opened his mind to hers, allowing her to see what he saw. The scene below made her heart almost stop in her chest.

It was a sea of the dead.

Aasarak's army stretched almost as far as she could see. The wraiths were led by Azmathous who sat astride steeds of darkness. Eerie mists eddied and flowed around the army, wisps of the foul magic that had brought them into undead life. They were human, faelin, halfen, and oroc. Even some oorgs and trolags filled the ranks. They swarmed over the landscape like a pestilence, and Adrianna imagined that she could smell the stench that surely arose from the plain. She realized that it must be the Plain of Antipithanee in the realm of Cortubro. It was the largest swath of grasslands on the western side of the continent.

<I will maintain my link with you as we begin our assault,> said Xebrinarth.

Adrianna gave a mental nod of agreement just as she felt a hand settle onto her shoulder. Turning around, she saw it was only Naemmious. She glanced beyond him to find that the rest of the group had come to a stop behind her. Almost a farlo ahead, Sirion looked back, an expression of concern written on his face. She would need to do better from now on, especially if Xebrinarth was going to maintain their link throughout the battle. Even now she could sense him in her mind, and if she focused just a little more, she could hear him strategizing with the other dragons about how to proceed. The Azmathous had noticed them, and some had stopped to watch the dragons winging in the sky above. Meanwhile, Adrianna was able to retain awareness of her own surroundings.

Adrianna indicated that nothing was amiss and once more fell in behind Sirion as he led them deeper into Aasarak's lair.

For quite some time the group walked. Adrianna had an uncanny sense of where they should go, and she indicated to Sirion that they continue past the peripheral hallways while keeping to the main tunnel. A sense of evil pervaded the place, and became stronger as they progressed deeper into the mountain. Stalactites descended from the ceiling, and similar structures arose from the floor. It reminded Adrianna of another time and another cavern not too long ago beneath the city of Sangrilak. Back then, Zorg and Bussimot had still been alive...

Adrianna knew when the dragons began their attack on Aasarak's army. They swept at the undead in waves, releasing their fiery breath upon the masses. As the first group of dragons pulled away, the next group proceeded with their own sweep. Many of the wraiths were incinerated with one pass, but hosts of others continued onward despite the scorching they had endured. Many of the Azmathous had crossbows, and they began to shoot the bolts at the dragons as they swept overhead. There were at least two sorcerers, and they would soon cast their first spells...

With a bit of effort, Adrianna returned her focus to the cavern. They didn't have much farther to go and her belly clenched in fearful anticipation. After all these years of preparation, the time had almost come.

Aasarak paced agitatedly in front of the pool. Upon its scummy surface, he could see the expanse of his army and the dragons that flew over it. He could sense that the sorceress Adrianna and her group were close, and he would soon have to deal with them.

This was unprecedented. Dragons had not been seen in Shandahar for hundreds of years. The Pact of Bakharas forbade it. Obviously, these dragons had disregarded the Pact. It was possible that they didn't even know that such a thing existed. Aasarak growled as he turned away from the pool. He had assumed that events were going to take place much as they had in the previous Cycles. He was disturbed to realize that they would not.

From the confines of her cage, Amethyst watched. Something bothered the sorcerer, but she didn't know what it was. She sat there quietly, barely breathing. She had been scrutinizing him, looking for any signs of weakness or vulnerability. Unfortunately, she had found none. The death-knight watched Aasarak as well. Amethyst glanced where he stood at the wall near the entrance to the chamber. It was the one who had taken her during the battle, the one Aasarak called Hodorin. He had been standing there for hours without moving. She figured it was because he was dead and didn't feel the need for such basic activity. Hells, she still should have seen at least a twitch here or there in spite of the lack of necessity.

Much to her surprise, the knight suddenly did just as she imagined he should. Hodorin pulled himself into alertness, and then turned to look towards the entrance. Aasarak did the same, and a tense expectancy began to fill the chamber. Amethyst instantly realized what was happening. The Wildrunners had finally come.

Moments later, Adrianna and Sirion slowly entered the large room. The rest of the Wildrunners fanned out behind as they stepped inside. Torches were dropped onto the floor as they entered, for sconces built into the cavern walls held flames for them to see by. It was still dim, but the area was made slightly brighter by the torches that now burned on the floor. From her place across the chamber, Amethyst could hear the sounds of weapons being drawn. Her heartbeat increased its pace as tension rose. It wouldn't be long now...

Adrianna saw that the cavern was much the same as the rest of the cave, only much larger. Many stalagmitic structures grew from the floors, wider at the base and becoming narrower as they rose upwards. Many of them were as tall as Naemmious. Silence reigned for many moments as the dark sorcerer watched them from across the chamber. Adrianna didn't take her eyes off of him, but she hoped that her comrades were viewing the layout of the battlefield. Sirion was a bastion of strength beside her. Before entering the chamber, he had pulled her close to share one last kiss. Adrianna knew he would protect her with his dying breath, but she prayed that it wouldn't come to that.

All of a sudden, there was a flurry of motion. Adrianna felt a swift change in the energy that surrounded them and knew Aasarak was casting his first spell. As her companions darted in every direction, Adrianna began to cast one of her own spells, one that she hoped would offset the sorcerer. It was an interesting spell, one that she had learned from one of the multitudes of books that Tallachienan kept within his vast libraries. Once the spell was chanted, small shallow portals would come into existence. She would be enveloped by them, and would then reappear in another place in the chamber. However, the spell would only last a short while. She hoped that, in the fleeting space between portals, she would be able to do some bit of good. She was afraid that Aasarak would have some immunity to many of her spells, and even have the ability to absorb them, or possibly deflect them back at the group. She knew she would have to take a risk, but hoped that any peril to her companions would remain minimal.

As Adrianna finished chanting the words to her spell, she saw Aasarak suddenly recoil. He stumbled backwards, and she knew that his spell had miscast. She couldn't see his face, hidden as it was within the depths of his black hood, but she could only imagine his anger. She knew what had happened... Triath had used his psionic powers.

Sorn rushed over to the glowing cage that surrounded Amethyst. He wasn't one who usually prayed, but for her, he had done it. He had supplicated himself to the gods to plead for her life, and now that he saw her there, hale and whole, he felt revitalized. Out of the corner of his eye he saw Armond engage the death-knight that stepped out of the shadows, and he wished the bladesinger well. Once reaching the cage, Sorn examined the lock. From within, Amethyst waited patiently with eyes

bright with the prospect of freedom. He had even brought a dagger for her, optimistic about finding her alive. He passed her the weapon through the bars of the cage. She accepted it silently and then watched him work.

It was an enchanted lock. Sorn quickly surmised that nothing about the cage, itself, was magical. It was the lock that caused the bars to glow, and probably made them resistant to any type of ordinary or arcane tampering. He began to work on the lock. It was complex, but he was skilled... very skilled. It had taken him years to gain the proficiency to remove the traps from chests, doors, locks, and various other objects. It had taken him even longer to acquire the aptitude to remove magical traps from such items, and then even longer to unlock them. It was the Talent that no one knew about. Just as Armond used his Talent to infuse magic into his weapons, Sorn used his own gift to imbue such arcane capacity to the lockpicks and other devices used in his craft.

However, Amethyst was perceptive. She had suspected before, and now those suspicions were verified. She watched in awe as Sorn deftly removed the lock. The bars ceased to glow, and became normal lackluster steel. She put her hand on Sorn's shoulder as she stepped out from within the cage, and then whispered into his ear. "He has something that is of value to him. I am going to lift it."

Sorn nodded his agreement upon hearing the conviction in her voice. He could sense it was something important. "I will be right behind you."

From her new vantage point, Adrianna watched as Aasarak recoiled from another of Triath's attacks. Just like the last time, the psionicist had waited until the sorcerer was halfway through a spell. It was disrupted when the *Mindblast* hit him, and this time, Aasarak screamed in rage. In her mind's eye, she could still see what was happening over the Plain of Antipithanee. While the dragons recovered from the use of their breath weapons, they fought the army on land. She hadn't realized the amount of time that needed to pass before they could access their flames again, and she was concerned about the proximity that her dragons had to utilize in order to fight the army. Through their link, she reminded Xebrinarth that they had to either obliterate or dismember the enemy lest they rise to fight against them again.

Adrianna stood several foot lengths from the location in which she had begun. She saw the cavern from a new angle, saw Armond as he fought the death-knight, and Sorn as he freed Amethyst of her prison. The girl blended into the shadows, and Sorn followed. Gods only knew what they had in mind to do. Adrianna watched Dartanyen and Anya shoot at Aasarak with their enchanted arrows, only to see them fall away from the sorcerer before they could hit.

Aasarak quickly recovered from Triath's attack. Fortunately, the miscast spells hadn't spun out of control, but simply fizzled away once the caster's concentration was broken. Again, Aasarak began an incantation, but Adrianna suddenly felt herself subject to her own spell and encompassed by a portal. When she reemerged from it, she found herself on the other side of the cavern. She was behind Aasarak, a rather strategic place to be. She had rather hoped she would be ready for something such as this, but didn't know that the randomized portals would bring her into such a position so soon. She hadn't enough time to prepare herself for a rear attack, but she began to make the effort anyway.

Just as Adrianna was about to start her incantation, she stopped. At her left, she spied a ledge upon which sat a variety of artifacts, many that were of the arcane variety. There was one to which she felt strangely drawn. It was a crystal... a plain, unadorned crystal. She picked it up and held it between her thumb and forefinger. Nothing happened. She didn't feel even the slightest twinge of magic. She went ahead and placed the crystal in her pouch. It was pretty, and she felt drawn to it. It seemed to feel at home there within the pouch, and she patted it as she returned her focus to the battle.

It was then Adrianna noticed Amethyst slowly sneaking up behind Aasarak, and realized it was a good thing that she hadn't cast a spell. The girl would definitely have been caught in it. Adrianna also saw Naemmious as he rushed towards the dark sorcerer, his mace arcing through the air above him. The rest of the group followed suit, bringing the fight closer to the enemy. With some ability he possessed deep within, Aasarak managed to block his mind to Triath's next psionic attack. As such, the sorcerer was finally able to cast his spell, and Adrianna watched as the Deathmaster lifted his arm and pointed two of his fingers in the direction of the Wildrunners. In horror, she saw the minor disturbance the magic made, warping the air as it swept towards the group, saw it train upon Naemmious. The big man stopped midstride as it hit him forcefully in the chest.

*Oh gods...*

The half-oroc fell heavily to the ground. Tianna dropped to his side as the rest of the group continued to rush the sorcerer. Adrianna felt the portal encompass her yet again, and when she reemerged, she found herself near the cage in which Amethyst had been held. Shaking her head, she quickly overcame her mild disorientation, wishing that she had thought to practice this spell more often whilst she was at Tallachienan's citadel.

Amethyst was surprised with the ease in which she lifted the puzzle

175

artifact from the sorcerer. She attacked him from behind, and when he reached around to pull her off his back, she put her hand into his robes. He didn't even feel it. With supernatural strength, he threw her away from him. She flew by Triath and Sirion as they continued to lead the rest of the group towards the enemy. She landed heavily on the ground, the wind knocked out of her. Still, she at least had enough presence of mind to keep the puzzle hidden. As she recovered from her landing, she drew the artifact out from beneath her.

It was elaborate in its décor, intricate in all of its detail. At first glance, it appeared to made of bone. However, on closer inspection, it was clearly made of that and a variety of other metals she was familiar with, and mayhap a few more she wasn't. Amethyst scooted across the floor until she reached the wall near the entrance of the chamber. There she began to work the puzzle. With hands bloodied by her fall, Amethyst manipulated the artifact this way and that. She was quick to recognize that it was a thing meant for sorcerers. No matter how well she manipulated the thing, without the incantations and components that accompanied it, she couldn't access the secrets. Yet, that realization didn't deter her. She blocked out the battle that waged just a few farlo beyond, concentrating all her efforts on the construct in her hands.

Adrianna felt herself *Blinking* to yet another region of the chamber. This time, she was behind the group. Before her, Tianna tried to resuscitate Naemmious to no avail. He was dead, and beyond her ability to repair. On one side, she saw Sirion attack Aasarak with his swords, and on the other, Triath and Anya struck at him with theirs. With merely a blocking hand all were deflected. At her left, she saw Dartanyen shoot his arrows at the death-knight that Armond fought. Both arrows embedded themselves within the areas uncovered by platemail. However, just as Dartanyen saw his arrows strike their mark, he was dropping his bow to draw his sword. He rushed by Adrianna on his way to Aasarak, hoping that he could aid in the fight.

Adrianna cast her spell, a simple *Flamesphere*. As she released it, she hoped that he skill level had made the spell more powerful than ever. However, just as it was about to reach Aasarak, it fell away. Adrianna cursed. She had thought that this might happen, but felt compelled to give it a try anyway. At least it had not been deflected and used against herself and her companions.

As the next portal took her, Adrianna saw the destruction of Aasarak's army. The dragons had begun another pass, and the fire seemed to be having a rather devastating affect on the wraiths. The Azmathous were becoming desperate, fighting the dragons with all the power at their disposal. As Adrianna reappeared in a place to the right of Aasarak, she saw that he was reacting to the destruction. His hood had fallen away from his face to reveal a countenance that was ravaged by evil and corruption. He had once been human, and that fact didn't surprise Adrianna as much as the realization that he might have once been a druid. She could see a mark on his face that attested to that fact. It was one Father Dremathian said that the druids on the eastern side of the continent gave to those who achieved the highest ranks.

Aasarak was divided. He knew his army was being attacked and that much destruction was taking place. He was not wholly focused on the battle before him. Adrianna would have liked to believe that made him vulnerable, but when he unleashed his next spell, she knew that it was not the case. Most of the group flew backwards with the power of the *Concussive Force*. Anya and Triath took the brunt of the spell; Dartanyen was just behind them. Not too much farther away, Tianna had still been working over Naemmious, desperately praying to her goddess. She too, was caught up in the power of the spell, and when the group slammed into the far wall of the cavern, she was the first to hit. Sirion and Sorn were the only ones who remained standing. Sirion's blades were crossed before him, and Sorn stood just behind the ranger. Stalker had deflected the spell, and it backlashed against the sorcerer. Yet, only a portion of the spell's energy had been deflected, not enough to send Aasarak very far. He quickly rose from the floor, his eyes only briefly glancing at the two men before searching out Adrianna.

Amethyst worked the puzzle as fast as her hands could move. They could barely keep up with her mind as it unraveled the secret that had begun to unfold. The answer wasn't in the runes, or in the patterns, but it was in the mechanism deep within. By holding the artifact lightly within her fingertips, she could feel that mechanism as she manipulated it, and if she really concentrated, she imagined that she could hear the little clicks as things began to snap into place. If she could balance the tiny springs and levers just right...

Within moments it was done. Complete, the magic inherent within the mechanism began to emerge. From the palm of her hand, Amethyst watched in awe as the artifact began to emit a bright light. She stood from her place next to the cavern wall, the wind that began to gust around the chamber blowing her short brown hair around her face. Then, she could hear nothing but the sound of the wind. She could feel the power of the artifact begin to sweep over and then into her, plunging deep into the core of her being. It was raw and vast, something that she could never possibly have fathomed.

Sorn ran towards Amethyst as though in slow motion. It seemed that time had stopped for that one moment as Amethyst held the Azmathion within the palm of her small hand. "No!" he heard himself scream. "Amethyst, no!"

The glow of the Azmathion swept over her, shrouding her body within a luminous haze. Her eyes were affixed onto the object in her hand, seemingly unaware of the danger she faced. But Sorn knew. Every Talent in the cavern knew what was about to happen. They could feel the shift of energy in the air around them. It gravitated towards the young girl. Sorn had felt a shift like this only once before... when the original Wildrunners sent the daemon Tharizdune back to the Hells, and Sirion was swept away within a magical vortex. But this time the energy was so concentrated, one could almost choke on it.

Sorn heard himself cry out one last time–

Then it happened. The energy rushed into Amethyst, filling her to capacity. She glowed so brightly that he had to shield his eyes. Still, he kept running, hoping that he would reach her in time so as to knock the Azmathion from her hand. But when he was able to open his eyes again, Amethyst was gone, and the energy was still. All that remained was a pile of dust. On top of it sat the Azmathion.

Adrianna watched as Aasarak tore at his robes, desperately seeking the Azmathion that had once resided within. Sirion had stepped back from him, and Sorn was running towards Amethyst. Arcane energies had coalesced and now swept towards the girl. Glancing over at her, Adrianna could see the glow that had begun to suffuse Amethyst. Great concern flooded Adria, but she dared not keep her eyes off of Aasarak for long. Looking back at him, she saw that something had begun to happen to the dark sorcerer. A strange mist surrounded him and was beginning to pull away. It had formed a path, *and it led directly to Amethyst.*

Adrianna began to make towards Sirion and Aasarak. Sirion was much too close, and she feared that something could backlash against him. The mist continued to pull away from the sorcerer, and she could see that he was struggling against it. Suddenly, there was a mild compressive force that impacted the air. The mist broke away from Aasarak entirely, and Adrianna heard Sorn cry out in denial. The energies stopped gravitating and became still. Just as Adrianna reached Sirion and began to pull him farther away from Aasarak, the sorcerer screamed in rage. She heard him uttering an incantation, felt the energies in the cavern once more answer to his call. With unbelievable speed, Aasarak cast his spell, and Adrianna roughly pulled Sirion to the ground. The bright missiles of crackly magic swept over them. Adrianna lifted her head just in time to see one of them strike Tianna in her torso. The other hit Anya in the chest. The two women fell next to Triath and Dartanyen, who had not risen since they had been hurled into the cavern wall.

With a heavy heart, Adrianna began to speak the words to her own spell. It would be one similar to the one Aasarak had just cast, although not quite as powerful. Sirion rose from his place on the floor and moved himself in front of Adrianna. She would have just enough space around him to cast her spell. Just as she finished it, Aasarak had completed yet another of his own. He knelt onto the floor and touched it with his hand. Adrianna half expected her missiles to fall away from the sorcerer, just as her *Flamesphere* had before. However, just as the rocky cavern floor began to *Transmute* to mud, each one of the missiles hit their target, one right after the other.

Aasarak rocked back from the force of the *Magic Missiles*. From the other side of the cavern, Adrianna heard a loud string of curses. It sounded like Armond, and when she took the chance to glance around, she saw that he was trapped within the wide muddy swath that now encompassed a large portion of that side of the cavern. She quickly turned back to Aasarak. She felt weakened and knew that she had cast the last of her spells. She wouldn't have the energy for another.

Aasarak slowly advanced towards her and Sirion. The sorcerer seemed different somehow, not quite what he had been when they first entered the cavern. Lying on the floor in the distance, Adrianna saw the Azmathion that Amethyst had once held in her hands, instinctively knew what its power had done to her. Everything abruptly clicked together in her mind and she realized what happed to Aasarak, why he now seemed so vulnerable.

He was bereft of the Azmathion's power.

The mist that Adrianna had seen... it was the power that the artifact had once bestowed upon Aasarak leaving him to go to another host. That host had been Amethyst. She had been unable to house power of that magnitude, and didn't possess any Talent. As she became consumed by the awesome power of the Azmathion, she probably didn't even know what was happening to her until it actually happened. Truth be told, she probably didn't realize it even then.

Adrianna steeled herself as Aasarak prepared to cast another spell and Sirion moved so as to completely block her. As Aasarak let loose his spell, Sirion raised his swords before him. In a shower of sparks, the spell deflected off of the blades and raced back towards the sorcerer. Contorting his face into a rictus of rage, Aasarak screamed as the electrical energy struck, but undeterred, he immediately advanced upon

Adrianna and Sirion once more. Wisps of smoke rose from his black robes, but with inhuman speed he was upon them. Before they could even comprehend his immediate proximity, the sorcerer placed a hand on Sirion's shoulder.

Adrianna fell back as Sirion cried out in agony. She stumbled and fell to the floor, the uneven surface cutting into one of her palms. Aasarak stepped past a fallen Sirion towards her, malicious glee reflecting in his dark, soulless eyes. Adrianna reached across herself and grasped the hilt of her sword. The wound on her hand burned as it came into contact with the hilt, but she didn't even flinch as she began to draw the blade free of its scabbard.

Aasarak loomed above her. He was larger than life, blocking out the glow cast by the fires in the wall sconces. "You have done well, my dear... much better than the last Cycles. It has been a pleasure defeating you once again, and I look forward to our meeting in the sixth."

Heart pounding against her ribs, Adrianna completely freed the blade of its sheath, clenched her jaw in determination, and embedded the sword in the dark robes at Aasarak's belly. She watched as the sorcerer's eyes widened with incredulity. She felt the power within the blade, the magic to which Sirion had alluded the night before. She felt it pour from the weapon and into her enemy, watched as it began to destroy him right before her eyes. Around the hilt, her hand throbbed with waves of pain that began to shoot down her arm. As the pain became greater, she gave an agonized cry. She tried to remove her hand, but it was fixed to the hilt, blood from the wound on her palm dripping onto the beige fabric of her trousers.

Through her pain, Adrianna watched as Aasarak withered away into nothing but a blackened skeleton and crumbled to the ground. The sword continued to glow for only a moment longer before the light faded away. Adrianna dropped the blade, brought her hand to her chest, and then turned to Sirion. An invisible hand squeezed her heart painfully until she turned him over and put her face close to his mouth. She sighed with relief when she felt him breathing. She then looked around her, saw her companions lying on the floor of the cavern and Armond kneeling at the edge of the muddy river that encompassed the entire left side of the chamber. With tears in her eyes, she regarded the skeleton of one of the most wicked sorcerers who had ever lived and kicked it. The bones scattered about on the floor like the bones cast in a game of Shockwave. When Adrianna went to rise, she felt the answering pain in her hand. She tried to tear away some of the fabric of her tunic, but when she found that she wasn't strong enough to even do that, she merely pressed the deep laceration into her thigh. She slumped down next to Sirion and opened her mind to Xebrinarth.

Adrianna called for her Bondmate so that he could come and carry her home.

# PART TWO

## PROLOGUE

T ime seemed to stand still as the Historian appeared at his next destination. The moment he arrived he knew where he was in spite of the pitch darkness that pervaded, the mystical feeling about the place settling deep into his weary bones. He mumbled a string of words beneath his breath, and a wide cavern was thrust into relief. From the ceiling, an explosion of tangled roots wove into and out of the walls. Onto these, thick pillar candles were set, weeping wax in white waterfalls and stoic stalagmites. A tiny flame now burned in the center of each candle, flickering brightly. In the middle of the chamber, a cluster of roots entwined into a thick column to descend into a peaceful pool of water.

With giddy excitement, the Historian walked up to the pool. He had been torn away from the final moments after Aasark's final battle to this place for a reason. Finally, after over five thousand years, the Cycling of Shandahar was over, and the world was at the dawn of a new era.

The Historian knelt before the pool and found himself looking down into a perfect mirror. Cold radiated from it in waves, and within, he saw an image of himself, seeing him, seeing himself, into infinity. Over the centuries, legends had been written about this pool, a pool that had blossomed into existence the moment that the High God, Odion, had placed his wretched curse upon Shandahar. The holiest of priests had been the first to find it, called to its hidden location deep within the bowels of the world beneath the western edge of the Ratik Mountains, and they named it "The Memory of the World".

As ancient and powerful as the Historian was, he still felt the pull to touch the surface. For most people, once the surface was touched, the pool would show them everything they had ever been or would ever be. For him, it would show him the life of any person in the world he wished to see, in any of the five Cycles they had gone through. It would also show him the present, show him events they were happening around the world all at the same time. No other being, mortal or no, could withstand such a deluge; only his mind could contain it all. That was why he was the Historian.

Suddenly, the world bucked and heaved. The waters of the pool shuddered, disrupting the image of himself. The Historian just crouched there, hands splayed upon the rock floor, as the quake continued. Debris rained down, accompanied by the crash of stalactites as they fell from their moorings along the ceiling. With a shanking finger, he reached out to touch the rippling waters, opening his mind so that it might show him what it chose...

With a birdseye view, The Historian found himself looking down at an immense plain. What had once been a vast, verdant grassland, was now a barren waste teeming with the living dead. The Plain of Antipithanee was not the scorched place he had recently left behind. Rather, it was a scene from a time before the dragons came. It was the place where Aasarak had found the bulk of his army, the poor souls who had lost their lives in the epic battle that had once been fought there. He watched as tens of thousands of the undead formed ranks, then fractured into three factions. The first went northeast into the Misemba Hills, the second northwest into Cortubro, and the third south towards the Sheldomar Forest. It was a familiar view, one had had observed near the end of this Cycle and the Cycles that had come before.

This Cycle, it was the westward-bound faction that would never reach its destination. Adrianna's dragons would intercept it and lay it to waste before it could reach the river and cross it into the realm of Elvandahar.

But this wasn't the entirety of Aasarak's army. There were other factions scattered about the continent, originating at the scene of one site or another. Many of them were old battlefields, others graveyards. And after razing the villages and towns the undead encountered, Aasarak would come, and he would raise the newly dead and add them to his ranks. Only now, without the Deathmaster to control them, the living dead wantered aimlessly across the plains, within the forests, and through the mountains. The months and years that lay ahead would be terribly dangerous for anyone wishing to travel anywhere in Ansalar.

This scene was Aasarak's army at its apex. In the Cycles before this one, it contiued to grow, to ultimately become the scourge that destroyed Shandahar. In this Cycle, this was it. The Deathmaster was dead, and over time, the remnants of his army would finally be eradicated.

Time sped up for a few moments, and the next scene the Historian saw was the Wildrunners. His mind reeled in shock, for he got the distinct impression that he was seeing the future. It wasn't an ability he'd had before, and he could only speculate why it was manifesting now. He imagined maybe it was because the world had never really had a future to envision before. The group was no longer languishing in the mountain cavern where he had just left them. Rather, they were arriving in the silver glen of Krathil-lon. The druids had been ready for them. Two shrouded figures were being released from the clawed embrace of silver and gold dragons, and three wounded lifted from their backs. Adrianna dismounted her dragon, watched the proceedings for a moment, and then turned back to her Bondmate. The Historian couldn't hear what was being spoken between them, but imagined what it must have been when she took a harness from her pack and began to settle it over Xebrinarth's shoulders.

"Adria, what are you doing?" Sirion's tone shifted from concern to alarm. "You aren't going back out there?"

"I must. My dragons are waiting for me."

Sirion's arms lifted from his sides. "Need you where?"

"Aasarak's army." Adrianna paused in her task to look him in the eye. "They need leadership. They need me to be there to keep the course."

Sirion's expression was pained for a moment before it shifted to resolve. "Then I am coming with you."

Adrianna turned back to the harness. "Don't be silly. You have been injured."

Sirion's jaw clenched almost imperceptibly. "The Deathmaster's spell could only touch me so deep. Your spell kept me safe from him, Shendori."

Adrianna seemed to flinch from his use of the term of endearment. "You are needed here. Your losses..."

"...are nothing compared to what I would suffer if I lost you!" He struggled to rein in his emotions before continuing. "I am your protector, Adrianna. Let me do my job."

She stiffened and stopped again, finally turning to regard him intently. "Alright, you can come with me." She then began to remove the harness from Xebrinarth and moved to the closest dragon, Mordrexith. The dragon lowered himself to the ground as she approached and allowed her to situate the harness over his shoulders the way she had begun to do with her Bondmate.

"Why aren't we riding Xebrinarth? Has he been wounded?"

"No, he's fine. But I will be riding him alone. It is too much for a dragon to carry two riders into battle, so you will be riding Mordrexith."

Sirion's briows creased into a frown. He stood there for a moment, watching Adrianna afix the complicated ropes of the harness onto the other dragon. Once realizing what it was, his frown deepened. "Don't you need that to ride Xebrinarth?"

"Not as much as you will to ride Mordrex."

"No, I will not have you sacrifice your safety. I will ride..."

"NO!" Adrianna's voice reverberated throughout the clearing. All who were in proximilty stopped their activity for a moment to see what was happening. "If you want to come with me, *Protector*, you will do it under my terms. Do you understand?"

Sirion stood there for a moment, his jaw ticking with the effort of keeping in clenched. "I understand, Warrior of Destiny."

Suddenly, it felt as though a weight was lifted from Adrianna's shoulders. She released all her tension with her next exhale, and regarded Sirion from weary eyes. "Thank you. It will be good to have you by my side."

Sirion's stance instantly relaxed and he reached out to pull her close. "I wouldn't want to be anywhere else."

Several moments passed before they finally stepped apart. "Come, let me get you into this harness."

Adrianna showed Sirion how to board the dragon's back, and once there, she strapped him into place with the complex series of loops and buckles that Xebrianrth had devised in order to keep her safe whilst in flight. Father Dremathian appraoched as she was finishing and gave her a hearty embrace. He uttered not a word, simply offered her his strength and support. She handed Sirion his travel pack, then shouldered hers and went back to Xebrinarth.

The two dragons crouched low, and when they were ready, they vaulted into the air...

Time sped up for few more moments before the Historian found himself soaring with a small fleet of dragons. Below was a faction of Aasarak's army. They had entered the Misemba Hills, making an aerial strike a bit more difficult, so some of the dragons settled around them where they could, and attacked.

High above, Adrianna circled over the melee, instructing the other dragons on how and where to assail the enemy. The Degethozak sprayed the foe with the flesh and bone consuming acid they spouted from their sharp-toothed maws, and the Rezwithrys their lightning strikes. Both destroyed the undead as well as any flame the Helzethryn could produce. Leading the adversarial bands were troupes of Azmathous. Despite the demise of the Deathmster, they had remained with their contingents. These foes proved to tbe the most difficult.

Despite the lack of harness, Adrianna kept her seat on Xebrinarth well. But as the spells from the ground intensified in frequency, that became more and more difficult. It hadn't long before the Azmathous recognized who was the dragon's leader, and began firing their most powerful spells in her direction. Xebrinarth had taken quite a bit of damage, his golden hide riddled with scorch marks and streaming rivulets of blood.

And then his right wing became paralyzed.

Xebrianrth began to plummet. The paralyzed wing had retracted close to the body, but as the other one attempted to slow their fall, they began to spiral. Adrianna clung to her Bondmate, her body pressed as close to his back as possible, and closed her eyes tightly shut.

<Zahara!> Her Bondmates's voice ringing through her mind opened her eyes. <You must jump from my back! Hurry!>

She looked arround her, saw Mordrexith flying just below them.

<Do not tarry! Go now!>

Despite her unwillingnesss to leave her Bondmate to an uncertain fate, she did as he bid. She positioned her feet on his back, and with all the strength she had in her legs, vaulted from his back.

For a moment she was floating, but only a moment.

Then she was falling again, falling without anything to hold onto anymore. She saw the ground far below, getting cloer, closer closer...

Suddenly there was a shadow above, followed by the sensation of sharp claws closing around her. She clutched at the claws as Mordrexith swept up and away, leaving the treacherous ground below her. She saw Xebrinarth lying on the ground, his golden body lying there so still. Agony ripped throug her and she screamed.

<Zahara! He has not left you!> Mordrxith's voice was in her mind, a deep voice that gave her comfort even in the face of such heartbreak. <Look deep within your soul and you will find him there still. He is simply unconscious!>

Adrianna did as her friend bid, and just like he said, her Bondmate's pulse was still there, his life force strong and sure. Her eyes remained riveted upon him as the undead began to mobilize towards him, slowly closing the distance.

<Mordrex!>

<I see, Sister. We are going down.>

The Historian watched as the dragon landed amid a sea of the undead beside his fallen companion. Sirion clambered down from the dragon's back and joined Adrianna in a fray that looked like it would never end. Their only reprieve was the gouts of flame that Mordrex breathed on the foe, stopping them only long enough for the faelin to get their bearings before they were overwhewlmed once more.

As the bodies piled up around them, the undead moved to surround her and Sirion. His blades were a flurry of motion, hacking and slashing into the mindless horde. There was no blood when he struck, and the enemy didn't stop. Even without arms, even without legs, they would continue, not stopping unless their heads were removed from their shoulders. Adrianna cast spell after spell, and realizing that fre was the best weapon, used all she had in her arsenal in order to keep them at bay.

All except one. That one she saved, along with the strength she would need to use it when the time arose. *Xebrin, please wake up. Please.*

But the enemy kept coming, and there was nowhere to retreat, the dragons behind them keeping them locked into place. It wasn't long before Sirion fell. In truth, he had lasted longer than she thought he might, his warrior will far exceeding any expectation, any hope, any dream she may have ever had.

So, it was natural for her to take a new stance. She planted one foot on eaither side of Sirion's hips, standing over him to keep him safe with her body as long as she could hold. In her mind, she could sense a struggle within Mordrexith⬚ his desire to see her to safety. It was a thing Xebrinarth would expect from his best friend. When Sirion fell, the struggle increased, Mordrex's desire to fight for his friend warring with the desire to make certain his friend's Bondmate lived to see another day.

Standing over the body of her beloved, Adrianna cast the spell she'd been saving. An invisible force projected outward in a half-circle, striking all who attacked. The enemy flew back, falling into a heap several farlo away.

It was then Xebrinarth awakened.

Adrianna could feel it in her mind, Xebrin's consciousness once more filling hers. She slumped to one knee, the power she had used in that spell alone making her feel dizzy. <Sister, we must retreat now!> said Mordrex.

Adrianna dug within for any energetic resources she might have left, sluggishly looping one of Sirion's arms around her shoulders to try and lift him from the ground. But Mordrex was already there, carefully lifting Sirion with his massive claws instead. <Hurry, get on my back!>

But the enemy was moving too quick. They reached her a moment later, one slicing its sword into her unprotected side.

<Zahara!>

Adrianna felt the burn as she fell, landing among the burned and decapitated enemy force that now surrounded her. Her teeth chattered as she took her hands away from her side to see them covered in blood. A gout of flame rushed past overhead, charring the enemy where they stood, swiftly replaced by the looming shadow of her Bondmate. He picked her up from the ground, his talons closing carefully around her body. <No! Sirion!>

<Worry not Zahara. He is safe with Mordrexith.>

Only after hearing his words did she slip into unconsciousness.

The Historian rose from beside the pool and swiftly made his way out of the cavern. He suddenly knew how the druids knew about the arrival of the Wildrunners, and he had some travel time ahead of him.

# WHEN TIMES COLLIDE

<T allachienan, we have a visitor and he doesn't look very happy.>

The sorcerer looked up from the book he was reading and frowned. It wasn't often he received a visit from the man, and when he did, Charlemagne was the epitome of friendliness. For him to be here now, and upset enough for Pylar to take note of it, meant that something was seriously amiss.

<Bring him to me.>

Pylar gave a mental nod. <We are already on our way.>

Tallachienan drummed his fingertips on the arm of the sofa. *Hells, what could it possibly be?* Just two days ago the Curse of Odion had finally been broken. With the Wildrunners' defeat of Aasarak, the world had been freed from the centuries of incarceration it had endured with the Cycling. Unfortunately, a new threat had emerged.

The Pact of Bakharas had also been broken.

Tallachienan nodded to himself. That must be it, the reason for Charlemagne's visit. There would be many upset by the unexpected event. With the dragons' attack on Aasarak's undead army, they had irrevocably changed the history of the world. Just as Trebexal had feared, the ancient pact between dragon and daemonkind was now rendered null and void. With the breaking of the Curse, and then the Pact, the world was suffering a series of cataclysmic events, heralded by quakes, volcanic eruptions, massive storms, and other natural disasters. Adrianna and the remaining Wildrunners had taken refuge in the mountain glen of Krathillon. There they would be safe from the natural disasters currently taking place. Of course, the druids who lived there were well aware of what was happening.

Meanwhile, the world was once more open to the insurgence of dragon and daemonkind. The ages old power struggle between the two races would resume upon the battlefield of Shandahar. Unfortunately, humans, faelin, halfen, and orocs would be caught in the middle. It was a frightening time in the history of the world, but Tallachienan couldn't help being selfish. He felt it was good that things were changing in the world again. For far too long Shandahar had been made to stagnate.

Tallachienan rose as Pylar opened the doors wide to admit Charlemagne. Choler surrounded him like a cloak, and it blazed in his blue eyes. He strode purposefully across the chamber towards Tallachienan, and spoke before Tallachienan could articulate a greeting.

"Tallachienan, we have a very big problem."

Tallachienan nodded. "Yes, I agree that the dissolution of the Pact of Bakharas does pose quite a dilemma. I have been ruminating over it quite a bit myself."

Charlemagne stopped half a farlo from Tallachienan, a frown creasing his brow. He shook his head. "I am not referring to the damned Pact of Bakharas! I am talking about my own personal, hideous mess that I am forced to deal with! What in all Nine Hells were you doing while your apprentice was wreaking havoc in my timeline!"

Tallachienan raised his hands in supplication. "Charlemagne, I understand why you are so upset, but let me explain..."

Charlemagne slapped his hands against the sides of his legs. "Are you serious? There *is* no explaining! There is no explaining because it doesn't matter! It is only a matter of time before your apprentice goes completely insane!"

Tallachienan felt his heart lurch in his chest. He closed the remaining distance between them and planted his face right in front of Charlemagne's. "What are you talking about?" he growled.

Charlemagne shook his head. "No! You aren't the one asking the questions here! I am! And I will ask again, what the Hells..."

Tallachienan interrupted with a shout. "The citadel was under attack! I didn't know Adrianna was gone until after the battle was over... until Death no longer loomed over me!"

Charlemagne was instantly taken aback. Silence reigned for a few moments. With the wind taken out of his sails, Charlemagne then stepped back a couple of paces. "I didn't know. I'm sorry."

Tallachienan remained silent as Charlemagne shared the details of what was happening, something very serious in order for him to say what he did about Adrianna. The god finally gave a deep sigh of frustration. "All I know is that if I had never done you that crazy favor of allowing you to go back in time to train your apprentice, this would never have happened. Now I am stuck with an, albeit small, population of people who remember Adrianna from, what was it? Fifty years ago?"

Tallachienan shook his head. "I can understand why you would perceive this as a mess in need of cleaning up, but why would it cause Adrianna to go insane?"

Charlemagne narrowed his eyes. "This is more than a mess. This is a catastrophe. Not only was Adrianna very memorable to a lot of people, she changed history while she was in the past. The Adrianna we know and love so much remembers only the 'old' history she experienced before coming to live with you here in your citadel. However, Adrianna was born in the 'new' history that was created, an Adrianna who has no recollection of ever having met these people before. That is because she didn't. It was *our* Adrianna who met those people.

"The realization that something was wrong started when you sent Adrianna forward into the time in which she actually belongs. However, with the pall generated by the Curse of Odion hindering my vision, I wasn't able to clearly see what had happened to cause the vast disturbance I was sensing in the linearity of my timeline. It wasn't until after the Curse was broken that the pall lifted and I was able to see exactly what had happened. The disturbance is growing every day that passes. It not only affects Adrianna, but every single person with whom she came into contact.

"Starting from the moment someone first remembered Adrianna from the past, the disturbance begins. From that point, history begins to waver. The people affected have no solid memory of what took place. Right now, as we speak, Adrianna's mind is trying to cope with the inconsistencies, just like everyone else's. It won't take long for it to buckle."

The grim reality of what was happening swept over Tallachienan like a tidal wave. He sat back down on the sofa behind him and put his head in his hands. He remained that way for several moments before finally looking back up at Charlemagne. "Is there nothing we can do?"

Charlemagne nodded. "I have been thinking about this for the past two days and nights since the Curse was broken. We can't fix the situation to make everything the way it was before she changed history because it would cause too much disturbance in the timeline before our goal would be accomplished. It would have consequences about which even I am unsure. The best thing to do would be to cast a spell through time, a spell that would affect the people with whom Adrianna came into contact, causing them to forget that they had ever met her. So then, when she goes to Elvandahar for the first time, no one will remember her, and thus not cause the initial disturbance to the timeline."

Tallachienan nodded. "That sounds good. I will start on something right away."

Charlemagne frowned. "There is just one thing for which I have yet to find a solution."

Tallachienan immediately sensed the solemnity emanating from Charlemagne, and he had a sense of foreboding. "What is it?"

"Adrianna will not be one of those affected by the spell. She has nothing to remember, so she has nothing to forget. At the same time, 'our' Adrianna will remember everything. I am not saying there are two Adrianna's out there right now, just a timeline that is no longer linear. Adrianna exists in two histories right now, two histories that we need to merge as best we can so that time may continue unhindered from here on out. In short, when the histories become merged, so will Adrianna's memories. My fear is that her mortal mind will not be strong enough to endure the merge."

Tallachienan swept a hand over his face. He had worked so hard not to lose her. And now here he was, in the new future she and her companions had just made for the world, faced with that very same possibility. Tallachienan's voice was strained as he asked the same question he had posed several moments before. "What can we do?"

This time Charlemagne sadly shook his head. "I don't know."

Tallachienan struggled to swallow past the lump that had lodged itself in his throat. This couldn't be happening, not now, not after they had fought for so long... Tallachienan wracked his mind for something, *anything*, that could save Adrianna.

Then he had it.

"What if I told you she was one of us? Descended from the ancient bloodlines?"

Charlemagne's gaze suddenly became piercing. "What?"

Tallachienan nodded. "I did the research. She is descended from the line of Ilistia."

Charlemagne nodded thoughtfully, but a moment later was regarding him intently. "Who is her sire?"

Tallachienan couldn't hold back his frown. "The very same who is my own."

Charlemagne raised his eyebrows in surprise. "Ilistia and Odion? Really?" He hesitated for the briefest of moments before continuing. "Yes, there is definitely a chance for her! The mind of a simple mortal would be too weak to withstand the merge, but in spite of the dilution, her lineage may save her."

Tallachienan smiled as Charlemagne reveled in his newfound information. He considered telling his friend how Adrianna had the power to withstand his *Persuasion*, but then thought against it. Charlemagne really didn't need to know about that. But then he had a thought. "How will we aid Adrianna during the merging of the two histories?"

Charlemagne became thoughtful. Then, "Mayhap nothing. Either her mind will endure it, or it will not."

"There is nothing anyone can do to ease the merge? Or perhaps to warn her of the mental hardship she will endure?"

Charlemagne gave a resigned sigh. "That is right. I tend to forget how attached to her you are."

Tallachienan shook his head. "You seem to forget that we will be conducting two different actions. The first will be a spell that we will cast through time to make those involved forget Adrianna. The second will involve Adrianna as she endures the merge. This has less to do with attachment than the fact I wish to preserve the mentality of someone who could be of great import one day. The girl has awesome Talent."

Charlemagne regarded him intently. Then he nodded. "Since you feel so strongly, we will both go to her."

Tallachienan nodded his agreement. "When do you want to get started?"

Charlemagne pursed his lips thoughtfully. "As soon as possible. There is no time to waste."

Tallachienan nodded and rose from the sofa. "Let us proceed to my laboratory."

## 4 Jicaren CY594

For the third time, Adrianna stopped to put a hand to her pounding skull. The headaches were only getting worse, and her increasing use of talsam powder was becoming a bit disturbing. After another moment or two she resumed her slow walk through the silver forest of Krathil-lon. The gentle wind brushed the unbound hair from off of her shoulders, and when she lifted her face into it, she could smell the barest hint of warm weather to come. She felt little joy, her thoughts dampened by feelings of loss and despair. Within the apoptos, one of her companions lay near death. Two others had been brought back to Krathil-lon draped in shrouds, and two more had been too wounded to even lift themselves from the battleground. Only Adrianna, Sirion, Sorn, and Armond were able to limp out of Aasarak's lair under their own propulsion.

The dragons had arrived just in time to get the group out of the mountain before the quakes brought it down around them. Soon after Aasarak's demise, a great compression had rocked the world, similar to one that was created when Triath used one of his psionic abilities, only a hundred times stronger and more pervasive. It set into motion a series of shakes that shook the mountains all around them. However, Adrianna and Sorn were only two, and they couldn't even begin to pull their comrades out from the lair alone. So they waited. By the time the dragons came, Sirion had roused, and Sorn had been able to pull Armond out of the mire that encased the bladesinger's lower legs and feet.

As the dragons lifted them from the mountainside, parts of it had begun to tumble with the next shake. After, the group rode for hours at a time without stopping, those who were well enough struggling to maintain a hold of their wounded companions. Those who had died in battle had been wrapped in blankets and carried within the clutches of dragon claws. When they stopped, it wasn't for long. Despite the field dressings, the wounded only became more pallid. Adrianna had bid her Bondmate haste despite knowing his exhaustion. She wouldn't see more of her comrades die, refused to believe that Aasarak would take yet another life.

When they had arrived at Krathil-lon, the druids were there. Somehow, they had been made aware of their imminent arrival and were ready with their most accomplished healers. The dead were respectfully set aside until the appropriate time came to attend them. The wounded had been swiftly taken away while the rest of them were treated with herbal teas and replenishing food.

That is, except for Adrianna and Sirion. They had left with the dragons to go back into battle to fight another fragment of Aasarak's army.

The battle had been a brutal one. Once the two of them had returned to Krathil-lon, they were taken to the individual chambers in which they had resided before going to Aasarak's lair and their wounds treated. Even after sleeping most of the ride back to the druid stronghold, Adrianna had been so tired she slept throughout the following night and day, besieged with vague dreams about the past. When she awoke, her skull ached with a ferocity she had never experienced before. Thinking back on the dreams, there was precious little she could remember about them. More disturbing, when she thought back on the past, there were events she could no longer quite recall. She tried rationalizing it to herself... the strain of the most recent set of events to take place in her life was astounding. But she still couldn't help feeling that something was terribly amiss. Once more, the tears came. Unchecked, they fell down the sides of Adrianna's face and she fell to her knees. She was so concerned about herself when there were those who had been lost in the fight.

It was hard to believe that she would never see Naemmious again, hear his funny stories as they sat around the campfire, or look into those gentle eyes. He had more than proven himself to be a faithful friend and a great warrior.

It was equally as difficult to believe that she would never get to see Amethyst again, watch her grow into the woman she had already started to become. Adrianna would never forget what the girl had done for the group, how she had ultimately turned the tide of the battle in their favor.

The third person to meet her demise in their fight was Anya. Out of all of them, Sirion's loss was mayhap the greatest and Adrianna's heart went out to him. Not only had he lost his sister, but he had also lost four other comrades within the past year: Naemmious, Arn, Laura, and Breesa.

Adrianna thought back to the time she first met the Wildrunners. Oh yes, it had been within the first few days she had returned to Sangrilak after her studies in Andahaye. It was also the first time she had met Sirion. Even then, when he had been covered in several days' worth of travel dust, she had recognized the attractiveness of the man. But it hadn't been until after his ordeal in the form of Cortath that she really got the chance to know him. When she and the rest of the group went with him to Elvandahar...

Adrianna cried out and clutched the sides of her head. The pain was excruciating. She sensed Xebrinarth's distress through their link, but she didn't have the capacity to make much response. *Oh gods, what the Hells is wrong with me?* She collapsed onto her side and curled in upon herself. *I can't remember. Why can't I remember?* She closed her eyes and screamed in silence, opening her mouth wide but allowing no sound to issue forth. She didn't want anyone to hear, for her companions didn't need any more of her drama. Just like the Travel Sickness, this would pass. She had only to endure it for a while...

Adrianna lay there for several moments, just breathing. It was strange... she hadn't really forgotten the past, only that it had become so difficult to recall. And when she did manage to bring forth the memories, they seemed somewhat nebulous and interspersed with images she never recalled experiencing. There was a vagueness that pervaded throughout and she wondered if perhaps she was losing her mind.

"Adrianna?"

She hadn't realized anyone was there until she heard his voice. "Adrianna, wake up. Lord Charlemagne and I are here to help you."

In disbelief she blinked her eyes open. Master Tallachienan knelt above her, his hands along both sides of her face. She placed her hands over his. "Tallachienan, what is wrong with me?" She refocused her eyes as another man knelt beside him. Chin-length blond hair hung alongside his face, and his blue eyes regarded her with deep concern.

"Adrianna, you must listen to me," said Charlemagne. "What is happening to you is a result of your journey to Sangrilak and Elvandahar while you were studying Dimensionalist magic in the past. You changed history, and as such, created a disturbance in time. I can help you, but you must endeavor to remember your past while keeping your mind open to the new past that was created when you changed history. Do you understand?"

Adrianna nodded. "I will try, but what about Xebrin?"

The man gave a brief nod. "He might be confused by what he sees in your mind through the link you share. He may also be affected by the turmoil he senses. You should tell him that he should disengage himself as much as possible." He shook his head. "I err on the side of caution because I don't really know what might happen. I have never had a situation such as this arise before." Adrianna opened her mind to her Bondmate, and understanding everything Charlemagne said, Xebrinarth sent her a brief mental caress before blocking his mind from hers.

Charlemagne gave another nod. "Come, let us begin now for we have no time to waste."

Suddenly afraid, Adrianna gripped Tallachienan's hands more tightly. "But what if I can't do it? What if I can't remember?"

Tallachienan leaned forward to place his forehead against hers. "You will remember," he said. "That is one of the reasons why I am here. I will be your strength when you feel you have none left."

Adrianna let the import of his words sink deep. For him to be here like this, offering to stand by her, meant that she was in a dire situation. She swallowed past the sudden lump in her throat while tears streamed down her temples. This was all her fault. If she had never chosen to fall into his well that night, she would not be in this situation now. She knew he was placing himself at risk... anything to do with casting spells through time was risky. "You would do that for me?"

Tallachienan gave her a small smile. "Of course. You are my good friend, are you not?"

She nodded solemnly. "I would like to think so."

"Well, now you *know* so."

Adrianna looked into his lavender eyes for a moment, and then took a deep breath. She had come to know the real man that lay within Tallachienan Chroalthone, and she believed in him. "I am ready now."

The man with blond hair stood overhead, his hands poised in the air over them. He then began the words to his incantation...

Sheridana followed behind as the rest of the group began to make their way out of the portal chamber and into the corridor that led to the outside of the cavern. After almost three weeks spent in Krathil-lon, they finally decided that it was time to return home. It had been just enough time for Tianna to heal from the terrible injuries sustained in their fight. Meanwhile, the world had settled down enough for them to feel safe enough to travel. The quakes had receded, as well as the tornadic storms that had swept across the continent. The druids explained that it was all because the Curse of Odion had finally been broken. For the first time, the world was able to pass into an era it had never experienced before.

Sirion was the first to exit the chamber, followed closely by Dramati. Out of all of them, Sirion had been affected the most by their losses, and his demeanor had changed considerably. He had always been a solemn individual, but Adrianna had been able to draw him out of the shell within which he had always encased himself. However, the shell had come back, along with a seemingly impenetrable wall of despondency. She couldn't really blame him, for not only had he lost many of his companions in the past several moon cycles, but also his sister. His good friend, Tianna, had been terribly wounded in their fight. Then there was Adrianna herself. Sheridana had been made aware of many of the things with which Sirion had to come to terms. Those things would be difficult for any man. For Sirion, with everything else he had on his mind, it might not be possible.

Sheridana swung her gaze to Adrianna. It was easy to see that her sister was also having a difficult time. After arriving in Krathil-lon after Aasarak's defeat, something had happened to her, something Adrianna had yet to explain. Armond had found her lying on the ground quite a distance from the apoptos. She was unresponsive to his voice and touch, and her complexion was terribly pale. He had carried her back, and Father Dremathian was at a loss as to what caused her to remain in the comatose state. Sirion had been beside himself with worry, and Adrianna remained that way for almost two days before awakening. Afterwards, she claimed not to remember what had happened, but Sheri couldn't help feeling somewhat doubtful.

The group walked through the corridor leading to the outside of the cavern. Sheridana remembered when they had been there last. It was before their battle with Aasarak, before Adrianna had returned from her training with Master Tallachienan, before Triath's final dominion over the daemon within him. For her, life had just become more complicated with the realization of her pregnancy. It was what ultimately led Adrianna, Sirion, Triath, and Tianna to act against her.

Of course, Sheri felt betrayed. Hells, who wouldn't? Her comrades had taken away her free will. She knew why they had done it. She supposed she might have done the same if it were Adrianna. *Maybe.* She could rationalize it in her mind all she wanted, but the result was still the same.

Sheri had awakened later that day after the group was long gone to Aasarak's lair. She recalled the confusion that reigned in her mind, and at first had wondered if she was dreaming.

*Sheridana sat up and saw their druid guide sitting before a small fire. Beside her lay Dinim, his body enveloped within a cocoon of furs. She blinked a few times in an effort to normalize her vision. By the time she could see clearly, the druid was watching her intently from brown eyes.*

*She frowned. "Where the Hells am I?"*

*The man's expression was impassive. "We are still in the mountains. It shouldn't be very much longer before we have more griffons to help us back to Krathil-lon."*

*The response was like a splash of cold water. "Wh...what?"*

*The druid simply sat there. She glanced at Dinim and then back at the* druid. *"Where are the others?"*

*"They are on their way to Aasarak's lair."*

*Sheridana shook her head. "No, that can't be. I am supposed to be with them."*

*"You were ill. They were forced to make the choice to proceed without you."*

*Sheri continued to shake her head and deepened her frown. "Do I look sick to you? We have to go back. They need me!"*

*The druid shook his head. "I'm sorry. It is already too late."*

*His words hit her like a sack of rocks. She felt her heart begin to race in her chest. No, this couldn't be. This had to be a dream. And the fool sitting there at the fire didn't exist either. Sheri made to rise from her place, but the moment she stood, she put a hand to her forehead. The pain pounded throughout her skull and made her feel dizzy enough to vomit. She reeled and was about to fall when she felt a pair of arms wrapping themselves about her shoulders and easing her back onto the bedroll.*

*Sheri sat down and shrugged him away from her. If this were really a dream, the pain wouldn't have been so profound. Her mind staggered with the recognition that her situation was indeed a reality. "Who the Hells are you, anyway?"*

*The druid rose from her side and looked stoically down at her. "My name is Markon. I am certain Father Dremathian announced that before we left Krathil-lon."*

*Sheri squeezed her eyes shut, still hoping this wasn't real and that her comrades really hadn't left her behind. The last thing she remembered was arguing with Adrianna about her participation in the upcoming fight. Then Triath was there...*

*It wasn't difficult for Sheri to make the connection.* Triath had done something to her.

*Sheridana looked up at Markon, her eyes certainly reflecting the betrayal she felt. She managed to speak only a few words before her throat closed up with emotion. "What did you people do to me?"*

*Markon frowned and shook his head. "What do you mean?"*

*Sheri struggled to blink tears out of her eyes and she cleared her throat. "I'm not an idiot. I know that the group did something to me. Don't tell me you don't know what I am talking about."*

*Markon expelled a gush of air and placed his hands at his sides. "Honestly, I have no idea what you are talking about. You should try to get some more sleep. Obviously, your illness is making you delirious."*

*Sheri sniffed and looked away from the man standing over her. By the tone of his voice, she could tell he was offended by her accusation. Maybe he didn't know. Maybe it was just Adrianna and Triath who were in on the secret. Or maybe everyone knew except Markon. Oh gods...*

*Saying nothing more, Sheri proceeded to lay back down on the bedroll. She turned on her side with her back to Markon. She sensed him still standing there above her but she didn't look up. He would see the wetness on her face and the terrible hurt reflected in her eyes. She didn't want him to know how little her sister and companions thought of her to do something so heinous as to incapacitate her so that she would appear unable to fight alongside them.*

Sheri brought her attention back to the present. She had spoken only once to Adrianna about what they had done, and it was then she explained that only she, Triath, Tianna, and Sirion knew the truth. As far as the others knew, Sheri had been sick. Adrianna explained that Triath had used his psionic ability in order to render her mind unconscious long enough for them to be long gone before she awoke, as Sheri had suspected.

As the group reached the mouth of the cavern, Sheridana stumbled and caught herself against the wall. She found that she had become quite a bit clumsy as of late. She glanced up to see if anyone noticed and found her gaze meeting Markon's. She gave him a lopsided smile and he returned it with one of his own. In spite of her despondency, and the sometimes-aloof demeanor she had exhibited during the remainder of that journey back to Krathil-lon, he had made every effort to be friendly. Mayhap he'd recognized that there was something wrong that made her that way, or perhaps friendliness was just a part of his personality, but his perseverance won out in the end and they had developed a camaraderie by the time they reached their destination.

For some reason, Markon now accompanied the Wildrunners back to Elvandahar. He claimed it was because he had family there whom he wished to visit. However, she had caught the shuttered glances shared between Markon and Father Dremathian, glances that made Sheri think something more was going on. Dremathian had seemed a bit loath for them to leave when he made allusions to Tianna's weakened health, and he had even approached Adrianna in regards to their leave-taking. Adrianna provided him several reasons, one of which happened to be Fitanni. Another was the fact that Sirion needed to be with his mother so they could mourn together over Anya's loss. Of course, the druid leader could not contest their reasons, so it was with great concern he watched the group step through the portal that would take them away from the sanctuary of Krathil-lon.

Sheri followed the rest of the group out of the cavern and into the surrounding wood. It wasn't the most pleasant of terrain, since they traveled the area where the western edge of the Selmist Forest met the northeastern edge of the Bryton Hills. It was particularly rocky, and trees and other forest scrub could make footing uncertain. However, it wouldn't last long, for within a day of moving due north they would be at the outskirts of the forest. Less than a day longer and they would reach the Denegal River. Once across, they would be in Hinterlean territory. They would have several days of travel through Elvandahar, but at the end of that journey would be the Sherkari Fortress and Fitanni. Gods, how she missed her daughter. Sheri could hardly wait to have the child in her arms again. She had been away for far too long.

As the first to manage the evening watch, Gareth stared into the flames of the evening fire. Licking about themselves and the wood on which they fed, the flames wavered and danced. He remained careful to not look too deeply. During times like these, when the breeze was just right, he imagined he could see things. The images seemed so real, and what made them terrifying was that he sometimes witnessed them become a reality. It might not be until the next day, or mayhap not until several weeks had passed. Sometimes the reality never came about, either that or he simply had not been there to witness it. Regardless, he knew to be wary, for the phenomenon was something that had beleaguered him for a long time.

Gareth gave a deep sigh and glanced about the encampment. His companions were slowly settling themselves down for the night. The Savanlean were far out of their mountainous element, aiding him on his monumental task, a task he had promised his mother's sister he would undertake for her. From out of the western arm of the Sartingel Mountains they had accompanied him, across the Tusbirian plains and then across the Plain of Antipithanee. On the morrow they would finally reach the Lordis River. There they would finally part ways. Gareth and the boy would venture into northwestern Torimir while his cousins would make the long journey back from whence they had come.

Gareth gave a deep sigh. He didn't relish traveling alone, but the men had come so far. He knew they hated to leave him, but they all had families back in Aldehirra. After crossing the river, he would reach the city of Entsy within only a day of travel. Once there he would find a suitable inn and then proceed to ask the locals about what they might know about a Cimmerean man by the name of Dinim Coabra, for it was the last place Sharra had seen him.

It was the *only* place she had seen him.

A feeling of melancholy swept over Gareth as he watched the last of his comrades prepare for sleep. From a smaller bedroll nearby lay the sleeping form of the boy who was his young charge. Talemar, Sharra's son. She had loved him dearly, and once realizing she was sick beyond healing, she had asked her nephew to take the boy to his father. Gareth had balked at the seriousness of such a responsibility, but as he proceeded to watch Sharra decline so rapidly, he agreed to her last wish. He figured it was the least he could do for the woman that had taken him in for so many years after arriving in Aldehirra, the woman who had cared for him as his own mother would have done.

His mother, Gemma Farwyn had been deceased for many years. As Gemma's sister, Sharra had been one of his last connections to her. During the years after leaving Sangrilak, Gareth had struggled to find a place for himself and finally chose to go to the land of his mother's birth. The people of Aldehirra had accepted him easily, for he was the nephew of their beloved eldranza... soothsayer. Not only that, Sharra was sister to the heir of the Aldehirryan throne. Everyone loved her for her youthful vibrancy and genuine kindness. Her terrible sickness and subsequent death had been devastating to so many. It was her loss that reminded him so strongly of the family he had remaining, sisters he had left behind so long ago.

Sisters he had left behind with their maniacal father...

Gareth's eyes lingered on the boy. Talemar was perhaps one of the most handsome children he had ever seen. He had known the boy his entire life, for Sharra had given birth to Talemar soon after his arrival to Aldehirra. That had been over six years ago, and Gareth had spent every day within that time with his young cousin. Gareth would miss Talemar greatly once he was in the custody of his father. In some ways, Gareth had begun to see himself as a father figure to Talemar and had told Sharra this when she first told him her desire to see the boy in the hands of a man Talemar had never met. Sharra had been very pleased to know he felt so strongly for her son, but it still would not deter her from the desire that Talemar be taken to his rightful parent. She explained to Gareth that it wasn't that she didn't feel he would make a good father to Talemar. Deep in her soul, she knew the man, Dinim Coabra, deserved to know he had a son.

Gareth turned back to the waning flames. Picking up the branch lying beside him, he poked at some of the outlying embers. If he found no useful information in Entsy, he would go to Sangrilak. Once there he would reunite with his sisters, as he should have done years ago. He knew it would have taken him away from his family in Aldehirra, but Sheridana and Adrianna deserved so much more than what they probably got at the hands of their father. *Especially Adrianna...*

Gareth shook his head slowly. Yes, Adrianna had been in a very bad situation when he left. From the moment of her birth Thane had hated the child, although Gemma's death really hadn't been any fault of Adria's. Even without the birth of the second twin, Gemma could have died from the severe blood loss that eventually took her life. But Thane was Hells-bent on blaming someone for the death... *anyone*. His own daughter had been an easy target. Everyone around him knew that Thane wasn't in his right mind, that Gemma's loss had done something to him. Gareth had been selfish to leave his small sister behind. One day he hoped to make it up to her.

## 25 Jicaren CY594

Adrianna glanced about her as they rode through the silver trees. The thick canopy of Elvandahar's forest loomed high overhead, blocking out much of the sunlight that sought to venture through. It also blocked her view of Xebrinarth, who flew high above it. Thanks to Tallachienan and Charlemagne, the pain of the headaches she had suffered after returning to Krathil-lon had receded into the back of her mind. She didn't remember what the two gods had done to help her, only that when she finally awoke from whatever ordeal she had endured, two days had passed while she lay in comatose slumber. Her companions, especially Sirion and Sheridana, had asked her what had happened. She'd been only partly honest when she told them she didn't recall, deliberately leaving out the fact that Tallachienan and Charlemagne had saved her from what she had come to realize was the loss of her sanity.

Adrianna took a deep breath of the cool air. She was glad to be back in the Silverwood, albeit a bit sad as well. The last time the group had been there was after Thane's demise, a time still fraught with memories of their battle with Sydonnia and the other lycanthropes that had been making trouble for the villages surrounding the principal city of Alcrostat. Sydonnia had died at the hand of his own nephew, Sirion.

She sighed and swept a hand over the pale curling tendrils of her hair that had escaped the thick plait hanging over one shoulder. The strain of the knowledge Adrianna carried still weighed heavily, and she fervently wanted to divulge all of it to Sirion. It was more than just her past relationship with Master Tallachienan, but the fact that she had gone back in time and met his uncle, a man who hadn't always been the monster Sirion remembered. Unfortunately, now wasn't the time, for he still mourned the loss of his sister.

And Adrianna mourned the loss of Sydonnia.

Adrianna looked ahead to the beginning of the procession and Sirion walking beside Dramati. Just behind them were Triath and Tianna. Her friend looked so frail sitting there atop her lloryk. Adrianna couldn't wait for the day that the vibrancy that characterized Tianna would return. But for now, she was still recuperating from the injuries she had endured, injuries that would remain with her for the rest of her life. Father Dremathian had pulled Adrianna aside whilst they were still in Krathil-lon and explained the severity of Tianna's situation. Adrianna had instantly realized the other woman would need a good friend to see her through the hardship the knowledge would cause, for the druids had determined that Tianna could never be able to have children.

In all honesty, Adrianna could scarcely imagine what that meant, for she had never really thought about what having children would be like. However, in the course of all their conversations together, Adrianna recalled several times that Tianna had mentioned having a family. It was something that Tianna considered of utmost importance, something she considered a high priority in her life. Adrianna remembered a time that Tianna wanted to share that responsibility with Sirion. However, once meeting Triath, that had changed.

Adrianna momentarily elaborated on the thought of having Sirion's children. She had never considered it before because of the precarious nature of her future. Thane had been on her heels for so long, and then she had the looming battle of Aasarak overhead and the reality of the Cycling of the world. But now there was an entirely different reason... the terrible injuries she had sustained from the brutal rape she endured in the Sheldomar Forest all those years ago. She only vaguely recalled what the priests in Andahye had told her when she was finally healed enough to leave their care, but she got the distinct impression they felt it would be unlikely she would heal properly enough to sustain a pregnancy.

Adrianna had never questioned that assessment. But now, thinking back on it, she wondered if their judgment had been accurate. She wondered because she had been touched by the magic of one of the most powerful healers upon all of Shandahar... a unicorn. The unicorn had saved her life, and then healed her enough so that her body would endure the remaining journey to Andahye.

Adrianna shook her head. Even if she could have children, now wasn't a good time to do it. With the Pact of Bakharas broken, the world had been plunged into a new era of darkness. The druids had told them about it several days into their stay in Krathil-lon. The newfound knowledge was dumbfounding, especially for herself and Dinim. Hells, they had been the ones to bring the dragons into Shandahar. Ultimately, it was their fault the Pact was dissolved.

Adrianna was ashamed to wonder... would she have made the same decision to call the dragons even if she had known about the Pact?

Since leaving the silvery glen, their journey had been a relatively effortless one. She was glad of it, for they had been through so much in so short a time. In another three or four days they would reach their destination. Once at the Sherkari Fortress, everyone would decide where they would go from there. She already knew that Dinim planned to return to Master Tallachienan's citadel for a while. Sorn wanted to go to Sangrilak, and Triath and Tianna were contemplating the same. Dartanyen and Armond remained undecided. Adrianna hoped that she would find a niche for herself and Sheridana within Elvandaharian society. Her hope was that she would be there as Sirion's wife, but she worried about her Bondmate. She wanted Xebrinarth to be happy, and wondered if there was a place in Elvandahar that could sustain the existence of a dragon.

Adrianna was pulled away from her thoughts when she felt her larian slowing to a halt. She glanced ahead, past Triath, Tianna, Armond, and Dartanyen to the front of the procession. She saw Sirion standing there with Dramati alongside, staring into the trees before him. It was then she noticed it, a familiar musky odor tinged with a predatory undertone. The hairs at the back of her neck began to rise in response to some unseen danger, and by the tense expectancy of his stance, she could tell Sirion sensed it too. However, instead of reaching for his weapon as he ordinarily would, Sirion stepped forward with his hands at his sides, saying something she couldn't quiet decipher in spite of her excellent faelin hearing.

Adrianna felt her breath still in her chest when a figure strode from out of the trees. He was large, much larger than she remembered him to be when last they met. He stood at least a full foot-length taller than Sirion, and his muscle mass was nearly doubled. Her mouth went dry and her eyes widened with shock. *No, this can't be. This man died several moon cycles ago at Sirion's hand.*

It was the very man she had just been thinking about... Sydonnia Timberlyn.

Adrianna felt herself almost fall from the back of the larian. as her mind swirled away within a vortex of memories. Suddenly it all came back: Tallachienan hovering over her where she lay on the grass, Charlemagne's spell, the disparity of the memories her mind fought to reconcile. For there wasn't just one set of memories she had anymore, but two— one from the timeline that she had experienced before falling into Tallachienan's well, and the one that came about after she changed history. Sydonnia's timeline had drastically altered, and as such, had changed hers too. In the second timeline, she never met him that day at the Inn of the Hapless Cenloryan: he never gave her a message for Sirion, and she, Tianna, and Dartanyen never met him in the alleyway in the

Sangrilak. In the second timeline, the group never met him and his pack when they entered Elvandahar for the first time: the group was never asked to contend with the lycan pack, she was never abducted by them, and Sirion and Sydonnia never got into the battle that would end in Sydonnia's death.

*By the gods, what have I done?*

Adrianna's thoughts then swept back to the time she had spent with Sydonnia and Servial. She had tried so hard not to do something that would alter the course of history as she knew it. It was clear she had not been successful, and Charlemagne and Tallachienan had already made her aware of that fact. Her friend now stood before them, very much alive. She could only wonder how many other changes had taken place, and how dire they might be for the future.

However, her mind refused to grasp those things. At that moment, all it could understand was that Sydonnia was alive. She hadn't lost him after all...

Adrianna slipped down from the back of the larian. Her movement caught Sydonnia's gaze and his eyes met and locked with hers. She could see the astonishment reflected in their deep, brown depths and his body became still. To him, more than fifty years had passed since he last saw her in his home village of Merithyn. In spite of her efforts to be careful, something must have happened whilst she was in the past, some twist of fate that had brought about this new reality. Only she wasn't certain exactly what that reality was, for she had yet to take the time and sort through the combined memories that were now in the fore of her mind.

Sirion turned to see what captured his uncle's attention. He stood solemnly by as she passed him on her way to Sydonnia. For a brief moment she wondered what he might be thinking. For some reason, the battle between Sirion and his uncle had not taken place. Either that, or the battle simply hadn't ended in someone's death. Since the two men were not currently tearing one another's throats out, some semblance of peace must exist between them.

Adrianna's mind warred with the complexity of the concepts thrust before it. A whirlpool of emotions churned about, both negative and positive. The positive ones made their way to the forefront and she couldn't help holding back a tentative smile. She knew Sydonnia wasn't the same man she had befriended so long ago. He was a monster who had wreaked havoc throughout Ansalar for decades. But he was still *Sydonnia*, and she couldn't believe that not even a small part of the man she once knew still resided within.

Adrianna stopped when she stood before Sydonnia. Silence reigned for a moment before he finally spoke, his tone solemn. "I always knew I would see you again."

Adrianna struggled with the sudden emotion that arose, so she didn't immediately make a reply. For so long she had thought he would die, and to see him standing there before her now was nothing short of a miracle. "I thought you were dead."

His eyes twinkled. "This isn't the first time you have been erroneously informed."

Adrianna saw his stance begin to relax. She felt a surge of happiness sweep through her and the corners of her mouth pulled up into a smile. Despite his transformation, Sydonnia bantered with her as though only a day or two had passed "Yes, I think you are right," she said. "It's about time I sent my advisor away. Besides, for someone who doesn't know very much, *he is so expensive!*"

Sydonnia closed the short distance between them and took her in his embrace. Adrianna found herself enveloped by familiarity, for she had been in this man's arms before. Once again, her breath caught in her throat as she laid her head against his leather vest and wrapped her arms around him. Through the thick material she was somehow able to hear the rapid beating of his heart. He whispered in her ear words that made her chest ache with their magnitude. "I have missed you my friend..."

# Son of the Beast

Xebrinarth soared over the silvery canopy. As always, Adrianna took in the beauty of the scene as they flew towards the place where she and Dinim had chosen to build their school. The Medubrokan Academy would be the first place upon all of Ansalar besides Master Tallachienan's citadel to acquire training in Dimensionalist magic. With Tallachienan's funding and support, they got to work right away on the construction, meanwhile thinking of the mages whom they would consider as instructors. Adrianna liked to believe it wouldn't be long before they were searching for the Talents who would be trained there.

Several weeks had passed since their return to Elvandahar. It had taken awhile, but everyone began to settle into their lives again after so long. During their journey home, Triath and Tianna had decided they wanted to be married. It was a human term, but very similar to the ceremony of the Hinterlean faelin after having been Promised for several weeks. The Hinterlean peruven, or ceremonial priests, honored the request and it was only two weeks after their arrival that Triath and Tianna were granted an audience.

The ceremony had been wonderful. Tianna was the epitome of beauty in her traditional Hinterlean ceremonial attire. The soft white leather vest was decorated with intricate beadwork, as was the matching long skirt and ankle boots. Her chestnut hair had been brought up from the sides of her face by decorative clips, and the cloak that trailed behind was clasped to her reinforced shoulders with the traditional Elvandaharian silver oak leaf. Sirion had stood beside Adrianna throughout the ceremony, and she couldn't help but yearn for the day they would share the experience together as those wed.

However, that day didn't seem to be coming any nearer.

Since the moment Sydonnia had stepped out of the forest to reenter her life, Adrianna's existence with Sirion had become vastly more complicated. Much to Sirion's disgruntlement, Sydonnia had walked with her for the remainder of the afternoon as they traveled. Much to his credit, Sirion never interfered even though he very much wanted to. Even though the mental connection they had once shared before her training with Master Tallachienan was gone, she had felt the animosity emanating from him in waves. The fact that Sydonnia remembered her was confusing, for Adrianna had rather thought that the spells Tallachienan and Charlemagne had cast would have taken care of that. It left her wondering how the rest of Elvandahar would respond when they saw her again, and the thought scared her. She'd explained everything to Sydonnia as they walked, starting from the very beginning. She told him about his fight with Sirion, and that he had died. She continued with telling him about her arcane training in the past, and her magical journey to Sangrilak. Of course, he remembered what happened after that, up until the time she left with her 'brother'. She explained that she must have somehow altered history, and that it was the only reason he walked beside her...

Adrianna hadn't been surprised when Sydonnia was silent for a long while before telling her he needed to take some time to think about what she had divulged. Not only that, but he could feel Sirion's mounting anger just as easily as could she. By the time Sydonnia left, the group was stopping to set camp for the night. Once Sydonnia was gone, Sirion had taken her a distance from the group. Once far enough away that no one would hear him shouting, he turned on her.

*"What the Hells is going on? How do you know that man? What else haven't you told me, Adrianna?"* His eyes reflected the betrayal he felt, and she felt her chest constrict with the hurt she'd inadvertently caused him.

*Adrianna stood there with as much calm as she could muster beneath his emotional onslaught. "Remember when I said there were many things I needed to tell you, but that I just didn't know where to begin?"*

*Sirion said nothing, just stared at her impassively.*

*"Well, this was one of those things. I've wanted to talk to you about so much since our battle with Aasarak, but I just didn't know when. You've been so swept up by your losses, I didn't want to thrust even more on you with my convoluted history of the past several years I've been gone."*

*Sirion just shook his head. "You didn't think that this was something I needed to know in spite of any 'losses' I've sustained? Gods, Adria! How is it that you possibly know my uncle? Please enlighten me!"*

*She had then explained everything to Sirion, just the way as she had done with Sydonnia. He listened without interruption, and when she was finished, he was pensive for a few moments before he spoke. "Why didn't you confide in me when you were suffering so much from the headaches? I thought we were a partnership."*

*"You were going through so much of your own hurt, I didn't want to bog you down even more with mine."*

*Sirion shook his head. "Adria, you can't protect me from these things. How can we be a solid entity when we are busy keeping secrets, no matter how unintentional? When we are wed, we are supposed to be two halves of one whole. How can we be that whole unless we know all there is to know about one another?"*

*She had lowered her eyes contritely and apologized. "I'm sorry Sirion. You're right. It's just that I've forgotten what it's supposed to be like..."*

Adrianna now shook her head free of the memories. She watched as the forest canopy below swept past and looked for a clue that would tell her how close they were to their destination, her thoughts having made her lose track of the passage of time. Much to her relief, the rest of Elvandahar had no recollection of her from the past, including Sirion's mother, Lilandria. Again, she had wandered why Sydonnia remained immune to the spells, and eventually decided it had something to do with his lycanthropy. Even now, Sirion still struggled with her friendship with a man he hated so much, a man who had committed so many crimes against the Hinterlean people. Adrianna understood Sirion's desire to remain distant, but had hoped that he might come to understand her affinity for Sydonnia. He also struggled with the death of his sister, a woman who'd had so much life left to live. He'd told Adrianna that he had always imagined that one day they would be home again, and that her children would play among the silverwood trees with his. They would be a family in a way he'd never experienced before with his father and mother. It was a dream that had been broken the moment Anya lost her life to Aasarak.

And it probably didn't help that she'd shared some of what had taken place between she and Tallachienan during her apprenticeship. The darker aspects, she'd left out. However, her fall to temptation and the circumstances surrounding that, she'd made certain to tell him about. Much to his credit, Sirion had been very understanding and forgiving, but she couldn't help thinking that maybe he just didn't believe in her so much anymore.

With that painful thought in mind, Adrianna saw the break in the canopy that told her they were getting close to the construction site. The natural clearing was the perfect place for them to build the tower, large enough to sustain the school as well as a few dragons. Since the first day of breaking ground, extensive work crews had been there almost day and night. It was a daunting task, for the large stones first had to be gathered. Master Tallachienan had been a great help with this monumental endeavor. There was no possible way they could have collected so much stone in so little time, a smooth, dark stone that, with his Dimensionalist skill, had been taken from the vast Kynerian Mountain Range in Shayamalan, Shandahar's mysterious continent to the east. The stones were being placed in such a way that there was minimal space between each one. And whatever space did manage to exist was filled with a substance made out of the sand and gravel created by the crushing of some of the more misshapen rocks that were found. Mixed with water and some other substances with which Adrianna wasn't very familiar, a thick slurry was made. Not only did the material make a good filler, but it seemed to also bind the stones together to make the structure stronger.

Adrianna smiled as Xebrinarth began his descent. Not only did she see the customary presence of Armond and Dartanyen, but Triath was there as well. His bare back glistened with the sweat of his labor and his face had an expression of grim determination. Adrianna glanced about the area, expecting to see Tianna somewhere nearby. By the time Xebrin landed she had come to the realization that her friend wasn't there. With the help of his foreleg, Adrianna slipped from the back of her Bondmate and onto the ground. She was instantly greeted by those who worked close by, all of whom were accustomed to her golden dragon friend. She stepped up to the men, sharing brief conversation before moving on to the next group. It was in that fashion that she made her way over to her comrades. She enjoyed the interaction, asking some of the men about their families while asking others about other pursuits they enjoyed outside of working at the construction site.

Adrianna smiled when she reached Dartanyen, Armond, and Triath. They stopped their work, each one enfolding her in a brief embrace of greeting. As always, she was pleased to see them. However, she knew the men had other duties to which they had to attend besides this one. Dartanyen had acquired a position as one of the elite palace isterian. His prowess with the bow had been instantly recognized, and in spite of his differing heritage, he was brought into the fold. Meanwhile, Armond had taken to teaching the art of bladesong. Already he and Adrianna had found a boy and a girl endowed with the Talent necessary for such instruction. Armond seemed happy with this newfound task in life, and it pleased her to know that he would be staying in Elvandahar with the rest of her comrades. Sorn had been the only one to leave, returning to his home in Sangrilak. Since the battle, he had seemed smaller within his brittle shell. The loss of his appretice had broken him in a place very deep inside.

After talking for a few moments with the others, Triath pulled Adrianna aside. "Adria, I need your help."

Immediately concerned, she frowned and looked deep into his eyes. "What is it?"

He shook his head. "There is no reason to be worried yet, but I have begun to accept the very real possibility that the Daemundai are searching for me and will eventually discover my whereabouts. In all honesty, I don't want to place Tianna, you, or anyone else here in Elvandahar at risk on my account."

Adrianna felt her frown deepen. "So, you want to leave, then?"

Triath shook his head. "That is the reason why I am asking for your help. I don't want to leave. Tianna is happy here, and for now I have chosen Elvandahar as my home. However, I feel that I need something that will keep the Daemundai from discovering my location."

Adrianna nodded thoughtfully. "All right. Let me see what I can do." Triath gave her a wide smile. "I knew I could count on you." Adrianna shook her head. "But why the secrecy?"

Triath gave a brief shrug. "I just don't want the others to worry."

"But don't you think they deserve to know? I thought we were all supposed to have each other's backs? How can we do that if you don't tell everyone what's going on?" Adrianna briefly recognized the irony of her words, for she had just been reminiscing about Sirion having said the same thing to her after realizing her affiliation with Sydonnia.

Triath regarded her intently for a moment. She could tell that he was weighing her words. "All right. I will be out with it then. I don't want *Tianna* to worry. She's been through too much recently to fret needlessly about me. She needs time to take care of herself for a while instead of giving all she has to others. It is the trait I love most about her, but I see how it can be damaging. I love my wife, and I don't want her to suffer over something that can be easily remedied by a few of us."

Adrianna took in the man standing before her. Triath Solanar had changed so much since their first meeting. According to Sirion, Triath's actions had always tended to revolve around himself and whatever benefit he might derive from any given situation. Now, to hear him speak solely with Tianna's wellbeing in mind, made Adrianna realize exactly how much he cared for her.

Adrianna nodded. "You have a valid argument there, Triath. You are right to believe that Tianna has much healing still to do. Worries for you should not be in her mind right now. I shall keep this between us, Sirion, and Dinim. Sirion always seems to know when something is going on, and Dinim may have some good ideas about what we should do."

Triath grinned. "Like I said, I knew I could count on you."

Adrianna returned the smile. "Come back here in a few days and I should have something to tell you. If I have something sooner, I will come to you instead."

Triath nodded, and they shared a brief embrace. Then Triath stepped away and rejoined Dartanyen and Armond, while Adrianna turned to make her way towards the base of the structure that would one day be the main tower of the academy. She saw Dinim approaching and met him several paces later.

"What was that all about?" he asked.

Adrianna continued towards the tower foundation and Dinim turned to walk beside her. "Triath is concerned that the Daemundai are searching for him." She paused and gave a small sigh. "He is probably right. Surely Sabian had communicated Triath's discovery to his brethren prior to his banishment from Krathil-lon. Being the only one of his kind, Triath would be a commodity to the Daemundai, no matter how hard he was won. They might stop at nothing to have him in their grasp."

Dinim said nothing for a few moments. Then, "An ordinary anti-scrying device might not be enough against the Daemundai. It is rumored they have a loose affiliation with the Brotherhood of the Konshue. Over the centuries, those people have devised ways to persevere against many ordinary devices. They call it 'technology'. They are powerful, and often very manipulative and cruel. It is no small wonder they dominate most of eastern Ansalar."

Adrianna frowned. "Then what other choice do we have? Without a means to keep him hidden, Triath will be forced into hiding. What kind of life is that?"

Dinim's gaze was somber. "We must consult Master Tallachienan. He will know what to do."

Joselyn stood near the periphery of the work area with the two clerics who had also decided to donate their time and skill. It seemed that everyone throughout all of Elvandahar had learned of the tower dedicated to magic that was being built at the border of Kleyshes and Nedmar a few dozen zacrol north of Alcrostat. Most of the men were being paid for their labor, but there were others, such as the druid and cleric field medics, who had been asked to offer their time so as to help treat any wounds the men might sustain. The construction site was a dangerous place, massive amounts of rock being broken down and used to build the tower and surrounding structures. Several injuries had been mended the day before, and this day was proving to be no different.

Joselyn narrowed her eyes as she watched the interactions between Adrianna and her friends. The other woman seemed very familiar with the men she spoke with: first the handsome human man with shoulder-length brown hair and tight-fitting trousers, followed by the Cimmerean man wearing an intricately designed burgundy tunic and billowy trousers. She surmised that the latter must be the one they called Dinim, the one that Adrianna had named her partner in the tower-building endeavor. Looking at the young woman, Joselyn could easily see why Sirion was attracted to her, for Adrianna was exceptionally beautiful. Actually, Joselyn had never seen one that looked quite like her before. It was no small wonder what Sirion was so besotted, as well as most every other man who had laid eyes on her. For Joselyn it was nothing short of disturbing.

Joselyn slowly began making her way over to the tower foundation where Adrianna and Dinim were headed. She was compelled to meet the woman who had become her nemesis, her primary competition for Sirion's affection. She was certain that, without this woman, Sirion just may have taken her back in spite of her relationship with Sydonnia. By the way she spoke to him, Joselyn could see that a close connection existed between Adrianna and Dinim. It was a bit out of the ordinary for a woman who was in a romantic relationship with another man. Joselyn couldn't help smiling to herself, for this observation could serve as fuel to the fire she would create when she encountered Sirion next.

Since the first time she had laid eyes on the daring Hinterlean ranger, Joselyn had known he would be a part of her life. It wasn't just fanciful musings that entered her mind based on simple attraction; it was an ability she seemed to have, one that the Order of Reshik-na had found quite intriguing. They had first met in the small silverwood glen located in the southern Sartingels. She had gone to Krathil-lon for the experience of meeting druids from other orders and to see how they prioritized their lives. When she arrived, Sirion had been there for several weeks already, a ranger who had decided to think beyond his training to embrace the teachings of a druid master, Father Dremathian. It was an unknown practice, for druids and rangers had been at odds with one another for almost a century. It was what made Sirion a clear cut above the rest.

It wasn't until after she had begun her work in and about the city of Entsy that she got to see Sirion again. Not long after, their relationship had become physical. As the moon cycles passed, he would seek her out whenever he was nearby. They were always happy to indulge in the sexual satisfaction they could offer one another, and Joselyn reveled in the attention

They went about his way for quite some while, several years to be precise. But the time finally came when they needed to make a decision— to either continue their relationship and take it to the next level, or to focus on their individual professions without the distraction that hindered them. A seemingly mutual agreement had been made, that they would each endeavor to rise in the ranks of their chosen vocations. Sirion had gone his way to pursue the life of a ranger, and she went hers in pursuit of a master's status in the order.

However, the agreement wasn't as wholehearted as it had been intended. It took barely a year for Joselyn to recant. In her mind she felt that Sirion must have surely realized the same, so she waited for him. For many years she waited to no avail...

Then Sydonnia came.

Joselyn had warred with herself. Somehow, in spite of what Sydonnia was, she was attracted to the man. She didn't know if it was because of his relation to Sirion or some other strange cause, but she chose not to overthink it much. When she went to Sydonnia's bed, it was with the hope that Sirion would discover her 'capture' and rush to her rescue. He would then realize how deeply he loved her and they would finally be wed like they were always meant to be.

Unfortunately, events didn't play out that way. Sirion had discovered an alternate destiny in Adrianna. Now Joselyn was faced with the monumental task of winning Sirion back in spite of the deplorable action of sleeping with his uncle. Her strategy would be multifaceted, focusing not only on Adrianna's weaknesses, but also the possibilities of infidelity and her inability to understand Sirion's true nature. Meanwhile, Joselyn would build herself up, make herself so much more than what he remembered, so much more *desirable*.

Adrianna and Dinim looked up when Joselyn stepped up to them. She made sure that she offered an affable smile, followed by some words of greeting. "Good day to you both. I hope it has been as pleasant for you as it has been for me."

Joselyn noticed their expressions of surprise before making a reply. Dinim was the first to smile and offer his hand. "It has, milady. What brings you here?"

Joselyn smiled and grasped his forearm. "I am one of the druid healers on duty today. I can only pray there won't be as many injuries as there were yesterday."

Dinim nodded. "Indeed, I had heard about that. We are fortunate to have those of you who have offered to aid in the progress here." Dinim inclined his head. "Thank you."

Joselyn inclined her own head for a moment before turning to Adrianna. The other woman regarded her intently. Adrianna spoke before Joselyn could formulate anything to say. "I recall someone pointing you out to me." Adrianna cocked her head to the side. "Joselyn, right?"

Joselyn nodded, struggling to hold back her expression of dismay. "Yes, that's right."

Adrianna only nodded, her expression shuttered. Joselyn felt a twinge of vexation. Sirion must have said something, for only he would mention something negative enough for Adrianna to respond so dispassionately. Regardless, she felt compelled to continue.

"Who was it, may I ask?"

Adrianna's brows drew slightly together. "It was Sirion."

Joselyn only nodded. "Ah, I see. How does my old friend fare?"

Adrianna's response was abrupt. "He is doing well considering all he has lost."

Joselyn nodded. "That is good to know." She paused for a moment and then continued. "Well, I hope your day is a good one. May the sun shine upon you both."

She nodded a farewell to Adrianna and Dinim, then walked past them in the direction she had been moving before they met. The meeting didn't go quite as she had expected, but truthfully, she hadn't known what to expect at all. But it was a start, and she would have some leverage when she happened to see Sirion again. She would make certain it was sometime soon...

Lilandria impatiently waited for Sydonnia. She had already considered getting up to pace the solar, but then he would instantly know something was wrong. He would then make her even more nervous than she already was by demanding to know what was amiss, and then she would feel the pressure of his gaze as she struggled to collect her scattered thoughts. It was something she wouldn't be able to handle, not for this. It would be a moment of truth after so many years, and she didn't know how he would respond. Always before she had backed down at the last moment. But this time she was determined–

Lilandria was startled away from her thoughts when she heard his mildly sarcastic voice from across the chamber. "Lilandria, there must be a good reason for you to call me here." Sydonnia walked into the solar and glanced around. "Especially since you have never called me here before." He focused his attention and pinned her with his feral gaze. "Something must be amiss."

Lilandria blinked a few times in succession and her heartbeat accelerated. This was precisely what she had hoped to avoid. It was interesting how this scenario had come about in spite of her passive efforts to make it otherwise. Sydonnia's presence dominated the room, and she felt way too small sitting there in her chair. She rose from her seat only to find that she felt almost just as small standing up. She frowned to herself and recalled precisely who it was darkening her doorway.

In vivid detail, Lilandria remembered the first time she discovered what Sydonnia had become. The events that followed were burned into her memory forever, and they were the reason why he was standing before her now.

# BREAKING DESTINY

Lilandria turned to look behind her for the third time since she arrived at the path that would take her to the heated springs. The pools were a boon to the people of Alcrostat and Merithyn, for none like them existed anywhere else within the realm. Usually, she had no problem with the walk it took in order to reach them. But today she couldn't shake the feeling she was being followed, and she was beginning to feel nervous.

Several moons had passed since Servial and a small contingent of surviving rangers returned from the banks of the Terrestra River. She was distraught to find that Sydonnia was not with them. He was proclaimed missing, for his body had never been found. She lamented the loss of her friend, for they had become quite close during the moon cycles leading up to the call to duty... a mission that ended in staggering defeat. The details were kept from her and most of the others who awaited the return of their husbands, brothers, and sons. Three fourths of those men never returned. It was a historical moment for all of Elvandahar, and the mourning was great.

But at least Servial had returned from the ill-fated assignment. He had yet to say much about his brother, but she knew that it was only a matter of time before he would confide in her. In spite of her own feelings of loss, she knew that Servial's were so much greater, and she vowed to be his bastion of support when he finally broke down. She was initially taken aback by his lack of emotion concerning Sydonnia, but in the end realized it was simply his way of coping with the loss. She respected that, and she would be there for Servial when he finally came around.

Finally, Lilandria reached the springs. Within the center of each of the four heated pools, water bubbled up from within the ground and mist rose into the air. It was the perfect place for people to get together and mingle whilst they bathed. More often, women visited in the mornings while men did so in the evenings after a hard day at work. Even though she had arrived closer towards midday, she was surprised to find herself alone. It was an uncommon occurrence, and it took her slightly aback. Today would have been a good day to have companionship...

Lilandria slowly set her pack on the ground. She then seated herself atop one of the flat rocks situated around the pools. She had always wondered if they had been placed there by natural occurrence or faelin one. She hesitated to begin removing the gown she customarily wore to the springs and then admonished herself. By the gods, she was being so silly. What had gotten into her? She would have known it if someone were following, and why would anyone do such a thing anyways? It simply wasn't civilized.

It was then that her skin began to prickle, and immediately after, Lilandria felt the unmistakable presence of another person there with her.

She would have loved to believe it was someone whom had come to bathe, someone much like herself who had a late start. But she instinctively knew it wasn't the truth, for her body reacted as though imperiled. She sensed danger emanating from the presence behind her.

Lilandria slowly turned in place. She fought from closing her eyes, an immature reaction... for if it can't be seen, it must not really be there. Then she saw him standing among the trees, a man she had thought deceased. Sydonnia.

She mouthed his name without speaking, and her eyes widened with disbelief. Lilandria thought she must be dreaming, but her physical response to his presence was not imaginary. She rose from the rock with a hand to her chest... a subconscious attempt to stop her racing heart. He then began to step towards her, a hand outstretched, and she rushed to him without considering her body's earlier warning of danger.

"By the gods, is it really you?" She spoke the words so low they were almost a whisper. The feel of his arms around her wasn't like she remembered, the embrace seeming stronger somehow... more powerful. The scent of him was familiar, but carried a strong musky undertone.

"Did you miss me?"

His voice carried a bantering quality, and she thought the question a strange one, especially from one who had been considered lost in battle. She pulled back, and through the tears in her eyes Lilandria took in the handsome face. It was much the same as it had always been: the cut of jaw, the shape of his lips, and the arch of his thick brows. But something was different, something she couldn't quite place.

"Sydonnia, where have you been? They went out looking for you, but..."

He placed a hand at her lips and she stopped. Lilandria felt a shift in his demeanor, and once more her skin prickled.

"Sssh. It doesn't matter now. I am here," he said solemnly.

His voice was deep, deeper than she recalled it to be. The breath caught in her throat. What was happening? He had disregarded her inquiry without a shred of care or thought. She shook her head. "It does matter! I thought you were dead!"

He regarded her thoughtfully for a moment but then grinned disarmingly. "Well, now you know that I'm not."

Lilandria frowned and took a step back, wracking her brain in order to discern the slight changes she noticed had taken place. "Sydonnia, that's not good enough. I need to know what happened." She paused and then continued. "Does Servial know you are here?"

Lilandria sensed it immediately. It was a shift in the very air surrounding them. His brown eyes focused piercingly upon her, eyes that seemed almost feral. She thought it strange that particular word popped to mind, and she slowly began to feel a pervading sensation of peril. However, it suddenly tempered, and she watched him swallow heavily and shake his head.

"No. And it might very well be better this way," he said in a low voice.

Lilandria shook her head and drew her brows together into a slight frown. "Sy, what's wrong with you? Servial is your brother and deserves to know! He has missed you so much these past-"

Sydonnia interrupted her. "No. My presence here is only between you and me." Sydonnia shook his head. "You must promise me, Lily."

He regarded her intently and awaited her response. The air crackled between them, testimony to the energy lying there. It didn't take her long to realize he would be long gone before she had any opportunity to tell Servial of his presence. Sudden realization washed over her like a wave. By the gods, he was one of those whom everyone spoke so much about, one of the monsters that wreaked havoc on the outlying villages and towns all across Kleyshes and Filopar.

He was a lycanthrope...

Sydonnia closed the gap between them and took her by the arms. "Don't you see? It doesn't matter where I've been... only that I am here now." He paused and then continued softly, "I am not the same man I was when I left."

Lilandria nodded slowly, her head lowered. "I know. By the gods, Sydonnia, I can feel it," she said in a near whisper.

"But I still want you the same as I always have. My feelings for you have never subsided."

Lilandria looked up at him, her brows pulling together into a frown. "What are you saying? I never knew-"

Sydonnia placed his fingertips at her lips, once again interrupting her. "You did know. You just didn't stop to realize it. But now I'm telling you. Don't be afraid to look deep, Lilandria."

She took a deep breath and became still. A moment passed, then another.

Oh gods...

Her barriers finally came crashing down, barriers she never realized were there. Everything that had ever existed between them was thrown into stark relief, and all that mattered was here and now. She recognized that she cared about him, had always cared about him. And now she wanted him, wanted him with the same passion and intensity he seemed to feel for her. When Sydonnia kissed her, she tasted an untamed wildness she knew she would never experience again. His scent was overwhelming as he laid her down onto the mossy ground, a scent that beckoned to her of what was to come. And she may not have been able to resist it, even had she wanted *to.*

After that day, Sydonnia left Elvandahar. Lilandria never told anyone about his visit, and the tryst they had shared she kept buried deep in her mind. Over the years, knowledge about his terrible exploits reached Elvandahar by the stories that the rangers and other travelers heard told in the closest villages, towns, and cities in the neighboring realms of Torimir and Karlisle. It hurt her to know Sydonnia was capable of such horrific acts, and as time passed, a part of her learned to hate him. But there was always that part of her that would never forget...

Lilandria tore herself away from thoughts of the past to focus on the present. Sydonnia stood there before her, watching her intently. That day had changed her life forever. Sydonnia had been right... there was something between them, quite a bit of something. But it hadn't mattered because he had become a monster, a scourge that would inflict mayhem wherever he went. All they had was that one day, that one time. And with no small amount of difficulty, she had borne the result of their union...

Lilandria swallowed past the painful lump in her throat and spoke in a low voice. "Sydonnia, why did you come back here? Why?"

She could see that her question took him aback by the expression of surprise that passed over his face. He hesitated to reply, mayhap not really knowing what to say, or how to say it. Then his expression shifted to agitation as he scowled and placed his hands at his waist. He gave a shrug of nonchalance. "Why not? I figured it was about time I came home."

Lilandria stared at him through wide eyes. Sydonnia had waited approximately fifty years to return. Within that time, he had victimized scores of villages and towns, killed hundreds of men, women, and probably even children. He had murdered his own brother in cold blood, mutilating Sirion that same night and leaving him in the wilderness to die. The boy had been found by the scouts of a traveling caravan and taken to the nearest Hermodian temple. Once he was able, Sirion told the priests he hailed from Elvandahar and asked them to send a message.

Lilandria supposed she could have been a bit more upset when she discovered what had befallen Servial. She had been enraged when she found out about what her son had endured.

*And her hatred of Sydonnia grew.*

Lilandria had so much wanted Sirion to come home, for it had been so many years since Servial had taken him from her. But he never returned until many moon cycles after she had learned of his death during his last mission with the Wildrunners...

But Sirion wasn't dead, never had been. He was very much alive. By then Sydonnia had already made his first appearance in Elvandahar after so long. With him he had brought his druidess consort, one of Reshik-na's most promising acolytes. After he and his 'pack' had terrorized the druids, he had decided to take her as his prize. Lilandria didn't think Joselyn gave him much of a struggle. Hells, Lilandria wouldn't be surprised if the union hadn't been a bit of Joselyn's devising.

"Why have you stayed?" she asked solemnly.

Once again Sydonnia hesitated. Then, "What is this about, Lily? Surely you didn't bring me to your solar to talk about why I am still in Elvandahar."

Lilandria swallowed heavily. "Why didn't you kill Sirion when you had the chance? You were almost finished with him. What kept you from making that last move?"

Sydonnia regarded her intensely from animal eyes. She had seen that same look recently in the eyes of her son. She wondered what had been passed from father to son and what it might ultimately do to Sirion. She knew about his transformation to survive the arcane vortex at the climax of the Wildrunner's fight against Gaknar and Tharizduun. She didn't think that the transformation was purely coincidence.

Sydonnia's words interrupted her thoughts. "I'm not having this conversation with you. I'm leaving."

Sydonnia turned to make his departure, but quicker than she ever thought possible, Lilandria leaped forward and grabbed his arm. "No," she shouted. "You knew this would come up sometime. You can't run from it anymore, and neither can I."

Sydonnia turned, his expression incredulous. "What the Hells are you talking about, woman? Running from what?"

Lilandria released his arm and stood back. She spoke in a calmer voice. "I want you to look back and remember why you didn't deliver that killing strike."

Sydonnia's eyes darkened with increasing anger, but she could tell he did as she asked. Several moments passed before he finally shook his head. "Lilandria, I don't know. I have asked myself the same thing a few times over the years. I have only vague and fragmented memories of what happened after I made my complete transformation. It is always that way after the change is made." He pursed his lips and continued to shake his head. "I tore Servial to pieces. My hatred of him had grown so much over the years. He was an arrogant bastard to the very bloody end. And Sirion... well, I don't even think I intended to harm him at all. I can only imagine he must have made some kind of attack and I retaliated..."

Sydonnia let his voice trail away and his expression was thoughtful again for a few moments. Lilandria just watched him, waiting for any sign that he might make the realization for himself. He finally gave a deep sigh. "Lily, please tell me what is going on. Why am I here? What do you want from me? Remorse? Fine, I can give you that. There have been many times I have regretted that night. Am I sorry that Servial is dead? No. The man was a..."

Lilandria silently held up a hand and Sydonnia stopped speaking. He just stood there and waited, waited for her to tell him what it was she wanted from him. But she didn't want anything. She only needed him to know the truth.

"Have you spoken to Sirion any time recently? Did he tell you about the conflict he and the Wildrunners experienced against Gaknar?"

Sydonnia frowned. "What conflict? Who is Gaknar?"

Her question answered, Lilandria moved on. "At the end of the struggle there was a magical crossfire and Sirion was caught in it. His faelin body was unable to endure the torment the vortex imposed, so it transformed into that of some type of wemic. He stayed that way for several weeks until he was helped out of that state by his druid friend, Dremathian Klavisic of Krathil-lon."

Sydonnia nodded. "Yes. I know Father Dremathian." He narrowed his eyes and became thoughtful. "And no, I wasn't aware of this transformation." Sydonnia then regarded her with mild consternation. "You of all people should know Sirion and I are on speaking terms only when it is in regards to the welfare of Elvandahar."

Lilandria couldn't help feeling disappointed and shook her head. Drat, the man was focused too much on the fact that he and Sirion didn't speak on normal terms. Hells, she had been so certain Sydonnia was intelligent enough to–

The sound of his voice penetrated her thoughts. "You say that he transformed into a wemic?"

Lilandria's breath paused and she watched him from lowered lids. All of a sudden, his hand snaked out and it gripped her upper arm. Her eyes rose to meet his and they locked. He knew...

Sydonnia regarded her from a face that had become leached of color. "Lilandria, are you trying to tell me something?" he growled.

Silence reigned for a moment. Then, "I feel it is the reason why you left him there." Lilandria trembled within his grip. "Somewhere deep within, you recognized that he was yours..."

Sydonnia's grip tightened and his voice was deeper than she had ever heard it before. It caused her to shiver, for her body had begun to sense danger.

"No! Servial had already taken you to his bed many times! I had you only once. Once!" He shouted the last.

Lilandria felt her lower lip begin to tremble. "I counted the days.

Servial never touched me near the time I spent with you because he had been injured during patrol. He had been attacked by–"

Sydonnia interjected. "Me. We fought and he skewered me with his dagger."

Lilandria shook her head. "No, I don't recall you having any wounds that–"

Once again, he interrupted, finally releasing his bruising grip on her arms. "That is because I heal very quickly." Sydonnia shook his head. "Servial had hoped to kill me with that thrust. I became angry and threw him into a nearby tree. The impact must have..."

Lilandria nodded and continued, "... broken him. Yes, he came home with a fractured leg and several broken ribs. I always wondered what animal would have caused that type of injury. In my mind I just decided that he didn't want to tell me about the fight he had with a fellow ranger, or mayhap a friend he had wronged in some way."

Lilandria chuckled humorlessly. It was interesting, even then she had never given Servial the benefit of the doubt. She should have recognized that. But she had loved him so much...

Sydonnia just stood there while the full impact of the revelation washed over him. Everything fit together like the pieces to a puzzle. The horror of it gripped him the way it had her for so many years. If Sydonnia was a lycanthrope, had been a lycanthrope when Sirion was bred, then what was Sirion? Was he faelin? Was he lycan? Or was he some unknown thing that lay somewhere in between?

Sydonnia brought his gaze up to meet hers. She could see the acceptance reflected there. He stepped towards her until there was barely any space separating them. "Does anyone else know?"

Lilandria shook her head.

Sydonnia took her in his arms and pulled her close to his chest. "Not even your husband?"

She shook her head again.

He was aware of her response even without seeing it. "Isn't your husband supposed to know everything about you?"

Lilandria hesitated a brief moment before shaking her head for the third time. She accompanied it with a vocal response. "No."

Sydonnia gave a deep sigh. "Why did you marry Thalios?"

She hesitated again before making a reply. "He is a good man."

Sydonnia lowered his chin to the top of her head and nodded. "And a king."

Lilandria stiffened in his embrace. "You have become such a lloryk's ass, Sydonnia."

He chuckled in her ear. "I agree."

"After all this time, I just thought you should know you have a son. That is the reason I brought you here. You can go now."

Sydonnia chuckled again. "Tsk-tsk. You think to be rid of me all of a sudden? Just because you have a husband? Hellfire, we have a child together..."

Lilandria struggled to pull away. "Let go of me, Sydonnia. I..."

Suddenly she fell back. Once righting herself she looked up to find him smiling sardonically. "As you wish, milady."

She just stood there and regarded him without expression. She watched as he finally decided to collect himself. Sydonnia cleared his throat, and returned to his more solemn state. Only then she spoke. "I think we should let him know."

Sydonnia pulled his thick brows into a frown. "No. He hates me."

Lilandria cocked her head. "Whose fault is that?"

He ground his teeth together. "You would be making a mistake to tell him. I've witnessed his state of mind as of late. There is something wrong there, I can feel it." Sydonnia shook his head. "Mayhap it has something to do with whatever horrific thing I passed on to him. Regardless, this knowledge will not help him right now. He needs to be in a better place in his life, a better place with himself..."

Lilandria nodded her agreement. "Fine. In this I will defer to you. I can only hope you are right."

Sydonnia nodded. "Me too."

Sirion walked silently among the looming trees. It was hot and humid beneath the silvery canopy, and he growled beneath his breath when sweat ran down the center of his back under the sleeveless leather vest he wore. They were approaching the hottest time of the year, so it wasn't unexpected. However, it didn't mean he had to like it.

Actually, Sirion had very little to like since returning home. He felt as though he hung upside down by the heel of one foot and that he little or no control over anything in his life anymore. What had happened to those more carefree days when all he had to consider was himself? Those days when his greatest concern might be the next village where he would make a stop, or the next lycan he would begin to hunt? Since joining his sister and the Wildrunners, all of that had changed. It hadn't been just about himself anymore, for he'd had the group to think about. But now... now it was so much more than even that. Now he had much more than he ever bargained for.

Sirion suddenly stopped to smell the air. He was instantly on the alert and his mood shifted from sour to angry. Sydonnia had recently been in the area. Several momths ago when Sirion had last been in Elvandahar, he and his outcast uncle had made a pact. So now, by continuing to stay within the limits of Alcrostat, Sydonnia was breaking that agreement. This fact angered him more than it should, for Sydonnia had been causing no trouble for anyone, and it even appeared that he kept away from other people as much as possible.

Well, almost everyone. Adrianna was an exception.

Sirion had been dumbfounded to discover the relationship that existed between his betrothed and the uncle who had been his nemesis for so many years. Watching Adrianna walk forward to greet the man who had caused him so much anguish for so long had been shocking. Then, to see her embrace Sydonnia was almost gut-wrenching. Following so swiftly behind the death of Anya, Sirion's response had been less than cordial, and Adrianna had suffered his emotional backlash. Later that evening, after the rest of the group had settled down for the night, he had pulled her aside and she told him the story of how she had met his uncle. It had been rather fantastical to say the least. But he had to admit, most everything about Adrianna had become that way since her return from training.

And that led into the next thing that weighed so heavily upon him. During their stay in Krathil-lon, while awaiting the healing of their comrades, Adrianna had told him about her Master, Tallachienan, and the relationship that existed between them.

Sirion was devastated by the knowledge she had imparted. He understood that it wasn't her fault, but it didn't take away the fact that the woman he loved more than any other had been in the bed of another man. She had told him that he was right about her not being the same person she had been before leaving for training. She had described the day of her revelation at the citadel, and that the memories of herself from past Cycles had been infused into her mind. The memories had made her confused for a few days after the revelation, and it was during that time that she had gone to Tallachienan's bed. The memories were what also gave her mastery of the sword, for in other Cycles it had been her weapon of choice.

After several moments, Sirion continued walking. He wished that his problems ended with Adrianna. However, since coming home, the reality of his sister's death had hit him so much more strongly, and the issue of the Elvandaharian throne was once more thrust before him. His mother expected him to accept Thalios' offer to be his heir, and Thalios himself hoped for the same. Meanwhile, he had his uncle to deal with... and then the issue of his former paramour, Joselyn Quemirren.

Joselyn. Yes, he could smell her too. Her scent had been more and more prevalent as of late, and he suspected she had been 'visiting' his patrol area with the intent of capturing his attention. A part of him felt her behavior somewhat irksome, for he thought he had made it very clear that he wanted very little to do with her. However, the other, more conceited and prideful part of him reveled in the attention. It wasn't that he cared less for Adria, or that he felt she didn't return his affection. It was the fact that he felt so overwhelmed by that relationship, and he recalled everything being so easy between himself and Joselyn in the past. Being no fool, Sirion knew the ease of their relationship sprang from the fact that he and Joselyn had borne no real expectations from one another. Unlike his relationship with Adria, deeper levels of emotion had never surfaced. Well, at least not for him.

As Sirion walked, Joselyn's scent became stronger. It wasn't long before he recognized that she was still in the area. The knowledge was a bit disconcerting, but he didn't have long to ponder it before she was stepping out onto the path before him. He stopped the moment he saw her, and solemnly watched as she closed the distance between them. As always, she moved with a slow seductive gait, and her eyes beckoned him to her bed furs. He maintained his aura of indifference as she approached, keeping in mind how silly she was to play these games with him. He wasn't a young man anymore, a man who had the indiscriminate appetite of a boy who often had his thoughts in his pants. Those years were long gone and he had become a man with other desires that didn't necessarily involve those of the flesh. Much to his pleasure, Adrianna more than fulfilled that particular requirement...

Sirion waited patiently as Joselyn approached. Finally, she stopped and regarded him intently for a moment. "Hello, Sirion. It's good to see you."

He kept his expression emotionless. "What are you doing here, Joselyn?"

She pouted her lips and furrowed her brows. "You were never very good with greetings, Sirion. Honestly, I thought you would have learned a bit more decorum by now."

He narrowed his eyes slightly. "Yes, actually I have learned quite a bit over the years. However, I don't see how it pertains to you."

Joselyn was quiet for a moment. "It seems you have also become rather harsh."

Sirion shook his head. "Only when I feel it to be a necessity."

Joselyn gave a gusty sigh. "My intent isn't to argue."

He narrowed his eyes. "Then what *is* your intent? You've been lurking around my patrol area for weeks now."

"That bothers you?" she asked.

Sirion frowned. "I told you that I wanted you to leave me alone."

Joselyn pouted again. "I can't do that."

It was Sirion's turn to issue a deep sigh. "Why not?"

Joselyn shrugged and her demeanor shifted into one of nonchalance. "I've met her, you know. She's nothing what I expected she should be."

Sirion became still. Silence reigned as he stared at her. The possibility that Joselyn had gone out of her way to accost Adrianna bothered him. "I want you to leave her alone."

Joselyn cocked her head. "Why? Are you afraid I told her about us?"

Sirion's frown deepened. "There is no 'us'; whatever relationship we had ended long ago. I thought I explained that to you."

Joselyn gave him a small smile. "I can't help questioning it. I heard you speak the words, but I saw you looking at me the time or two you have noticed me about the souk." She shook her head. "That is not indicative of a man who truly believes an ending has taken place."

Sirion regarded her intently as he pondered her words. She was right, he *did* take note of her the two times he saw her about the extensive marketplace along the eastern side of Alcrostat. However, it wasn't what she claimed it to be, only that he had wondered what she was doing there. Of course, she would throw it in his face now, and the reason why he found it disturbing was because she was making him question himself.

Sirion chuckled condescendingly. "Your arrogance still tends to get the best of you, I see."

Joselyn raised a delicately arched brow. "You are actually refuting me?"

"How could I not? You are spouting idiocy."

Joselyn stepped closer and lowered her voice. "Am I really? I find that so hard to believe after the things you have done to me in whatever privacy we could find at the time."

Sirion narrowed his eyes. Of course, he remembered what they had once shared together. They had been more than delighted within each other's company and had often sought one another out more than once in any given day. They had quite a physical relationship, and it was only after he began to have feelings for Adrianna that he realized that was all it had been between him and Joselyn...physical.

Joselyn moved even closer and placed a hand on his chest. "I can tell that you remember," she whispered. She moved her hand upward to caress the curve of his jaw. "You were good, very good."

Sirion's reply was scathing. "As good as my uncle?"

Joselyn stiffened and she dropped her hand away. He could see the conflict in her eyes as she pondered her next words. Her relationship with Sydonnia sickened him, especially since she used it as an excuse to get him to come back to her after they had mutually decided to part ways many years before. She had been in the bed of an abomination, a man who had killed so many people. No matter how attractive Sirion found her to be, Joselyn was despicable and more than unworthy of him.

Joselyn's jaw tightened almost imperceptibly. "I worry about you, Sirion," she said in a solemn tone.

Sirion stepped back and placed a hand on each hip. "I worry about me too, but I am certain it is for entirely different reasons."

Joselyn cast him a withering glance. "She isn't what you think her to be."

Sirion said nothing.

"I sense something about her, something profound."

Sirion pursed his lips. "That tells me nothing. I already know that there is more to Adrianna than what meets the eye." He paused and then continued. "Like I said, I want you to leave her alone. And it has everything to do with what you might tell her. You are a poison, Joselyn, and I don't want Adria affected."

Joselyn's complexion had paled and she regarded him intently. "You think you know everything. I suppose some things are bound to remain unchanged."

Once again, Sirion said nothing, knowing she was goading him.

"I can tell she is hiding things from you and I have seen the way she looks at the man who has become her partner in the building of the tower. You are a fool not to make this realization for yourself."

Sirion flinched inwardly and could only hope Joselyn didn't notice that she had struck a chord. Even after he had witnessed the kiss they shared before casting the spell to open the portal for the dragons, Adrianna had assured him that there was nothing between herself and Dinim. However, sometimes he found it hard to accept in light of all they shared together. He liked to believe that he was the sole recipient of Adrianna's love. Regrettably there were times, especially now, he found that belief difficult to capture.

Sirion felt his temper flare. "Go away, Joselyn. I know you speak only out of jealousy. You wish that it was you for whom I care so deeply. Go back to my uncle. I am certain he will have you in his bed again if you beg him."

Sirion saw the trembling of her lower lip just before she turned away. Within moments Joselyn had disappeared back into the trees from whence she had come. A part of him considered feeling sorry for her, but an even larger part couldn't bring himself to do it. This was the third time she had approached him since coming home, and he had come to the realization that she was very manipulative. He hated to think that she might say or do something to hurt Adrianna, and he realized she had just done that to him.

Unfortunately, in his current state of mind, Sirion was more easily influenced. He felt so overwhelmed in his life already, and anything more might just send him over the edge. He waited for the day things would begin to look better for him, but as of yet he hadn't seen the light at the end of his dark tunnel.

He couldn't help wondering if it would ever come.

# Secrets Revealed

Sheridana slowed her pace even more as she approached the practice hall. Her belly spasmed for what seemed like the tenth time since she made the decision to approach Armond with the secret she had been keeping from him for so many weeks. She knew he was already at bit put out by her avoidance of him, and she was uncertain as to whether he would even bother to give her a moment of his time. She supposed she couldn't blame him for she would probably be the same way if their places were reversed.

Sheri stopped at the entry to the chamber and brought herself close to the wall. Silently she watched as Armond spoke to the two young people where they sat in the middle of the room. She didn't really pay attention to what he said, but the way he said it, the gestures he made as he explained his words, and the tone he used. The boy and girl listened with avid interest. Both seemed to be near adolescence at about fifteen years of age, and it was obvious they had much respect for Armond by the way they willingly gave their undivided attention.

Sheri couldn't help but smile sadly to herself. It was very apparent to her that Armond would be a good father. Not for the first time she felt how unfortunate it was that they were so indecisive about one another. It was the reason she waited so long to tell him about the baby. Since returning to Elvandahar, a part of her wished he could be the male figure in Fitanni's life, but another part of her rejected that idea based on how she would always be at odds with him. Her heart ached with what she faced now, a man who had only enjoyed her company in the bed furs. Their relationship had been purely physical, with very little intent to get to know one another as more than just a warm body at night to satisfy lusty cravings. She had known what she was getting into when she bedded Armond for the first time, and she was fine with that until she realized what their union had conceived.

*Oh gods...*

Sheri felt the tears come to her eyes. She hadn't allowed Armond to touch her since he and the rest of the group returned to Krathil-lon after their battle with Aasarak. After a while of avoiding him, he was finally able to back her into a corner. He had made a show of concern for her, but she saw his underlying reason for detaining her reflected in his eyes. Mayhap she'd thought too harshly of him, but her despondency made her more pessimistic than usual.

She imagined that he'd gone to the beds of other women to satisfy himself. The thought bothered her but she wasn't deterred. She didn't want him to notice the changes that were taking over her body, not prepared to lie in order to explain them away for they would only make her sound shrewish. Besides, if she happened to succeed in those lies, she didn't want him to think her to be a *fat* shrew instead of just a shrew...

In the meantime, she had missed him more than she thought she might. And now here she was, spying on him from the entry of his own practice chamber.

He must have sensed her watching, for it was then Armond glanced up towards the entryway. She saw him do a double-take as his gaze swept past and then went back to her. She heard his words falter, and for a moment longer he continued his lecture before dismissing his students. Sheri nodded to both the boy and girl as they made their way out of the chamber, and then watched as Armond rose from his position on the floor.

Armond slowly made his way across the space separating them. He regarded her stoically, and once close enough, he spoke. "Why are you here?"

Sheridana swallowed heavily. She was nervous in his presence and her hand shook as she swept a damp palm over the thin fabric of her trousers. "You are good with the children."

With a brief sarcastic chuckle Armond shook his head. "So, you are willing to speak with me now? After shafting me for so long?"

Sheri hesitated and glanced at the floor. "I have something I need to tell you."

Silence reigned for a moment. Then, "What makes you think I even care what you have to say?"

Sheridana gazed back up at him solemnly and shook her head. This could be her easy out. If he refused her, she could claim he never allowed her to tell him...

"Nothing. There is nothing that I can do that will make you want to listen." Sheri paused and then continued. "But I am *asking* you to."

Armond crossed his arms over his chest and pursed his lips. She had to admit he was rather handsome and it reminded her of why it had been so easy for her to go to his bed. His black hair was pulled back at the nape of his neck, and it hung over his shoulder. He was tall, but muscular, and she could see the planes of his chest beneath the thin fabric of his summer tunic. He shook his head and turned away. He walked across the chamber and picked up the swords leaning against one of the walls to return them to the chest situated at the far side. With a heavy heart she watched him perform this task and was about to turn away in defeat when she heard his voice call out to her.

"I am listening."

Sheri felt her heart begin pounding in her chest. She knew it was silly to feel so afraid, but she couldn't help it. She had never experienced this before, telling a man that he was going to be a father when he didn't expect it. *Because Ian was long gone before she ever realized she was pregnant with Fitanni.*

Without meaning to, Sheridana struggled to speak the words she knew she wanted to say. Her mouth moved but no words issued forth. From across the chamber Armond had turned to give her his attention. She could sense his consternation a few moments later when she still had yet to say anything. With a deep sigh he walked back towards her. In spite of what she was about to tell him, she was glad she had decided to wear one of the looser fitting garments that had begun to characterize her attire over the past moon cycle. With all her energy, she kept her hands at her sides in spite of her desire to place a hand protectively over her slightly swollen abdomen.

Armond stopped only when he stood directly in front of her. Personal space held no meaning for him as he closed the distance so that barely any separated them at all. He looked down at her intensely from green eyes. "Come out with it, Sheridana. I haven't got all day."

She swallowed again as she continued to look up at him. He seemed so imposing standing there above her and she vaguely recalled when he would never have intimidated her the way he did now. Her belly spasmed yet again in response to the anxiety she felt. But this time it was it was stronger than it had been before. She took a deep breath as the realization washed over her. What she was feeling was not her body's response to the stress of her situation, but the tiny movements of the child within.

By the gods, Armond was going to be so angry when he realized how long it had taken her to tell him...

Armond looked down at the woman standing before him and frowned inwardly. Sheridana Darnesse had become an enigma to him, more so than she had ever been before their battle with Aasarak. It began when the sickness started, at least a fortnight or two before the journey to Aasarak's lair. When he had first asked her about it, she had assured him that she suffered from frayed nerves and that it was nothing to worry about. Of course, it never stopped him from being concerned. Hells, the woman shared his bed furs! How could he not be concerned? He had even gone so far as to be a bit more solicitous of her whilst they were together, making certain he remained gentle.

The sickness had only become worse as the days passed. For a while he saw her vomit at least once every day. After so many times of inquiring and being given the same vague response, he ceased asking and just remained vigilant. Then the day came that Sheridana became unconscious. Tianna had looked over her and announced that she was sick, only she didn't know what the sickness was from. Sheri was in a coma and Tianna was unable to bring her out of it. He remembered the terrible feeling that gripped him, and he hated leaving Sheri behind whilst he and the rest of the group moved on to Aasarak's lair without her.

After the horrific battle, Armond was anxious to make it to Krathil-lon. He knew it was foolish for him to worry so much for Sheridana, but he couldn't seem to help it. He had always thought they shared very little together, only the lustful union of which they partook on a nightly basis for so many weeks. But he soon recognized he was woefully wrong. The woman whom he had disliked since the first day he met her had somehow become a part of him whether he liked it or not.

Much to his dismay, once reaching the sanctuary of Krathil-lon, Sheridana had behaved very differently with him. It didn't take Armond long to realize she was avoiding him like a plague, and when he finally got the chance to talk to her, she was distant and aloof, treating him as though there was nothing between him. It was like a splash of cold water and he promptly left her alone. He accompanied the group to Elvandahar, but several times since then he had considered leaving. Nothing held him there, and it would be easy for him to get hired on as a mercenary somewhere else. But then Adrianna had approached him with an idea she and Dinim had for a school dedicated to Dimensionalist training. Somehow, she had roped him into helping out with the construction. In all honesty he didn't mind, for it was something to keep him busy until he devised a more solid plan for his future.

It was then she found them. Somehow, Adrianna had a knack for perceiving the Talent of others. Rikon and Dahlia were brought to him and it didn't take him long to come to the same conclusion. Both were secondary Talents, and ripe for the type of training Armond had the capacity to offer. Initially he questioned his ability to teach others. Such an endeavor took time and no small degree of patience. It didn't earn him a living, his help with the construction did that. But it was fulfilling, for he felt he had a chance to affect the future of the young people who sought out his expertise.

Regarding the woman standing before him now, he saw a lot of Adrianna. He had always been physically attracted to her, and with Sheri it was no different. It was strange because the sisters were colored so differently. Where one seemed to be made of the light, the other was dark. However, the lighter complexion of the two, Adrianna, had the more solemn personality. Sheridana, the one with darker hair, had a more free-spirited attitude. Armond had noted this a time or two and thought how interesting it was that the sisters were so very disparate. However, as he looked down at Sheri, he couldn't help thinking there was something amiss. She had never looked at him this way before, with an expression tinged with dread. It was almost like she thought him a miscreant that would take her by the throat and beat her at any moment. It was so different from what he always knew Sheri to be, a very strong, forthright woman. Her apparent inability to speak to him now took him aback, for he was unaccustomed to such hesitancy from her.

Finally, she spoke in a tone he had never heard from her before. "You are aware I have been sick for a while now."

Armond frowned and even moved back a step so he could better his view of her. He was about to say something but decided to respectfully maintain his silence so as to await her next words.

"I lied when I told you it was frayed nerves that were making me so ill."

Armond deepened his frown, not liking the direction her words were heading. He put his hands at his hips and just stood there, not really knowing what to say.

Sheridana tried to clear away the dryness in her throat. His expression was intimidating to say the least. No longer able to win the struggle, she placed a hand against her belly with the hope of quieting the movements of the baby, movements she was certain had much to do with her current confrontation.

Sheri shook her head. "I... I'm sorry it took so long for me to tell you, but I just didn't know how. Our situation with Aasarak was so consuming, and I knew that it would distract from that..."

"Tell me what?" Armond's face had visibly paled, and his gaze was intense.

Shaken by his response, Sheridana blinked away the tears that threatened. "I'm pregnant."

Armond stepped back as though he'd been struck a physical blow. He rubbed his hand down the front of his face to stop at his mouth and regarded her from eyes wide with shock. Once again, silence rang throughout the chamber. Sheridana felt a tear finally manage to escape to run down her cheek. Oh gods, he was going to hate her more than he did already...

Finally, Armond composed himself enough to take his hand away from his mouth. She could see him putting the pieces together as he determined an approximate time the child my have been conceived, followed by when she may have become knowledgeable of it. He then realized that it may have been the reason why she didn't accompany them to Aasarak, and that others in the group were aware of her condition.

His eyes flashed with sudden anger and his voice was gruff. "How long has it been?"

She hesitated a brief moment before answering. "About six moon cycles."

Armond nodded. "And how long have you known?"

"M... maybe four moon cycles."

Armond nodded again. Sheri swallowed heavily and continued to watch the play of emotion on his face. "And you waited this long to tell me?" Armond's voice rose to a shout and his eyes blazed green. "We have been free of Aasarak for almost two moon cycles! Who else knows about this?"

Sheridana shook her head and placed an arm protectively over her belly. Her voice quavered. "Only Adrianna, Sirion, Triath and Tianna know. It was their actions that kept me from aiding the Wildrunners against Aasarak. They worried about my welfare, as well as that of the child."

Armond just stood there and regarded her for a few moments. Then he slowly shook his head. "You must think me such a dimwit. You come in here and interrupt my training session. Then you tell me you are pregnant with a child, *my* child. You expect me to just accept this even though you and half the group has known about it for many weeks." He raised his hands into the air and brought them down to slap the sides of his legs. "Why bother telling me at all? Obviously, you were doing just fine when you were keeping this from me." Armond took a deep breath and then expelled it. "I can't believe I actually started to care about you."

Sheridana just stood there as Armond tuned away and walked out of the practice room. Tears ran, unchecked, down her face only to drip onto the floor. The child lay quietly within, almost as though it knew its father had departed. She was astounded by Armond's reaction, knowing he would be angry but never thinking he would walk away from her.

Sobbing pitifully, Sheridana crumpled into a distraught heap on the floor. The terrible reality of her situation washed over her and she was afraid. In about six moon cycles she would deliver another child. It would join the first one without a father. Meanwhile she would be without a husband, without someone to share such a burden. With what money would she support her family? Carli would help care for the children when Sheri was able to find work, but three mouths to feed and shelter was a big responsibility to manage alone. Meanwhile, Hinterlean society would find it easy to shun her, not only because of her race, but because she had borne two children out of wedlock with two different men.

Adrianna might be able to offer some help, but her sister had yet to find a means of supporting herself without even considering Sheri and her dependents.

Since returning to Elvandahar, the harsh reality of life had come crashing down on her and she had nowhere to turn. For now, crying seemed to be the best course of action...

Dinim walked along the interconnecting bridges of Alcrostat. As usual nowadays, he held a parchment in his hands, his eyes perusing it every now and again even as he was walking. This time it was the original plan Adrianna had drawn for the tower and surrounding school. The endeavor had been something they had entertained between one another for a few weeks before she chose to execute it, and once seeing the plan for the first time, Dinim had been quite impressed. He never would have taken her for an architect, but she had drawn most structures to scale, taking into consideration the support materials that might be needed for each one. Of course, it wasn't near perfect... one would need to be an expert for that. But it was *good*.

Dinim's thoughts shifted to he and Adria's recent visit to Master Tallachienan. Via the Travel notebook, Dinim had told the Master about the anti-scrying device they hoped to acquire for Triath, and within a day or two he had responded and brought them to the citadel. They hadn't been there long, only about two days. Triath had gone with them, for the device Tallachienan created was to be constructed especially for him in order to make it more powerful. Adrianna had been immensely grateful for the care master Tallachienan put into the artifact, for it would be something Triath would need to wear for a very, very long time. Right away Dinim had noticed something between them, a strange dynamic between master and apprentice he had never experienced before. It was the way they behaved around one another, as though Tallachienan considered her more a peer than a subordinate...

Dinim continued along, taking first one bridge and then the next that would take him to the daladin he shared with Armond and Dartanyen. It was located a bit closer to the fortress than he would have liked, but it had been one of Dartanyen's requirements. The man wanted a home near the place where he would be spending many of his waking moments, day or night. Armond really hadn't cared one way or another, but Dinim would have preferred something a bit further away from the near constant bustle. Dinim grinned to himself. Once the construction of the main tower was complete, he would make his residence there as the remaining academy was built. He knew no one would care, not to mention there was a benefit to someone staying on site during the darkest hours of the night.

Dinim was about to turn down another bridge when he suddenly noticed someone standing in his way. He had almost collided with her when he swiftly drew himself to a stop. With some measure of irritation, he brought his eyes up to her face, but once seeing who it was, he allowed his ire to dissipate. He had met her once before during the initial construction of the tower. What was her name? Oh yes, it was Joselyn. He remembered it because he had thought her rather pretty.

The druidess offered him a smile. "I'm sorry, I didn't mean to be in your way." She cocked her head to the side questioningly. "Dinim, right?"

Dinim nodded and offered her a smile of his own. "I remember you as Joselyn. Am I correct?"

She widened her smile and inclined her head. "Indeed, you are. You have a good memory."

Dinim chuckled. "It seems you do as well."

Joselyn shrugged. "I have always been that way. It is easy for me to remember names and faces."

Dinim nodded. "Well, it's good to see you. Are you still volunteering your time at the construction site?"

Joselyn nodded. "Every once in a while. However, I have other duties to the order, and many times I must conduct my work elsewhere."

"That's easily understood. A person can only give so much of their time away. I have been in similar situations before."

Joselyn cocked her head to the side. "Really? When?"

"Actually, not very long ago. It was a mission I undertook with the Wildrunners. You probably know of them."

Joselyn nodded. "Indeed, I do. You must have been working with Sirion Timberlyn."

Dinim grinned. "You know him, then?"

"He is actually a good friend of mine."

"Oh yes, I think I recall that being mentioned when we first met. It's strange though, I have never heard him speak of you." He paused the briefest of moments, instantly recognizing that wasn't the right thing to say. Then, "Of course that means nothing, for Sirion happens to be one of the most private people I know."

Joselyn seemed to have taken no offense. "Yes, I have noticed the same." Dinim simply nodded, glad he had diverted a potential small disaster.

"I have also noticed some other things," she continued.

Dinim found his interest piqued. "And what is that?"

Joselyn shrugged. "Only that your friend... what is her name...

Adrianna? I don't know if you realize it or not, but she has a liking for you."

Joselyn smiled inwardly when she saw that Dinim was taken aback. In her mind's eye, she could see the unfolding drama. She hadn't volunteered her time at all to the construction site since meeting them there, instead spending her free moments watching them. In reality, she had seen the reverse... that it was Dinim who felt an affection for Adrianna.

But it didn't mean that Adrianna didn't feel something similar, for her close relationship with the man was quite noteworthy.

He recovered his composure and offered a small chuckle. "What?"

Joselyn nodded. "Yes, I can see it clear as day." She maintained her aura of seriousness as she watched the myriad expressions pass over the man's face, and he shook his head in hopeful denial. He was handsome, even for a Cimmerean, and she briefly wondered what he might be like in the bedchamber.

"No, that can't be right. She has Sirion," he responded.

Joselyn shrugged again. "I'm only telling you what I saw."

He gave another small chuckle. "Well, what exactly is that?"

Joselyn feigned lack of knowledge. "I saw her watching you a bit more intently than one might a mere friend. Honestly, I had no idea Sirion was involved," she lied.

Dinim was silent as he became introspective. Joselyn waited patiently, her mind continuing to see a set of events soon to take place. Her primary goal at this time was now complete. Dinim would seriously consider making a play for Adrianna's affection, and if she kept working on Sirion, he just might slip up. Adrianna might never forgive him, and he would be Joselyn's for the taking.

Unfortunately, Sirion had been gone for the past couple of days... Joselyn became thoughtful. But mayhap she could use Sirion's absence to her benefit. Mayhap it would give Dinim that much more impetus to pursue Adrianna. Mayhap it would be Adrianna who slipped up, and Sirion wouldn't find it in him to forgive her... *much as he hadn't forgiven Joselyn.*

"Well, it is good to see you again," said Dinim, finally recovering from the deluge of thoughts that had momentarily overwhelmed him.

Joselyn smiled widely. "It's good to see you too. Good luck with the building."

He nodded as she stepped around him to proceed along the bridge. She walked several paces only to turn around and see him still standing there. She smiled again and continued along. Next, she needed to pay a visit to

Adrianna.

The daladin was probably like most of those that belonged to the unmarried men in and around Alcrostat. It was small, yet easily had the capacity to house two people comfortably. It was modest, with spartan furnishings and it was more than just a little bit messy. Besides the fact that it was not located as close to the academy as she would like, it was one of the reasons why Adrianna did not stay there full time. The other was that Sirion had not really invited her to.

Adrianna frowned at this as she set her bags down on the nearest chair. It had been strange with Sirion the past few moon cycles, and to be honest, she hadn't given herself much time to consider it much. She knew it was more than just the time constraints that had beset her since the building of the academy had begun, it was the fact that a part of her simply found it too painful to contemplate.

The presence of one Joselyn Quemirren didn't much help matters.

With a deep sigh, Adrianna made her way to the bedchamber. There, she found the blankets and furs in the disarray which she had come to recognize as normal. They needed to be laundered again, and if she didn't do it, the task simply wouldn't get done. Sirion was not prone to bother himself with such things, so it was up to her to do it if she wanted a clean place to sleep when she stayed at his daladin. Her frown deepened, uncertain of how she should feel about it.

Adrianna sat on at the foot of the bed, her thoughts returning to Joselyn. The young druidess had approached her just that day under the guise of helping to get work done at the building site. Somehow the topic of Sirion had arisen, and Adrianna, plagued by the reality that things were not right between the two of them, was easily affected by anything the woman had to say.

*"I know Sirion, and he has needs."* Adrianna raised an eyebrow, not believing what she was hearing. *"How can you see to those when you are always here?"*

Astonished, Adrianna had just stared at the other woman. Certainly, she understood the words Joselyn spoke, but Sirion wasn't the only one with needs. Didn't Adrianna have them too?

After the conversation was over, Adrianna had walked away from Joselyn feeling dejected, wounded, and somehow sullied. She couldn't understand the last part, why she would feel so dirty. She didn't want to understand it; she just wanted it to go away.

But it didn't, and now Adrianna sat there on Sirion's bed, feeling worse than ever, tears streaming down her face.

For several moments she simply remained there, waiting for the tears to dry, her heart heavy. The thoughts running through her mind were disjointed, not really making much sense. All she could really glean from them was that she was beseiged by saddness with glimmers of anger.

Adrianna heard movement in the front room, telling her that Sirion was home. She squared her shoulders and took another deep breath, rising from the bed to meet him. When Sirion saw her emerge from the bedroom he gave her a cursory smile that didn't quite reach his eyes and continued to take off his vest and tunic that were dirty from the last few days spent on patrol.

It appeared she would have to launder those too.

Adrianna just stood by and watched him. The muscle on his bronze chest and back rippled across the contours of his body as he moved, and his crimson hair, gathered at the nape of his neck, lay in a tangled mess between his shouder blades. More than anything, he needed a good bath, but as of late, he seemed to care less and less about his state of cleanliness. It was almost like he was reverting to some animal state, but even animals bathed when they needed to.

"How was your day?" The words resisted coming from her mouth, for, in that moment, like so many others that had happened upon her more frequently as of late, she felt as though she was talking to a stranger.

Sirion shrugged noncommittally. "It was like all the others I suppose."

Adrianna just nodded. He seemed so distant, more distant than ever, and she so much wanted to bridge that gap. She hoped that maybe he would ask her about her own day; at least it would be somthing, something better than *this*.

Sirion walked past her and into the bedchamber, moving aside the blankets and lying down with a gusty exhale. Adrianna could sense his fatigue. He worked on patrol from early mornming until late into the afternoon. Sometimes he worked into the night, barely pausing to even take a meal.

She stood there and just stared at him. His eyes were closed, his body relaxed. She considered simply leaving him there to rest, but the feeling of wrongness between them bade her stay.

"Sirion, is something wrong?"

One eye cracked open to regard her and a slight tension could suddenly be felt in the air. "Why do you ask?"

She shrugged. "You just seem so distant... not yourself. I was hoping you might tell me what's bothering you."

He closed the eye and sighed. Silence reigned for several moments before he spoke again. "I don't see how I've been any different since we first got back here."

Adrianna nodded, thoughtful. "You are right. You haven't. You are different since the battle with Aasarak." She was quiet for a moment to gather her courage. Then, "Are you angry with me for some reason?"

Once again, there was silence. Adrianna shifted in place, taking his lack of response as affirmation of his anger. For the life of her, she couldn't figure out what would have made him upset. They spent most of their time apart, granted, but it wasn't just her work schedule that made it that way. He worked just as much, if not more, than she did. She didn't come to his daladin every night because he had never insisted she do so. She only came when she felt the need to see him, not because of any words spoken by him that he might like to see her. She wanted... no, *needed*... for him to tell her he wanted to see her too. Was it something she was supposed to do that made him upset? Something that he expected from her that she wasn't aware of?

Once realizing she wasn't going to get a response, she spoke again. "I don't understand. What didn't I do?"

Sirion opened both of his eyes then, pinning her with their intensity. "It's not what you didn't do. It's what you did do."

Adrianna frowned. "Alright. What was it? Why haven't you told me about it?"

"Why would I? You don't tell me things. Why would I bother to tell you things?"

Adrianna recoiled from the scathing tone of his voice, and her heartbeat stuttered in her chest. "I... I thought we discussed this. I apologized to you. I told you that I would do better, that I would tell you things moving forward."

Sirion pursed his lips and shook his head, staring off into the air beside him. "Well, maybe it's just not enough."

Her lips began to tremble. She fought from crying, didn't want to break down in front of him and show him her weakness. A painful lump formed in the back of her throat, and it was all she could do to just swallow past it. "What do I have to do to make it enough?" she whispered.

"Do you love him?" Sirion's tone raked over her from across the room, leaving deep rents in her heart.

Adrianna had to think about who Sirion was talking about, swiftly concluding that it must be the Master. "I told you I did. That my self from the last Cycle loved him deeply. I told you it wasn't like that this Cycle, that my love for you was far greater than anything I felt for Tallachienan."

"Yet you went to his bed." Sirion's jaw pulsed with tension.

"I told you why that happened. I □"

"You didn't love me enough to resist him."

Adrianna's heart stuttered again, filling with dread. "No! It wasn't like that!" Unable to keep the tears in check any longer, they began to course down her face. "The memories were so vivid, I thought I was myself from the previous Cycle. All I could feel was what she felt. But I came back to my senses! I thought of you and everything I hoped we could share together!"

"And after that?" Sirion pinned her with his gaze once again. "You went back to his bed. You lived as his mistress for weeks."

Adrianna stood there, stunned as the realization washed over her. Sirion couldn't forgive her for what she had done because he had been able to resist Tholana while she couldn't do the same with Tallachienan. Despair washed over her and she turned away from his accusing glare. She stumbled away from the entry to the bedchamber and back into the main living area, sinking down onto one of the chairs situated around the table. She cried silently, her body heaving with her sobs. The sadness poured out of her with the tears she shed, dripping onto the floor beneath her feet. Of course he was right. She hadn't been strong enough.

"Oh gods, I'm so sorry. I should have been stronger. I should have been stronger. I should have been better. Please, gods, please save me from myself. Please." Adrianna whispered the words to herself, hoping, praying that the agony in her heart would somehow cease. She was losing Sirion, and it was all her fault. *If only I could have been stronger. If only...*

A gentle hand touched her shoulder. "Adria?"

She trembled beneath Sirion's touch, winced at the soft tone of his voice, a tone now devoid of the hate she'd heard not long before.

"Adrianna, I'm sorry, please don't cry anymore. It hurts me when you cry."

The sobbing continued. She just couldn't seem to stop it, feelings of guilt and powerlessness washing over her in wave after wave. They stripped her soul bare, leaving it lying there open to the elements.

"Adrianna, I'm so sorry. I know you tried. I know how difficult it must have been. Please, come and lay down with me. Let me hold you to show you how sorry I am, and that I love you."

She allowed herself to be helped up from the chair and walked into the bedroom. Sirion urged her down onto the bed, and once she was situated comfortably, he joined her, laying beside her and wrapping a strong arm around her waist. "I was wrong to doubt you, Shendori. Please believe me when I say I'm sorry. I am just hurt, bleeding inside. But I'll get better, and I'll help you get better too. I promise."

Finally, the sobing receded and she was able to breathe normally again. By that time, Sirion had fallen asleep, his breaths a rhythmic warmth at the back of her neck. She lay there in the darkness, her eyes closing in response to her own fatigue, and her mind played over her last weeks in

Tallachienan's citadel once again.

It was right as sleep began to claim her that Adrianna realized something. Day after day she had studied and practiced Dimensionalist magic in Master Tallachienan's presence. Not for one week, or two, or even several. She had lived in his citadel for almost seven years. During that time, she never buckled, not until the bitter end.

# FAMILY REUNION

With no small amount of worry, Gareth regarded the Hinterlean rangers that surrounded them. Jaysim cast him a withering glance, probably wondering why his insanity had dictated that he accompany Gareth and Talemar through to the end of their journey. Gareth appreciated the monumental gesture, pleased that his uncle would want to be certain they remained safe. Of course, Gareth was certain Jaysim did it more for his deceased sister than for any allegiance he had to his young nephew. Yet the result was still the same, for Gareth reaped the benefit of his actions.

One of the rangers stepped closer, his crossbow trained on Gareth where he sat astride his lloryk. "Please state your name and your business here within the realm of Elvandahar."

Gareth nervously glanced about and cleared his throat. "We were told that a man by the name of Dinim Coabra resides in one of the villages close to the city of Alcrostat. We come bearing a message."

The ranger thoughtfully considered his words. "I see. What might this message entail? I am curious as to why you have come to bring it yourself as opposed to via messenger hawk."

Gareth frowned slightly. "The message is only for Dinim Coabra to hear."

The ranger nodded. "So, who are you, then? Have you met Master Dinim before?"

Gareth shook his head. "My name is Gareth Darnesse. And no, I have never met him. However, he will find my message of supreme importance."

The ranger nodded again. "These are difficult times. We are required to escort you into the city."

Gareth nodded. "Of course. Please proceed with your protocol. We have no objection."

The ranger continued to regard him speculatively. "You say your surname is Darnesse."

Gareth nodded and deepened his frown. "What is it to you?"

The ranger shook his head. "Nothing. Only that I have heard it before."

"Really?" Gareth's interest was immediately piqued.

The ranger's gaze became hooded. "Maybe. I can't really know for certain." He paused for a moment and Gareth was about to speak again when the ranger turned and gestured into the trees ahead. "Come. The city lies this way."

"How much longer do we have before we make it there?" asked Jaysim.

The ranger shrugged and cast a quick glance at Talemar where he sat in front of Jaysim on the other lloryk. "Two days of ordinary travel with a minimum of stops."

Gareth and Jaysim both nodded and followed the rangers. The journey was easy, and the rangers a bit more amiable than they originally thought. The rangers allowed them to share their evening fires, a courtesy that extended to the food they brought for the evening meal. Some of the men took an interest in young Talemar, and showed the boy how to hold his bow, how to nock the arrow, and then to aim at his target. It was apparent that Talemar enjoyed the attention when his cerulean eyes alighted with pleasure. Gareth couldn't help smiling to himself. He liked to see the boy happy, for Talemar had felt little of that particular emotion since Sharra's death.

The rangers also had some very large canines. The corubis were companions to some of the rangers, and shared the space around the evening fires. Gareth and Jaysim found them quite disconcerting, while Talemar readily accepted them near his person. Much to Gareth's extreme anxiety, the small boy even went so far as to touch the biggest one. The animal was gentle, much more so than Gareth ever would have imagined. It even appeared that the beast enjoyed the attention Talemar paid, and before long Gareth also became acclimated to their benign presence.

By the time they reached the city of Alcrostat, Gareth had decided that he very much enjoyed the forested environment offered by the Silverwood. Even though he had found family within the mountainous reaches of the most populated of Savanlean strongholds, he had finally discovered how much more comfortable he felt among the trees. Throughout their long journey from Aldehirra, Gareth had considered staying in Elvandahar for only a year or so while Talemar adjusted to his new life. But now that had changed. He thought maybe, just maybe, he could make a life for himself here... and he would never have to leave his little cousin behind.

It was midmorning when the rangers stopped. The leader, Shumon, approached them. "I have sent two of my rangers ahead to notify Master Dinim of your arrival and the reason for your visit. They should be returning any moment."

Gareth nodded. "I suppose now is the time for me to tell you how appreciative we have been to have your escort. Your guidance has been a boon, and you and your men have been exceptionally kind to myself, my uncle, and my little cousin." Gareth gave a brief bow. "Thank you for all you have done for us."

Shumon's eyes shone with the praise. "I am pleased you have enjoyed our company. Believe me, there are so many others who pass through here who consider us bothersome and intrusive."

Gareth cocked his head. "That is strange, for I only see a group of men who are trying to do their duty." Then he smiled. "And you have gone above and beyond. I would like to offer my gratitude." Gareth held out his arm, palm up.

With a smile, Shumon accepted the arm and grasped it whole-heartedly. "Thank you, my friend. Your words are kind."

"My words are the truth," replied Gareth as he gripped Shumon's forearm.

Both men turned when the two ranger scouts suddenly appeared. They immediately jumped down from their corubis and approached Gareth and Shumon. Meanwhile, the large dappled canines settled themselves wearily to the ground. "We have been instructed to bring our guests to the Academy."

Shumon nodded and turned to Gareth with a smile. "Follow us. Your journey is nearly over."

Gareth vaulted into the saddle and followed immediately behind the rangers. Jaysim and Talemar rode behind. Gareth and Jaysim agreed that it should be Gareth who would do the talking. Both of them knew that they would be entering a delicate situation, facing a man who had no knowledge of his son.

It wasn't long before the great silver oak trees gave way to a clearing. At its center rose a magnificent tower. The structure rose higher than any of the great oaks, and at the top there was a spire that rose even higher. By the gods, the manpower and materials used to build such a thing was unimaginable.

The rangers stopped in the clearing. Gareth dismounted his lloryk and waited for barely a moment when, from around the side of the tower, there emerged a woman. Gareth was surprised to see that her hair was colored the palest gold, a color one might see in one who was of Savanlean descent. As she approached, he could see that she was very beautiful, possibly the loveliest woman he had ever seen.

Finally, the woman stopped before Shumon and Gareth, her dark brown eyes assessing them speculatively. Her gaze was solemn and she immediately got to the point. "Good morn, Shumon. I hope you don't mind, but it was I who gave permission for our guests to come here." She then turned to Gareth. "Is it you who carries the message for Master Dinim?"

Gareth found himself in a state of shock. He struggled to speak, his mouth moving with no words issuing forth. *The young woman standing before him was an almost exact replica of his dead mother.*

Adrianna stood before the young man whom Shumon had brought. She couldn't help but think there was something familiar about him. He was quite handsome, with light brown hair and slightly canted blue eyes. It seemed he was at a loss for words, his mouth opening and closing the way a fish's might once it had been caught and brought above water. She noticed Shumon glancing back and forth from herself to the man, his expression one of extreme interest.

Adrianna frowned slightly but maintained her patience in spite of having very little to give in light of the events of the past few days. "What is your name, and what type of message do you bring?"

Finally, the man managed to speak, his voice emerging as a croak. "My name is Gareth Darnesse, milady."

Adrianna felt her heart still in her chest for a moment. Her eyes widened and it was then she knew why Shumon was so interested. Not only did this man have the same surname as hers, but there were unmistakable features they shared in common, features that one didn't see very often, features that defined an individual who carried both human and faelin heritage. Adrianna slowly moved forward to close the distance between herself and the young man who stared at her incredulously from blue eyes, eyes as blue as Sheri's.

She stopped only when she stood right before him, then tentatively reached out to touch his face. She spoke in a whispered tone. "Brother, you have been gone so long I didn't recognize you.'"

"Adrianna, you... you've changed."

She gave him a sad smile and dropped her hand. "That is what happens to people when they grow older."

He shook his head. "You look just like Ama."

Adrianna breathed deeply and was about to make a reply about Thane saying the same thing, but held her tongue. Now was not the time to speak of their deceased father. Besides, there was a reason why he was there... Dinim. How her brother knew her Cimmerean friend she didn't know, but she was about to find out. "What brings you to Elvandahar, Gareth?"

She could immediately see that he was taken aback. The fact that he had just met his sister after so many years spent apart had encompassed the entirety of his mental capacity. Adrianna supposed she had become a bit hardened over the years, especially towards those who had made it so easy to leave her behind so they could endeavor to accomplish their own goals. She knew that this reality weighed on her more than usual because she was under a lot of strain with Sirion's absence. In fact, she even pitied some people whom she encountered on a consistent basis, they having to endure her wrath more so than anyone else.

Gareth struggled for a moment with his reply, but much to his favor, he was able to set aside his personal issues to address the one at hand. "Like you said, it is a message I bring for Dinim Coabra."

"And how do you know Master Dinim, may I ask?"

Gareth shook his head. "I don't milady. I simply carry the message."

Adrianna took note of his formality, but frowned when he stated that he did not know Dinim personally. "I am Master Dinim's good friend. Currently he is unavailable, but he allows me to take his messages. What is it you need to impart?"

Gareth turned to look behind him and another lloryk stepped from behind the line of rangers that pervaded the area. It seemed that everyone had a vested interest in the outcome of the delivery of this message. Sitting astride the animal were two others, one a Savanlean man, and the other a black-haired boy of about seven summers. For the second time Adrianna felt her eyes widen.

"After leaving Sangrilak, I traveled around Ansalar for a while until I decided to go north. I knew that our mother was a from a place called Aldehirra, and after asking around and finding the most accurate maps, I found the city on the northern side of the western arm of the Sartingels.

"Once making it to Aldehirra, our mother's sister, Sharra, took me into her home. I was easily accepted into Aldehirran society and, in deference to my skill with the blade, given a place as one of the patrolmen who would defend the city gates if the time to defend them ever arose.

"Sharra was already pregnant when I arrived there. Several weeks later, she gave birth to a son. Since the moment of his arrival, Talemar has been like a brother to me. When Sharra became terribly sick a few years later, I was one the who took responsibility for the boy, and when Sharra realized she was dying, she imparted to me her ultimate desire... that I take Talemar to his father."

Adrianna was silent as she took in Gareth's words. By the gods, this child was her cousin and Dinim's son. Fate had been mischievous this time, for how likely would it be for their families to be bound in such a way? Adrianna finally nodded and then asked the obvious. "Dinim is this boy's father?"

Gareth nodded silently.

Adrianna trained her gaze upon the small boy. The Savanlean had dismounted the lloryk and was currently taking the boy into his arms and bringing him to the ground. She slowly began to walk towards them. The child was beautiful, his pale complexion a stark contrast to his black hair. Then there were his eyes, cerulean eyes so crystal clear it seemed they could pierce the soul...

Once standing before the Savanlean man, Adrianna looked him in the eyes. He was quite bit older than Gareth, and it was easy to see that they shared familial ties, mayhap as an uncle or an older cousin. The man courteously nodded, the expression in his gaze telling her that he was aware of their kinship. He solemnly stepped back and the small boy was left at the fore. Adrianna instantly crouched before him and smiled.

"Hello, boy. What is your name?"

The child regarded her intently. He spoke formally in a small voice. "'Tis Talemar, milady."

She nodded. "Do you know why you are here?"

The boy nodded. "I am to meet my father."

The boy didn't move as she slowly reached out to touch the shock of silver that ran the length of his hair, the same characteristic Dinim sported. There was no doubt in her mind that this boy was indeed Dinim's son. "Where is your mother?"

The boy gave a half-hearted shrug. "She is dead from the fever, milady."

In spite of his youthfulness, and the fact he had limited understanding of the world around him, Adrianna could see the hurt reflected in the boy's eyes. Instinctively she took him by the shoulders and drew him into her. She felt an affinity for the child as he melted into her embrace. It was more than the fact that he was her cousin, her own flesh and blood. It was the call of a child who no longer had a woman to mother him. Without fully understanding why she felt so strongly, her heart ached for this boy, and she wanted to bring him into her protection.

This boy who also happened to be Dinim's son...

Gareth watched his sister embrace Talemar. To him the gesture was monumental, for it told him that Talemar had already been accepted into Hinterlean society before he even had the chance to meet his father. He couldn't believe how Adrianna had grown over the years, morphed into the exceedingly beautiful woman he saw before him now. However, in spite of the warmth she showed Talemar, there was a coldness about her, a chill he never recalled from their earlier days as children.

It was then he heard a distant voice. "Adrianna, who have we here? What is the occasion and why wasn't I invited?"

Gareth's eyes swung towards the sound and saw a Cimmerean man approaching the small gathering from a distance. Adrianna released the boy and took Talemar's small hand within hers. As she rose from her crouched position, Talemar instantly placed himself slightly behind her and pressed himself against her legs. Gareth was astonished at the

behavior, for the boy had known this woman a scant several moments. Although, Gareth had to attest that there was something about Adrianna that he could see might draw people to her. Sharra had had the same ability and had always called it one of her gifts.

Adrianna projected her voice a bit to be certain the man heard. "Dinim, these good men have come from afar to deliver a message."

Gareth felt a moment of relief, for it seemed his sister had chosen to take on the task of informing Master Coabra about the boy. It would save him an uncomfortable confrontation, not to mention the possible ire he might be forced to endure. As Dinim got closer, Gareth saw that the man's friendly expression was alight with curiosity and a smile of greeting played about one corner of his mouth. Dinim raised his hands from his sides. "All right, enlighten me then."

Adrianna kept her position as she made her reply. "There is someone here you should meet."

Dinim finally made it to the group, nodding first to the surrounding rangers followed by himself and Jaysim. He then turned towards Adrianna, his glance flicking to the boy for the briefest of moments before settling onto her face. His smile widened and Gareth could easily see that he cared for her.

"So, who is this person I need to meet that made people came from so far to be certain I did so?"

Still holding Talemar's hand, Adrianna stepped aside to reveal the boy. Dinim's gaze was confused as he looked down at the boy and then back up at Adrianna. "Dinim, may I introduce to you your son?"

With a questioning expression, the Cimmerean man brought his gaze to rest upon Talemar once more, his easy smile slowly fading away. Gareth could see Talemar fidgeting slightly beneath the scrutiny but didn't move from his place in front of Adrianna.

"What? What is this? Some kind of jape?"

Gareth chose that moment to step forward and speak up. "Please, my lord... are you Dinim Coabra?"

The Cimmerean man nodded brusquely.

"I have traveled far to find you, and to bring to you this boy. His mother succumbed to Dreyfus Fever a few moon cycles ago, a woman by the name of Sharra Farwyn. She knew you had no knowledge of the boy, so I understand this comes as a surprise to you. As she lay upon her deathbed, the lady Sharra requested my promise to deliver this boy to his father." Gareth spread his hands out before him, palms upward. "So here we are. And I am blessed to know that my duty to my mother's sister is accomplished."

Dinim nodded mutely, his lips pressed into a thin line. "I knew Sharra for only a short while sometime after my apprenticeship with Master Tallachienan. It was about eight years ago in the city of Sangrilak. We were together only a handful of times before I felt my destiny calling me elsewhere." Dinim shrugged. "So, I left. I had no idea..."

Dinim looked down for a moment and then back up at Gareth. "You say that Sharra was sister to your mother. That would make you a cousin to this boy."

Gareth nodded. "And just today I have found my sister after so many years apart." Gareth gestured to Adrianna.

Dinim's eyes became wide as he turned to Adrianna. "Is this true? Is this man your brother?"

Adrianna nodded haltingly. "Indeed, he is. Until now, I haven't seen Gareth for many years."

Dinim's brows pulled into a frown. "That means that this boy is cousin to you as well," he stated.

Adrianna only nodded.

Dinim looked back down at the boy. Gareth could easily see that the Cimmerean had no idea what he was going to do with the child, not to mention that he was probably recovering from both the shock of Sharra's death and the fact that a son had been borne as a result of their union.

Adrianna turned to Gareth and spoke into the pervading silence. "Brother, you and your comrade are welcome to stay with me until you are once again ready to travel. The daladin belongs to Sheridana, but it is large enough to house all of us." Adrianna then turned to the Cimmerean. "Dinim, why don't I take the boy home with me while you finish your work here? You can come by the daladin when you are through."

Gareth watched as Dinim smiled in relief. Meanwhile, he was pleased to know that he and Jaysim had a place to stay for the next few nights until he could decide what he should do next. More than ever, he had reason to stay here in Elvandahar, but he knew that Jaysim would be against it. There would be a fight, and Gareth wanted to delay that if possible.

Dinim looked down at the small boy standing beside Adrianna. There was no doubt in his mind that the child was his. Why the Hells had Sharra never bothered to try locating him? Or had she tried without success? He supposed he wasn't the easiest person to track. Memories of Sharra flitted through his mind. Now that he thought of it, he realized that Adrianna looked much like her. Both shared the same pale blond hair and the same shape to the mouth. They even both shared the gift of foresight. Damn, he couldn't believe he'd never recognized it before. Mayhap the similarity had caused him to develop an affinity for Adrianna so quickly. Or perhaps it was more basic than that and he just liked women with light coloration.

The boy looked up at Dinim from wary eyes. He was surprised to see that they were a brilliant shade of blue. He was so accustomed to lavender eyes set in a face that was so obviously Cimmerean. But there were other differences that were much more subtle, such as the position of the tapered ears. As opposed to the more vertical position characteristic of most Cimmereans, this boy's ears swept backward in a position indicative of his Savanlean heritage. His skin tone wasn't quite as pale, and the shape of his eyes had the distinctive Savanlean cant. Aware of everyone's attention on him, Dinim knelt before the boy. The child took a nervous step back and clutched at Adria's long-tunic with his unoccupied hand. Dinim had never considered himself intimidating before, but it was obvious that this boy felt him to be so. He tried to speak in a mild voice, but he wasn't certain he succeeded. A situation such as this thrust upon him so suddenly beat at nerves that were already frayed by other recent ordeals.

"Boy, do you know who I am?"

The boy nodded his head and replied in a small voice. "You are my father."

"What are you doing all the way over there?" Dinim indicated to the boy's position half-hidden behind Adrianna. "Come here and tell me your name."

Dinim saw Adrianna give his hand one last squeeze before letting it go. She then just stood there and watched. Dinim appreciated her silence, for she could very easily have coddled the boy, reassuring him that Dinim was a 'nice' man and that he had nothing to fear. Instead, she chose to let the boy conduct his own actions without her influence.

The boy hesitated. It was obvious he was afraid, but a moment later he slowly closed the gap between them. Finally, the child stood directly before him. Dinim made more of an effort to lower his voice and make it less authoritative. "You seem to know more about me than I do of you. What is your name?"

"'Tis Talemar, milord."

Dinim nodded. "Your mother gave you a good, strong name... worthy of respect one day." Talemar continued to stand there but Dinim thought he saw the boy pull himself up just a bit straighter. "Where are you from?"

"Aldehirra, milord. 'Tis a place that lies far to the north."

Dinim nodded, pleased that the boy chose to add an extra piece of information to his reply in spite of his reticence. It told Dinim that his son was able to overcome his fear in the face of adversity and that he would one day have the ability to speak upon his own behalf even in the most tenuous of situations.

"Why are you here, then?"

Talemar frowned. "Why, 'tis because my mother wished for me to come here. She told me that you would care for me when she was no longer able."

Dinim swallowed heavily. "Where is your mother now?"

Talemar glanced back at Adrianna before making his reply. "That lady looks very much like my Ama." He paused and then continued. "I know that my mother is dead. She is gone forever and will never come for me. But I have my uncle, and the lady that looks like Ama, and you." Talemar's expression became determined. "That will have to be enough."

Dinim sat back on his heels. In all of the years he had lived, he had never heard a boy so young speak with such wisdom. It wasn't only the words he used; it was his understanding of the complexity of his situation. Dinim was only left to wonder how well Talemar would *accept* it...

Dinim slowly stood. "You should go with the Lady Adrianna. She will take you to her daladin, and later I will come for you." Dinim hesitantly placed a gentle hand on Talemar's narrow shoulder. "I am sorry that you lost your mother. She was a good person. But just like you said, the rest of us are here for you." Dinim put a finger beneath the boy's chin. "You are not alone."

Sheridana nocked an arrow and pulled back the string. She set her sight to the target in the distance and let fly. The arrow struck just outside the center and she hissed an expletive beneath her breath. Since her belly had become larger, her aim had become poorer. She really didn't understand such a crude dynamic, but supposed she couldn't really fight it. 'Twas a shame actually, for she would have liked to address the issue with more knowledge at her disposal.

"Ugh!" she cried. "What's wrong with me?"

"Your center is off."

Sheri turned at the voice of a man behind her, immediately recognizing it as the one belonging to Markon.

She gestured angrily towards the target. "Well, that's easy to see." He chuckled. "No, not that center. Your body's center."

She put one hand on her hip while turning the longbow and planting one end of it into the ground. "Why would you think that?"

He shrugged. "Mayhap because my sister suffered the same indignity when she was pregnant with my nephew."

Sheridana looked away from him and wiped a hand over her sweaty forehead. "How did you find out about the baby?"

Markon shrugged. "I've been suspecting. With your response just now, you verified my musings."

She gave an inward sigh. For a moment she had thought that Armond must have said something to someone who, in turn, said something to another. If that were the case, gods only knew how many people were privy to her condition. "I see."

Markon put a hand on her shoulder. "What's wrong? You don't seem very happy."

She shook her head, wondering how much she should say. She and Markon had developed a friendship during the moon cycles following the Wildrunners' recovery in Krathil-lon. She realized she didn't want him to think poorly of her, but didn't understand why she cared. For some reason, it mattered that Markon keep his good opinion of her...

Sheridana brought her eyes back up to meet his. "That's because I'm not."

Markon's expression became questioning. "Why? It might be considered a bother for many moon cycles while the babe resides within, but children are such a blessing. Certainly, you realize this, for you have a child already."

Sheri swallowed heavily and nodded briefly. "You're right." She looked away from him again, this time casting her eyes to the ground while she struggled to staunch the tears that threatened. "You must think me a terrible wretch."

Markon was silent for a moment before placing a hand alongside her face. "No, I would never think that. You are a good person, Sheri. I am not blind; I know it's hard for you. I want you to know that I am here if you need me."

Sheri felt her lower lip tremble. Oh gods, she so much didn't want to cry. It was so good of him to stand there and offer her support when he knew so little about her. But he was a druid, and those people were inherently like that, people who offered aid to those living things that needed it the most. To Markon, she had become one of those things. The thought was somehow disheartening, for she didn't want him to help her out of simple professional obligation. She wanted him to help her because...

"Sheridana, look at me."

She immediately obliged. His gaze was intent and his demeanor solemn.

"I don't offer you my help because I feel I have to. I offer it because I *want* to."

Sheridana blinked in surprise. How had he known what she was thinking? Markon gave a small smile. "I could tell what you were thinking. It was written all over your face."

Sheri hesitated before offering a smile of her own. A moment later she was quietly laughing. "So I am that readable?"

Markon's smile widened. "To me you are."

Her laughter continued as she stood on the tips of her toes to wrap her free arm around his neck. "Thank you. I would sincerely appreciate your help. I know it's silly, but sometimes I feel so alone."

Markon put his arms around her to return the embrace. "Well, try to remember that you're not."

"Like I said, it's silly. I have my sisters. Adria and Carli help me all the time with Fitanni. With this child, it should be no different."

Markon tightened his arms for a moment before releasing her. He then took the bow from her hand. "Here, I am really good with the longbow. Maybe I can demonstrate some things you might not already know."

She cocked her head to the side with a doubtful expression.

"What is it?" he asked.

"I suppose I am willing to entertain any wise words you might have to offer me," she replied.

Markon raised an eyebrow. "So, you think you know as much as I do?"

Sheri nodded. "Most definitely."

"All right, we'll see about that."

Armond silently watched the camaraderie between Sheridana and Markon. Jealousy surged through him, and his anger towards Sheri increased. He couldn't hear what was being said, but he could imagine what it might be. What the Hells was the woman doing by accepting the overtures of another man when she had approached him not more than several days ago? Beside him, Dartanyen sighed a deep breath. Armond turned to regard his friend. "What?"

Dartanyen shrugged. "You look like you could kill somebody."

"Yeah, that bastard over there," he replied, indicating to Markon.

Dartanyen frowned. "Why? It's not as though you've made any of your own advances."

"Surely you are joshing me!" said Armond in an irritated tone. "The woman is carrying my child. She has no right to cozy up to other men."

Dartanyen deepened his frown. "Well, I don't see it that way. Sheri is a woman, a pregnant one at that. She needs someone to help care for her needs and those of the infant she carries. You have yet to step forward to accept the job. As such, she feels compelled to find someone who will. Sheri is a beautiful woman. It will be effortless for her to—"

Armond put his hands up. "All right, stop," he growled. "I don't need to hear any more. It's easy to see you are on her side."

"Her side? Do you hear yourself, man? There is no *her side*. I merely state the truth, and you are a fool not to recognize that!"

Armond stared at him for a moment. Then, "Keep your voice down lest you wish to give our presence away."

Dartanyen shrugged. "What do I care?"

Armond pinned him with a pointed glare. "As my friend you should. I understand you have some loyalty to Sheri as well, but–"

"Damn right I do! And I'm going to say it as I see it. If you want her, then go get her. She won't wait for long because she doesn't just have her unborn to think about. She also has the child that came before. Sheri needs a man, and if you aren't willing to step up and be that for her, she will surely move on."

Armond's brows drew together into a frown. "Move on with Markon?"

Dartanyen gave him a dung-eaten look. "Yeah, maybe. He certainly seems up for the task."

"You are a lloryk's ass, you know that?"

Dartanyen gave him a sarcastic smile. "The best kind!"

Armond rolled his eyes and looked back to Sheri and Markon. The druid had his arms around her, his hands positioned atop hers on the bow. Sheri was perfectly capable of wielding the weapon on her own. The scenario was sickening...

"If it bothers you so much, mayhap you have a vested interest that goes beyond the child," said Dartanyen in a lower voice. "Perhaps you should just go to her."

Armond shook his head. "I wish it were that easy."

"Who said it would be easy?" said Dartanyen. "Most things in life worth having are never easy."

Armond shook his head. "We have had too many differences in the past."

"So what?" said Dartanyen. "That is the past. The future looms ahead of us, a future for which we paid dearly." Dartanyen gave a humorless chuckle. "We can make of it what we choose."

Armond was silent for many moments. He looked down and away in defeat. Then, "I don't know. I just don't know."

Dartanyen shrugged. "There are things I don't know either. But one thing I *do* know is that Sheri needs you, whether she realizes it or not." Dartanyen clapped him on the shoulder and turned to walk away. Armond continued to watch Sheri and Markon for a few moments more before doing the same. He had to accede that the two had a good rapport. It would be natural for them to develop something more.

Armond needed to decide how much that realization meant to him.

# DANGEROUS LIASONS

Numbly, Adrianna glanced around the main chamber of the daladin, seeing that most everything remained as it was when she had last been there a few days ago. It was the last time she had seen Sirion before the short assignment that would take him away from Alcrostat. She had spent the night in his arms, and when she awoke the next morning, he was already gone. Two mornings later she had heard from some of the others rangers that he had returned, and throughout the day had expected some type of message telling her where he would be later that evening. She had received nothing, and after inquiring here and there, learned that he had left again. She had thought it strange, but not beyond the realm of possibility, for Sirion was often called away at barely a moment's notice.

That had been over three days ago.

Adrianna slowly continued her perusal, finally making it to the bedchamber. It was then she felt the ache, a terrible soulwrenching agony that made it feel as though her heart was being ripped from her chest. The bed was just as she had left it, the blankets and pillows left in the disheveled state since she had left so hastily in response to the late morning hour. Everything else was also as she left it, all except one thing. *Stalker was gone.*

Adrianna placed a hand to her mouth, a silly effort to minimize the sobbing that would soon issue forth. Sirion tended to take his favored weapon only when he would be gone a while, and she distinctly remembered the staff leaning against the wall closest to the bed when she left the daladin a few mornings before. When Sirion had returned three days ago, he had obviously made preparations for a lengthy time spent away without even bothering to send her a message...

Adrianna swiftly stepped over to the armoire that characterized the far wall of the chamber, opening it to reveal that the contents had been strewn haphazardly about, most likely in an attempt to find the few items of clothing that were the most comfortable for travel. The terrible sensation in her chest only became more intense, and for a moment she struggled to breathe. By the gods, this couldn't be happening. Sirion couldn't possibly be gone. There was no way that he would leave without even a word of farewell.

With the back of a shaky hand, Adrianna wiped away the tears that trickled down her cheeks. Thinking back, aside from the one miserable evening they had experienced together, she had sensed nothing amiss. At least, nothing that was out of the ordinary from what she had been seeing from Sirion for the past several weeks since returning to Elvandahar. He had been somewhat withdrawn and lackluster, his moods easily affected, and he had become a bit thin. He worked most of the day and often well into the night, taking extra patrol shifts when they were offered. She knew he was having a difficult time fighting his internal daemons. She hated that some of those were because of her, that the events that had taken place during the months they had spent apart battered at a mind already compromised by the loss of his sister, the disturbing presence of Sydonnia in Alcrostat, and the looming responsibility of his succession to the Elvandaharian throne.

In spite of his hurt, he had still professed his love for her. And she had believed him.

Adrianna looked upward, more tears streaming down her face, her heart breaking into a million pieces. *Oh gods, why? Why is he doing this to me?*

"Adrianna?"

Startled, she jumped where she stood in front of the armoire. Looking towards the entryway, she saw Sydonnia standing there. His expression was one of deep regret, an expression one might see on the visage of a 'normal' man. But to see it on *this* man was a rarity, for it wasn't often he felt any kind of emotion pertaining to another being. Sirion had explained it to her, for it was simply the way of lycanthropes... often brutal beyond caring for the individuals they had once been. But with Sydonnia it was different. She didn't know how much of that was her, or mayhap something that existed already deep within him.

Regardless, it made him come to Sirion's daladin, a place where he thought she might be.

Adrianna just stood there, regarding her friend from tear-filled eyes. Within moments she was bring wrapped within his powerful arms, an embrace she was certain had killed many. But right now, at this time, she didn't care. All that mattered was that Sydonnia was there for her.

And he hadn't killed for many moon cycles.

He spoke in a concerned tone with a soothing edge. "I'm sorry, Adria."

Adrianna allowed herself to be pulled close to her good friend, and she cried pitifully onto the shoulder of his leather vest. He stood there and allowed himself to be her pillar, patting her back with a reassuring hand. For several moments she thought no thoughts, just simply let the emotion wash over her. When she had collected herself sufficiently, she stepped back and looked up at Sydonnia.

"Where is he?" she asked in a wavering voice.

Sydonnia shook his head. "I don't know. I knew he had left, but I didn't realize no one knew of his whereabouts until today. I came looking for you, thinking that surely you would..." He stopped speaking and sighed. "Adrianna, I'm so sorry. I can't help thinking this is my fault."

She frowned. "Why? Did something happen?"

He shook his head again. "I knew that my presence here placed a significant amount of strain on Sirion. I should have left, given him time to deal with some things before placing the added burden of myself on him."

Adrianna solemnly nodded her understanding. Sydonnia was right; maybe he should have left, even for just a little while. But it may not have been enough, for she knew that Sydonnia was just a small part of the plethora of things that made up Sirion's problems.

"You can't blame yourself for this." Adrianna paused and then continued. "He left because he wanted to." Her throat closed up as she lowered her eyes to the floor. "I wasn't enough of a motivation for him to stay."

Adrianna felt a finger beneath her chin and her head was brought back up. She looked into Sydonnia's warm brown eyes. "My dear, you would be enough for *any* man. Never believe otherwise."

She felt another tear fall down her face. Sydonnia regarded her intently, his gaze running over her face. She could see the hurt reflected there, hurt he felt on her behalf. "I will find him for you, Adria. I will talk sense into him and bring him home."

Adrianna thought about that for a moment. Yes, Sydonnia was an excellent tracker. Even if Sirion was hiding his trail, Sydonnia would be able to find him. But what if Sirion didn't want to be found? What if he didn't want to come home? She realized she didn't want to be the one to tell him to stay with her. She wanted, *needed*, Sirion to make that decision on his own.

Adrianna shook her head. "No, Sy. Don't do that. Sirion will return when he is ready." She gave him a tremulous smile. "Your offer is very thoughtful. Thank you."

Sydonnia inhaled deeply and put his fists against his sides "You know, I may never come to understand you."

This time the smile reached her eyes. "I know. But it makes me so much more interesting, does it not?"

Sydonnia nodded. "Indeed."

With a grimace, Adrianna turned and glanced around the chamber. She instantly noticed the presence of many of her things. However, she no longer wished to use the daladin if Sirion was no longer there. Besides, her presence there so often had been noted and it had already given her somewhat of a negative reputation in Hinterlean society. She had never really cared all that much, for she was soon to be wed to the man to whom the daladin belonged.

Adrianna felt a sudden twist in her gut. Damnation, Sirion hadn't even bothered to go through the haldrith ceremony. It was a ritual performed by the most powerful of the Hinterlean priests that would make them husband and wife for all of eternity. Somehow, he had escaped that obligation, most likely because she had never placed undue pressure on him, not to mention he already reaped the benefits of such a union without having gone through the motions...

Adrianna struggled to swallow past yet another painful lump in her throat. Oh gods, she was so lucky to have escaped unscathed. Much opposed to poor Sheri...

"Well, since you are here..." Adrianna let her voice trail off for a moment as she continued to get a grip on her emotions, "and since you are of the masculine variety, mayhap you can help me take whatever is mine from this daladin to the one I share with my sister located closer to the academy?"

Sydonnia gave her a brief bow. "Whatever you wish, milady."

Adrianna turned back to find him stoically watching her. Once again, she smiled and placed a palm to his face. "You are like a brother to me, Sydonnia. I am so glad I have you."

The big man placed his hand atop hers, his countenance remaining solemn. "The feeling is mutual."

Sydonnia had spent the remaining morning with Adrianna, helping her with the tasks for which she needed him, as well as offering himself as a bastion of support during the difficult acceptance of Sirion's desertion. Sydonnia hated what his son had done to his good friend, never really imagined the man would abandon the one whom he seemed to love so greatly. Sirion's rare relationship with the beautiful woman he had brought home with him from Sangrilak had mystified so many people in the neighboring villages. Sydonnia had once asked her why no one seemed to remember her from the visit she had made so many years ago. She went into some amount of detail, explaining that a spell had been cast, a spell that would make people forget. For some reason, Sydonnia had not been affected, and she surmised it might be because of his lycanthropy.

Now, as Sydonnia went about his patrol, he took a moment to ponder the past. Adrianna had affected him in so many ways. Somehow, within the short amount of time allotted to them, they had become comrades. And he couldn't help but believe that, because of her, he had become a better man. A cruel twist of fate had brought that foul sorcerer to him that day in the forest. Even now he could remember the agonizing touch of the clawed hand at his neck that made him into a monster...

...and through all of the despicable years before his eyes settled upon her face once more, he always remembered Adrianna as the one person in his life who had wholly accepted him for who he was.

That wasn't counting Lilandria.

Near the end of his patrol, Sydonnia sensed the approach of one of his own. Closing his eyes and breathing deeply of the air, he recognized the scent of Melvyn, one of his finest warriors, a sentinel who set his territory on the eastern banks of the Terrestra River within the realm of Torimir. Sydonnia stopped and waited for his pack member to approach. Melvyn completed his transformation into faelin form as he stepped out of the trees. It was easy to see that he had traveled far without stop, for his breathing was labored, his flesh pallid, and his eyes red-rimmed. Sydonnia was instantly alarmed.

Melvyn spoke right away. "Sydonnia, Bordrigan moves closer to Elvandahar."

"How far away is he?"

Melvyn was stoic. "He enters Randall's territory."

Sydonnia shook his head. Bordrigan offered Elvandahar more of a threat than Sydonnia ever had. It was true that Sydonnia had made an unmistakable mark in his homeland, but it was nothing like the harm Bordrigan and his dread pack could inflict. By now they had probably become quite large, and there was strength in numbers. Although many of those whom Bordrigan had turned would manage to live only a few moon cycles, it would be enough for him to devastate Elvandahar and make the realm weak to any attack that might come after, be it from monster or human.

Sydonnia was silent for several moments. Then, "How many?"

Melvyn's eyes expressed the desperation he felt. "At least a hundred."

Once again silence reigned. Then, "I need to go see for myself..."

Melvyn quickly interjected. "No! You don't have the time to waste! We all need to leave as soon as possible and divert him!"

Sydonnia shook his head. "You know we don't have a large enough force. His numbers will crush us!"

Melvyn nodded. "I know. You must tell King Thalios. Maybe he will know what can help–"

Sydonnia shook his head. "No! Thalios knows nothing! There is nothing he can do for us!"

Melvyn was quiet. Sydonnia stared angrily into the space before him. He had known this day would come eventually. Bordrigan had always hated him because Sydonnia was another dominant male, capable of acquiring the glory that Bordrigan had just begun to achieve. Sydonnia imagined that, under slightly different circumstances, he might have borne the capacity to counter Bordrigan, to be the type of being that would lay absolute waste to the place he called home. In light of Bordrigan's mentality, it would be only fitting for the other lycan to take away Sydonnia's home territory. Not only would the act bring Bordrigan the simple pleasure of death and destruction, but it would serve to break down his nemesis.

Sydonnia struggled to think of something that might help them. His mind kept returning to the fact that his son was a lycan hunter of some renown. Maybe, just maybe he would be able to garner the loyalty of any forces Sirion might have, and along with the highly specialized forces Sydonnia had at his disposal, maybe they would have a chance. Maybe.

Sydonnia shook his head. That would mean having to track down a man who might not want to be found. And there was also the terrifying possibility that the lone Sirion could come across Bordrigan and his pack...

Sydonnia finally nodded. "Melvyn, you are right. I need to speak to Thalios. He at least deserves to know about the approaching threat." Sydonnia intentionally kept his thoughts regarding Sirion hidden, for he didn't want any unnecessary talk. "You should go and rest. I will let you know what develops."

Melvyn nodded, turning around to swiftly melt back into the background from which he had come. Sydonnia remained standing there, the light given by the descending sun surrounding him. Any other time, he may have awaited the next day. But with a matter of this import...

...there was still enough daylight left for him to bother the king.

Sirion stopped, listening to the surrounding environment. He could hear the birds calling in the canopy overhead, the insects singing in the lower lying brush, the soft steps of the leschera to his right and those of the alothere to his left. A burbana merely glanced out of the home it had made in the hollowed core of a felled tree for a brief moment before disappearing back inside. It felt so good to experience these things... especially since he was *free*.

He had left the confines of his monotonous prison behind, choosing instead the life he was meant to lead. Sirion wasn't made for coming home every evening at the same time, waking up in the same place every morning, and walking the same paths day in and day out on patrols. There were constant remainders of the sister he had lost, the strain of his lycan uncle's presence in Alcrostat, the frustration of his past flame, and the reality that the one to whom he was Promised was an object of desire for almost every man in Alcrostat.

And he definitely wasn't made to be a king.

Sirion had managed to escape, the call of the wild having become so fervent within the days prior to his leave-taking. It had consumed all rational thought, making him forget any good things he might be leaving behind...

For only brief moments at a time, he remembered the woman he loved, the one for whom he had once made the decision to remain in his prison. But something had changed in him. It was a slow change, one that had begun to gnaw at him from the inside. A part of him thought it might be the many pressures that had begun to characterize his life. But another part of him thought it might be something more, so much more.

Sirion continued his brisk walk, a reticent Dramati following behind. Soon they would reach the forest outskirts. Already the trees had begun to thin out and became smaller. More light could be seen reaching the forest floor, making it possible for an abounding variety of things to grow there. Such diversity made it easy for them to find a meal. Once out of the trees they would travel across the small plain that characterized the V of the Terrestra and Denegal Rivers. They would keep to the east and probably reach the shore of the Terrestra within two days. Once across they would be in a location approximately a day or two from the city of Sangrilak. By then Sirion would have made the decision to travel north to that city, or to journey south to the port city of Yortec.

It all depended on how far he felt he needed to go in order to make certain his escape, and he had plenty of time to decide.

Not for the first time, Sirion felt Dramati query him through the connection they shared. The corubis was confused, wondering why they had left home so precipitously. He wondered why they planned to leave Elvandahar, for didn't Sirion want to be at home within the trees? Dramati liked it there so much, not to mention, there were other corubis with whom he could spend his time.

Sirion didn't really know how to make his reply. Dramti would never understand his need to escape. Besides, the animal loved Adrianna, and he had formed a bond with Sheridana's daughter, Fitanni. Dramati loved to have the baby crawl over his back and grip his fur in her tiny hands. Inasmuch, the beast liked the idea that Sheri would have another baby so that he could have the same experience all over again in a few moon cycles.

Sirion wondered about these emotions he gleaned from the mind of his furry companion. He imagined what might have brought them about, and thought that mayhap Dramati had sensed a female approaching her estrus just before they left. Sirion felt a twinge of regret, for Dramati deserved to experience many of the things that other corubis did, things that were basic to any animal. But he didn't feel rueful enough to turn back, instead continuing his trek south across the domain of Filopar. As yet, no one had taken notice of him, and one day, when he returned to Alcrostat, he would inform the king of the laxness of the rangers there.

Of course, that might be quite a while.

Sirion inhaled deeply. His sense of smell was better than it had ever been, as were his senses of hearing and sight. His reflexes during the hunt were superb, and he wondered how good they might be in battle. He never bothered to stop and think of the reason why, merely accepted it for what it was. As he moved ever farther away from Alcrostat, his connection with his amplified senses only grew, and he liked the sensations that were evoked. More and more it became that much easier to shrug away any responsibilities he might have had there. It was so profound, he even managed to forget every once in a while.

He had felt this way once before. His good friend, Father Dremathian, had saved him, freeing Sirion so that he could live another day. It was the time he spent in the form of an animal after the Wildrunner's battle with Gaknar and Tharizdune, when his body had transformed into something Shandahar had never seen before. *Adrianna had called him Cortath....*

Lilandria slowly wandered along the bridge. It was one of many that made up the walkway system of the Sherkari Fortress, and the one that would ultimately join the bridge leading to her solar, a small personal alcove that she used throughout the day as she conducted her business. It was her favorite place, one that Thalios had given her after they were wed, a place she could call her own. The king was a fine man and a magnificent leader. He was also a good husband, much better than Servial had ever been. Many times since their union, she'd wished she loved Thalios the way he did her. Certainly, she cared for the king, cared greatly for him. But the flame simply wasn't there...

Lilandria pursed her lips. Sydonnia had requested an audience with Thalios, and she wondered if it was about Sirion. Her son had left Elvandahar without a word to anyone, and once again she was faced with disappointment. Of course, he had every right to be upset with his lot in life; the severity of his trials rivaled her own. However, she had yet to run away from her problems, and Sirion seemed to have no qualms about taking that action. Not only had he left Lilandria behind again, but also the group of people who had arrived in Elvandahar at his side after their costly battle with Aasarak.

One of those people also happened to be Adrianna Darnesse, the woman whom Sirion had claimed as his love interest.

Lilandria came to a stop, turning to grip the rope that made up the side of the bridge. She glanced around the area, took in the sight of the other alcoves that comprised the fortress. She had to admit, she wasn't overly fond of the relationship. Sirion was many years Adrianna's senior, and Lilandria had often wondered throughout the past few moon cycles why her son had chosen her. The young woman was also one of mixed descent, a half-breed. Both humans and faelin tended to keep distant from these people, for their bloodlines couldn't be as easily traced. In Hinterlean society, one's ancestry was very important, and another reason why Lilandria wondered about her son's choice for a wife. She just had to remember, much like his father, Sirion was never one to conform. Lilandria breathed a deep sigh. She supposed she shouldn't be one to speak. She had borne a son and a daughter from two brothers, one of whom had just discovered the truth of his son's parentage.

It was so odd, she had noticed Sydonnia's interest in Adrianna as well. Not of the romantic type, but something that seemed almost *brotherly*. It was almost like he'd known her before, but Lily knew it just wasn't possible. She'd considered asking Sydonnia about it a time or two, but never brought herself to do so. Strangely, it was just another reason for Lilandria to dislike the young woman...

But recently they had something in common; Sirion had left them both behind.

Lilandria found that her interest in Adrianna was piqued more than it ever had been before. She wondered how the other woman dealt with the abandonment and if she felt anything near what Lily had felt when Servial left her all those decades ago. Of course, it wasn't the same, for Lilandria had borne Servial a daughter, and Adrianna had no children with Sirion. *Gods be thanked for that small concession.* Lily could only imagine what it would be like to have a grandchild of her bloodline born out of wedlock.

Lilandria pulled away from the side of the bridge and continued towards her destination, her thoughts on her daughter. Anya had meant the world to her, and now she was gone. It was hard to imagine never seeing her again, and every night Lilandria lay awake wishing she could catch just a glimpse of her beautiful face one last time.

With a sense of disquiet, Triath glanced around the torch-lit chamber. Two armed isterian stood alongside each of the two entrances, as well as one in each corner of the room. He had no idea what the Hells was going on, only that he had followed the instructions written on the parchment that had been left at his daladin not long ago. The message was written in fine print and sealed with the wax insignia of the King of Elvandahar. The contents were brief, expressing the need for secrecy, even from one's spouse. It also asked for the recipient to arrive at the south entrance of the Sherkari Fortress just after the sun set.

Triath looked towards the nearest entrance as the door was suddenly opened from the other side. He was surprised to see Armond escorted inside. Triath rose from his chair and met his friend halfway across the room. He noticed the confused expression on the other man's face, an expression that must be very similar to his own.

Armond grasped Triath's arm in greeting. "Do you know what this is about?"

Triath shook his head. "I probably know only as much as you do."

Armond arched one dark eyebrow as he noticed the isterian standing around the chamber. "Hells, it looks pretty serious to me."

Triath nodded. "Mmm yes, I was thinking the same just as you entered."

Once again the door opened and both men turned to watch as Dartanyen and Markon were escorted through by the same guard who had done the same for them, an isterian wearing the additional tattooed embellishment to the arm tattoo all isterian sported. It signified him as one of higher rank, one of the palace elite.

The isterian approached behind Dartanyen and Markon, politely waiting for the friends to greet one another. Then he spoke. "King Thalios will be with you shortly."

Triath nodded and indicated around the chamber. "May I ask the reason for the extra guards? Surely you do not take us for assassins."

One corner of the isterian's mouth pulled up into a brief smile. "Of course not, my lord. We definitely do not take you all for assassins. They are here for an entirely different reason, one that will be revealed to you shortly." The man gestured towards the table and indicated the casks of wine and mead set there by the silent hralen who had entered unawares. Already the household staff were leaving the chamber. "Please sit and have a drink until the king arrives. It won't be long."

Triath nodded and moved to the table, sitting back down in the chair he had occupied prior to Armond's arrival. The other men followed suit, positioning themselves around the table. Markon seated himself next to Triath, while Armond and Dartanyen sat at the other side. Triath turned to his companion and nodded. "It is good to see you again. Have you heard from Father Dremathian recently? How does he fare?"

Markon nodded. "It is good to see you as well, albeit strange under these circumstances. And yes, I received a message from Father Dremathian just yesterday. All seems to be well in Krathil-lon, although..."

Markon allowed his voice to trail away, shifting his gaze to the surface of the table.

Triath frowned in concern. "What? What is it?"

Markon gave a deep sigh. "I don't know if I should be telling you this, but in light of Sirion's noted absence the past fortnight, I feel compelled." He paused for a moment and then continued. "Especially since the lady Adrianna wasn't aware of his leave-taking herself until he had been gone at least four or five days."

Triath pursed his lips, very aware of the circumstances surrounding Sirion's absence. It baffled him that Sirion had departed so precipitously and without an indication to anyone that he would be leaving. What made the situation so saddening was that his silence encompassed Adrianna as well. "Speak freely. We are all friends here."

Markon nodded. "Father Dremathian has expressed great concern for Sirion. Even before we left Krathil-lon he sensed something was amiss. If you recall, he even went to far as to urge you all to stay, using Tianna's infirmity as an excuse. However, he understood your collective desire to return home, so he didn't pursue it. Instead, he chose me to accompany you here, merely as someone with whom he could keep in touch in regards to Sirion's welfare."

Triath was silent as he took in this revelation. Dartanyen and Armond were similarly affected.

"Damnation, that explains a lot," said Dartanyen. "In spite of the excuse you used to see your family, I wondered about your being with us."

Armond nodded. "As did I."

"What was it about Sirion that disturbed Dremathian so much?" asked Triath.

Markon shrugged. "I'm not entirely certain, only that he mentioned sensing an uncharacteristic vehemence about Sirion, an intensity he may have felt once before several moon cycles ago when Sirion and the rest of you came to him for help. I recall that time myself, the time that Sirion was no man at all but a beast..."

Once again Markon's voice trailed away. Triath looked over at Dartanyen and Armond, saw the haunted expressions on their faces. Triath, Sorn, Anya, and Naemmious hadn't yet joined the group when Sirion was under the influence of the beast they had called Cortath. He had only heard about it in stories told to him more recently in the moon cycles since they had returned to Elvandahar after Aasarak's defeat.

Triath shook his head and returned his gaze to Markon. "I need more specifics. Why would Father Dremathian think about that time?"

Markon became introspective. "Dremathian seemed to feel that Sirion was behaving more aggressively than usual. He noticed it especially when it came to Adrianna. Sirion was more protective of her than ever, even before the battle with Aasarak. Dremathian mentioned a restlessness about Sirion, one that indicated a call from the wild that many rangers tend to feel before they have been tamed by the woman who will ultimately serve as the one who will keep them anchored. Dremathian sensed Sirion pulling away from the mainstay that Adrianna offered, and felt that it wasn't a good thing." Markon shrugged again. "Every man needs something that will ground him, no matter who he is or what he has become."

Silence reigned in the chamber as the men considered what Markon imparted. Several moments passed before the door to the main entry was being opened once more. The men all glanced towards it as King Thalios swiftly strode into the room. He wore the traditional deep green satin robes of his station, as well as the bejeweled crown that rested atop his head. Each of the five gems symbolized each of the five domains of Elvandahar: Filopar emerald, Mirpur ruby, Nedmar sapphire, Medea topaz, and Kleyshes diamond. In deference, the men rose from their seats and offered a half bow.

Thalios' expression was grim as he approached. With a downward sweep of his hand, he indicated they should all resume their seats. The men silently obeyed, each one's gaze riveted on the King as he also seated himself at the table. "I want to first thank you all for coming. I know this was a bit sudden and unexpected." Thalios looked at each of them in turn before continuing. "It is in regards to a matter of great importance that I have asked you here, and it will require some dedication of your time until the situation can hopefully be resolved."

Triath frowned and hesitated only briefly before speaking. "My lord, please excuse my interruption but, what do you mean by 'hopefully'?"

King Thalios gave a deep sigh. "That question, unfortunately, is better answered by the man who asked me to bring you here."

Triath's frown deepened and he shook his head. "So, you aren't really the one who is behind this meeting?"

Thalios also shook his head. "It is with a heavy heart that I have done this, for I feel that I have betrayed you in some way." Thalios glanced at the isterian standing at the entryway at the other side of the chamber and nodded. The isterian promptly took the cue and turned to open the door. "Allow me to bring in the man who will be leading your mission."

Triath and the others looked towards the door and were deeply dismayed. Silence rang throughout the room as Sydonnia strode in, flanked on each side by a man. The three of them walked to the table and promptly seated themselves. A sense of unease had begun to permeate the air, and casting sidelong glances at his comrades, Triath could see the horrified expressions on their faces... including the overly stoic Armond.

Triath took the initiative. Standing from his seat, he indicated to the shirwemic sitting alongside the King with an irritated wave of his hand. "What the Hells is going on? What is the meaning of this?" he nearly shouted.

Thalios was about to stand, but Sydonnia laid a polite hand on the King's shoulder. Triath could sense a sudden increase in the pervading enmity in the chamber, the surrounding isterian tensing at the physical contact. "Please allow me to speak."

Thalios nodded at the request, and with a brief flick of his hand, commanded his guards to relax their stance. Meanwhile, Sydonnia began to address Triath, Armond, Dartanyen, and Markon. "The reason I have brought you here is one that means just as much to you as it does to me. Accept it or not, we are working on the same side. The enemy is not someone sitting here today. In fact, it is someone who is much more powerful than I would like to believe."

Sydonnia cocked his head to the side, taking in Triath's malicious glare. With an expression of determination he said, "Let me ask you, in all honesty would you have come here if I requested it? Even had I expressed dire need of your help?" Sydonnia raised his hands from his sides. "Well? Would you?"

Triath and the other men finally shook their heads in the negative.

Sydonnia nodded. "I didn't think so. Inasmuch, I asked King Thalios for help. Ordinarily I wouldn't care, but the man did me a favor by bringing you here for me. Please consider keeping him apart from this." He paused for a moment but then continued. "We are here for a mutual goal☐ to see our home kept safe from those who would seek to destroy it. I understand that you have heard things about me, and most of them are probably true. However, I just want to say that any threat I may have posed to Elvandahar in the past is nothing compared to what is coming."

Triath shook his head and then sat there for a few minutes, tuning Sydonnia out. Hells, he had no desire to sit there and listen to this guy talk, especially knowing Sydonnia's hideous history. Triath had no reason to believe anything the monster had to say. However, his attention was suddenly grabbed when the man spoke Sirion's name.

"So, when was the last time any of you saw Sirion?"

The four men glanced at one another for a few moments. "I'm not entirely certain, but mayhap about a fortnight ago? Maybe a day for two less," said Dartanyen.

"Me too," said Triath in agreement.

"And I," said Armond.

Markon nodded his head. "I will have to say the same."

Sydonnia shook his head and gave a condescending smirk. "Damnation, I'm glad my friends aren't like my nephew's. Hells, any of mine would have become concerned and gone looking for me already."

Sensing a ring of truth to Sydonnia's words, Triath instantly felt defensive. "Who the Hells do you think you are?" he shouted. "Who are you to judge Sirion's friendships? At least those were borne of mutual care and respect as opposed to one man biting another and having them act as his subservient. What do they call that again? Oh, yes... siring. How many dung-eaten fools have you bred by now?"

All of a sudden, the two people sitting at Sydonnia's other side jumped out of their seats. Their feral eyes were bright with fury, and he could imagine the beginning of their transformation beginning to take hold. Triath lurched back from the unleashed power emanating from the other side of the table. Meanwhile, his comrades had sensed it as well and rose from their own seats, each man drawing his weapon of choice: Armond the longsword, Markon the scimitar, and Dartanyen the crossbow. Only Triath made no move for his weapon, and Sydonnia was similarly calm.

Just as it seemed the shirwemic would bound across the table, Sydonnia stopped them with an abrupt shout. He spoke in Hinterlic, so Triath only caught brief bits and parts of what the man said. The two lycan instantly relinquished their offensive and stepped back from the table at Sydonnia's gruff command. King Thalios simply sat there, his head in his hands, obviously reacting to the tenuous situation in the chamber. Meanwhile, the isterian had surrounded the table, their own weapons drawn. It was obvious that, if things had progressed, the results would have been messy indeed.

Sydonnia returned his attention to Triath. "Touché. Although, I must say that you have a bit of a misconception about the relationship between myself and my pack members." Sydonnia shook his head. "But that is another conversation, one not meant for this meeting."

"Then why *are* we meeting, Sydonnia? Have out with it," said Triath.

Sydonnia scowled. "As I have already told you, a threat approaches Elvandahar. His name is Bordrigan, a lycan who has sired hundreds. Where I practice some measure of discrimination, Bordrigan does not. I try to choose those who are strong and will withstand the nature of the curse for many years. Bordrigan has no such compulsion. For him it is a numbers game, and so far it has worked. With sheer numbers alone, he has decimated entire towns and villages, overcome multitudes of caravans, and murdered untold sums of women and children. Take what you know about me and increase it tenfold... then you will have Bordrigan."

Triath turned to look at his companions. During Sydonnia's talk, they had lowered their weapons but remained on alert. They had also listened to what he had to say. "What makes you think we believe you? For all we know, you are diverting our attention elsewhere so that you can make any move you have in mind successfully without opposition," said Dartanyen.

Sydonnia nodded solemnly. "You are right. Indeed, I could be planning a coup. However, if you really think about it, why would I have waited this long? And why would I have given you any reason to believe I was planning such an event by having this meeting? Instead, I would have created a diversion somewhere else in Elvandahar. I then would have brought my primary pack into Alcrostat and taken over the city within the small space of several days." Sydonnia sighed. "In all honesty, if that was what I wanted to do, I would have done it long ago."

Dartanyen nodded, as did Armond. Triath shook his head. "All right, we understand that a threat approaches, but why the secrecy? Why are we here? What else is going on?"

Sydonnia pursed his lips and also nodded. "Yes, I suppose it's time to get to the point. Unfortunately, it seems I must spell it out for you," he growled. "Believe it or not, Bordrigan is coming to Elvandahar, and he will lay waste to this realm if it is not defended. This need not become common knowledge if we can find a way to divert the threat. Meanwhile, I conducted a preliminary search earlier today and discovered that when Sirion left, he was moving in a southeasterly direction. Bordrigan and his pack are currently located in central Torimir, slowly making their way here. It is very possible that Sirion will come into contact with them, for Bordrigan sets a wide periphery. Sirion is well known in lycan circles for his lycan-hunting prowess. He is a dead man walking if he enters Bordrigan's scouting range."

Silence reigned. Triath took in all that Sydonnia had spoken. A part of him didn't want to believe Sydonnia's words, but the other, more rational part, couldn't help but do so. The monster had once been a scourge upon all of Elvandahar, but in recent years, Sydonnia had become relatively benign. The possibility that Sirion was in such grave danger scared Triath. Triath and Sirion had come a long way since they had first met all those years ago, and a mutual respect had eventually developed. That and so much more. His good friend was out there alone somewhere with no one to watch his back.

In Triath's estimation, they had no choice but to trust Sydonnia and go after Sirion. He hated being forced to place his faith in someone so chaotic. Hells, for all he knew Sydonnia would have another shift in loyalty and turn against them at the last moment. In essence, he needed more information...

Triath looked back up at Sydonnia. "So what course of action do you propose?"

"I suggest that we follow Sirion. Maybe we will get lucky and catch up with him before he meets up with Bordrigan. By then I am hoping we will have come up with a plan on how to create enough of a diversion that the enemy will shift his focus elsewhere."

Triath shook his head. "If that is your intent, why are you still here? What do you need us for?"

"Like I said, Bordrigan has numbers on his side. In spite of the superior abilities of my pack members, it will never be enough. So I thought to incorporate Sirion and his wellspring of knowledge, hoping to find some measure of equality. In addition, Sirion has an excellent support system." Sydonnia paused and then continued. "Unfortunately, Sirion is not here, most likely entering a dangerous situation, a situation he never would have seen coming."

Armond nodded. "Well, I have no problem going after Sirion and dealing with the situation as it arises."

Sydonnia grinned. "Good, we should leave as soon as possible."

Triath shook his head. "It is only the company we have a problem with."

Sydonnia's smile instantly dissipated and his gaze darkened. "You won't have a choice."

Triath cocked his head to the side. "And why do you say that?"

Sydonnia smiled widely, a smile that displayed sharp canines. "Because I am the only one who can track Sirion."

Triath sat back. Damnation, Sydonnia was right. Only someone as good, if not better, than Sirion would be able to find someone... *as good as Sirion.* Triath shuddered at the thought of traveling alongside the monstrosity and his minions. However, he couldn't refute Sydonnia's claim. It was common knowledge how good most lycan were with their tracking, and Sydonnia even more so. Triath hated to be forced to rely on someone he hated on so many levels.

Sydonnia regarded him with a wry smile, knowing he had Triath cornered. "Listen, let's make a compromise. Whatever grievance you have with me, and I with you, let us set those aside for a while and tend to the task before us. Only after our mission is through will we all return here to continue our mutual hatred of one another." Sydonnia cocked his head. "What do you say?"

Triath gazed at the shirwemic through narrowed eyes. In spite of the despicable nature of his predicament, he had no choice but to relent.

"Fine, let's get on with it then."

Sydonnia nodded. "Good. We will give you two hours to gather whatever personal belongings and other supplies you might need. We will then meet you approximately a half day's journey to the south." Sydonnia widened his grin. "We will leave a trail easy to follow, even for you."

Triath frowned. "What do you mean, 'we'?"

Sydonnia returned the frown. "What, you didn't think I wouldn't bring my own people with me, did you?"

Triath was about to respond when Armond interjected. "Do you really think that is wise? The situation here is relatively benign, yet we were about to kill one another in cold blood not long ago. Imagine how much more tense it might be out in the open with none of King Thalios' men here to mediate."

Sydonnia was adamant. "The truth remains that we have no chance of success without all we have at our disposal. I would be a fool to leave my pack out of this mission, and you equally foolish to believe we can make it without them."

Dartanyen chose that moment to speak. "I don't think I am going with you."

Triath raised his brows and glanced over to the other man. "Why the Hells not?"

Dartanyen shook his head. "I should remain here. It is my ultimate duty to protect the realm, and I can't do that if I am away fighting an enemy that may never make it here."

Armond nodded. "Yes, but by helping us find Sirion and fight Bordrigan, you will be fulfilling the same duty."

"I know, but my instincts tell me to stay. Besides, it seems that the women folk will be left behind. Who better than one of the Wildrunners to protect them?"

"They will have Dinim," Markon pointed out.

Dartanyen gave a small smile. "He is too focused on his work at the academy. Adria, Tianna, and Sheri need someone who is focused solely on their welfare, as well as that of their children."

Markon nodded. "Then what of Gareth, brother of Adrianna and Sheridana? Does he fit into any of this at all?"

Once more there was a moment of silence. A moment later Triath shook his head. "Word has it that he and his uncle will be leaving Elvandahar within the next few days to journey back north."

Sydonnia also shook his head. "Perhaps I should have thought to bring him here."

Triath gave a humorless chuckle. "By now I am certain he has heard of your exploits. It is for the best you didn't think to contact him."

Sydonnia frowned. "Maybe."

Armond gave a hiss of frustration. "Let's just be done with this meeting already. We are wasting time bickering over things that don't matter right now."

Markon nodded. "Yes, Armond is right. But in spite of the rush, we should be allowed at least a full day or two to prepare and rest. Our families will miss us while we are away, and we will be on the move almost constantly once we are in pursuit. They deserve at least that much."

Sydonnia's frown deepened for a moment before neutralizing. "Fine. Another day will give me more time to gather my pack and warn them of your presence before we begin our merger. By then, Sorn Sikondar will also be that much closer."

Triath widened his eyes in surprise. "Sorn is on his way here?" Sydonnia nodded and gestured beside him. "Courtesy of King Thalios."

Triath nodded his head in satisfaction. It seemed that Sydonnia had thought everything out rather well. He supposed that was a good thing, for their mission would certainly meet dismal failure if everything wasn't taken into consideration. Meanwhile, Thalios had remained silent throughout the exchange. Everyone now looked to the King. He rose from his seat and waved a hand. "This meeting is adjourned. You are all dismissed."

Triath bowed before the King before turning away. He had almost made it to the doorway when Sydonnia's voice made him pause. "The morning after this one we will meet you in the location I described."

Triath only nodded before stepping through the door the isterian opened for him.

# TENUOUS ALLIANCE

Jaysim regarded Gareth with an expression of disbelief. "Are you seriously considering this?"

Gareth nodded. "I feel that this is where I belong."

Jaysim shook his head. "Nephew, you say this only because you fear you will miss the boy overly much."

Gareth gave a deep sigh. He had known this was going to be a fight. Jaysim had come so far, chosen to complete the journey to Elvandahar with him and Talemar with the knowledge he would be bringing his nephew back home. But Gareth had finally reunited with his sisters after so long, not to mention he found he so much preferred the wooded paths of Elvandahar over the rocky ones that characterized Aldehirra. Gareth had even gone so far as to think that mayhap this had been Sharra's design all along, for she had always seemed to know things about a person and his or her future. Gareth couldn't help but believe he was meant to come here, and that it was one of the reasons why Sharra had been so adamant that he bring Talemar to his father.

But that also meant she had somehow known Dinim was in Elvandahar. Why wouldn't she have imparted that information to him? Did she think that it might deter him in some way? He would never know.

Gareth shook his head. "I feel good here, that I am meant to stay. It's not just about Talemar, but Sheridana and Adrianna as well. Sheri will be giving birth at the beginning of the new year, and Fitanni is already accustomed to me." He paused and then continued. "Jaysim, my family needs me."

Several moments passed as Jaysim regarded him with an expression of solemnity. Gareth chose to speak again. "Uncle, I would welcome it if you would remain here, at least for a while. Then, when I return, you can decide if you would like to stay for good."

Jaysim frowned. "What are you talking about? Where are you going?"

Gareth knew this question would arise, so he had already formulated an answer. "Adrianna's betrothed is in some trouble and a group of us have been asked to aid him."

"Who is this man?"

"Sirion Timberlyn."

Jaysim's frown deepened and his expression shifted to incredulity. "The heir to the Elvandaharian crown?"

Gareth nodded and struggled to keep his face impassive. "It's a long story."

Gareth watched as Jaysim came to grips with everything that had been imparted. Gareth had done the same just the day before. Shumon had come to him, telling him that something was amiss.

*Gareth shook his head. "Listen, I don't know what's going on, but it has nothing to do with me. I'm actually supposed to be leaving on my journey back north in a couple of days."*

*Shumon raised an arched brow. "I would think it should have everything to do with you. Your sisters are involved."*

*Gareth stared at him for a moment. "What?"*

It was then he had learned about Sirion Timberlyn and his abandonment of Adrianna several days ago. The word was that he had come across some trouble, trouble about which even the man called Sydonnia was concerned. A group had been put together, a group whose goal was to find Sirion and snuff out the terrible trouble he had found. But as Shumon understood it, the group could use as many members as possible...

So, Gareth had gone to Sydonnia, a man he had already learned was a monster. Only he had found that the man probably cared more about his family than anyone else in Elvandahar, a truth that won Sydonnia Gareth's instant loyalty.

Unfortunately, the man Sirion had managed to gain Gareth's intense disapproval and dislike.

"When are you leaving?" asked Jaysim.

Gareth was swift to reply. "The morning after tomorrow."

"That was the day we were supposed to go home."

Gareth nodded. "I know." A few moments went by. Then, "So, will you stay?"

Jaysim wore an expression of reluctance, but he acceded. "Fine."

Gareth smiled and placed a hand on his uncle's shoulder. "Are you certain? You will stay here to stand by our family until I make my return?"

Jaysim returned the gesture and placed his own hand atop Gareth's shoulder. "Yes, I will stay."

Gareth's smile widened. "Thank you." Jaysim only nodded in response.

In the silence of the daladin, Sheridana stared contemplatively at the sword in her lap, rubbing a soft cloth over the shining blade. She hadn't seen to Defender in quite some time and felt the weapon that protected her so assiduously was due for some well-deserved cleaning and polishing. It was shameful of her to neglect the sword as she had, but the memories she knew it would incite were not ones that were easy for her to endure. But this day she chose to be strong. Just as the sword was in need of a good coat of polish, Ian was in need of some remembering.

*It was hot as Sheridana made her way down the cobbled street towards the inn. For the third time she swept her tongue over her upper lip, tasting the blood of miserable defeat. She couldn't help thinking that Thane had set her up for failure, she who had won all of the competitions previously set before her. This last opponent had been way out of her league, obviously much more skilled. If her father thought to give her a lesson in humility, he had done more than that. He had taken away her dignity as well.*

*"Sheri!"*

*She kept walking, not wanting anyone to see how the humiliation affected her.*

*"Sheridana, wait!"*

*It was her uncle, but she didn't care even for his benign presence. Her body ached too much, and her mind was a roil of negative emotion. Ian didn't deserve the verbal lashing she might inflict if pushed too far.*

*"Sheri, didn't you hear me calling you?" Ian gripped her elbow and pulled her around to face him. She refused to look him in the eye but could tell that he was taken aback by her dejected countenance.*

*"I heard you."*

*Ian regarded her silently for a moment before leading her down the street in the direction she had been heading before he stopped her. It wasn't long before they were walking through the front door of the inn, Ian calling out for a hot bath as they headed up the staircase. He walked her to her room, and once there, held open the door so she could enter.*

*She felt Ian's eyes on her as she walked across the chamber to seat herself on the chair near the window. She stared silently at the rays of sunlight that passed through the glass, her mind ruminating over the failed swordfight. She had been soundly defeated, with more cuts and bruises than she would care to admit. She recalled the expression of concern on Ian's face, along with the one of mock disapproval on Thane's. Really, what did he hope to accomplish? Why would he seek out an opponent merely to crush her spirit, to make her loath to enter the circle again? Why would he want to sully the good reputation she had begun to acquire for herself?*

*Sheri was only half aware that Ian had moved to stand behind her. He was silent for a few moments before he spoke. "Your father has many reasons for the actions he chooses to take."*

*Sheri frowned. How in the Hells would Ian know what she was thinking? And how was it that he was such a sudden solid bastion of support to Thane? In spite of the camaraderie that had begun to develop between them the past several moon cycles, she supposed Ian's first loyalty was to her father. The two men were brothers, after all.* "I don't recall asking for your words of wisdom, Uncle." *Sheri gave a heavy swallow, hating the words she had chosen to speak. Yet, she felt somewhat righteous, for it was she who had suffered the indignity that day.*

*There was a period of silence before he made a reply.* "You are right; you didn't. But I choose to offer them anyway, because I can explain what Thane did today."

*Sheri shook her head.* "Well, maybe I'm not ready to hear it. My body aches abominably, and I'm grimy from a decent accumulation of dirt, sweat, and blood."

"Hence the bath I ordered for you."

*Sheri gave a grudging sniff.* "I suppose I could thank you for that."

"None is needed."

*The chamber was silent for a few moments until Ian spoke again.* "Come, let me help you out of that armor."

*When Sheri didn't move from her place, Ian gave a sigh, grasped her upper arms, and pulled her up from the chair. She had never cared before to recognize how strong he was in spite of his lean frame, and she felt her eyes widen in mild surprise. Ian then set himself to the task of relieving her of the arm and shin guards she tended to wear in competition, followed by the studded leather vest she wore over her sleeveless tunic. If she had the gold, she would have a chestplate to match, but for now, the studded leather sufficed. The armor had definitely seen its better days, but it had quite a bit left in it before needing replacement.*

*By the time she was stripped of her boots, the bath was being brought. A pair of burly men brought the tub, followed by a small legion of buxom serving wenches that would later tend the common room that eve. The women filled the tub with steaming water and left behind a bar of soap and a cloth before exiting the chamber and closing the door behind them.*

*Sheri only stared at the bath, her body unwilling to move from the place in which it seemed rooted. Once again Ian gave a sigh and led her to the tub.* "Lift your arms."

*Sheri barely hesitated before doing as he commanded. The man had seen her naked more times than she could count, albeit not in the confines of a bedchamber. Regardless, she thought nothing of it as he pulled the soiled tunic over her head. She unfastened the strings of her trousers and allowed them to fall to the floor before stepping out of them. She then removed her smallclothes before stepping into the warm waters. She sank down into the deep tub until the water touched her chin. Meanwhile, Ian had taken the soap and made a lather with the cloth. With a brief gesture he motioned forward and she exposed her back. He rubbed the cloth over her in gentle circles that eased the taut muscles. When he was through, she took the cloth for herself and washed the rest before submerging herself once again, this time into a mass of bubbly soap suds.*

*Ian watched her through fathomless blue eyes for several moments. When he spoke, he broke the pervading silence, his voice sounding louder than it may have if there had been any sound to be heard at all over the past hour. "So, are you willing to hear what I came to say?"*

*Sheri frowned. "Do I have a choice?"*

*Ian paused and then shook his head. "Not really."*

*Her frown deepened. "Then why bother asking?"*

*Ian shrugged. "Merely out of formality, I suppose."*

*Sheri grunted. "You care about formality when you have seen me naked in the private confines of my bedchamber?"*

*He gave a gusty sigh. "When did you become so difficult? You were such an amicable child."*

*Her eyes narrowed. It figured he would mention the fact that he was almost two decades her senior. "And you weren't such a pushy uncle."*

*Ian pursed his lips and nodded in acceptance before speaking the words he needed to say. "Despite what you might believe, it wasn't Thane's design to subjugate you today."*

*It was Sheridana's turn to give a sigh, albeit one with a tone of exasperation. She swiftly rose from the bath, taking her long hair and wringing the water out of it before reaching for the towel hanging nearby. When her hand came into contact with it sooner than she expected, she looked to see that Ian had unfurled the length of it between them. She mumbled a brief word of thanks as she took it and wrapped it around herself before heading to the travel pack that rested on the bed.*

*"His intent was to show that you still have so much to learn. He felt that you had become overly confident and that you needed a lesson to show that you must never underestimate an opponent."*

*Sheri looked over her shoulder. "Humph. That 'lesson' was a bit harsh, don't you think?"*

*Ian nodded slowly. "Indeed, it did seem a bit more severe than I imagined it should be."*

*Sheri turned back to the travel pack. She withdrew clean smallclothes, tunic, and trousers. She dropped the towel and donned these, not turning back around until she was finished. Ian's gaze on her was intent, yet gave away nothing of his musings until he spoke again. "You are very good at what you do, my dear," he said solemnly.*

*Sheridana retrieved her belt and placed it about her waist.*

*"Thane sincerely felt you needed the lesson and I agreed with him."*

*Sheri's eyes snapped up to meet his. Ian's gaze was unwavering in his conviction and her belly churned sickeningly. She couldn't believe what she was hearing. Damn, if Gareth had been there, he would never have allowed this to happen. But Gareth wasn't there...*

*Suddenly wanting only to escape, Sheri headed for the door. She made to sweep past Ian, but his hand reached out and caught her arm above the elbow, holding her in place before him. "I agreed with him because I saw how quickly you were learning the skills set before you, and I feared you might become complacent." He hesitated for the briefest moment before continuing, his hand tightening about her arm. "I would never forgive myself if something happened to you."*

*Sheridana looked from the hand on her arm to the man who owned it. His cerulean eyes spoke volumes, much more than the words he uttered. She suddenly felt herself breaking apart at the seams a little, and she wondered what it was she was feeling...*

Sheridana wiped a hand across her eyes and sniffed away her tears. Typically, at this time of day, Ian's daughter would be found sleeping in the next room. But Carli had taken Fitanni away, telling Sheri that she expected her to get some much-needed rest. Lately Sheri had been having a difficult time sleeping, and she was certain much of it had to do not only with her progressing pregnancy, but Armond's obvious rejection. And then there were her unresolved issues concerning her past with Ian. Thoughts of him had been infiltrating her dreams more and more, and she knew this time was bound to come.

Sheri gently caressed the blade with the tips of her fingers. She felt the runic designs engraved in the metal, knew they were part of what gave Defender his magic. Even at the terrible end, the sword had worked to defend his user, his magical glow lighting the darkest hour of her life... the moment of Ian's demise at the hands of his own brother.

Thane had slowly disemboweled Ian right before her eyes. Her father's gleeful visage at seeing the suffering he'd wrought was burned into her mind forever.

"I hope you aren't planning to use that sword anytime soon."

Sheridana was so startled, she almost cried out. She clamped a hand over her mouth as she looked up to find Armond leaning there at the entry to her bedchamber. She had been so engrossed in her thoughts, she hadn't heard his approach.

Seeing the alarm on her face, Armond's expression was instantly contrite and he pulled away from the wall. "I'm sorry. I didn't mean to frighten you."

She would have loved to tell Armond not to be silly. Of course, he hadn't frightened her. But compounded with the horrifying thoughts that had overtaken her mind just before he announced his presence, she had experienced that very emotion... strongly. Sheri struggled to control her wildly beating heart, and when the tempo didn't slow as readily as she thought it should, she wondered how much of it was a reaction to Armond's handsome presence.

When she didn't say anything, Armond slowly entered the chamber. He looked slightly ill-at-ease and she wondered why he had come. Peeling her shaking hand away from her face, she asked him precisely that. "Wh...why are you here? Has something happened?"

Armond regarded her with intense green eyes. "If you mean, 'Has Sirion returned?' then no, nothing has happened."

Sheri nodded and continued to sit there for a moment. She was almost afraid to ask again. "Then, why are you here?"

Armond's gaze intensified and he gave a slight shake to his head. "But if you are referring to anything else, then yes, something has happened."

Sheri nodded silently and waited. Once again, he appeared somewhat discomfited. He untied a coin pouch from his belt and placed it on the nearest surface, which happened to be her nightstand. "I realized that you might need some extra money while I am away. I know you won't be able to find much work right now, so I want to help."

Sheri swallowed heavily and looked at the fat coin purse. It was obvious there was quite a bit inside. She considered questioning him about it, but she found herself more concerned with the statement he had just made. "Where are you going?"

Armond shook his head. "I'm not certain, but it has something to do with Sirion." He rolled his eyes. "Really, I don't understand what all the secrecy is about."

Sheri frowned. "Who else is going?"

"Just myself, Triath, Sorn, and Markon."

With mention of the last name Sheri noticed that his gaze intensified for a moment. Then, "Oh yes, and your brother chose to come with us."

Sheri was taken aback. "Really? Gareth is leaving as well?"

Armond slowly nodded.

Sheri was quiet for a moment. Then, with sword in hand, and forgetting that she wore only her sheer night-shift, she rose from her position on the floor. Armond's eyes immediately swept over her and she belatedly realized her mistake. Her gaze swept the chamber for something to cover herself, but the robe lay on the other side of the bed.

Armond tore his gaze away and indicated to the bared blade in her hand. "You looked so sad as you sat there with your sword. I was wondering what made you feel so..." Armond shook his head. "No, never mind. It really isn't..."

Sheridana interrupted. "It once belonged to Fitanni's father."

Initially surprised, Armond glanced into her eyes. She knew he had heard the story from Adrianna, and his expression seemed as though he regretted saying anything. She lowered her eyes to the floor, and once picking up the scabbard, she sheathed the blade within. He said nothing as she went to the chest at the foot of her bed and placed the weapon inside. Then remembering her state of undress, she leaned across in order to obtain the robe that lay on the other side.

Sheri had just taken hold of the garment when Armond took her forearm in his grip. She turned to find that he had moved to stand beside her. "What are you doing?" he asked.

Sheridana looked up at him, saw an expression she couldn't entirely decipher. "I... I just thought I should put on my robe."

Still holding her arm, he cocked his head slightly to the side. "Why? You know I have seen you in a state of undress much more revealing than this before."

Sheri stared at him for a moment before making a reply. "I didn't want to seem rude or inappropriate."

He gave a brief, somewhat humorless, chuckle. "Surely you are joshing me." He proceeded to pull her towards him and placed his other hand against her distended belly.

Sheri's thoughts raced. *What does he think he's doing by touching me this way? After so long of shafting me, Armond decides to come into my bedchamber, give me some money, and then have his way with me?* The thought wasn't as appalling as it should have been, and the moment she realized that fact, she resisted.

Sheri twisted her arm free of his loose grip and stepped away. "What do you think you're doing?"

Armond's dark brows pulled down into a frown and shook his head. "I don't know. What do *you* think I'm doing?"

Sheri regarded him from wide eyes, not expecting this response. But then, she should have come to expect the unexpected with Armond Hovardin.

"You think you can just come in here and grab me like you own me?"

Armond put his hands to his hips. "Last I recall, you are carrying *my* child, is that not correct?"

Sheri swallowed heavily and nodded, knowing where this was going.

"As it appears to me, there is a part of you that I *do* own, at least for now."

She was silent for a moment. "That may be true, but you forget that I shared the truth of my condition with you at least two weeks ago." She hesitated for a moment as she struggled to hold back her emotion. "You left me standing there and I haven't seen you since." She swallowed again, this time past the painful lump in her throat, and she shook her head. "What do you expect? Arms open wide with welcome?"

Armond just stood there, regarding her from eyes reflecting the turmoil she had caused in his mind. Then he slowly closed the distance between them. Nervously she stood her ground and waited to see what would happen. Once standing before her, Armond spoke in a low voice.

"I concede. This time you have the right of it." He paused for a moment and then continued. "But you have to recall that you did the very same thing to me, only for much longer. You took me aback that day, and I just needed some time." Armond's expression shifted. "Now I would like to lay claim to what is mine."

Sheridana took a jagged inward breath. His gaze intensified as it once more focused on her naked body beneath the sheer fabric of the nightgown. "But you already know the child is yours."

Armond reached out and once more took her arm in his grip. He then gently pulled her towards him, his gaze slowly making its way back up to her face. Just like before, he placed his other hand against her belly. This time she didn't move, simply allowed him the freedom to do as he wished. When she felt the child within suddenly begin to move, she placed her own hand just below his.

Armond's eyes met and locked with hers, the wonder of what he was feeling beneath his palm making them so much more piercing. For several moments he just stood there, experiencing the tiny movements of the child in the only way he could. Finally, the movements slowed and Armond moved his hand until it rested on top of hers. Entwining his fingers through her's, he then brought her hand up to his chest. Sheri couldn't help closing her eyes, reveling in the closeness for which she had been yearning for so long.

When Armond finally kissed her, it was unlike anything she had experienced with him. It wasn't the wild, often abandoned touch she had always known before. It had somehow become the tamed caress she felt now. It felt wonderful, but she pulled away. He had already hurt her once. She didn't need for it to happen again.

"Armond, what are you doing?" Her voice was almost breathless as she spoke, somehow forgetting that he had answered that question for her already.

Barely a moment passed before she felt his hand beneath her chin, raising her head so that she would be forced to look him in the eyes. His gaze smoldered with barely suppressed emotion and his grip on her arm tightened. Sheridana felt her heart skip a beat just as Armond once more brought his lips alongside hers. His breath caressed her jaw and his voice was low as he made his reply. "Only claiming what is mine."

The group left central Alcrostat in the early hours of the morning before the sun began its ascent. Gareth rode the larian upon which he arrived in Elvandahar, as did his uncle. When Gareth had told Jaysim they needed as many people as possible, the man felt compelled to volunteer. Jaysim was taken very aback to discover the truth of Sydonnia's true form, but had somehow been able to look past it to the greater good that needed to be achieved, and decided to join the ranks.

Sydonnia just seemed pleased to have another warrior to replace Dartanyen, who had remained adamant about remaining behind in Alcrostat. "Adrianna is here, and Sheri, and the children," he'd said. "If something were to happen to them, and I wasn't here, I'd never forgive myself."

Much of the first day, the group moved south in the direction Sydonnia had told them to go once leaving the city. Upon meeting up with Sydonnia, they moved even farther south for the remainder of the day before finally stopping to erect an encampment. As the sun completed its descent to the horizon, Sydonnia's pack began to converge in the campsite. Almost immediately, tensions began to rise. Gareth could only sit back and watch the drama unfold.

They crept upon the scene, large wemic varying from shades of pale gray to pitch black. Then they would shift, their bodies transforming into the form they had been originally... most of them faelin, a couple of them halfen, and even one of orocish descent. Watching it all happen before his very eyes, Gareth saw that the transformation wasn't as easy as the lycan liked to make it out to be. From what he could see, the pain was extraordinary.

As the lycan numbers grew, so did the group's unease. That evening, after the evening meal had been eaten and the watch set, Sydonnia and two of his pack members sat on the opposite side of the fire from himself, Triath, and Markon. Armond and Jaysim had taken to their bedrolls, hoping to find an early rest since they would be waking early for the third watch. One was a Hinterlean male and the other a halfen woman, her hair bound in a pattern of multihued thick locks that reached to her shoulders.

Gareth watched as Triath's frustration grew. Finally, the man spoke, his eyes narrowed into slits. "What the Hells are you all doing sitting here at my watch-fire"?

Sydonnia regarded him askance. "We need your permission to sit where we choose?"

Triath did the same, his head cocked to the side. "You realize you are pushing your boundaries with us. It is difficult enough already to have you in our midst. Now, for you to sit here at our fire..." Triath shook his head. "Need I really explain this to you?"

Sydonnia nodded. "It seems to me that you have every intention of telling me and my pack where they can and cannot go. That does not sit well with us."

Gareth sensed a rise in Triath's normally calm demeanor. "As I recall it, *you* were the one asking for *our* help. The least you could do is to keep your filthy pets on a leash and maintain your distance until we become more accustomed to your presence."

Triath's words immediately caused a stir. The halfen woman rose from her place, an expression of anger on her face. "How about I take that effing leash and put it up your ass? I will shove it up far enough so that I can pull it out your effin' nose and hang you from a tree before beating you with the nearest stick, you worthless piece of dung!"

Sydonnia grabbed the woman just as she was about to leap across the fire. Meanwhile, the one Gareth heard Sydonnia call Melvyn had also risen from his place and was moving to help his leader. She tried to claw her way free of the men who restrained her, wickedly sharp fingernails leaving deep scratches on their hands and arms that bled almost immediately. "C'mon, Sy!" she growled. "I've had enough of this pile of umberhulk dung. We don't need any of the likes of him with the pack anyway! Let me kill 'em so we can end this farce now!"

Sydonnia finally got a good hold of the woman and tackled her to the ground. Triath and Gareth just glanced at one another in dismay, wondering about the situation they had gotten themselves into. Sydonnia spoke to her in Hinterlic, leaving them unable to understand what was being said. However, by the soothing tone of his voice, Gareth knew Sydonnia endeavored to calm the woman. He also heard Sydonnia use her name... Simi.

Finally, the woman was under control. As she was led away from the fire by Melvyn, she turned her head for one last look at Triath. Her angry gaze was predatory and her mouth pulled down into a frown before she allowed Melvyn to urge her onward. Gareth turned back to Sydonnia where he continued to stand beside the fire, his chest rising and falling with the deep breaths he continued to take after subduing his pack member.

Triath was the first to speak. His brows pulled into a frown, he indicated towards the retreating Melvyn and Simi. "Case in point... your pack members are no more ready to deal with us than we are them. You do everyone an injustice by forcing such close quarters."

Sydonnia was silent for a moment before nodding his head. "You are right. I forget that not everyone is like me. Over the years one would think I would have learned this by now."

Gareth watched the shift in Sydonnia's demeanor. At that moment, he reminded Gareth of the man he approached when he learned of his family's involvement with Sirion, a man who, under the facade of strength and domination, was more like the rest of them than he cared to let on. Of course Gareth could see that Sydonnia was still an ass, and always would be an ass. But he was an ass who cared about Gareth's family, an ass that would protect his sisters with his life... especially Adrianna.

Gareth sat there as Sydonnia melted away into the surrounding darkness. With thoughts of Adrianna on his mind, it was all he could do. In spite of his efforts to make some kind of connection with her since his return, Adrianna had rebuffed him at every turn. It seemed she wanted to have nothing to do with him, and the day before he left, she'd finally told him why.

In spite of knowing the hatred that lay within Thane's heart, Gareth had deserted his young sisters, leaving Adrianna to continue to suffer Thane's contempt and Sheri to come under his influence, an influence that ultimately took her away from home. Aside from Mairi, Adrianna had been alone. For a while, life had ceased to have much meaning. The days had run into one another, as well as the nights. Eventually, Adrianna had met an old man by the name of Nahum. Only then did a whole new world open...

*A world without a brother, without a sister, without a mother or father. A world that involved only herself and the Talent inherent within her.*

The group moved quickly across the steppes. They were relieved to be on dry land again after spending the entirety of yesterday crossing the Terrestra River. Sorn had been there to meet them on the other side. Triath had instantly sensed the maelstrom of emotions the other man felt and knew the reason why. Sorn was remembering an ill-fated river crossing, and as Triath recalled, it was *this* river that had almost killed Sirion, Sorn, Dramati, and Amethyst. Amethyst... unfortunately, Sorn wasn't just remembering the failed ferry ride.

Sorn had been shocked to discover the company the group kept. He was even more appalled to learn that it was the lycan leader who had been the one to send for him. Sorn managed to say a few choice words to Sydonnia before taking himself as far away from him as possible. Even now he remained at the group's rear. Triath understood Sorn's ire. He would have felt the same if placed in such a predicament. Sorn hated to be made the fool, and felt he had been deceived by the King when the royal seal had been affixed to the message he'd received to join the group at the necessary location.

Meanwhile, prior to Sorn joining their ranks, tension between the lycan pack and the group had begun to subside as they traveled. A general understanding had been reached, one that dictated that the pack make a separate encampment every night. Their encounters were minimal, for the pack journeyed ahead of the slower moving group during the day, acting as a scouting party for anything that might be approaching. It was in this manner that they discovered the presence of a large party of priests moving in their direction.

"If we stay on our present course," said Sydonnia, "we will meet them by eventide."

With a sense of foreboding, Triath was quick to speak up. "What do they look like? How many are there?"

"They don't appear to be the typical variety. Their robes are dark and they are at least thirty strong." Sydonnia shook his head. "I wouldn't ordinarily suggest this, but I feel we should avoid them. I sense a malevolence about these people."

Triath gave a gusty sigh. He rubbed his hand along his upper arm, feeling the band resting there. He had nursed the hope it was constructed in time for the Daemundai to lose track of him. Unfortunately, it seemed they had divined his general location before Master Tallachienan was able to construct the armband that would keep him invisible to scrying devices. *"Damn..."*

He didn't realize he spoke aloud until Sydonnia was standing before him, the lycan's thick brows drawn into a frown. "What is it? What do you know that we don't?"

Triath regarded Sydonnia intently for several moments. Then, "I am quite certain these are the priests who have been searching for me since they discovered the truth of my identity."

Sydonnia cocked is head to the side. "And what is that?"

Triath kept his gaze impassive. "What? My identity? Or that of the priests?"

Sydonnia narrowed his eyes. "Both."

"They are Daemundai, priests belonging to a cult dedicated to bringing daemon-kind back into Shandahar. Now, with the Pact of Bakharas broken, that feat is much easier to perform than it used to be." Triath paused for a weighty moment and then continued. "Just as you are no longer wholly faelin, I am not entirely human. During a battle I once had with a daemon, our spirits somehow merged. I acquired many of the abilities that daemon possessed. As the only one of my kind, I have become a commodity to the Daemundai."

Sydonnia stared at him for a moment. "And what is 'your kind'?"

Triath shrugged. "Something Shandahar has never seen before."

Sydonnia pursed his lips and became silent. Meanwhile, Triath was introspective. These Daemundai would continue on to Elvanadahar. Gods only knew what chaos would ensue, what destruction they might cause. In his right mind, Triath couldn't let that happen. Those priests were after him, and once he was in their custody, they would turn around and leave Elvandahar alone.

This revelation scared Triath. However, he would give himself to the Daemundai if it meant Tianna would be safe, as well as countless others that might be affected by the dark priests' passing.

Triath shook his head and turned to the group. Sorn, Armond, Gareth, Jaysim, and Markon stood around him. "I have to go. They outnumber us, and I don't want them to have any reason to cross the river."

Armond frowned. "Surely you are joshing me. You can't just give in like this."

Triath nodded. "Yes, I can. The odds are deplorable. Besides, you can't get involved. You have to move ahead to find Sirion."

Sorn shook his head. "Sorry old friend, but that isn't going to happen. Sure, I want to find Sirion, mayhap more than any other man here. But your solution to this problem doesn't sit well with us."

Triath frowned. "Sorn, this isn't up for discussion. I'm leaving."

Sydonnia's voice suddenly cleaved the air. "No, my pack and I will eliminate them. We will devise an ambush. They won't know we are there until it's too late."

Triath and the other men looked at Sydonnia in surprise. So taken aback by the offer of aid, at first he didn't know what to say. Then, "Why would you place yourselves at risk like that? You don't even like me."

Sydonnia shrugged. "My pack has been itching for a good fight since leaving Elvandahar. And in spite of their strangeness, I am certain these unwanted interlopers will taste just fine."

Triath pursed his lips. "I'm being serious. These men are dangerous."

"And I am equally serious," Sydonnia replied solemnly. "Let me do you a favor to pay you back for the one you are doing for me."

With a deep sigh, Triath nodded in agreement. "All right. We will travel an hour longer and then find a suitable encampment. We will await your return there."

Sydonnia only nodded before disappearing into the tall grasses.

Little more than an hour later, the pack crept upon the priests unawares. Obeying the commands Sydonnia had given, everyone silently maneuvered themselves into position. Then they waited. Just as Sydonnia had predicted, the men weren't alert of the presence of the shirwemic until it was too late.

Everyone moved at once. Sydonnia watched as the pack leaped at the unsuspecting enemy from out of the shaggy grasses that characterized much of central Torimir. Within the blink of an eye, wemic Simi tore an arm off of one of the clerics, followed by rending his abdomen to allow his entrails to spill onto the ground. She then turned and bit the hand off another that was reaching for his sword. Wemic Azreal landed on a cleric close by and tore out his throat. Melvyn charged into the fray in hybrid form, and with his mighty broadsword, cleaved the head off one imam priest and impaled a cleric struggling to draw his mace. Hybrid Evelyn took careful aim and shot an arrow from her bow into the head of the man that had his hand bitten off by Simi, then swiftly sent another arrow into the chest of the imam priest trying to help him.

By then, the element of surprise was lost. An imam priest cast a spell that sent a volley of glowing darts at Simi. Another was nearly finished casting his spell when several short swords pierced his chest, the blades springing out from behind. Hybrid Nosram then sliced off the head. A cleric approached Melvyn from behind, raised a huge battle axe high above his head, and was about to slice into him when the priest was picked up of his feet and slammed hard onto the ground. The grotesque sound of crunching bone could be heard amid howls of pain. Once finished, Ragnarov stood over the priest to survey his destruction. Azreal howled when a cleric managed to slice into him with his sword, but an arrow or two from Evelyn felled him soon after.

Finally, Sydonnia entered the skirmish. He swung at the first priest he encountered and broke his lower jaw. He could tell by the way the bone gave way beneath his knuckles, followed by the cries of the man as he fell to his knees with his face in his hands. Sydonnia then swung around and punched another priest, breaking the nose and knocking out a few teeth. Ragnarov was there to see an end to both men by striking them with his mighty flail. Meanwhile, Simi was being pulled away from the fighting by Nosram. Azreal was also wounded and lay about a farlo away. Sydonnia hoped the man wasn't too terribly injured as the second wave of his pack surged out of the grasses. He grinned as the sounds of battle picked up again. He heard first one howl, and then another as the shirwemic gained the upper hand. The dark priests made a good stand, but they were nothing against the might of his pack.

Sydonnia stood by and watched as the battle swiftly came to a close.

His grin widened when everyone turned towards him with expressions of anticipation, waiting for his next command. With a wave of his hand, he gave it and the pack converged upon the dead that littered the battlefield. The sounds of mass gorging could be heard all around and Sydonnia was pleased... very pleased indeed.

# SEAS OF DESPAIR

Sydonnia stared down at the ravaged body of a corubis. Flies buzzed around the terrible wounds that had been inflicted before death, wounds that Sydonnia was certain had been endured for the sake of Dramati's dearest friend. Sydonnia hated the knowledge of the animal's passing, for it was just another loss on top of all the others Sirion would be forced to endure... or not, depending if Sydonnia could draw his son out of the convenient escape he had found.

It was an escape in the form of a beast, a beast Adrianna had once called Cortath.

*Paws barely touching the ground, Sydonnia ran back to the group, his mind in turmoil. The rest of his pack followed behind, Randall and Makenna in the center. The two of them were tired, and weakened from wounds that had never been given a chance to heal. The information they had shared shook him to the core, giving him more speed than usual. Sirion was in terrible danger. If they were to have any chance of saving him, they needed to make haste. Against the odds Randall described, there was little chance the man was still alive. Sydonnia couldn't bring himself to accept that reality.*

*The men were startled as Sydonnia rushed into the encampment. His eyes sought out Triath as he shifted into faelin form. By the time the complete transformation had taken place, Triath was walking towards him, his expression one of concern in spite of Sydonnia's nudity. "What is it? Has something happened?"*

*Sydonnia nodded. "I have received word of Sirion. Two of my pack members, Randall and Makenna, approached me less than thirty minutes ago. Ahead of us by nearly five days is the scene of an attack. I think that Sirion must have come into contact with Bordrigan's periphery patrol, and the lycan thought he might be an interesting bit of sport. The way Randall tells it, there were quite a few chasing after him by the time he and Makenna happened upon the scene. The lycan finally caught up to Sirion at the same time as Randall and Makenna. A conflict ensued, and in the middle of it, Sirion changed. He... he..."*

*"Became a wemic," supplied Armond in a monotone.*

*Sydonnia looked around to see that the rest of the group stood around him.*

*He nodded a moment later. "Yes, something like that."*

*"Where is he now?" asked Triath.*

*Sydonnia shook his head. "We don't know. But Randall and Makenna offered enough of a distraction for Sirion to get away..."*

"Hey everyone, over here! I think I found something!"

Sydonnia shook his head free of the memory as Gareth's voice reached his ears. He turned away from the body of Dramati and rushed over to find the man crouched beside a travel pack. Sorn stepped up and lifted it from the ground. The straps had been broken, but the rest seemed to be whole.

"You go head and open it, Sorn. You were closest to Sirion. Maybe you can find something inside that might give us an idea of what he was thinking when he left," said Triath.

Sorn shook his head. "I doubt I will find anything. In more recent years, Sirion was always against keeping a written log of his personal accounts."

"Please take a look anyway."

Sorn nodded and went about the task. Meanwhile, Sydonnia approached Triath to tell him about Dramati. The man's eyes widened with the implication of what Sydonnia divulged. "Oh gods, no. Dramati would have fought at Sirion's side until the end."

Sydonnia gave a sigh. "I know."

"Can you get a scent of him? Find out if he was able to escape like Randall and Makenna hoped?" asked Triath.

Sydonnia nodded. "That's what I am about to do. But I just wanted to tell you what I found." Triath's shoulders slumped as Sydonnia turned and strode away. He removed his clothing, stuffed the tunic and trousers into his travel pack, and shifted into beast form. He knew the trail would be old, and it would be easier for him to discern anything with his nose closer to the ground.

Sydonnia gave his thoughts free reign as he methodically perused the area. Bordrigan. The sire had been an enemy since the first time they met. By that time Sydonnia had been away from Elvanadahar for many moon cycles. He was a loner, those whom he had sired during the first several moon cycles after his transformation all finally deceased. A part of him had wished he would endure the same fate, but Death never came for him. He had wondered about those poor wretched souls, why they had been unable to survive when he was forced to live a hideous existence he didn't want.

They met by chance, at least Sydonnia always thought so. By then he had learned of the existence of other lycanthropes like himself, lycan that had the ability to sire, or transform, other lycan. Not all were wemic; some were kyrrean, alothere, and bruin. They had all been created the same way as Sydonnia... by the wicked claws of a hideous cloaked man. He had also learned that not all of those sired died within a year or two after transformation. Their minds didn't degrade, and as such, their bodies remained strong. He endeavored to know the secret of such successful transformations, for he had quickly tired of the transient lifestyle he had lived before.

However, Bordrigan didn't seem to have the same qualms. His pack was large, much larger than any other Sydonnia had encountered in his travels. Most of the changelings were sickly, each undergoing mental degradation at different rates. However, Bordrigan also had the allegiance of other sires. That fact made him a force to be reckoned with, a force Sydonnia had wished to avoid.

Unfortunately, such evasion wasn't meant to be. Sydonnia encountered Bordrigan in the city of Ames located north of the Balcazon Hills within the realm of Durnst. In a dark alleyway in the heart of the city, Sydonnia had found himself suddenly surrounded by lycan he had sensed closing in on him only brief moments before. Once Sydonnia was properly detained, Bordrigan had made his approach. Sydonnia had stood silently by as the shirbruin gave an elaborate speech detailing the reasons why Sydonnia should join his ranks. Sydonnia had given the impression of being attentive and thoughtful, but when the time came to give a reply, Sydonnia had responded in the negative.

Needless to say, Bordrigan had been quite put out. It wasn't every day that he was turned down, especially with such a well-developed oration. Much to Sydonnia's benefit, a contingent of the Ames city guard had happened to pass through at that moment. Bordrigan and his minions had quickly dispersed, and Sydonnia similarly disappeared into the shadows.

A few years passed before they met again. By that time, Sydonnia had begun to develop his own pack, a group of individuals he had chosen carefully from those he met on his travels. Through trial and error, he had begun to discern who might be capable of withstanding the transformation. Chaysin was his first, followed by Melvyn, Randall, and much to his surprise, the female Makenna.

This time a fight had broken out. The skirmish was grueling, but in the end, Sydonnia and his small 'specialized' pack agreed to a stalemate with the larger, much less coordinated one that belonged to Bordrigan. Sydonnia had lost his first pack-mate, Chaysin, and another one he called Boslow. Bordrigan had lost several more, but had many others to spare. However, rather than continue and suffer more deaths, the two groups parted ways, knowing they would eventually meet again...

Sydonnia stopped and sniffed again, his focus shifting back to the present. The scent was unmistakable. Beyond a shadow of doubt,

Sydonnia knew Sirion had passed in this direction. *Blood never lied.*

Sydonnia came to a halt and lifted his voice into a howl. Within moments he was answered by the rest of his pack, the voices of over thirty strong. They would bring Triath and the rest of the group to his location, then they would make a decision on how they would proceed.

The group walked through the dilapidated hamlet. Most of the buildings were little more than shanties, and even those were pathetic. The people they passed were very obviously destitute, castoffs of society that no one wanted or cared about. They had found one another and settled here, somehow existing with the meager resources at their disposal.

Triath urged his lloryk to increase its pace. He felt uncomfortable by the stares of the women and children they passed, people that knew more hunger in one day than he had ever felt in the entirety of any one year of his life... because even as a thief on the streets of Sangrilak he had lived better than these people. Unlike a normal village, where the children would often come running to surround the travelers, these just stood there and stared silently from wide eyes, their bodies gaunt beneath the ragged clothing they wore. The women watched them with glares of suspicion, for not many passed through.

Finally, they reached a ramshackle building standing at the village outskirts. It was larger than any of the others, most likely an old storage house. Sydonnia raised a hand as they approached and the group stopped when they were about a farlo behind him. A moment later he glanced back. "My senses lead me inside here."

Triath dismounted his lloryk and went to stand beside Sydonnia. Armond, Markon, Gareth, Jaysim, and Sorn followed suit. "We are coming in behind you."

Sydonnia gave a brief nod and moved towards the building. Once inside, Sydonnia immediately went to the rear of the structure. Traith's eyes struggled to adjust to the lack of lighting, for all they had was the sunlight that filtered through the intermittent cracks here and there. The building was empty but for a moldy smattering of grain in one room and a small desiccated pile of wood in another.

"By the gods..." Sydonnia's voice brought him up short. Triath rushed forward to stand beside him at the entry to the darkest chamber they had encountered. In the far corner lay the form of a large animal.

Armond came to stand behind Triath and looked over his shoulder. "Hellfire, it's Cortath."

Triath swallowed heavily as Sydonnia slowly approached the fallen animal. The scent of blood permeated the air, noticeable even to his human senses. He was certain it belonged to the beast. Triath could scarcely believe it was really Sirion laying there. What the Hells had made him that way? What made him suffer such an affliction? Triath watched as Sydonnia went to his knees beside the animal. The lycan seemed unusually affected by the scene, and Triath attributed it to the fact that the form Sirion had taken was so similar to Sydonnia's own.

Sydonnia's agonized voice rent the air. "He's bleeding to death."

Triath felt a jostling from behind as Markon shouldered his way through. The druid went to kneel beside Sydonnia and laid his hands on the blood matted fur. Triath realized he had moved along behind the man when he recognized that he could discern such detail within a room as dark as this one.

It wasn't long before Markon spoke, his voice reeking of exasperation. "I can't work like this. I need more light."

Triath turned back to the rest of the group who still stood at the entry. "Come on in. This place will be our encampment for the next few days."

Gareth set down his pack and removed a torch. He lit it and brought it to Sydonnia. Markon nodded and gave a more thorough perusal of the beast lying before him. He solemnly shook his head. "He is severely wounded, and has been for at least two or three days. If not for his healing capability, he would have died already." Markon paused for a moment before continuing. "There is very little I can do right now, for the wounds have already begun to seal shut. Some of them have infection beneath them and need to be reopened."

Sydonnia regarded him intently. "Then what are you waiting for?"

Markon shook his head again. "He is very weak." He pointed to the dark stickiness that characterized the floor beneath the animal. "He has lost so much blood already. I'm not certain he can withstand the opening of so many wounds."

Sydonnia frowned. "How many?"

Markon pursed his lips, clearly undeterred by Sydonnia's stern demeanor. "It doesn't matter. You just need to take my word for it."

"But will he withstand the infection?" Sydonnia asked.

Markon shook his head. "Probably not."

"Then what have we to lose?"

Markon breathed deeply inward. "He will suffer the pain of my incisions, and even if I reopen the wounds and place antiseptic poultices, it is no guarantee he will persevere."

"Have you no prayers to offer your gods so they may bless him with healing?" asked Triath.

Markon shook his head. "I am not a priest. My skills lie in the natural remedies that can be found in the world around us."

Triath swallowed heavily and shook his head. He so wished Tianna was there with them now. With prayers to her goddess, she surely could have saved Sirion's life. Then she would have sealed the deal with her remedies. Really, why hadn't she been included in this excursion? Why hadn't he spoken on her behalf? He knew the answer even before he asked himself the question. It was all about fear. He had been afraid that she would get hurt, and even more afraid that he wouldn't have the good fortune of seeing her escape the terrible wounds she might incur. He couldn't help feeling that way, for he'd almost lost her the last time.

And now Sirion's life was forfeit...

"Do it," said Sydonnia. "The pain is worth the chance he could live."

"That is easy for you to say," said Markon. "You are not the one having to endure it."

Sydonnia's thick brows pulled into a frown. "So, you would rather he continue to lie here and die? Surely he is in pain even now."

Markon nodded grudgingly. "You are right. It is worth the try. I just hate the fact that he will suffer."

Sydonnia laid a hand on the druid's shoulder, his demeanor instantly calmer. "I know you do. Thank you for that."

Markon nodded. "All right, bring that light closer so I can get to work."

*Adrianna's dark eyes brightened with wonderment. Sirion felt himself responding in kind with a small grin of his own. He couldn't help it, for he loved to see her smile. The small spotted hawk perched on his forearm rustled his dusky green feathers for a moment before subsiding. The feisty birds were customarily hooded when brought before someone unfamiliar, but Sirion felt confident enough in his ability to handle the hawk without the hood. He was unusually adept with creatures such as these, and he probably would have done very well as an aerie-keeper if he hadn't chosen the life of a ranger.*

*Or more accurately, if Servial hadn't chosen the life of a ranger for him. Sirion stopped before Adrianna. Her eyes were riveted on the hawk, and he could easily see the appreciation reflected there. "Oh, Sirion! He's so beautiful!" She brought her gaze back to his face. "How do you manage him so well?"*

*"I have been trained to handle many kinds of animals." He gave a brief shrug. "And perhaps I have a propensity for them. The animals like me, always have." He paused for a moment before asking the question that came to his mind the moment she spoke. "How do you know the hawk is male?"*

*Adrianna became thoughtful for a moment before eventually giving her own shrug. "I don't know. Am I wrong?"*

Sirion felt his smile widen. "No, you are right. I was just curious."

Before he could say not to, Adrianna unexpectedly sidled close to his side to get a better look at the hawk. Sirion struggled to keep his calm in spite of the fear that her sudden proximity would unsettle the young bird. However, much to his delight, the hawk seemed unaffected by her closeness, and even seemed to be expressing an interest in her. The bird turned his head to the side and watched her intently from one red eye.

"He likes you, I think," Sirion said.

"How do you know?"

Sirion regarded her for a moment and then pulled the extra arm guard he had brought out of his belt pouch. At the time he hadn't really known why he bothered to take it, for he would have never thought he would even consider doing what he was about to do. "Here, put this on your arm the way I have mine."

Adrianna inspected the padded piece of leather beneath the sharp talons of the hawk and then fastened the guard on her forearm. Then, very slowly, Sirion brought his arm with the hawk close to hers. "Hold your arm perpendicular to your body just as I am. He will consider it a nice place to perch if you do it just right," he said in a low voice.

Adrianna did as he instructed. Sirion held his breath, wondering if the bird would really do what he thought he might. He brought his arm just below Adria's so that her padded arm just barely touched the hawk's legs. He released the jesses as the bird effortlessly stepped from his arm onto hers without hesitation.

Adrianna gave a soft inhalation of wonder. She slowly brought her forearm close to her body and the hawk stepped along the guard until it reached the edge of the padding near her elbow. He then turned his head to the side to look up at her, his eye watching her with interest. She crooned to him in a low voice in a language Sirion didn't comprehend, and once again, before he could utter a nay, she had brought her other hand up to the bird and gently ran a fingertip along his chest.

Much to Sirion's surprise, the hawk did nothing and allowed the brief caress. "He's so soft!" she exclaimed.

He shook his head in bewilderment. Who was this woman? How was it that she could handle a bird that many rangers could not? Rangers who had been born in and of the forest, rangers who had been taught the skill to handle creatures such as these? What was it about Adrianna Darnesse that made her so special? She had become so precious to him within the past several weeks since she and her sister had defeated Lord Thane. Sirion never imagined he would care for anyone as deeply as he did this woman...

She was his soul-mate, that person in his life that made him whole, the one who would set right anything that was wrong, the one who would be *there by his side for all of the days of his life. She was the better part that would love him even during his darkest hours...*

Sirion felt pain, terrible pain that cut into his flesh like daggers. And he was cold, so cold he shivered in spite of the fur that covered him. He opened his eyes and saw nothing but the darkness of an enclosed space. He heard vague murmurings at the periphery of his auditory senses, but he couldn't make out any of the words that were spoken. He felt the pain again and he cried out...

## 11 BRINAREN CY 594

Adrianna lay within the crook of her Bondmate's foreleg, the rest of his body and tail curved protectively around them. Xebrinarth slept peacefully and she was glad, for he deserved the reprieve. His efforts towards the tower construction had been awesome to say the least, and joined by Saranath and Mordrexith, the three dragons accomplished more in one day than any group of faelin or humans could have done in weeks. It was wonderful that the two dragons had come for a visit, but the circumstances behind it were a bit disturbing.

The fractioned remainders of Aasarak's army were still at large. In spite of the militaristic efforts of the surrounding realms to eradicate what was left of the wraiths, the group invariably heard of more contingents that had laid waste to another village or town. Thinking on it now, mayhap it had been the reason that made it easier for Sirion to leave so abruptly without a word to her. Maybe it was his objective to make an end to the undead that threatened so many.

Of course, Adrianna would love to believe that, but who was she fooling? It would have taken Sirion barely a moment to compose some kind of message to send. Hells, since leaving Elvandahar on his own mission, Triath had already done that for Tianna. But then she remembered... Oh yes, those two were married, much unlike herself and Sirion. In light of that fact, she supposed Sirion owed her nothing, except perhaps ownership of her heart, which she had foolishly given away to him in spite of the lack of ceremony.

The thought made her sick to her stomach.

Xebrinarth stirred. <Zahara, why do you persist in tormenting yourself? You had no idea things would end this way. Please, I love you so dearly and I can barely stand the censure you make yourself endure day in and day out.>

Adrianna's reply was less that satisfactory, much of it based on the fact she got very little sleep since Sirion's departure, not to mention the resultant malaise she had begun to feel the past several days. <Is not Sirion's silence similar to what you treated me when you first learned of my destiny? Did you not deny me the camaraderie I needed at that time? Did you not ignore the pleas of your Bondmate in order to keep yourself from further disappointment?> Adrianna frowned. <Don't bother giving me advice on this matter when you were so hasty to deny me yourself in the face of terribe adversity.>

Silence rang throughout their link. Adrianna immediately felt awful about her thoughtless response. <Oh, Xebrinarth... I am sorry. I didn't mean to...>

Xebrinarth shook his head. <No, you are right, Zahara. I deserted you when you needed me most. I will never forget that. But I have learned from my mistakes. I only wish that Sirion had learned the same before he met you. Obviously, that is not the case and you are now forced to suffer. I want you to know that I am here for you, and just like your lycan friend said, you are 'enough for any man.'>

Adrianna gave a wan smile at Xebrinarth's attempt to make her feel better. He had been a bit over-solicitous of her of late, but she knew it was only because he loved her. Now, as she lay there under the protection of her dragon, she recognized how wise he could be. One day she hoped to catch up with him and mayhap they could be intellectual equals. With her head lying against his side, she heard the rumble of his laughter before it became auditory, sensing it from deep within his body before it emerged into the air.

<You think too highly of me, Zahara. I am not at all what you perceive me to be.>

<But you are close enough,> she replied.

Xebrinarth only shook his head and lay back down to sleep. He enjoyed the touch of the sun's rays, yet protected Adrianna from them with a partially extended wing overhead, stating that she was much more fragile than he, and that her thin hide simply couldn't sustain such rays without damage. Of course, she felt him to be overprotective and silly, but it endeared him to her nonetheless, for he sincerely believed all he told her. Mayhap one day he could explain it to her.

But for now, she would think of Sirion and all she had lost. In spite of her newfound love for the boy, Talemar, little else seemed to have meaning and it was difficult for her to rise from bed every morning. Dinim had been forced to undertake the bulk of the building supervision, for she had become too sickly to help much anymore. She knew that she was going down a path of self-destruction, knew that most people didn't react this way to similar situations such as hers. But she couldn't help how she felt, like a bleeding leschera after being mortally wounded with an arrow... slowly suffering through the last moments that precipitated inevitable death.

It was so strange that everything had begun to happen at once. A few days after everyone realized Sirion's absence, Triath, Sorn, Armond, and Markon had also left Alcrostat. It was a mission that had been declared top priority, not to mention, very secretive. Somehow discovering the import of the situation, Gareth had opted to go along. Dinim might have accompanied them had he not been knee deep in the building of the academy, and as one of the elite palace guardians, Dartanyen had chosen to remain at the home front.

Adrianna had not been apprised of the details, and she hadn't been asked to go. Somehow, it just didn't seem to matter. Besides, Tianna was there, and Sheridana. And, of course, she had Xebrinarth.

The same day, she had discovered that Sydonnia was also leaving Alcrostat. She imagined it had something to do with the mission in which the others participated. She didn't ask, and Sydonnia didn't say, but at least he had the decency to offer her a farewell.

Adrianna slowly rose from her place in the crook of Xebrinarth's foreleg. Not wanting to disturb him, she then crept away into the nearby trees. Paying no heed, she just walked, her thoughts floating around in a sea of memories. How had it come to this? She supposed she shouldn't really be all that surprised. Her life had already proven to be fraught with adversity, beginning with the night of her birth when her mother died and her father wanted nothing to do with her. She had suffered many more trials in her childhood before her horrific ordeal on the road to Andahye. And once in the mystical city, she had been beleaguered even more as she tried so hard to find a master who would take her, and then even more when she struggled to find her place within Master Tallek's household.

However, several years later Tallek had died, and Adrianna went back home to Sangrilak. That was when the severity of things ramped up a bit. Somewhere... somehow in the chaotic course of events that transformed her life, she had found Sirion. Since coming together, she had begun to think of him as the other half of the being that made her whole, that part of her that would continue to remain in spite of any differences that might arise between them.

However, Sirion obviously did not feel the same, leaving without even bothering to send her a message. He'd been gone almost six weeks now and she had yet to hear a word from him. As it turned out, part of that top secret mission had involved looking for Sirion. Gareth had been good enought to send messages about the ranger's welfare, reporting that he was hale and whole. She was relieved that he was well, but it made his behavior all the more despicable.

Instead of an inability to send some type of communication, there had been a choice not to. This reality burned her to the core of her being, leaving a vast hole where her heart had once been.

Adrianna continued to walk. Her thoughts were haphazard, but she allowed them to simply come and go as they pleased. The trees and shrubs blended together as she aimlessly moved, the sounds of the wood offering a pleasant backdrop to her scattered musings. However, after a while had passed, her thoughts finally settled again on the present. She slowly regained her awareness and came to the realization she didn't know how long she had walked. It could have been only a few moments, mayhap an hour, possibly a few... Somehow, in her melancholic state, she had lost track of the time. The canopy overhead made it difficult to tell where the sun had been positioned when she first started out, and even more so when it became dark with the approach of the night. She finally stopped to take a look around. The giant silver oaks towered overhead, and the scrub brush laying all around made it difficult to tell where she might be.

It didn't take Adrianna long to realize she was lost. Strangely, this didn't seem to bother her overly much. It was like many other things in her life... she simply didn't care anymore. Over the days since Sirion's departure, she'd become a shadow of herself. She had very little desire to eat or drink, to go anywhere, to speak to anyone, or to think about anything. She imagined that one day she might become invisible... unseen, unheard, untouched.

Nothing.

Adrianna sank to her knees on the forest floor. She thought perhaps this would be a good time to cry, but the tears didn't come. Mayhap she had finally cried them all out and none were left. She took note of the darkness that now pervaded the area and thought it odd that her Bondmate had yet to contact her. It was then she realized she couldn't sense their link. Her mind was as she remembered it before she had ever met Xebrinarth. The sensation was a strange one, but she didn't think much of it as she lay herself down on the ground. She didn't feel like walking anymore, didn't feel like thinking anymore, didn't feel like *feeling* anymore...

Then time seemed to no longer exist.

*For the third time that morning, Adrianna caught him watching her. The giddy sensation it elicited deep inside made her guts twist again, and she wondered what Sirion thought he was doing. He had kept his stares no secret, and she'd already noticed the pointed glances cast at her from other members of the group, especially those members with whom she was less familiar. She felt her cheeks flush and turned away, successfully hiding her face with the curtain of her unbound hair. She couldn't help grinning to herself, a silly smile that she didn't want him, or anyone else, to see.*

*The past few days had been some of the most emotional in her life. She had been faced with the mistaken reality of a romantic relationship between Sirion and Tianna, followed by her abduction by Sirion's diabolical double. The next evening, after having slept most of the day recovering from the poison used to subdue her, she and Sirion had argued. They had been rather cruel with one another, and rather than continue the verbal flaying, Adrianna had chosen the high road and retreated to her bedchamber.*

*Sirion had come to her. She had thought to resist the power of his seduction, but when he professed his love, her barriers came crashing down. Casting her fears aside, she gave herself to him, believing he would never hurt her. And true to her conviction, he hadn't, ending their passionate liaison before it could proceed to that ultimate union. He had told her that he wanted to give her the time she needed to become accustomed to his touch, to realize he would always have her best interests at heart. More than words could say, she appreciated his gesture, and it endeared him to her.*

*The next evening, after the group had prepared themselves for travel, Sirion had brought his belongings to her chamber, sheepishly explaining that Sheridana had taken over his place in Dartanyen's room. Adrianna had frowned at the antics of her wayward sister, but opened the door wide, Sirion had then held her in his arms all the night through.*

*Now, as they traveled the road to Driscol, she was befuddled by what had begun to take place. While Anya took the initiative and scouted ahead of the group, Sirion stayed behind. It was plain to see that Triath, Sorn, and Naemmious were all taken aback by this shift in their comrade's behavior. It was obvious he wanted all to know his intentions towards her. When Adrianna finally raised her eyes again, she found her gaze caught by Triath. He wore a knowing smirk on his handsome face and she felt her eyes widen for a moment before looking away. She knew what he must be thinking and imagined the others assumed the same. Only her own close comrades might know differently, well aware of her unfortunate past.*

*Finally, Adrianna rode her larian over to him. Dramati had chosen to accompany Anya, so Sirion walked swiftly among them. His endurance was phenomenal, for she never could have walked at his pace for so far and not collapsed from exhaustion. His eyes brightened as she approached and she smiled in return. For a few moments she walked beside him, deciding what she wanted to say. But then, finding nothing of real value in her thoughts, she simply said the first thing on her mind.*

"Sirion, is there something you need to tell me?"

314

*He looked up at her where she sat astride the larian, regarded her from mischievous eyes, and shook his head. "No, I don't think so. Why do you ask?"*

*She gave a resounding sigh. "Then why do you keep staring at me? Everyone* is *wondering about it."*

*Sirion simply watched her for a moment before making his reply. "I stare because you are quite attractive and a pleasure to look at. And now that I know that you feel similarly about me, I am comfortable looking at you whenever I choose." Sirion shrugged. "And in regards to the others, who really cares what they think?"*

*Adrianna considered his words. Of course, she didn't really believe him about her comeliness, however she sensed the truth behind his second statement. Yes, who cared what everyone else thought? He regarded her solemnly as she reached this realization for herself, smiling when she glanced back at him. She gave a gusty sigh and said, "Well, can you at least tell Triath to keep his thoughts to himself?"*

*Sirion instantly frowned. "He said something to you?"*

*Adrianna pouted. "Well, no. But he didn't have to."*

*Sirion chuckled. "Yes, there are times Triath doesn't need to speak. His expression says it all."*

*Adrianna only shook her head and returned her focus to the road before them. Later that evening as they prepared an encampment, Sirion invited her to sparring practice. She eyed him askance as he beckoned her into the circle with only a curving of his forefinger, wearing a beguiling smile that spoke only of intimacy. She vaguely wondered what he was about as she entered the ring, but when he suddenly swept at her with his staff, she quickly resolved herself to battle.*

*It was more a dance than weapons exercise. At almost every move, Sirion was reaching out to touch her, to make any type of physical contact. Once realizing the game, Adrianna joined in. Dodge. Parry. Retreat. He curved an arm around her waist as he swept by, caressed her face, or touched her hand. Adrianna followed his lead. It was quite a difficult exercise, one that required the utmost of skill and focus. She wasn't able to keep up, but she did well enough.*

*Sirion's smile was triumphant when he finally stood over her with his staff against her neck, his chest barely a fingertip from hers. Sexual tension surrounded them in a thick shroud and she sensed that many of the others had stopped to watch them. She shook her head in bewilderment. "Sirion, what are you doing?"*

*He gave her a small smile. "I'm doing what I told you I would, making you accustomed to my touch." His gaze became intense. "I don't want you to fear me, Adrianna."*

*She regarded him intently as he got to his feet and held out a hand to her. She took it and he pulled her up. It was quite an effort to take her hand from his, however, once free she stepped back. "I will join you for the first watch," she said quickly.*

*Sirion nodded, and she turned away only to be captured by the knowing gaze of her sister. Adrianna walked towards Sheri on her way to her bedroll, and as she passed, Sheri turned to move alongside. Her sister waited until they had reached the bedroll to say anything, hunkering down beside Adrianna as she began to remove her boots.*

*"By the gods, Adria! What was that?"*

*Adrianna paused and brought her eyes to Sheri's face. "Sparring practice."*

*"The Hells it was! That was... that was something like..." Sheri paused, "pleasure play."*

*Adrianna simply went back to preparing herself for bed. Sheri stared at her for a few moments before speaking again, her voice low. "That man definitely has it for you."*

*Adrianna glanced back up. "Has what?"*

*Sheri smiled. "He wants you, dear sister. And it won't be long before he has you."*

*Adrianna shook her head and snickered.*

*"What, you don't believe me?"*

*"It's just that you are so dramatic."*

*Sheri sighed. "But I speak the truth."*

*Adrianna only shrugged. Sheri shook her head and went to have their bowls filled with the evening stew. For the rest of the evening, Adrianna thanked the gods for Sheri's silence. When the sun had almost completed its descent, she walked to the fire and gingerly seated herself next to Sirion. He greeted her with a friendly nod, but waited until the others had settled before turning towards her.*

*She cocked her head to the side. "Don't you think you were a bit forward today?"*

*Sirion slowly shook his head, placed a hand at her cheek, and brushed her lips with his thumb. "No."*

*Adrianna gave a brief gusty sigh. Hells, she had been forced to field the curious expressions of most of the group all evening long. Amethyst and Sorn had been an exception. Only they seemed to not really care about anything she or Sirion did. And then there was Tianna. The other woman had avoided her as much as possible.*

*Adrianna reached up to take Sirion's hand in hers. "I want to know about you."*

*Sirion furrowed his brows. "Know what?"*

*She shrugged. "I don't know. Anything you might want to tell me."*

*He regarded her intently for a few moments, seemingly at a loss for words. She waited patiently until he spoke. "I was born to one of the most influential families in Elvandahar. My mother is Lilandria, daughter to the Hamzin of Kleyshes, the largest domain in the realm. My father was a nobody from the outskirts of Alcrostat, one of the two sons of one of the most renowned rangers in the region. I was brought up knowing my heritage from the whispered stories my mother would tell Anya and I in the middle of the night, afraid my father would overhear and become angry. She would tell us of the friendship between the King and her father, how they had remained close even through the darkest days of Elvandahar's history, the days that took nearly half of the Hinterlean population during the Bloody Plague. She would tell us about the sacrifices the men made, the battles they fought, and the loves they lost together. My mother taught us much about our home, our people, and our duty to both. But I was enamored by my father. What boy wouldn't be? So when Servial came to take me on my first Run, I was excited to go. It was the last time I saw my mother for a long time."*

*Sirion was silent as he reclaimed his hand. He placed it alongside her face again, trailing the thumb from her lips, down her jaw, and onto her neck. The sensation was nice, easily distracting her from any other conversation. As she struggled to regain her senses, Sirion leaned in and kissed her. He brought his other hand to cup her face as the first one moved to her shoulders and pulled her into him...*

*For the remainder of that watch, they shared one another's embrace. Regardless of the effort it took for him to resist her, Sirion waited. The group journeyed almost a fortnight to reach the city of Driscol. Along the way they had passed through a few towns and villages, the people speaking about the swath of destruction being left by one Lord Thane and his deathly minions. By the time the group was at the outskirts of Driscol, Thane was near the city of Celuna. Meanwhile, Sirion had given her the time she needed. Each day of their journey he had built her up, making her yearn for the day they would finally be alone together.*

*That first night in Driscol, at the nearest inn the group could find once entering the city, Sirion finally broke down and showed her what no man ever had before...*

Adrianna awoke to a disturbance. She struggled to open her eyes and felt herself being turned onto her back. Then she heard a voice, "I've found her! She's over here!" It was dark, and she couldn't see the face of the man at her side, but knew the voice belonged to Dinim. She tried to rouse herself enough to speak, but she somehow couldn't find the strength.

She felt herself being picked up from the ground and subsequently held tight against his chest. By the scent alone, she knew it was the same man.

She struggled to make her way out of her all-encompassing lethargy. *Where the Hells am I? Why is it so dark, and why am I being carried around like an invalid?*

Dinim looked down onto the face of the woman in his arms. By the gods he was so glad he'd been able to find her. Adrianna was woefully pale, and her eyes circled with darkness. Her lips were dry and cracked, and her mouth probably felt the same. He could see her trying to focus on his face, but she was too weak. Hells, had she eaten anything at all since discovering Sirion's absence? She felt so frail in his arms, and it had been easy to pick her up in his arms, *too* easy.

Dinim stopped when he was met by the others that made up the search party. Dartanyen was there, as well as Tianna, Sheridana, Carli, and Xebrin in faelin form. The dragon was the first to step up to him, lovingly accepting his Bondmate from Dinim's arms. Dinim gave her away easily, knowing that Adrianna was better off in his care than anyone else. Tianna was a close second, and she walked immediately behind Xebrin as the group made their way to the nearest lift that would take them up into the trees.

Dinim had been shocked when Xebrinarth approached him in the middle of the night. The dragon was in faelin form so as to more easily navigate the newly built halls of the academy. Dinim had never seen a naked man more disturbed, or one so afraid, as this one. But when Dinim heard what Xebrin had to say, he couldn't help but be equally fearful.

Adrianna was nowhere to be found, and Xebrin's link with her had been severed. She wasn't dead, Xebrin would have felt it. But something terrible had happened.

Most of the next day, Dinim alternated between wracking his mind for a good spell to divine her whereabouts, and waiting for someone to come and tell him that Adrianna had been found. Neither happened. All he was able to come up with was an intermediate scrying spell that *might* work. Hells, with such magnificent Dimensionalist skill at his behest, he struggled over a simple scrying spell! Damnation, what was the use in that?

Later that evening Dinim cast the spell. He reeled from the effort, but was delighted to have it show him the way towards something. When it led him to Adrianna, he was ecstatic. However, the feeling was short-lived for she lay motionless in a sprawled heap on the ground. He rushed to her side and turned her over. He placed his fingertips to her neck, and upon feeling the slow but steady beat of her heart he began to relax. And it was then he called to the others...

Dinim followed behind as Adrianna was taken up into the treetop village of Taegryn. Once there, they took her to the nearest daladin. After explaining themselves to the residents, permission was given to enter. It would be much too crowded for everyone, so only Xebrin and Tianna went inside with Adrianna. The rest of them waited outside, impatiently wanting to hear how she fared.

Over the past fortnight since Sirion's disappearance, Dinim had fought an internal battle. He had wanted to go to her on so many occasions, but he couldn't release himself from the idea that he would be intruding upon a situation that didn't warrant his involvement. He hated what Sirion had done to her by professing his love, and then leaving without bothering to bind himself in wedlock. Adrianna deserved so much more, and he hated that he'd been sucked into Sirion's fabrication with everyone else.

In short, the man was a lloryk's ass to let someone like Adrianna go, no matter how difficult the situation seemed to be. For her sake he hoped that Sirion would soon return to give her the life she so richly deserved. It was blatantly obvious she suffered without the ranger. Many times, Dinim had wished it were himself that she loved so deeply. But it was not to be, and all he could do was be her good friend, champion her when the need arose, and stand by her side in a fight.

Dinim felt that his position in her life allowed him to be righteously indignant on her behalf. There had been times when the situation had not warranted such emotion. However, in this instance the feeling was definitely warranted. He would make great efforts to be certain this night never repeated itself.

No matter how much she fought against him, he would never let Adrianna be so alone again.

# EPILOGUE

J ust like many others of her kind, Tholana had followers of every race. Most of them were Cimmerean, for it was they who tended to gravitate the most towards the dark chaos she exuded. A few of them were Terralean, a few less Savanlean, and lesser still, Hinterlean. It was those forest dwellers who seemed most at odds with her anarchic ways, but there was the odd one or two that just didn't fit the typical mold.

Tholana had one such follower in Elvandahar, a woman by the name of Thessaly. She wasn't entirely of Hinterlean descent, but to all outward appearances she was. Tholana had met her when Thessaly was a much younger woman, a woman with a wayfarer's heart and a lust for the unattainable. Thessaly was beautiful and conceited, and in spite of their differences, Tholana was there to help when Thessaly languished in her darkest hours. It took a long time for Thessaly to recover from the trauma she had endured, but in the process, the woman became a devout follower.

Tholana had been shocked to learn that Adrianna and the Wildrunners were successful in their defeat of Aasarak. It was a difficult event to miss, for the aftershock rocked the world as the Curse of Odion broke. It seemed so strange that the world would not be repeating itself again, that the destiny told in previous Cycles would not come to pass. For the first time in so long, Shandahar had a future. A new era had begun.

Tholana didn't quite know what to do with herself.

It was through Thessaly that Tholana discovered the Wildrunners had come home. Of course, Adrianna Darnesse was among them. Tholana had found this fact rather disturbing even though she expected the girl would have most likely survived the encounter. It wasn't very much later that Tholana had learned Adrianna was with child. Rumor had it that the father was Sirion Timberlyn. Tholana wasn't so certain, *for it hadn't been very long ago that Adrianna was in Tallachienan's company.*

Tholana had gone into a frenzied rage. The blackened corridors would take weeks to reconstruct, and several lives had been lost in the inferno she created. She had briefly considered feeling a twinge of remorse for the lost souls, but never brought herself to do it. Instant death was simply one of the hazards of having the privileged luxury to reside behind the walls of her fortress.

By early the next morning, Tholana had gathered her cohort and was prepared for travel. She hated to journey on the surface, so she moved along familiar underground passages for as long as possible. In spider form, she and her retinue traveled quickly, much faster than they would by any other means. Even at the surface they moved quickly, and it was only when confronted by a waterway that their progress was slowed. They traveled mostly by night, and during they day they burrowed into the ground just enough that a thin layer of soil rested over them. Not only did it reduce fluctuations in temperature, but it kept them well hidden from any eyes that would be unaccustomed to the shocking vision of a spider much larger than the norm. Hells, such an event would be woeful indeed, for the owner of said eyes would certainly meet an unfortunate demise.

Once reaching Elvandahar, Tholana had left her cohort to proceed alone. It would be easier to travel this way, for their numbers would certainly draw the attention of the Hinterlean rangers. Once reaching the first large village, she shifted into faelin form. Her typically Cimmerean appearance was modified to blend with the other Hinterleans: sleek black hair was changed to a vibrant red, delicate pale complexion altered to a warm gold, and bright indigo eyes to a color of honeyed mead. Pride dictated that she stand out as an unusually beautiful woman, and she enjoyed the ogling she got from the men. To any stares she got from the women, she responded with malicious glares.

It didn't take Tholana long to reach the central city of Alcrostat. Through her communication with Thessaly, she already knew that Sirion had left many weeks ago. The reasons were unknown, but his departure had come as a surprise to many. As she traveled, she had also learned that a tower was being built, a tower surrounded by a school that would be dedicated to the arcane arts. Tholana could only assume what specialization it might be, and her thoughts were proven correct when she heard the word 'Dimensionalism' spoken in conjunction with the construction.

Tholana had been two days in Alcrostat before discovering that Adrianna was not in the city. Of course, no one knew where she had gone, and Tholana's resolve that Tallachienan was the true father of Adrianna's child was subsequently strengthened. The most obvious reason why no one would be aware of Adrianna's whereabouts would be if she had gone to Tallachienan's citadel. Tholana struggled to maintain her calm, and in the meanwhile came across a woman by the name of Joselyn Quemirren...

Keeping herself inconspicuous, Tholana had set about learning all she could about the druidess. The only reason she bothered was because she had heard the woman's name used alongside Sirion's. Purportedly the two had once been lovers. Their liaison had ended several years ago when Sirion began to make a bigger name for himself as a woodland tracker and lycan hunter. Tholana imagined that Joselyn might still harbor romantic feelings for Sirion, and her musings became a reality when she overheard the other woman talking to herself at the heated springs...

Patience was a virtue. Tholana had only to wait a while longer before things would begin settling into place. She knew she could make a visit to Tallachienan's citadel, but what would that action ultimately accomplish? If she waited, she just might have the opportunity to catch Adrianna unawares. And the woman Joselyn... under the right conditions, Tholana might find the opportunity to use her to accomplish her goals.

# GLOSSARY OF TERMS

Aertna (airt-na) – that place faelin-kind believe to exist within every man somewhere between his mind and his soul

Alcrostat (al-kro-stat) – the largest city within the realm of Elvandahar - residence of the Sherkari Fortress, home to the King

Alothere (al-o-thayr) – large porcines that are cousins to the wild boar – they live in the forests and steppes of the temperate regions of Shandahar

Andahye (an-duh-high) – mystical city located at the northern edge of the Sheldomar Forest – it is the place where many mages receive their arcane training

Ansalar (an-sal-ar) – one of the three continents of Shandahar – it is the most inhabited

Azmatharcana (az-math-ar-kana) – a mystical tome that delivers many necromantic secrets, including those contained within the Azmathion

Azmathion (az-math-ee-on) – the arcane artifact that gives Aasarak much of his power – it is a geometrical work of art, and one must work the puzzles contained within it in order to divine its secrets

Azmathous (az-math-us) – the most powerful of Aasarak's undead creations – with the power of the Azmathion, they are reborn and are able to retain the skills and abilities they possessed in life

Behiraz (be-heer-az) – a worm of gargantuan proportions, it lives beneath the ground finding it's prey by the vibrations they make upon the surface – swift and deadly, very few survive an encounter

Buffelshmut (buffel-shmut) – a slang term for buttocks

Burbana (bur-ban-uh) – a small ermine-like animal with exquisitely soft fur

Calotebas (kal-o-tee-bas) – a large foul-tempered herbivore that lives near swamps – the taste of their flesh is equally as repugnant as their personality

Cenloryan (sen-lor-yan) – a creature made of the twisted magic of the Kronshue, it has the lower body of a lloryk and the upper torso, arms, and head of a human

Chag (chag) – a drink made from the large seeds of the chagatha plant, which grows in the more southern regions of Ansalar

Chamdaroc (sham-dar-ok) – a shrub that grows within Elvandahar and other forested regions of northwestern Ansalar – it has small white flowers that are said to have intoxicating qualities

Cimmerean (sim-ur-ee-an) – one of the faelin sub-races – also known as 'dark' faelin, they live in vast labyrinths below the surface of the world

Common (com-mun) – the universal language across most of the main continent of Ansalar

Cortubro (cor-too-bro) – a realm situated north of Elvandahar

Corubis (kor-oo-bis) – large canines that have tawny fur with dark dappling – they live in packs headed by an alpha male, but many of them find companionship with faelin, especially Hinterlean rangers

Croxis (krok-sis) – a plant that has hallucinogenic properties, often making the person feel a false sense of well-being – the extract is called croxian

Daemundai (day-mun-die) – an organization of those who strive to give daemon-kind influence and power in Shandahar

Daladin (dal-a-din) – a Hinterlean house in the trees

Denedrian (den-ed-ree-an) – one of the human sub-races – they are largely nomadic, originating from the western plains and deserts

Dimensionalist (dim-en-shen-al-ist) – a sorcerer who specializes in other-worldly knowledge and travel

Doppleganger (dop-pel-gang-er) – a bipedal being once thought to be made of magic, it is a daemon that has the ability to shift its shape into any humanoid between four and eight feet tall – it is a master of trickery and disguise that works for the most powerful of sorcerers

Elvandahar (el-van-da-har) – large forested region in the vee of the Terrestra and Denegal Rivers – it is ruled by Hinterlean faelin, and bears the largest population of these people

Esfexanar (es-fex-an-ar) – a deadly poison often used to subdue someone – it causes the person to fall unconscious and to have after-effects such as slurred speech and tiredness

Eukana (yoo-kana) – a mixture of assorted nuts and dried berries that Hinterlean rangers carry on long trips

Farlo (far-low) – the equivalent of several feet

Filopar (fil-o-par) – one of the five domains of Elvandahar

Fistantillus bush (fist-an-til-lus) – a plant bearing poisonous thorns that can make a person violently ill for several days

Grang (grang) – slightly shorter than halfen, these small, bony humanoids live primarily on the steppes - they are primitive and voracious, but not very smart, their greed often getting in the way of thieving strategies

Griffon (grif-fon) – large animals that have both feline and avian features – they are friendly and intelligent, and can often be found in the company of druids

Hamzin/Hamza (ham-zin/ham-zuh) – the title given by the King to the one who rules within one of the five domains in Elvandahar

Helzethryn (hel-zeth-rin) – one of the dragon sub-races – at maturity their color ranges from pale gold, to deep bronze, to fiery red – they have the highest propensity towards *bonding* with other species

Hestim (hes-tim) – one of the three moons of Shandahar

Himrony (him-ron-ee) – a type of grass that grows abundantly throughout the central Ansalar – the preferred vegetation of larian

Hinterlean (hin-ter-lee-an) – one of the faelin subraces – they live in treetop villages within temperate forests

Hralen (her-ay-len) – the name used for the household staff within the Sherkari Fortress

Humanoid (hue-man-oyd) – any creature that walks upright on two legs (bipedal)

Hybanthis (hie-ban-this) – a vine that has poisonous blue thorns – poison has brain-based affects that heighten a person's emotional state, making emotions difficult to handle

Isterian (iz-ter-ee-un) – the name used for the guards that keep patrol throughout the Sherkari Fortress

Karlisle (kar-lyle) – the human realm neighboring Elvandahar on the other side of the Denegal River

Kleyshes (klie-shays) – one of the five domains of Elvandahar

Krathil-lon (kruh-thil-lon) – a forested glen located within the southern reaches of the Sartingel Mountains

Kronshue, Brotherhood of the (kron-shoo) – a 'technological' society that dominates eastern Ansalar

Kyrrean (kie-reen) – large blond felines with dark brown dappling and oversized paws – they make their existence on the warm temperate plains and borderlands

Larian (layr-ee-an) – with only minor differences, these are smaller cousins to the lloryk – they are able to carry faelin and most humans

327

Leschera (le-sher-uh) – very gentle, larian-sized, deer-like creatures that grace the temperate woodlands

Lloryk (loor-ik) – large muscular equine-like creatures that are able to carry humans and small orocs – they are omnivorous and beneath the top coat of silky fur, have modified hair shafts that appear similar to scales one would see on a reptile

Lycanthrope (lie-kan-throap) – one afflicted with the disease of lycanthropy – they are humans, faelin, or hafen that can transform into animals (beginning with prefix *shir* - wemic, althothere, or kyrrean) – the disease is spread through the bite

Lytham powder (lye-tham) – a component used in a spell that creates a noxious vapor

Mehta (may-tuh) – the title given to the leader of the daemundai

Meriliam (mer-il-lee-am) – one of the three moons of Shandahar

Merzillith (mir-zil-lith) – otherwise known as a mind flayer, this intermediate daemon is from one of the Nine Hells – it has psionic power, the ability to use the energy of the world in a way that is different from the Talent possessed by mages

Mirpur (mir-poor) – one of the five domains of Elvandahar

Monaf (mon-af) – the human realm neighboring Torimir on the other side of the Ratik Mountains

Morden (mor-den) – one of the halfen sub-races – they live in deep caverns within the mountains

Murg (murg) – an alcoholic beverage distilled from fermented cane sugar

Necromancer (nek-ro-man-ser) – a sorcerer who focuses on the darker aspects of spellcasting

Nefreyo/Neiya (nef-ray-oh/nay-yah) – the diminutive/familiar terms used for nephew and niece

Oorg (oorg) – one of the humanoid races of Shandahar, they are even larger than orocs and are often called giants – they often fight with brute strength alone, but aren't good with any type of real strategy

Oroc (or-ok) – one of the native races of Shandahar – they are muscular and broad, standing at least six to seven feet tall – faelin are their greatest enemies, and the two races find any excuse to maim and kill one another

Pact of Bakharas (bak-hair-us) – an agreement between daemon and dragon kind that does not allow one or the other too much influence over Shandahar

Papas fruit (pay-pas) – a small pink orb about the size of a nectarine – it grows on the papas tree, which is prevalent throughout the temperate borderlands of Ansalar

Ptarmigan (tar-mig-an) – a squat, grouse-like bird that is often hunted for its flavorful meat

Rathis (rath-is) – the leaves of this plant are known for their pain-relieving capabilities

Recondian (re-con-dee-an) – one of the human sub-races – they mostly live in the central regions of Ansalar

Reshik-na (resh-ik-na) – an order of druids that lives within the Elvandaharian domain of Filopar

Rezwithrys (rez-with-ris) – the largest of the dragon sub-races – at maturity their color ranges from silver to steel blue to metallic violet – they have a propensity for magic

Samshin/Samshae (sam-shin/sam-shay) – the son/daughter of the Hamzin or Hamza

Sangrilak (sang-ri-lak) – a very diverse city located in the northwestern quadrant of the realm of Torimir

Savanlean (sav-an-lee-an) – one of the faelin sub-races – they live in majestic cities built into mountainsides located in the more northern regions of the Ansalar

Shagendra (shuh-gen-dra) – the root from this plant can be used to make a person's mind vulnerable to suggestions – also causes general lethargy, dulls the senses, and slows reflexes

Shockwave (shok-wave) – a game that is popular throughout the continent – involves cards, bones, and no small amount of strategy and luck

Steralion (stir-a-lee-an) – one of the three moons of Shandahar

Tabanakh drink (ta-ban-ak) – a drink prepared by the druid elders as a right of initiation for their tyros – it has properties that exaggerate the visions of those who are so *gifted*

Talent (tal-ent) – (adj) the ability that some people possess to harness the energy of the world and use it – (n) someone who uses magic

Talsam (tal-sam) – the root from this plant is ground into a powder from which a pain-relieving tea is made

Tankard (tank-erd) – a vessel for holding liquid – it is the equivalent of approximately two mugs and is usually used in taverns

Terralean (ter-a-lee-an) – one of the faelin sub-races – they inhabit many of the borderlands between the forests and steppes and are the most widespread

Thalden (thal-den) – one of the halfen sub-races – they live within the temperate hills

Thritean (thrye-teen) – very large silver felines with black striping and six legs – they live in cold northern forests

Tobey (toe-bee) – a small, goat-like creature – many nomadic peoples breed them for the creamy textured milk they produce

Torimir (tor-eh-meer) – the realm neighboring Elvandahar on the other side of the Terrestra River

Tremidian (tre-mid-ee-an) – one of the human sub-races – they live on the eastern side of the continent

Travel Sickness – the discomfort a Dimensionalist will often endure after Travelling for any length of time between worlds – it is especially pronounced when one Travels ahead in time.

Trolag (trol-ag) – one of the humanoid races of Shandahar, they are tall and stooped, their long, gangly bodies covered with dark brown wiry hair – they have the ability to heal quickly

Umberhulk (um-ber-hulk) – large, stout burden beasts with thick umber colored skin virtually devoid of hair – used to pull carts in cities, towns, and many times even in caravan trains

Varanghelie Vault (vair-an-gay-lee) – a highly protected storage facility located within Andahye – it is where many people keep their most valuable possessions

Wemic (wee-mik) – in some places better known as wolves, these animals appear to be distant cousins to the corubis – they run in temperate to sub-arctic forests and have never been tamed

Wraith (rayth) – a corpse that has been reanimated – they are mindless, following the commands of their necromantic masters – their bodies are ravaged by the effects of decay and they wield only the simplest of weapons

Wyvern (why-vern) – a large snake-like creature with four stubby legs and a poisonous barbed tip on its long sinuous tail – it lives in shallow caverns in temperate climes

Zacrol (zak-rol) – the equivalent of about a mile

# ABOUT THE AUTHORS

**Tracy R. Chowdhury (aka Ross)** was born in the small town of Tunkhannock Pennsylvania in 1975 and moved to Cincinnati Ohio when she was twelve years old. Growing up, she was an avid reader, especially of fantasy and science fiction, and she loved to write. She attended college at Miami University in Oxford, Ohio and studied her other passion, Biology. She graduated in 2002 and worked in cancer research for several years. During that time she picked up her love for writing again, and in 2005, her first book, *Shadow Over Shandahar- Child of Prophecy*, was put into print. With the help of her co-author, Ted Crim, the sequel was published two years later.

Tracy currently lives in Montgomery, Ohio. She is married with eight children, a big dog, and four cats. She does home renovation work, and in her 'spare' time she continues to write and promote her books. In 2011 the novels were picked up by a small press, and her original duology was re-mastered and separated into smaller volumes to make a series. More books have followed, as well as several short stories. More information about the books can be found on her website at www.worldofshandahar.com, and she can be found on Facebook and Twitter.

**Ted M. Crim** was born and raised in Cincinnati Ohio. He spent most of his early youth in Over-the-Rhine, but moved to upper Price Hill when he was about eight years old. He was always interested in fantasy role-play, and enjoyed playing Dungeons & Dragons with his friends. When he was a junior in high school he went into a vocational program called Animal Conservation and Care located at the Cincinnati Zoo & Botanical Garden. He received his certificate in 1989 and worked in animal care for several years.

It was during that time Ted met his good friend, Tracy, and they shared an interest in Dungeons & Dragons. She was a writer, and it was upon the first campaign they played together that her first book, *Shadow Over Shandahar-Child of Prophecy*, was based. Together, they brought the world and the characters to life into a novelized format. Ted has been pivotal in the development of Shandahar, and he is in the midst of creating a role-playing module based on the world. He attends many of the conventions and festivals at which the books are sold, and goes by the moniker, Pirate Ted!

Ted is currently working on his new fantasy series and gaming system. More information about the books can be found on his website at www.worldofshandahar.com, and he can also be found on Facebook.

# OTHER BOOKS TO ENJOY:

The legendary Pact of Bakharas has been broken and daemon and dragon-
kind are free to make the world of Shandahar a battle-ground in an epic
struggle that has lasted centuies.

Young sorceress Aeris Timberlyn is burdened with the task of persuading
a new Talent to return to the academy to persue training in the arcane
arts. Accompanied by her brothe rand their companions, she travels
through dangerous lands in search of him.

Imagine living over one hundred years without a home, without a family, without responsibility. Imagine being alone in the wilderness with nothing but memories of the long ago past. Imagine dreaming of the day you might find something worth living for... worth dying for.

Elvish Jewel.

THE LEGEND OF FOX CROW:
I KNOW NOT
BOOK ONE

JAMES DANIEL ROSS

Picture a hero.

I bet he's tall, muscular, and chiseled... forthright and chaste with bright, shiny armor... takes on all challengers face-to-face... lots and lots of honor?

Yeah. I am not that guy. Am the antithesis of all of those things.

In this world, with so much gold at stake, with the most powerful people in the kingdom taking notice...

That shiny hero? Yeah, he dies.

I am the guy that can get the job done.

I am Fox Crow.

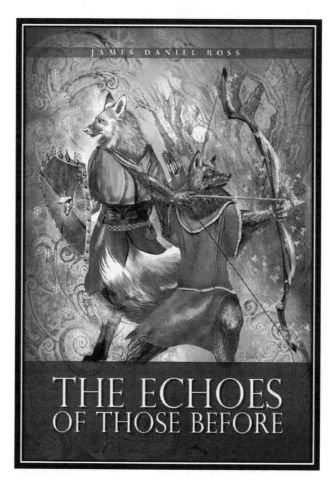

# THE ECHOES
## OF THOSE BEFORE

Hungry. Feral. Remorseless.

Demonic creatures have crawled from their hives for the first time in thousands of years. They seek their prey relentlessly, seemingly invincible, swarming across the world to blot out whole nations.

Two young men, an orphan and a maverick, will pick up one of the most powerful weapons ever forged by Those Before and stand against the rising tide of darkness.

Follow this pair as they venture from the safety of the Fox Vale, into the cold embrace of the big wide world.

In a world beset by nightmares, another is coming. Two of the mightiest nations in the world are clashing in a war that will shake the Great Veddan River Valley to its core. The fae elves and the bronze dwarves look upon one another as foreign and alien, their conflict fueled by dark powers and bigotry. Pride and misunderstandings foil peace at every turn, and two star-crossed lovers shall suffer as their people descend into bloodshed.

# AND FORTHCOMING:

Seth and Kaila: writing partners, friends, lovers. Their relationship is a rocky one, and an arguement sends Kai out into the night in tears.

An accident leaves Seth suddenly facing one of the worst days of his life. Deep within the embrace of a coma, Kai struggles for her life, her mind trapped within the world she and Seth have created. And as the days pass, she continues to weaken.

The only thing keeping Seth from insanity is the book he and Kai were working on, and as the love of his life slips closer to death, he is desperate to finish what they started together. As their darkest hour approaches, Seth finally realizes what might save Kaila's life, and it is a race against the clock before she is lost forever.

PUBLICATIONS

VISIT THE WEBSITE AT
WWW.WINTERWOLFPUBLICATIONS.COM
FOR

BREAKING NEWS
FORTHCOMING RELEASES
LINKS TO AUTHOR SITES
WINTERWOLF EVENTS

Made in the USA
Middletown, DE
08 September 2022

73519156R00194